Ebook ISBN: 978-1-956335-12-5

Audiobook ISBN: 978-1-956335-20-0

Paperback ISBN: 978-1-956335-19-4

Front cover design by Danielle Fine at Design by Definition.

Sword, gaming system, portal, and Lake Nacimiento drawings by Etheric Tales.

Luma map designed by Fictive Designs.

First published in 2024 by Ringtail Press.

www.melissajacksonbooks.com

 Created with Vellum

UNHOLY MAGIC

THE
CHARM
COLLECTOR

BOOK 3

MELISSA ERIN JACKSON

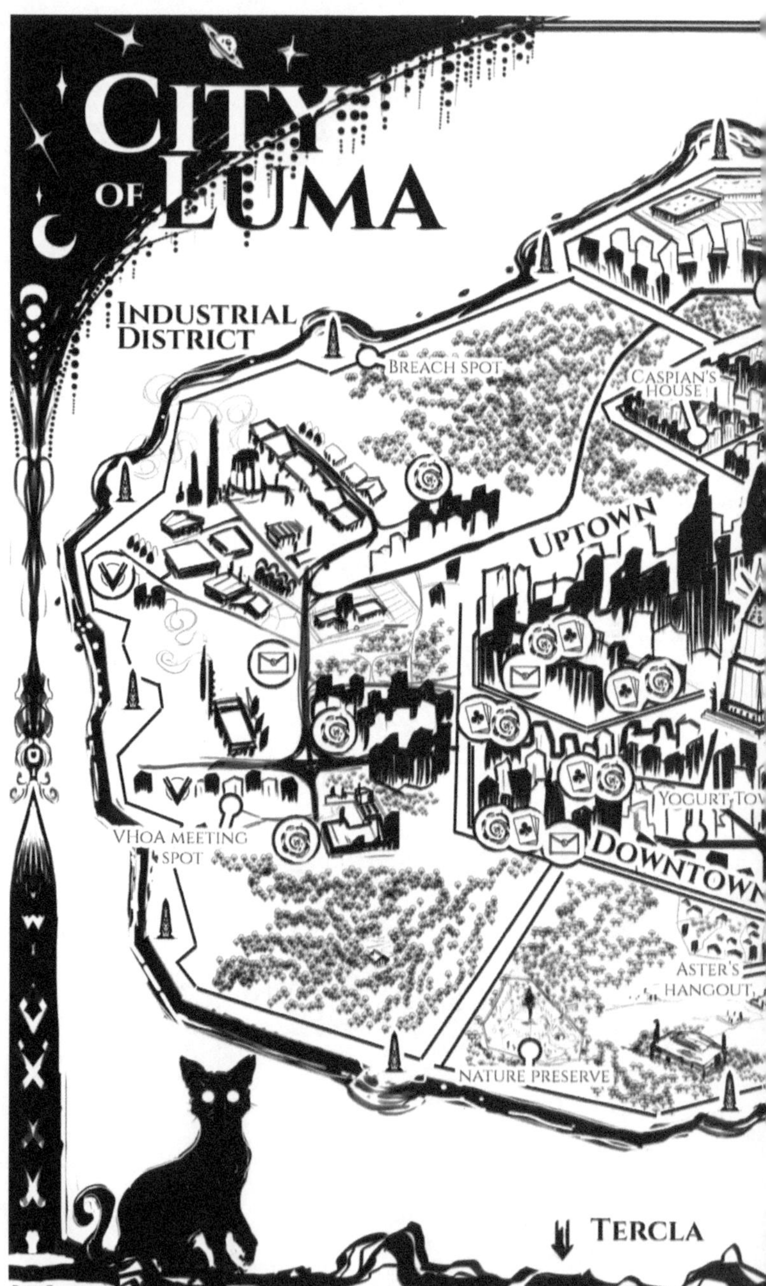

CITY OF LUMA
INDUSTRIAL DISTRICT
BREACH SPOT
CASPIAN'S HOUSE
UPTOWN
YOGURT TOW
DOWNTOWN
VHOA MEETING SPOT
ASTER'S HANGOUT
NATURE PRESERVE
TERCLA

WAREHOUSE
DISTRICT
CALIFORNIA
SACRAMENTO
SAN FRANCISCO
LUMA
LOS ANGELES
SAN DIEGO
ARDMORE
KAYDA'S APARTMENT
HENRI'S APARTMENT
AL'S BURGERS
APOTHECARY
MONTCLAIRE
VHOA HEADQUARTERS
NECROPOLIS
VEIL OBELISKS
TELEPAD STATION
CASINO
VISITOR'S CENTER
TELEPOST STATION
SORCERERS' COLLECTIVE HEADQUARTERS

CHAPTER ONE

HARLOW

I stood in the middle of the dirt entrance road that led into the Vampire Hunters of America's Washington headquarters, face tipped toward the cloudless sky. Light pollution obscured most of the stars, but there were far more than I ever got to see in Luma.

It was still summer, so even after eleven p.m., it was warm. Any faint breeze brought with it the scent of dust from the lot next door. Other than the occasional scrabbling of small mammals in the dried-out bushes dotting the otherwise desolate landscape, it was quiet at night. I'd walked far enough away from the warehouse that the voices tumbling out the open roll-up door were reduced to a faint hum but not so far that I couldn't haul tail back inside should something scarier than a mouse emerge from the withered vegetation.

I'd only been able to handle an hour or two of the boisterous gathering tonight and had excused myself to go to the bathroom. No one, not even my mother, had noticed when I'd left the table.

Three days had passed since the Collective contacted me and Caspian via courier bird. The message had been intercepted by Caspian's Collective-hating eagle, but we'd gotten the note all the same. After calling the number on the missive, a Collective sorceress named Rhiannon had brokered a deal: If I was able to track down my mother and bring her back to Luma with me, the Collective would call off their cats and bounty hunters. Caspian, the sword, and I would no longer be fugitives. Mom would no longer be in exile.

We could finally go home.

When Sorceress Rhiannon had first sent the note bundled into a plastic tube affixed to the leg of a hawk, she hadn't known I'd already found my mom. Well, Mom had found *me* when I'd been trying to escape a motel that was being attacked by a troll minion of an orc mob boss.

It had been a weird few weeks.

Yet even though Mom had agreed to come back to Luma to serve as their new vampire expert—my label, not theirs—we had yet to leave the VHoA bunker. Every time I thought we were going to hit the road, some new vampire-related crisis cropped up and Mom would take off again. I didn't think she was stalling, but I didn't think she was making leaving a priority, either.

Every night, while Caspian geeked out over runes with Arturo, I sat with Mom, Soren, and the other rowdier VHoA members, listening to them talk and laugh about that night's hunt or memorable skirmishes from the past. Caspian and I never tagged along on hunts. I wasn't built for combat unless absolutely necessary. Caspian could hold his own, but he'd rather have his nose buried in a book.

I was shown old scars and told tales about injuries invisible to the naked eye. The drunker everyone got, and the later into the night the post-hunt celebration went, the more tragic the stories became. I fell onto my cot every night with a head full of memories of people I'd never met and battles I'd never fought, yet the stories were part of my marrow now.

Which made me even more desperate to return to Luma. According to Kayda, a hybrid vampire had gotten *into* the city. The veils surrounding Luma—surrounding all forty-three hubs in the United States—had spells woven into them that were *supposed* to repel both pure and hybrid vamps.

One of the strangest things about all this was that Kayda said Lachlan Shade and the infiltrating hybrid had been friends. The vamp had been decapitated—by Jo's bizarro apprentice Erik, of all people—which had presumably put a damper on the friendship. Logic dictated that hybrids didn't suddenly have access to hubs and all the vulnerable humans and fae inside them. Lachlan— seeing as he'd not only managed to open a portal from another realm but had gotten through—was the reason the hybrid had stepped his necrotic foot on Luma soil. The mere fact that the possibility existed was yet another reason I balanced on the precarious edge of becoming a full-blown insomniac.

When some new nightmare or anxiety-fueled thought yanked me from sleep and I stumbled to the bathroom at three a.m., I often found Caspian still hunched over his books and notes. The guy lived for his research, but I could tell he wasn't just making up lost time with his beloved tomes. He was hoping to find solutions somewhere in Margaret Fengast's journal, or in all those textbook pages of rune theory, to both the Lachlan Shade problem and a way to wake up my sword's dormant twin.

Though I suspected Caspian reread Fengast's journal ad nauseam in part because he'd managed to develop a crush on her —this woman from decades past who'd been a second-generation sorceress. A woman whose direct ancestors had wound up in the earthen realm after the Glitch. A woman ahead of her time, who'd been skilled at runework and blacksmithing in equal measure.

At least Caspian's infatuation with runes had the potential to aid in stopping the impending crash of the entire hub system, if

Sorceress Rhiannon's ominous warnings could be believed. Me, on the other hand? All I had to offer was a dubious alliance with a sentient sword.

The sword in question spent most of its time in the back of my mom's SUV, along with Margaret Fengast's treasure chest and the sword's lifeless counterpart. It must have been doing whatever it could think of to wake the other sword. Caspian had tried to explain to it that until we had access to a significant heat source to reveal sentience-giving runes—and the privacy to accomplish the task—the second sword was unlikely to ever rouse from sleep. My sword, however, rarely listened to reason. I pictured the weapons like an old married couple, one-half of which had fallen into a coma—my sword vowing to remain by its spouse's side, whispering words of encouragement down the long tunnel of unconsciousness, hoping that one day its figurative eyes would flutter open.

Hell, even my delusional sword had more to offer in this fight than I did. Without my sword, I was just another powerless human …

I wasn't sure if my sense of hopelessness was causing the insomnia or vice versa. It was exhausting either way and resulted in many lost hours of playing solitaire on one of the VHoA computers while Caspian studied by electric lantern.

Or, on nights like tonight, my worries sent me outside so I could be alone with my thoughts. I doubted that being trapped in my own brain with only wild mice for company was a healthier option.

As usual, my anxiety-induced thoughts eventually strayed back to Lachlan Shade.

Kayda said the portal had snapped closed on the elf and lopped off his left arm at the elbow. Yet not even that had slowed him down. Lachlan could still cast rune arrays like a sorcerer. And even worse, the hybrid vampire who'd ambushed Kayda and her friends had *also* wielded magic. Vampires using magic made even less sense than them being inside Luma.

Lachlan, despite his exile—or maybe because of it—had amassed a cult in the earthen realm, recruiting elves, vampires, and who knew what else to his cause. Elves had formulated a way to manipulate veils to tear open holes in the magic. Holes anyone —even bloodthirsty vampires—could use to stroll right through.

The cult, better known as the Shades, had been working for months, if not years, to free their elf savior from the realm Collective sorcerers had banished him to nearly thirty years ago—an event my own mother had witnessed.

No one but his loyal followers knew where Lachlan was now, though.

Deep in my gut, I knew Lachlan's return was only the start of something bigger. He held a grudge against the Collective, and he'd allied with vampires to help mete out his revenge. I didn't trust vamps of any stripe, but ones in league with the elf terrified me on principle.

A swell of muted, raucous laughter wafted out of the warehouse behind me. I couldn't fathom why I was the only one this worried. Maybe this chapter of VHoA was so far removed from the hub system that it didn't feel like their problem—that it couldn't touch them. I supposed they could be *so* worried that they drowned themselves in booze to make themselves forget.

I refocused upward at the smattering of stars. It *did* feel as if I were on a different planet here. Even in the quiet, deserted places of Luma, it was hard to ever truly feel alone there. Magic itself existed in the very air, brushing against me with invisible fingers. If I stayed in the magic-free mundane world for long enough, got lost in the VHoA lifestyle, it would be easy to eventually forget what was happening in Luma and the other hubs. Not my monkeys; not my circus.

I sighed—a great gust of breath that rounded my shoulders.

I knew I couldn't let go of my life there, even if holding on currently felt futile.

The Collective had thought Lachlan's plan was impossible, so they'd been as blindsided by his success as everyone else. Mastery of portal magic had become so rare that the fanatical Shades had been treated as lunatics who had accepted a fallacy as truth—the hub system's version of Heaven's Gate. No one but the Shades believed Lachlan would be able to free himself, especially not when the price of opening said portal was sacrificing over a dozen innocent elf teenagers. But Lachlan had done it. The pile of obituary notices that had hit some bureaucrat's desk had proven it.

Lachlan could open portals and craft rune arrays, and he was fueled by almost three decades of spite. He'd gone mad along the way. He cared little for others, seeing them as a means to an end. His sister, Blythe, had been killed during the battle on the night he'd crawled through the portal. Kayda said Lachlan had been more upset about the potential death of his vampire friend than the *actual* death of his sister.

He didn't have much left to lose, which made him even more of a wild card.

I wasn't sure if Mom was concerned about Lachlan coming after her personally, but I had to assume that the list of people he wanted to cut down for banishing him to another world included her. Even if she hadn't been the one to push his psychotic ass through the portal, she'd had a front-row seat to the event. Hell, I had too, in a way: She'd been pregnant with me when it happened.

A shooting star silently streaked through the dark sky. I wished for some clarity of purpose.

Eventually, the faint glow of blue in my peripheral vision told me the sword had come out to check on me. It hummed softly, and I somehow knew it was asking if I was okay.

"I'm fine," I said, not looking over. "Just thinking."

The soft crunch of gravel a minute later told me Caspian had joined us, too. Actually, it was the faint whiff of Ocean Sunrise Body Wash that gave him away. He was running low on his beloved soap from the motel we'd been temporary residents in. Maybe he could put in a wholesale order from a hotel supply chain.

"Want company?" he asked, coming to a stop on my other side.

The last time he'd asked me that, we'd embarked on a road trip. Now we were rooted in place.

"Sure," I said.

He mirrored my stance: hands in pockets and face upturned. "Getting antsy again?"

"A bit."

"The offer still stands to leave and head back first."

I shook my head, just like I did every time he suggested this. A quick-moving satellite drifted across the inky sky. "We can't go back without her. The Collective wants *her* back; we're only bargaining chips." Sighing, I added, "I know being in Luma is going to tear open old wounds for her, and I don't want to rush her, but it feels like time is ticking by too fast." I sounded calm to my own ears, at least. Resigned, even. "I'm worried about Kayda."

"Kayda is more than capable of taking care of herself," Caspian said. "And she's got Welsh and Henri with her."

I tilted my head to look at him instead of the stars. "I *miss* Kayda," I amended.

He cocked his head to look at me, too. "I know."

I stared at him a beat before looking away, staring forward instead of at the sky. The dirt road was eaten up by darkness a hundred yards away.

An owl hooted somewhere far, far in the distance.

My sixth sense pinged a moment later. It wasn't a magical ability so much as one borne out of necessity. Even though a deer might be comfortable foraging in its well-known forest, it still kept its ears pricked at all times for signs of approaching danger. If a twig snapped underfoot, a bunny was sure to freeze, body poised to bound away. Doves were known to burst into flight in a raucous burst of noise to startle approaching predators. For me, my senses tingled. Almost like the sensation of a sleeping limb waking up—an all-over buzzy feeling. My back straightened, wide eyes scanning the area ahead of me.

"What is it?" Caspian asked.

The sword glowed cherry red on my other side. I couldn't tell if it sensed something, too, or if it was reacting to the tension in my body and the spike in my heart rate.

"Daughter of Camila," came a smooth-as-butter voice from nowhere and everywhere.

Caspian spun in a circle, searching. I didn't move.

"You are even more beautiful than I imagined," said the voice.

"Who are you?" I asked, damned impressed with myself that my voice hadn't shaken.

Ahead, the darkness shifted. Kayda said the hybrid vampire she'd met in the nature preserve had melted out of the shadows. I'd thought that description had been a bit flowery for her, but now I saw it had been close to literal. According to Welsh, the vampire had been dabbling in shadow magic. He could manipulate shadows to his will, creating illusions made of darkness itself. Shadows could be used for travel, too. That particular vampire was dead, but it didn't mean there weren't others who possessed the same unholy magic.

Mom told me pure vampires could cloak themselves in darkness—someplace between invisibility and shadow manipulation. Instead of molding himself out of shadows like clay, this particular vampire stepped out of the darkness as if he'd been wearing it like a shawl that had slipped off his shoulders. Not-there one minute, and there the next.

Caspian instinctively wrapped a hand around my forearm. The sword was the color of an ember now, but it hadn't shot forward yet. Did that mean it hadn't sensed an immediate threat from the vampire, or did it figure my odds of dying went up considerably if it left my side?

"I am Vaughn," the vampire said. "It's lovely to finally meet you, Daughter of Camila."

He hadn't attempted to approach us. From what Mom had told me, all vampires—pure, hybrid, *and* feral—were preternaturally fast. I'd only interacted with feral vampires in a hostile situation so far, and I could attest to how quick those little bastards were. I knew if this one wanted to close the gap stretching between us, he'd be on me before I could react. Caspian had his magic, and the sword had its murderous tendencies, and yet the vampire could probably tear my throat out before either of my companions could stop him.

"Harlow," I said, figuring it might be best to be polite. "'Daughter of Camila' is too wordy. Friends call me Low, but I don't think we're there yet."

Every muscle in my body felt like a coiled spring. Caspian still held fast to my arm. His free hand was behind him, his fingers working overtime to craft a small rune array.

"It is a pleasure to finally meet you, Harlow," Vaughn said. "Your mother spoke of you often."

I had no idea how to reply to that. "What do you want, Vaughn? There's a warehouse full of vampire hunters not far from here. If anything happens to us, the sword and all those hunters will be after you in seconds."

Even from this distance, I noted how Vaughn's scrutiny flitted to the sword hovering by my side, glowing as bright as a fireball, before returning to me. Expression unchanged, he said, "I do not wish you harm. I wish to offer you an invitation."

"An invitation to what?"

"I have been searching for your mother for a while now," Vaughn said. "She won't listen to what I have to say, but she *will* listen to her only daughter."

He spoke in a pleasant, even cadence, taking care with each word. It made me even antsier. Maybe when one was immortal and had all the time in the world, getting to the damn point already wasn't a driving force.

"The pure vampires know of the threat hybrids and ferals pose to your hubs," Vaughn said. "We know because they threaten us as well. A bite—sometimes a mere scratch—from a feral is fatal to pure vampires."

Marisol had told me as much, but it was still a bit of a shock to have it confirmed.

"We also know that the elf, Lachlan Shade, has amassed a veritable army of hybrids and their feral abominations to do his bidding ... whatever that bidding is." Vaughn eyed me and Caspian in turn. "While we have no vested interest in the well-being of the humans in the hubs, we're certain that once Lachlan perfects ripping away veils from hub cities like one tears a shower curtain from the rod, enclaves like Tercla will be next."

"Is that where you're from?" Caspian asked, speaking for the first time since Vaughn materialized out of nowhere.

Vaughn inclined his head. "I am from many places, but I met Camila Fletcher in Tercla, yes."

My eyebrows shot toward my hairline. My mom had been to Tercla? It was a hub made for pure vampires. There were humans in residence too who were in some kind of contractual relationship with a vamp. Had she signed a contract with one? Just how far off the rails had she gone when she lost Dad and then Naomi and then was exiled and cut off from me?

"So ... what is it you want me to tell my mother?" I asked, not sure I wanted the answer.

"I believe she can help us determine how to save both your world and ours."

"Why her?" I asked.

Vaughn was quiet for so long, I thought he wouldn't answer. "Because the leader of Tercla owes her a life debt, and it's high time she cashed it in. If she can convince the stubborn mule to treat this threat for what it is, it may convince him to approach the Vampire Council. Without the Council's help, pure vampires may very well be wiped from existence."

Caspian's fingers dug into my forearm.

I hadn't realized the situation had grown this dire for vamps, too.

A whoosh of air swept past my face just before something metallic clinked by my feet. A pair of talismans lay an inch from my tennis shoes. My gaze snapped up.

Other than a strand of Vaughn's dark hair that was out of place and draped over his forehead, there was no other indication that he'd moved. He gently tucked the wayward strand back into place. My heartbeat stumbled. The ferals had been fast—*too* fast—but I'd at least seen them coming. Vaughn had moved so quickly, I'd literally missed it when I blinked.

Vaughn said, "Those will get you into Tercla."

"There's only two of them," Caspian said.

"Correct. You are not welcome. The talismans are for the Fletcher women and the Fletcher women only. The note in your pocket, sorcerer, includes instructions on how the Fletcher women can contact me."

I shot a fearful look at Caspian. He abandoned his half-formed rune array to shove his free hand into the pocket of his jeans. He pulled out a folded slip of paper.

It hit me all over again that Vaughn could disembowel Caspian and me both in an instant. It could happen so fast that my mother and her armed-to-the-teeth hunters wouldn't hear it. I didn't trust Vaughn any more than I had when this creepy-ass conversation started, but now I knew he was actively choosing *not* to murder us. That was a solid half-point in his pro column.

"And when exactly did you want *the Fletcher women* to swing by?" I asked.

"As soon as possible," Vaughn said. "There are only a few of us pure vampires who see the writing on the wall. We don't know what Lachlan is plotting, but it must be substantial if he was able to convince the hybrids to get in league with him. Hybrids are loyal only to themselves; Lachlan must have offered them something they couldn't refuse. He's had decades to plan his return to this realm. I doubt he'll take longer than a few months, if not weeks, to enact the next phase."

One would think hearing someone voice all the same concerns

that had just been swirling in my head would be comforting. Hooray, I'm not alone!

The comfort level went down by a significant margin when that someone was a vampire.

I squatted to pick up the talismans. Caspian's fingers traveled up my arm as I moved away from him, as if he couldn't quite bring himself to let go yet. The sword tapped hard, twice, on the dirt road just inches from my reaching fingers.

"What?" I hissed at it, snatching my hand back.

Tap-tap.

Caspian squatted next to me. "I don't think the cutlass wants you to pick them up. Give me a moment."

"The talismans are exactly as I say." Vaughn managed to sound both poised and mildly exasperated as he added, "There is no tracking magic on them, nor will they melt the flesh from your bones as soon as you touch them. Your sorcerer may test their properties all he wants, but it is a wasted effort. Your time should be spent convincing Camila to return to Tercla." Vaughn took three steps back into the inky blackness behind him and disappeared from view.

My sixth sense wasn't pinging as loudly as it had been before.

"Spend your limited mortal time wisely," his voice said from everywhere and nowhere, making the hair on my arms stand on end. "Make no mistake that, without the pure vampires as allies, this is sure to be a war you lose."

The buzzy feeling in my limbs slowly faded away. Why did vampires have to be so damn dramatic all the time? I shook off a chill.

Caspian had evidently taken Vaughn's words to heart because, instead of beginning an exhaustive round of experimental spells, both talismans lay in his open palm.

We both stood.

I tightly crossed my arms. "What do you think?"

"I hate that I'm being left out of this. Not out of jealousy so much as ..." He huffed. "It's proof we're being watched. Your mother and her allies are well equipped. Despite being mundanes, I've never felt unsafe in their presence. Until now. We've been outmatched for an indeterminate amount of time and had no idea."

I couldn't say I liked any of that, either.

He searched my face, but I couldn't guess what he expected to find there. "Beyond that, I think we need to ask your mother why in the hells the leader of Tercla owes her a life debt."

I groaned. "Why couldn't I have a normal mother?"

Caspian slung an arm over my shoulders and guided us back toward the warehouse, the talismans still held in his open palm like he was a waiter offering hors d'oeuvres. "You realize how weird *you* are, right?"

The sword was flying ahead of us, so it had clearance to drop to the road and offer a tap of agreement.

"I don't know why I keep hanging out with either one of you."

Caspian pulled me closer, curling my body into his chest as we walked, and planted a quick kiss on my temple. He loosened his hold a fraction and kept walking, unfurling me back to my original position as if he hadn't done anything.

The show of affection was somehow wildly out of character for him—making my cheeks heat up so hot, it was a wonder my hair didn't catch fire—and exactly what I'd needed at that moment. It grounded me. It told me that whatever came next, he was with me.

Even if "with me" was metaphorical because the vampires were excluding him.

When we stepped into the warehouse, my mother was halfway across the floor. She came up short when she saw us. We halted just inside the door, and Caspian dropped his arm from around my shoulders.

After scanning all three of us, she closed the distance. "Everything okay?" She contemplated the talismans in Caspian's hand, her jaw tightening second by second. Her gaze finally met mine.

I arched a brow at her. "We need to talk."

CHAPTER TWO

HARLOW

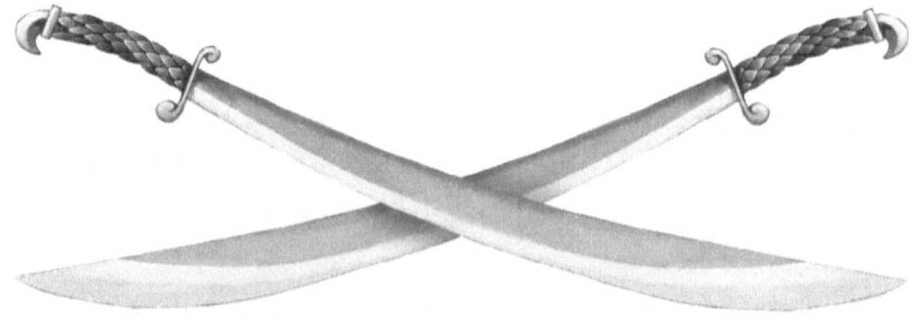

"Talk about what?" Mom asked cautiously.

I crossed my arms. "A vamp named Vaughn just swung by for a chat."

She stared at me, dumbfounded. Then she stalked for the door. I threw an arm out to stop her, causing her to take a few stutter steps back.

"He didn't touch any of us," I said. "If he'd wanted to kill us, he would have."

"How the hell did he find us here?" Her eyes darted around as she mentally assessed how secure this location truly was if a vamp could just stroll onto the property. "Tell me exactly where you saw him."

I complied, if only because she was using her Mom Voice, and I was powerless against it.

Backing up, she called into the warehouse, "Buckley! Glover! Possible tech failure on the western road! Check it out."

In record time, two ladies came trotting over. One had a large black bag slung over her shoulder. The other carried a rifle. Both had short swords strapped to their hips. They nodded at us before they slipped out into the night.

"Lomas! Hardwick! Play backup!"

A man and a woman jogged out the door next, this pair even more loaded down with weapons than the first.

Mom zeroed in on me again, arms crossed and stance wide. "Start at the beginning."

As I spoke, I wondered how much of this "life debt" business the others here were aware of. Was this the kind of thing she wanted them to know? Even so, she didn't shoo anyone away who crept up to listen. By the time I finished, Soren, Arturo, and a handful of others had made a semicircle behind my mom.

"And those are talismans to get into Tercla?" Arturo asked when I was done, jutting his chin at Caspian's still outstretched hand.

"Yes," Caspian said, which elicited murmurs from the small crowd. "But only Robin and Deanna are on the invite list," he said, using our aliases.

"It was only a matter of time before one of them came looking for you, Robin," Soren said. "I didn't think it would be because of this, though. Pure vamps going to war against hybrids, ferals, and elves was *not* on my apocalypse bingo card."

"So you've *actually* been to Tercla, Mom?" I asked, incredulous. "Why?"

Soren, behind her, winced. "Hey, who wants to help me scrub the toilets?"

The entire group behind Mom dispersed at once.

"Real subtle, Soren!" Mom said. Sighing, she studied me and Caspian in turn. "Let's have a seat." She walked away.

I glanced up at Caspian. He shrugged. The sword hummed.

"Why do I have a feeling this story is going to traumatize me?" I muttered as I trailed after my mom.

Caspian and I sat on one side of a deserted picnic table, and Mom sat on the other. The sword hovered nearby, floating in my peripheral vision.

Folding her hands on the table, my mom let out another weary sigh. "First, let me preface this by saying that I was drowning in guilt and regret."

Caspian asked, "Was that before or after your experience in Tercla?"

Mom barked a laugh. "Yes." Taking a moment to center herself, she said, "I've been fascinated by vampires since I was a teenager. And not because I thought they were sexy, either. A girl in my hometown went missing when I was in high school. A week later, her body was found near a trail that a lot of kids from my school used to get home. She had bites all over her body that looked both human and not. While most of her blood was gone, very little of it was found outside her body. The town went nuts over the story. It was all anyone talked about at school for months. They never found who did it. There was speculation about everything from a Satanic cult to a serial killer to a wild animal attack."

"And you had a feeling it was something supernatural," I said, having heard this story before. I guessed she was saying all this for Caspian's sake. Or maybe she just needed to warm up to the topic.

"Right," Mom said. "I turned into Nancy Drew over the whole thing. I never found actual evidence of vampires back then—and it's still considered an unsolved case in my hometown, as far as I know —but I'd found enough in the lore to have a pretty good inkling about what had killed her. A lot of the lore from popular culture got it wrong. Vamps don't have an aversion to sunlight, they don't turn into bats, and their reflections smile back at them in the mirror. They aren't all pale, and they aren't all good-looking. Becoming a vampire doesn't suddenly make you attractive. If you want to be a vampire with washboard abs, you have to do crunches like everyone else. Their blood diets help them slim down quick, but they can still eat human foods if it agrees with their constitution."

I tried to imagine a vampire sitting on a park bench in full sun, gorging his way through an entire box of doughnuts.

"Did they get anything right?" Caspian was leaning slightly toward my mom, so I knew he was intrigued. I considered tracking down one of his legal pads so he could take notes.

Mom said, "Like in most movies and books, vamps possess the power of compulsion—though most of us call it 'enthralling.' Let a vamp talk to you for long enough, and they can convince you to do damn near anything. Eye contact is to be avoided—especially if you find the vampire even remotely attractive. It's not just about looks, either. If you find humor attractive, the instant a vamp realizes this and makes you laugh? It's only a matter of time before your pants hit the floor or your veins are drained—sometimes both."

"Ugh. Gross, Mom."

"You say much worse on a daily basis," Caspian said to me. "*Hourly* basis."

"So? She's my mom. She can't say stuff like that."

Mom flashed me a mischievous smile I didn't like one bit, so I suspected she'd double down on the gross. "Their legendary prowess in the bedroom is due more to experience and a long life than some vampiric magic that turns them into virile lovers. Some vamps are crap in bed, but the enthrall power can convince you that you've just had the best sex of your life. And they can be very, *very* convincing."

Caspian coughed awkwardly.

I let out a pained whimper. Some part of me wanted to ask her how she knew all this, but if, during those years after Dad and Naomi were killed and her ties to me and Luma had been cut off, she'd spent that dark time under—or on top of—a bevy of vampire lovers, I really didn't need details. Really, *really* didn't need them.

Though I supposed that potentially horrifying information was still on the way whether I wanted it or not, given that she'd started this conversation with a disclaimer.

"Anyway," Mom said. "The obsession over figuring out just what these creatures were led me to vampire hunter groups, which is where I met Harlow's dad. He was just as obsessive about the history of vamps as I was."

"I find it very interesting as well," Caspian said. "A bit of my own research has revealed that vampires have existed in the earthen realm as far back as the 1500s, but they'd started as mere humans whose behavior caused a … kind of hysteria that resulted in the legends we have today. Is that correct?"

My mom smiled at him like she wanted to leap across the table and hug him. "Pretty much, yeah. There was a rare red blood disorder—something akin to sickle cell anemia—that plagued a subset of the population in Europe. The earliest records of the disease date back to the 1500s. This was also during the second wave of the Bubonic Plague, and since there were already concerns about a more virulent strain of the disease reemerging, when something as odd as this blood disorder showed up, it garnered more curiosity than it possibly would have otherwise. Chlorosis was first discovered around this time, too—which is a type of anemia that plagues young women and adolescent girls. It was discounted as a 'hysterical disease' for a long time.

"Like sickle cell, this odd chlorosis-like disease is inherited. Blood transfusions weren't performed with any real success until 1667. Blood transfusions were the best treatment for the disease, but because of how new they were back then, only the really wealthy or well-connected got them. Sickle cell patients typically get transfusions once or twice a month. For sufferers of the chlorosis-like disease, once a week was ideal. It got worse for women after puberty—which is why we think this disease got lumped in with the 'hysterical' women suffering from chlorosis. Their menstrual cycles made them even more anemic.

"The disease was reported to leave sufferers weak and lethargic. They also experienced vision problems, frequent infections, and developed ravenous hunger. The hunger component is what sets this disease apart from your run-of-the-mill chlorosis. Rumor has it that while a patient was getting her infusion the doctor spilled blood on his hand. The scent of the blood sent the woman into a crazed state. Like a suckling kitten, she latched onto the webbing of the doctor's hand and was so desperate for more blood that she bit him. She'd only been able to ingest a small amount of his blood before she was restrained, but *consuming* the blood resulted in a marked improvement in her condition. The doctor, Alonso Dario, started telling anyone who would listen that he'd found a cure for this rare disease, but, naturally, he was shunned for advocating the drinking of blood. Chlorosis had already been classified as a hysterical disease—you can imagine how well a campaign for blood consumption would have gone over.

"Injecting blood had varying levels of success, partly because people often had adverse reactions to infusions from the wrong blood type—blood typing wasn't discovered until the early 1900s. *Consuming* the blood worked regardless of blood type, though. Dario created an underground clinic that prescribed blood for those suffering from the disease.

"With a regular diet of blood, the disease was manageable. The body healed itself. By the mid-1900s, the disease was no longer fatal. What we now know as vampires are the descendants of these people who, through the consumption of blood, survived both their genetic diseases and three waves of the Bubonic Plague. Vampires are human in most senses of the word—they have a beating heart, they can eat, they emit waste … but they also consume blood. They live much longer lives than the average human because consuming blood heals their diseased or aged tissue. Their bodies evolved. Just like humans have incisors, canines, and molars because we're omnivores and have teeth that allow for both the tearing of meat and the grinding of plants, vampires evolved to have teeth that allowed them to better consume a blood diet. Hence the fangs. But because they can still eat human food, many have the kind of teeth one might find on a chimpanzee or bear."

I remembered the first feral vampire I'd seen—how there had been something almost dog-like about her face. "When magic and fae blood got introduced to this realm after the Glitch, that changed vampires even more." It was a statement, not a question.

My mom nodded. "That's right. The magic that entered their systems after they consumed fae blood was like evolution in over-drive—perhaps 'mutation' would be more accurate. You know that werewolves went extinct after the Glitch, right?"

Caspian and I nodded.

"Any idea how?"

I shook my head. I hadn't really ever thought about it.

"There weren't werewolves in the fae realm, at least not the way we think of them. They had something closer to dire wolves —giant dogs that stand as tall as a man. Well, on those massive canines were fleas, ticks, and other parasites, and they took a ride into the earthen realm on those wolves during the Glitch. The dire wolves' magic lured in the werewolves already here like a siren's song. Without their packs from their previous world, the dire wolves formed new ones here. Unfortunately, those parasites jumped from dire wolf to werewolf and infected them with magical blood-borne viruses that absolutely devastated the popu-lation. Within ten years of the portals closing for good, were-wolves were gone.

"There were groups of fae and human scientists who worked hard to find a cure for the wolves—and they found one. Only a year too late. They'd been able to cure the one werewolf they had in captivity and healed him, but he'd been outside his prime for procreating by then. Werewolves were genetically incompatible with mundane wolves. And despite the plethora of fiction that features mundane women mating with werewolves, they're not genetically compatible, either. He was able to leave captivity after he was healed but died unable to sire healthy pups."

I frowned. Dogs—*wolves*—weren't supposed to die in stories. My mom had to know that. *Everyone* knew that.

"The foreign parasites didn't just affect the wolves; they wreaked havoc on the native supernatural community in this realm, too. Those that weren't killed were changed. Mosquitoes brought disease with them. Thankfully the human population was immune, but a kind of magical malaria swept through the fae community a few years after the Glitch. For those who survived, it altered magical skills: enhanced some and demolished others.

"The pure vampires in Tercla aren't as pure as they want everyone to believe. Vamps like Vaughn survived the magical malaria epidemic and came out of it with an enhanced ability. Just that little bit of transferred blood from a mosquito almost killed him and also made him preternaturally fast. Thankfully not all pure vampires are that fast, or we'd really be screwed."

I heaved a sigh of relief. That revelation made me feel marginally better. "Ferals have evolved—*mutated*—so much over the years because they consume tons of fae blood, and then on top of them being, you know, feral, they're also basically venomous snakes to the pure vamps?"

Mom nodded. "Yes."

"This is *fascinating*," Caspian said.

"Nerd," I muttered, though I was pretty fascinated by it all, too. The idea of a tiny mosquito being able to cause that much change in a person was humbling. "You still haven't gotten to the part about owing a life debt to the *leader of Tercla*."

Mom gusted a sigh. "Since pure vampires are still human in most ways, they can have offspring, but only with humans. Female vampires can get pregnant, but the chances of being able to carry a baby to term increase exponentially if the father is mundane. If the father is a vampire, the female's body almost always treats the fetus as a disease to be eradicated, and the baby dies in utero. Because vampires are mating with magic-less mundanes, though, it's a crapshoot whether their offspring will inherit what's essentially become known as the vampire gene."

"Wait, can't people get bitten and turned into a vamp?" I asked.

Mom's head tottered back and forth. "Yes, but that's a shot in the dark, too. Vamps have their highly potent pheromones that ensnare their victim—which is essentially where the enthrall power comes from. They've evolved to have a kind of neurotoxin present in their saliva that paralyzes their victim, much like a spider. There's some serotonin mixed in there so their victim feels good about it while it's happening. But there's no guarantee a person will turn vamp after being bitten. To complete the possible transformation, the victim needs to drink some of the vampire's blood, too. Then there's gotta be something in the victim's genetic makeup that reacts to the blood of the vamp to trigger a change. Even if someone wants to be a vampire with all her heart, if her genes aren't predisposed for it, the change won't happen no matter how many times she's bitten or how much blood she drinks."

Yuck. *Hard* pass.

"Hybrids have a much better chance of turning a human with a bite, but the new vamps are then also addicted to fae blood because of it," Mom said. "Vamp hunters are almost exclusively dealing with hybrids and ferals, as those are the ones violating the Pact and/or indiscriminately killing and kidnapping. Those two types are also enemies of the pure vamps, so some of my jobs have actually come from them.

"My reputation got me on the radar of the ruler of Tercla, Vincent Roch. He has a daughter who didn't inherit the gene. About four years ago, he sent me a personal invite to Tercla to offer me a very lucrative job to essentially be his daughter's body-guard while she was in college in the mundane world. There's a lot of political infighting among the pure clans." She rolled her eyes. "My team and I stopped four kidnapping attempts and we killed a bunch of ferals that had been sent after her on several outright assassination attempts. Say what you will about vamps, but Roch adores that girl."

"Are you no longer on that job because she's out of school?" I asked.

"She was only in the States for two years before she entered a study-abroad program in Europe. My team and I escorted her to London and stopped yet another assassination attempt on the way to the safe house where we were handing her off to her British bodyguard team. Far as I know, she's thriving out there. I kept his kid safe, so he told me he owed me a life debt. I've got a contract written in his blood and everything."

I stared at her, remembering what she'd said about guilt and regret. "You hooked up with him, didn't you?"

The pause was like a deafening roar.

"Many, *many* times." Mom shrugged, but her cheeks darkened a little. "He claimed to be in love with me and said he wanted me to have his child since I was missing my own so much."

"*Please* don't tell me I have a long-lost vampire sibling …"

Mom laughed. "No. Being offered the chance to birth an elder vampire's child is a great honor in their culture. Once I explained to him that I couldn't have his child even if I wanted to—"

"Because menopausal?" I asked.

"Because menopausal," she said. "Menopause isn't an issue for vampire women, and the concept blew his mind. He also offered to attempt to turn me. I shut that shit down immediately. I got a life debt out of him instead."

"Oh my," Caspian said, because, really, what else was there to say?

She was my mom, but she was such a different person now, sometimes it was hard to see her that way. Now she was an emotionally scarred woman with tons of wild stories to tell about a life I knew next to nothing about. Six years apart felt like a lifetime.

Mom shrugged again. "So, daughter of mine, how do you feel about a field trip to Tercla before we go back to Luma?"

In my peripheral vision, the sword glowed a sickly yellow color I'd never seen before. It probably wasn't a good sign that even the murder-happy sword was leery of this plan ...

CHAPTER THREE

KAYDA

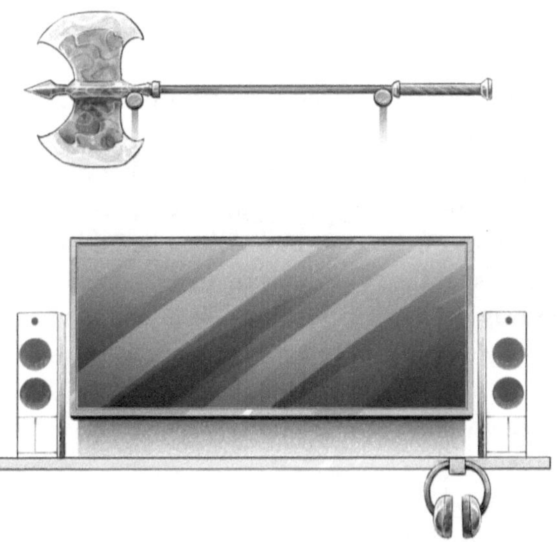

K ayda still hadn't gotten used to having a warm body next to her in the morning. Usually her nightly company—if she had any—left before daybreak. Or she did. But she didn't *want* to kick Henri out of her bed. It was still a marvel that he was there at all. Apparently, all it had taken for them to finally act on the feelings they'd been skirting around for a year was to go on a life-threatening journey together.

But even as she lay there, listening to his soft snores beside her, she couldn't forget that the reason they'd been thrown together in the first place was because Luma was in trouble. Harlow stealing that sword months ago had snowballed into Kayda being caught up in a nefarious plan cooked up by elves and vampires. Elves who, up until recently, hadn't really been on her radar—they were a people who largely kept to themselves. And vampires hadn't been on her radar at all, as they were the boogeymen outside the veils who couldn't reach her as long as she stayed in her beloved self-sufficient city.

Now the boogeymen had found a way in, and Kayda didn't know how anyone was supposed to plug the leak. Especially since now, no thanks to Kayda, the psycho who was Lachlan Shade roamed free.

Deep down, she knew she'd been so badly injured that she couldn't have stopped Lachlan even if she'd known what in the hells was going on. At the end of the day, she was only a draken. She had superior hearing, strength, and speed—and a badass battle-ax that spat lightning—but Lachlan had magic. Kayda was realizing that she wasn't as indestructible as she'd once thought. Sure, she was well suited for work as a bouncer or a security guard, where her bulk and menacing glare were usually enough to halt any mischief in its tracks. But against magic? She ended up wrapped around trees and dropped from heights that her bones didn't appreciate.

With Harlow, her mom, the sword, and Caspian set to return—eventually—Kayda wanted to learn everything she could about what they were up against. She wanted to be an asset in this fight, not just the muscle.

Stretching, she rolled toward Henri, watching him for a moment. He was on his stomach, his mouth was agape, and the side of his face was smashed into one of her pillows. They'd been up well past one a.m., so she felt bad waking him, but time was of the essence. She poked a finger into his side, which she'd discovered last night was a ticklish spot.

He snorted awake. "Wha?"

"Hey, Sleeping Beauty," she said. "Up and at 'em!"

"I really didn't p-peg you as a morning p-person," he grumbled.

She lifted the sheets enough to get an eyeful, patted his bare ass, and then deftly swung out of bed. "We're supposed to meet Welsh and Marisol in two hours."

"Two *hours*? Why are y-you up n-now then?"

"I need to go for a run."

Henri groaned, plopping face first onto the pillow again.

By the time she'd emerged from the bathroom with brushed teeth and clad in her workout gear, Henri had resumed snoring. Like most draken, Henri didn't have much hair. No tousled, messy bedhead for Henri. Instead, his white hair, which stood a mere half inch in length, was in mild disarray.

She left the apartment, letting him sleep.

By the time she got back from her ten-mile run, Henri was up and dressed and had made them breakfast. He looked mostly awake now, but the glasses perched on his nose were askew, and every time he yawned, it was a full-body affair.

"You work nights more often than not," Henri said from across the table as she shoveled bacon, eggs, and toast into her mouth. "How do you have this much energy at …" He checked his watch. "Seven thirty?"

"Old habits, I guess. I used to be a competitive cage fighter."

Henri choked on his sip of orange juice.

She tamped down a smile. "Have I not mentioned that?"

"I would have r-remembered that one," he said, coughing and giving his chest several hard pounds with his fist.

"Anyway, it's been a long time since I fought competitively, and I never really liked it, but I liked the workout routines. I run most mornings. It's nice around here really early. Most people are still asleep. The streets are quiet. It helps turn off my brain."

Henri nodded. "Turning off the b-brain seems like a g-good call lately."

Even though Henri had put on a brave face as they'd dealt with pixie swarms, vengeful elves, hybrid vampires, and potent glamour tinctures that turned him and Kayda into big-eyed doll people, Kayda knew the events as of late were starting to haunt him. How could they not? He was a nerdy, teddy bear of a guy who worked as a security guard because his sheer size was intimidating. He wasn't someone prepared to square off against a feral vampire with only an industrial flashlight as a weapon. Most people weren't.

But he was still here. He might have been freaked out by a lot of this—by *her* on some level—but he liked her enough that he stuck around.

"W-what?" he asked. "What are you s-smiling about?"

"Just thinking I'd be super down for a repeat of last night if we didn't have to go meet Welsh."

His skin flushed navy. "Would he be m-mad if we were l-late?" His face contorted, probably recalling that Welsh was mad most of the time. "Eh. Never mind."

She laughed.

Henri did the dishes while Kayda took a quick shower. As much as she'd like to entice him with one of her dresses—or nothing at all—that would be wholly impractical for the day's agenda, so she went with her usual choice: a black shirt tucked into black pants held up by a black belt. She stuffed her feet into her favorite black combat boots. Henri donned his standard outfit of a plain T-shirt and worn jeans. Time would tell if his tennis shoes would be sufficient. When people saw them together, did they assume she was his bodyguard—this giant, aggressive woman paired with a bespectacled gamer nerd? Maybe they'd think he was a tech billionaire.

When they made it out to the sidewalk and Henri slipped his hand into hers, she decided she didn't care what anyone thought.

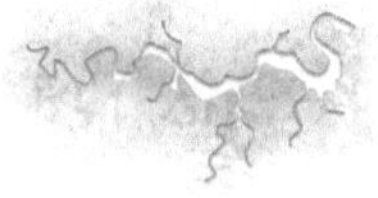

Even though they were meeting Welsh, Marisol, and some of her crew—including the triplets, Ben, Ollie, and Liam, who weren't related by blood so much as inseparable—they weren't going to VHoA's compound in the human neighborhood in the Necropolis. This morning, they were headed to the nature preserve where Kayda had faced Lachlan Shade. It was also where Welsh had been kidnapped and bitten by a hybrid vampire who'd had a specific craving for witches. Though the bite mark on his neck had healed, Welsh changed the subject every time she tried to get him to talk about it. Henri was remaining tight-lipped about it as well, out of respect for Welsh's privacy.

Henri, Jo, and her apprentice, Erik, had been with Welsh when he was attacked. Kayda and Grayson had gone after Lachlan by themselves.

Marisol hadn't suggested the preserve as some kind of aversion therapy—forcing them all back to a place of trauma to help them heal. It just happened to be a spot with a lot of open land that didn't get much foot traffic. The area had once been home to a zoo for some of the fae animals that had wound up marooned in the earthen realm after the Glitch. But the zoo had been closed and abandoned for years, reclaimed by nature.

Kayda rode on the back of Henri's three-wheeled motorcycle as he drove them to the preserve. Her now-cherished battle-ax rode in the sidecar. Henri didn't have a weapon of choice yet, but that was part of the reason for the meeting. They all needed to become better fighters if they had any chance of surviving what VHoA believed was an inevitable breach of the veils. And large-scale breaches at that—not the kind they'd experienced dozens of times already. Those breaches were made up of a few temporary holes in the veil that let in small waves of ferals at a time. Marisol was convinced that the day would come when parts of the veil would get stuck open, if not come down entirely, revealing their hidden magical city to the mundane world.

The idea of it rattled Kayda down to her bones.

She couldn't let it happen.

After Henri parked, she grabbed her battle-ax out of the side-car. She hadn't touched it much since the night of the battle. After cleaning it and sharpening it with supplies from Welsh, she'd mounted the thing on her wall above her TV. It watched her silently as she and Henri played *Mangrin's Gate* night after night. It felt good in her hand now. The magic-dampening hood was still snapped around the blade, as she didn't want to inadvertently zap herself.

Within ten minutes of Kayda and Henri's arrival at the preserve, Marisol, the triplets, Jo, Erik, and three semi-familiar VHoA members joined them. Had Grayson not been invited, or had he declined? Kayda hadn't seen the guy since that fateful night in the abandoned zoo.

Once the group was gathered behind Marisol's van, she flung the back doors open with a flourish. The walls of the van had been outfitted with wooden pegboards, and from those hung charmed weapons. Weapons the Collective would happily relieve Marisol of if they'd known she had them. Magic wafted out of the van like a fog, making Kayda's teeth buzz. There were short swords, hatchets, machetes, battle-axes, spears, morning stars, nunchucks, and daggers.

"Choose whichever weapon calls to you," Marisol said.

"Even us?" Liam asked, gesturing at himself and his two friends flanking him.

Marisol smiled, leaning against one of the open doors of the van. "Even you."

"Yes!" Ollie said. "I'm so sick of that training baton!"

Ollie and Liam practically dove into the van.

"They let us use cool stuff during the big breach," Ben said, as if in apology to Marisol for Ollie's complaints.

Just before Ben hopped into the van with his friends, Marisol grabbed him by the elbow. She pitched her voice low, but Kayda still heard the words easily. "I need you to take it easy today. If you pop any of your stitches, you're riding the bench for the next two weeks."

Ben huffed a dramatic sigh, then offered her a tight nod. He winced and groaned as he climbed into the van. He stood before the small collection of daggers, a hand pressed to his side. Ollie and Liam watched him warily but kept their mouths shut.

After only a moment of staring at Ben as if she were a mother goose and him her gosling, Marisol turned to the rest of the group. "Everything in there is Level 4 and under."

Level 3 magic, out of a possible 8, was as high as was safe for a human to use. Level 4 was where things started to get dicey. Marisol and the other VHoA members were all human. Anything over a 5 could zap one of them badly enough to send them to the hospital, if not the morgue. Kayda and the others were magic-touched and could handle higher levels of magic. But a Level 7 or 8 could be enough to flatten Kayda.

She guessed that when it came to sparring, the humans would be clustered in one area, with fae and magic-touched in the other.

Once the boys were done, Henri selected a giant machete. Welsh reached for more daggers, but Marisol shook her head and selected a sword for him instead. Erik happily grabbed a spear.

Kayda eyed Jo, honestly a little surprised the woman had shown up today. Jo's magic was formidable, making her more of a long-distance fighter. Jo selected a spear, then returned to her spot between Erik and Welsh.

As if she could sense what Kayda was thinking, Jo turned to her and said, "If this gets as bad as they say, I don't want to be a liability. I want to be ready if I have to fight hand to hand."

"Don't worry, Lady Josephine," Erik said, his smile more of a grimace—too many teeth. "Nothing will happen to you."

Kayda had always seen Erik as a sniveling little weasel of a man who looked down his nose at everyone but Jo. Turned out, he was a very powerful witch who didn't have the best control of his powers. Jo was helping him with that—and she was seemingly doing a good job of it because he practically worshipped at her feet.

"I'd never let anything happen to you," Erik said, more intensely this time. "*Never.*"

Welsh almost imperceptibly flinched. Zander Welsh was not a man who flinched.

It had been Erik who had finally slain the vampire who had targeted Welsh. Welsh had described Erik as one of the most ruthless fighters he'd ever seen, and that he owed Erik a life debt.

It made Kayda curious all over again about what had happened out here that night. One day she'd get the story out of one of them.

"All right," Marisol said. "First up, weapon drills."

For the next couple of hours, Marisol and her three VHoA crewmates wandered the assembled group as everyone else cycled through drills. They had to get used to the feel of their weapons before they could start hitting things. Kayda had held her own with this battle-ax days ago, but she'd been sloppy. Frankly, luck and adrenaline had been on her side more than any natural skill. It was nice going back to basics. It reminded her of her cage fighting days and the rigorous training her father had put her through. She found her swings were more powerful when she imagined *him* standing in front of her.

Later, a few of the VHoA members pulled fighting dummies out of their cars and erected them in the weed-choked grass. Welsh stood off to the side and cast his glamour magic at one of the dummies, turning it from a rigid figure made of magic-reinforced rubber to a feral.

The first time he cast his magic on the dummy, Kayda's heart had lurched into her throat. Welsh even made the glamoured dummy snarl like the real thing. Since he was only casting a kind of illusion over the figure, the feral couldn't advance—it just thrashed around in place like a nightmarish scarecrow come to life.

The group at large was sent to battle the unglamoured dummies. Then, one by one, fighters were summoned to where Marisol and Welsh stood near the falsely snarling feral. As the fighter attacked, Marisol made suggestions about stance and reaction time. Then the next fighter was waved over.

By the time they were done around midday, Kayda hurt all over. She relished the ache. Henri, Jo, and Erik, however, looked like they wanted to pass out on the ground and never get back up. Weapons were returned to the van, sweaty hugs and high-fives were exchanged, and then the group slowly dispersed. Henri and Kayda stayed behind to help Marisol and her crew load up the van.

The triplets had limped off together, with Ollie and Liam more or less carrying Ben to Liam's car. The kid was definitely getting saddled with desk duty.

When Kayda and Henri finished helping Marisol, Henri looked even closer to passing out.

"Want me to drive?" Kayda asked him.

All he did was nod before shuffling in the direction of his cycle. Kayda intended to follow him but stopped when Marisol called her name.

When she turned around, she found Marisol with a hip resting on the side of her loaded van. A horn honked twice, and the final car with a weary VHoA member behind the wheel headed off, leaving only Marisol, Kayda, and Welsh. Henri continued trudging toward his cycle, his path unwavering.

"What's up?" Kayda asked, resting the haft of her hooded ax on her shoulder.

"Have you given my job offer any more thought?" Marisol asked. "We need all the help we can get, and you've saved several of our asses more than once. I'd feel less bad about that if I could compensate you."

"Would it mean patrols every night?" Kayda asked.

"Most nights," Marisol said, nodding. "It wouldn't be many days off, but the pay isn't bad."

"Pay's better than your security gig at the casino," Welsh added.

"The security gig I would still have, no thanks to you," she said, but there was no bite. She'd largely hated that job anyway.

She wanted to ask how he knew what her pay had been but decided against it. Welsh just … knew things. She guessed it was from how often he wore glamours when he was out in the world, gathering intel while wearing any number of different faces. An army of spies inhabiting one body.

"With a bit more training, I'd be happy to have Henri join us, too. He's a little green, but he's got good instincts," Marisol said.

All of this was code for *"We know you just started dating Henri, but now you're hardly ever going to see him. At least you'll get paid!"* Welsh, she supposed, was here to gently bully her into saying yes if it looked like she might decline the offer.

Marisol had a good poker face, and her casual folded-arm posture suggested she couldn't care less about Kayda's answer. But thanks to Kayda's heightened senses, she could hear how fast Marisol's heart thumped, how the tiny rock by the toe of her shoe was getting ground into the dirt from Marisol's fidgeting, and the rhythmic tap, tap, tap of Marisol's finger against her side.

Kayda didn't doubt that what waited on the horizon for Luma —for all the hubs—was bad, to put it mildly. But the fact that levelheaded Marisol was wound this tight made Kayda even more anxious.

"When do I start?"

Marisol heaved out a breath and bent at the waist, hands on her knees. "Holy shit, Kay. You almost gave me a heart attack with that pause."

Welsh chuckled and patted Marisol's back. "Told you she'd say yes. Have a good day, ladies."

When Marisol finally stood straight again, her cheeks were flush. "Tonight at ten?"

Kayda nodded. "See you then."

She headed for Henri's cycle.

"Oh, and tell Henri we're planning to meet out here every morning, seven a.m.," Marisol shouted. "He's welcome to join anytime!"

Kayda thrust a hand in the air in acknowledgment. Even from a distance, she could see Henri draped over the seat of the cycle like a sack of flour thrown across the back of a horse. She thought he might be upset that she wouldn't get to hang out with him tonight, but given the pathetic groans issuing from him now, she surmised he would much prefer being sprawled out on his couch for the rest of his day off.

"Kayda ..." he said, his face still angled toward the ground. "Kayda, I have a very serious question."

She deposited her battle-ax in the sidecar. "What's that?"

"Am I dead?"

She laughed. "C'mon, let's get you home and into bed."

"I've waited a long time for you to say that to me," he said. "But today it doesn't feel very sexy."

Kayda wasn't sure if it was a good or bad sign that he was so tired his stutter had fled the scene.

After getting both of them seated properly, with Henri's arms wrapped around her middle, she started up the cycle and headed for his apartment. He rested his cheek on her back.

"Marisol said you can come back anytime you want," Kayda said. "You can earn the clearance to go on patrol with me if you put the work in. Training starts every day at seven a.m."

Henri softly whimpered all the way home.

CHAPTER FOUR

KAYDA

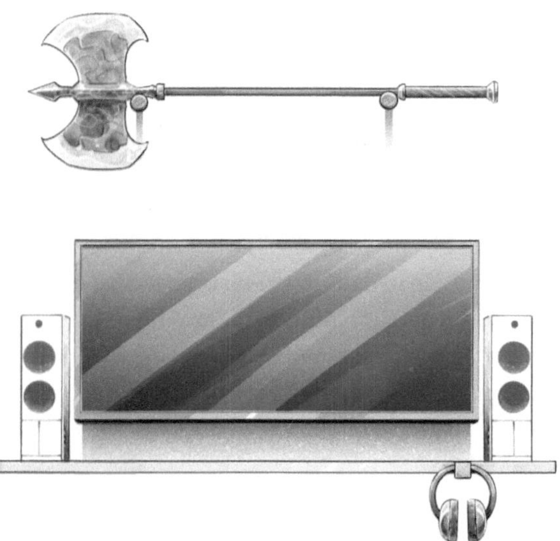

It had been three days since Kayda had officially accepted Marisol's job offer, and she was *wiped*. Since the breach the night Lachlan Shade had escaped, patrols had been almost as uneventful as her security shifts at the casino could be. It was making for very long, boring nights.

Some of Marisol's crew and a handful of Collective werecats had begun doing more patrols outside the veil, but even they reported that there were next to no ferals prowling around the city's perimeter trying to get in. And most of the ones the patrols *did* see got spooked the way a wild animal would and bounded away into the night.

Kayda couldn't help but feel like this was the calm before the storm. The hybrids who controlled the ferals had withdrawn their attack dogs in preparation for some fresh new hell. Kayda didn't think the wild beasts were curled up on dog beds before roaring fires, though. They were just out wreaking havoc somewhere else until they were needed.

It didn't take Kayda long into her first shift to learn that the various chapters of VHoA were well connected. They had an online forum and database that was updated constantly. Nest locations, battle stats, and any newly observed behaviors were logged into a system that updated in real time. Part of Kayda's job during the day was checking the forum and message boards for any new information that Marisol might need to know.

There was an active corner of the forum dedicated to deep discussions about lore and theories about the three types of vampires. Kayda had only dipped into this section a couple of times, but the threads about ferals were the most active by far. Useful, actionable suggestions weren't what was found there. Instead, those threads were where the most out-there conspiracy theories were voiced.

She'd seen Marisol's handle come up often, and Kayda wondered how much time her friend spent in that section of the forum. Maybe that was Marisol's go-to hangout when insomnia seized her—which was often if Kayda's assumptions were correct. It was the kind of place where off-the-wall speculations could only be made more outlandish with the aid of intoxication and/or an unhealthy lack of sleep. When Kayda got sucked into reading a lively discussion about how ferals were actually the victims of human cloning gone awry, using illegally exhumed bodies of celebrities as the source, she decided it wasn't the place for her. The theory that ferals were the genetic cousins of Elvis and Tupac was more than her brain could handle.

After only three days of scouring the online places that the *average* VHoA member frequented the most, it was clear the same thing was happening everywhere: Ferals were no longer breaching the veils in significant numbers. So what in the hells was going on now?

VHoA had spent much of their time over the last several months barely keeping their heads above water as they stemmed the tide of the veil breaches. Now that the breaches had slowed, they were realizing that they'd been merely treating a symptom of a much larger problem. Now their efforts were funneled into figuring out what exactly that problem was.

Kayda assumed this was all by design on the Shades' part. The Shades had slowly overwhelmed the hub systems with waves of feral hordes to keep the Collectives and their police forces preoccupied. It was reminiscent of the misdirection technique mundane magicians employed, and just like a wowed audience mesmerized by the actions of the magician's right hand, no one had seen what Lachlan's left hand was doing until it was too late.

She fought a small smile as she remembered that his literal left hand had been chopped off. Hopefully that would make life harder for the elfin bastard, but she doubted it.

Kayda feared another distraction was at play now. Clearly, Lachlan was a long con kind of elf. She supposed spending three decades banished to another world had something to do with that. Plenty of time to think and scheme.

The whole thing made her head ache.

Currently, she was seated at the bank of computers in the middle of the VHoA War Room, as she'd taken to calling it, wedged between two guys wearing chunky headphones. She yawned for the four-hundredth time as she scrolled through forum posts and message boards and sifted through the cluster that was mundane social media, searching for anything of note.

Just as she was about to extricate herself from her chair to take a power nap on the nearest available couch, a new post popped up on the forum page she'd been staring at for the last twenty minutes.

"Mulgrew's Veil Breached!" the headline of the post said. A cell-phone video was the entirety of the post.

Kayda did a quick search on Mulgrew, discovering that it was a small hub in Iowa. Her headphones had been resting behind her neck, so she pulled them up, fitting the cups over her ears. She hit play.

The person taking the video stood on a balcony that on one side overlooked an outdoor market in a massive parking lot and on the other a crowded downtown street. The videographer had a perfect view of the festivities below. Kayda guessed it was the balcony of a hotel.

In the direction of the market, the camera panned over tents, food trucks and, off in a corner, what looked like a petting zoo. The lot was swarming with people. The whole area was enclosed behind a chain-link fence hung with banners advertising local shops and restaurants. A line of people waiting to get in stretched down the tree-lined sidewalk. A pair of maroon tour buses were parked along the curb.

The video panned away from the festival for a moment, scanning down the street—perhaps to take in the hustle and bustle or the architecture of the surrounding buildings. Whatever this event was, it was popular. Music heavy on the saxophone wafted from up the street, and Kayda imagined a live band set up on the patio of a packed bar.

A series of shouts made the videographer swing the phone back toward the festival.

Large swaths of the crowd inside the fenced-in area had paused what they were doing and were now all facing some point in the middle of the lot. The stillness of that many people creeped Kayda out—especially since, even with her high vantage point, she couldn't see what had caused such an abrupt reaction. There were so many tents and trucks scattered around the space that Kayda figured most people couldn't see what was happening. After a moment, the folks in the middle of the lot began to scatter. A few started to run in the direction of the fence. Someone shoved someone else out of the way with such force they hit the ground. Kayda's wide gaze frantically scanned the scene, trying desperately to find the source. It was frustrating that her heightened senses could offer no aid.

Another shriek. A surge of movement in the middle of the crowd. Screams sounded off to the left, Kayda thought, where the sidewalks were filled with people shopping and searching for a place to eat. Then, from out of the frame, a fast-moving creature galloped up the sidewalk where waiting festival-goers stood in line. The creature launched onto someone's back. Another rounded the side of a bus. Two launched off the top of one.

Hysteria surged like a physical entity both inside and outside the fence as creatures who were somehow both humanoid and not came pouring in from all directions. They attacked indiscriminately. It took mere seconds for complete chaos to descend on the festival. The videographer kept up a steady stream of soft, disbelieving curses that mirrored the ones in Kayda's head. The camera swung to the right, where the festival was, then to the left, where the sidewalks had been clogged with people only a minute or two before. Bodies were strewn everywhere. Even from the height of the balcony, it was clear that blood soaked into concrete and asphalt. It splattered the banners lining the chain-link fence. It pumped out of torn throats and slid down curbs into the gutter.

The ferals just kept coming.

Parents ran by holding young children close to their chests. People ran hand in hand, dragging each other away from the carnage.

Even though swarms of people clad in black and camo showed up within five minutes, armed with swords, spears, and axes, those five minutes had been an eternity for the victims. Shortly after what looked like VHoA's arrival, werecats came loping onto the scene. With quick efficiency, the cats and vampire hunters took down dozens of ferals, their blackened blood mixing with the red blood already splattered everywhere. Ferals had to be running loose all over the city by then, though. It would take a while to find the stragglers. Assuming the ferals didn't just slip back out the way they'd gotten in, returning to the sides of their hybrid masters.

Kayda's stomach roiled. She wasn't sure she'd blinked in minutes.

Ripping off her headphones, she hastily got to her feet, sending her office chair hurtling backward. It crashed into one of the freestanding tool lockers behind her—a locker she knew was packed to the gills with charmed weapons. Would a locker's worth be enough if Luma was attacked like Mulgrew just was? Ten lockers? Twenty?

If her abrupt movement hadn't startled her fellow researchers into looking up, the crash of her chair did. There were only five people in here now—the night shift was the busier one.

Marisol had been pacing the room, her phone pressed to her ear, but upon seeing Kayda's no doubt freaked-out expression, she said, "Hey, I'll call you back ..." She pocketed her phone and took a few cautious steps forward, as if Kayda were a frightened animal who might bolt. "Kay ... what the hells happened?"

In a calm tone that sounded robotic even to her own ears, Kayda said, "Everyone, get on the forum and find the post about Mulgrew's breach."

The group at large only hesitated for a moment before hands sought for keyboards and mice. If they hadn't already been at a computer, like Marisol, they were at one now.

Kayda hastily clicked out of the video still on her screen. The post already had over a thousand views and fifty comments. It had been up for less than ten minutes. She stalked away from her computer.

She paced up and down the room as she waited for everyone else to watch the video. The level of devastation those things had wrought in such a short window of time was making her head spin. She'd fought ferals before, but she'd been ready for them. She'd always been armed.

Those people … those people probably had no idea this was possible. Maybe the ferals and their hybrid masters had left Mulgrew alone all this time. Their VHoA chapter would be aware of the threat the breaches posed, thanks to the VHoA network being so tight-knit, but maybe they'd never experienced a breach firsthand. How many of them had fought ferals before? Hundreds of people had been slaughtered before help could arrive. Did VHoA and Collective werecats across the country need to be stationed at every large event now? Should hubs not hold large events at all?

Kayda pressed a hand to her stomach as she paced, her mind filled with the anguished cries of strangers.

Gasps of shock, words of disbelief, and violent cursing started to slip out of her colleagues. After a minute, someone started weeping. Another tore their headphones off and stalked out of the room, leaving the door to the War Room open.

When everyone in the group had finished watching the video, an eerie silence settled over them like a blanket.

Kayda turned to Marisol, who was pacing on the other side of the room.

"What do we *do*?" Kayda asked.

"Start contacting the Mulgrew chapter," Marisol said. "Call all the numbers we have on file until someone picks up. Ask them everything you can think of. We've got a list of questions compiled that you can work from. We need as much information as possible. Add any new info to the corresponding files as you get it. Find out if they need help."

Kayda didn't want to sit around making *phone calls*. She wanted to punch something. She wanted to lop off heads.

"Kay. *Kayda!*"

She glanced up.

Marisol held eye contact without flinching. "Keep a level head.

Mulgrew is a tiny hub. They have resources, but not as many as we do. Our Collective already knows breaches are possible. They've added a bunch of werecats to the patrolling roster. We're safe for now. At the very least, if Luma is next, we'll get a warning. Right now, we need information. I know this is frustrating, but the more we know, the better equipped we'll be when the shit hits the fan here, okay?"

Kayda ground her teeth together so hard, she was surprised she hadn't reduced them to powder. She wasn't worried about Luma so much as she was worried about everyone who *wasn't* in Luma. There were small hubs scattered all over the world. Had they all been hit at the same time? Were they being hit now? Were hundreds of thousands of people getting torn apart by ferals while she sat in a too-small chair typing away at a computer?

"Kay ..."

"Yeah, yeah," Kayda said, wheeling her chair back into place and then plopping into it. "Your data monkey is back at work, see?" she asked Marisol over the top of her screen.

"If you behave, I may even give you a banana," Marisol said, then dropped out of view behind her monitor.

The guy next to Kayda chuckled, but he nearly choked on his tongue when she sent him a death glare.

Kayda picked up her cell phone lying by her keyboard. Given the madness of the last couple of months, at least Harlow had become less paranoid about cell phone use.

KAYDA

You all right?

HARLOW

If by all right you mean I haven't murdered Cas over his horrendous taste in music while on yet another road trip, yes. Know what's even worse? Mom LIKES the nonsense he keeps picking. What's up?

KAYDA

Ask your mom about Mulgrew when you get a chance. Shit's starting to go down, I think. Stay safe out there.

HARLOW

So is this a bad time to tell you that we got a personal invite to Tercla and we're making a pit stop there before heading to Luma?

KAYDA

...

HARLOW

I'll get you a souvenir! Do you want a T-shirt, a shot glass, or a keychain?

KAYDA

A shot glass, obviously.

HARLOW

Right! Silly question. I'll give you an update on Tercla once we get there ... assuming I don't end up as vamp food. Unless, of course, I get the hots for one of the bloodsuckers and enter into a contracted relationship.

KAYDA

You're giving me an ulcer.

HARLOW

Miss you, too!

CHAPTER FIVE

HARLOW

The surprise visit from Vaughn had been the push my mom needed to finally leave the VHoA warehouse, though it had still taken her nearly three more days. Mom held authority in the Washington headquarters, but several others were considered point people. Mom was respected because of her reputation, rather than her position in the organization, so her leaving wouldn't throw the group into anarchy or anything. Perk of being a traveling consultant.

Apprehensive about what might go down along the way, Soren had decided to make the trek from Washington to California with us. Soren had family and friends in California, and he claimed a trip to see them was overdue. It wasn't lost on me that he never gave specifics about where these people lived, nor did he make any active plans to see them.

Even though I'd been ignoring Felix's check-in texts, I sent him a message once we'd finally left the VHoA warehouse.

HARLOW

Hey. Me, my mom, and Caspian are headed back to Luma. Not sure when we'll get in since we're kinda sorta making a stop in Tercla first? Long story. We've got a date with Sorceress Rhiannon once we get to town. Does the Tower have a nice coffee shop? We could have a little reunion before I meet with the people who ruined my life and the lives of everyone I love!

FELIX

I have a mild heart attack every time you message me. One day I'd like to get a message from you that's a just link to a cute cat video. Not a werecat, either. Just a housecat. Playing with string or something. Why are you going to a vamp enclave?!

HARLOW

My mom's past is sordid and full of fangs

FELIX

I can't decide if I want details or not

HARLOW

You do not

FELIX

Things at the Tower are currently…a hot fucking mess. I can't really get into it right now. I'm heading out the door on a call. Def let me know when you're on your way to the Tower. Maybe I can help run damage control

Well, that was ominous.

I probably should have asked a clarifying question or two, but I was nothing if not an avoider of difficult things, so I shoved my phone into the front pocket of my backpack and watched the passing landscape instead.

We drove seven hours straight to an Oregon VHoA warehouse. It, like the Washington one, was in an industrial area. A fleet of black SUVs and Jeeps were parked inside the building, a bank of tables covered in computers sat in the middle of the room, and a sea of cots were spread out in the back of the space behind a series of freestanding curtained partitions. It felt like déjà vu being here. Mom said they modeled all the headquarters to look the same, so no matter where you were coming from or how new you were to that particular location, you'd still feel at home.

Despite that sentiment, we decided the sword needed to stay hidden while here. Mom trusted VHoA on the whole, but she hadn't spent as much time in the Oregon locations, so she didn't want to go blabbing to everyone in earshot that we were traveling with a sentient weapon.

Since she had done all the driving that day, Mom made the rounds to say hello, ate, then collapsed on a cot in the back.

The Mulgrew attack had happened a few days ago, so the place wasn't in chaos like the Washington headquarters had been when the news hit. That night, we'd huddled around a computer and watched three cell phone videos that had been posted to the VHoA forum.

It had been *the* nightmare scenario: innocent people being torn apart by monsters. No warning. No reason. Just pure carnage.

The vibe of the Oregonian headquarters was chill, though a bit subdued. To be fair, they could have been a more relaxed group than the Washingtonian one to begin with.

Shortly after Mom stumbled off to bed, Soren joined a group going out on patrol. His usual goofy energy had been dampened these last few days, sometimes hardening into something intense and a little scary.

I was wired after so many hours in the car, so sleep was out of the question, and Caspian practically frothed at the mouth in anticipation of returning to his books and journal. He couldn't read them in the car; he got carsick.

While Caspian found a quiet corner to settle into with his notes, I opted for hopping on one of the computers. I avoided even thinking about the VHoA forum. If I never saw the Mulgrew videos again it would be too soon. But some light research wouldn't hurt. Research was key. The key to what? I didn't know.

I played solitaire for an hour.

When I got sick of that, I considered making Caspian play actual cards with me. If this place really was set up like all the others, then the cabinet under the coffee maker would be jam-packed with board and card games.

Someone plopped into the chair next to me, startling me out of making a decision. I'd expected it to be Caspian, but instead I found a very attractive stranger. He hadn't taken up the spot next to me solely because it was the only open computer. Down the row, VHoA's logo slowly bounced off the edges of several dark, idle screens. The guy swiveled his chair toward me, propped an arm on the back, and flashed a disarming smile.

He was in his mid-thirties, I guessed. Dark skinned, maybe Indian. Wavy jet-black hair. Brown eyes. His gaze slowly roamed my face, his smile deepening. He wanted me to be flustered by his presence; he was gorgeous—and he knew it.

I mirrored his posture. With my chin propped on my fist, I asked, "What can I help you with …?"

"Samar."

"Deanna," I said, proud of myself for remembering my alias when that smile of his was making my brain short-circuit.

Caspian's alias was Caleb.

"Well, Deanna." Samar's voice was nice, too. "I just wanted to officially welcome you. Have you ever been to this HQ?"

"Oh, you can do better than that, Samar. Is that your version of 'Do you come here often?'"

He laughed. "Okay, fine. Is it true you're all from Luma?"

"Caleb and I are. My mom—Robin—used to live there," I said,

figuring that out of all the topics he could want to talk about, this was the safest.

"Is it also true that … Shade came back?"

Of course that rumor had made the rounds already. I was sure said rumor had gained even more recognition in the wake of the Mulgrew tragedy. "Yeah."

"Any idea why he chose Luma for his grand re-entry?"

I eyed him. "How would I know?"

He shrugged. "I've only been to Luma twice. Downtown is like Vegas—always swarmed with people, always active. The werecat guard force is three times the size of the one in Pinebough. Doesn't seem like the best place to try something as risky as opening a portal. But you live there. You're an expert on the place compared to me. You don't have any theories?"

"Luma might be big as far as hubs go," I said, "but the spot he picked is not only rural, it's basically abandoned."

Samar nodded absently. "That makes sense. It's just that his chances of getting caught would've been way less if he'd chosen one of the smaller hubs. Hell, Axia is in California too and has, what, a population of ten thou or less? He could have popped up there, and that sleepy little town wouldn't have known what hit it."

I considered this. "I think he chose Luma *because* there was a large risk of getting caught. He's got a big enough ego that he didn't doubt he could pull it off. Why not do it in a city that's got a Collective, a fleet of bounty hunters, a police force, *and* a ton of werecats? Not to mention a VHoA chapter. He wanted to be successful despite all that. And now, only a week later, someone in Oregon has heard about his impossible feat, right? Mission accomplished for him."

Samar grinned that disarming grin. "See, I knew you had a theory."

My face flushed. "It was also a fuck-you to the Luma Collective specifically."

Samar cocked his head. "Why?"

"It was a Luma sorcerer who banished him in the first place."

Samar whistled. "No shit?"

"No shit." There was a brief lull in the conversation as he continued to stare at me. "So did you mosey over here to flirt with me or to get intel on Luma?"

"Why can't it be both?"

He had the decency to strike up a normal getting-to-know-you conversation after that, whether or not he was actually interested in anything I had to say. He was funny, at least. Funny won me over more times than not. He was in the middle of telling me a story about his little sister when he suddenly stopped talking, scrutinizing something above my head.

I quickly scanned the area above me, worried the sword had grown bored and was floating there. All I saw was part of Caspian's face. I gave my chair a slow spin, so I was facing him instead of turned toward Samar. "Hey … Caleb. What's up?"

"Aiden just texted me. I'm going to be an uncle thrice over," he said without preamble.

"Uhhh … congrats?" I said, troubled by how tired he looked. I thought he'd slept in the car on the way here, but maybe he hadn't.

"He has not informed my parents yet. It appears we have bonded over our mutual frustration with our parents' disappointments in our life choices."

Samar coughed awkwardly behind me.

Caspian's eyes lost their glazed look, quickly recovering from his sleep-deprived fugue state. He offered me a tight smile. "I'm heading to bed. You might want to consider doing the same. Your mother wants to leave bright and early in the morning, and you have the disposition of a fire ant before ten a.m." His gaze flitted over my head to address Samar. "I apologize for not making your acquaintance, but I'm beat. Perchance I'll see you at breakfast."

He gave my shoulder a squeeze in passing as he walked away. Margaret's journal was tucked under one arm. As I turned my chair back to Samar, I glanced at the time in the bottom corner of my computer screen. It was after midnight. How in the hell had that happened?

Samar wore a curious little smile. "What's the deal with you two? I can't tell if he's your boyfriend or your stuffy attendant."

"The stuffy attendant thing is just because he's an academy-graduate sorcerer."

Caspian wasn't technically a graduate, but Samar didn't need to know that.

Samar nodded knowingly. Once you met enough sorcerers, it was easy to recognize the ones who'd made it through extensive sorcery schooling. "So ... do *you* need to go to bed?"

"That would be the wise move. I don't want to turn into a fire ant, after all."

Samar laughed.

I was about to get up when Samar awkwardly coughed again.

Easing back into my seat, I asked, "What's up?"

"I asked about Luma earlier because I've been working on a project the last few days with some people here. It's not a VHoA assignment, exactly," Samar said.

I tried not to sound suspicious as I asked, "Where else do you get your assignments?"

Samar hesitated. "I take on ... contract work for ... wealthy clientele."

It sounded like the diplomatic answer an assassin for hire would put on his resume. Considering I was keeping my own secrets, I opted not to press for details about his.

"What was this mysterious assignment about?" I asked.

With a grateful smile, he continued. "It's about vamps—shocking, I know. I was thinking of posting it tomorrow on the forum to gauge the reaction from the hive mind. This whole Mulgrew fiasco makes me want to post it even more. Do you ... want to see it?"

There was a hint of insecurity in his tone now, like he really wanted my opinion on whatever it was. Huh. Maybe part of the reason he'd come over here *had* been to flirt with me.

"Sure."

He bobbed his head and turned his chair toward the computer in front of him. He jiggled the mouse to wake up the screen, then deftly opened a browser, keyed in a password, and up popped a website with "Vampire Hunters of America Official Message Board" written at the top. The VHoA logo—a fanged mouth enclosed in a circle with a line running across the diameter at an angle—was stamped in the upper right-hand corner.

He clicked open a folder, typed another password, and then clicked on a post titled "Shade Map." A bright-red "DRAFT" was written next to the heading. "Do you know anything about Bliss?"

I snorted a laugh so loud, he flinched. "Sorry. Just saying 'yes' is an understatement, but yes."

"Good, that'll save me some time," he said, attention back on the screen. "Among VHoA, there's been a pretty popular theory for a while that Bliss is connected to vamps. Some chick named Harlow figured out a few months ago that Bliss's secret ingredient is vampire saliva. She discovered that around the same time half of Luma's chapter of VHoA got blown up during a vamp nest raid. *My* theory is the raid happened *because* of her discovery about the venom. She got too close to the Bliss cartel's biggest secret. The lead hybrid vamp of that nest had been using Bliss to drug fae girls and then used those fae girls as both food and as bait to lure in *more* food."

A little pang twinged in my chest at the memory of that explosion. It hadn't been half of Marisol's crew who had died, but two-thirds.

Instead of voicing any of that, I made the appropriate sounds of shock. "That's wild."

"Right? That confirmed what we've all been thinking for a while—that vamps were using Bliss somehow. A group of us have been combing the forum and message boards for everything we can find about Bliss. I've got contacts in … uhh … a bunch of hubs who find out what they can about Bliss in or around their cities, and then I add that to the message boards. On the side, I've been pulling as much info as I can on areas that have an abnormal number of missing fae teens and young adults. Luma can't be the only place where hybrid vamps are running fae-trafficking rings for whatever fucked-up shit they're doing."

"And you think these trafficking cases are connected to Lachlan Shade?" I asked, concerned we'd gone too far afield of our starting topic.

Samar nodded. "Yeah. If hybrid vamps and the Shades have been working with each other all this time, and the hybrids have this whole smuggle-in-Bliss and smuggle-out-fae scheme, it could all be connected. At first I was thinking it was just a way for hybrid vamps to make money and get their food supply from inside the hubs, but what if it's more than that?"

"Like what?" I asked, inadvertently leaning closer to the computer. Samar grinned over at me, and I sat back a bit. I'd picked up one of Caspian's habits.

"Shade used elf teens for his ritual to open that portal, right? And from what I've read from the Luma chapter's logs, those elf teens were going through skill tests for weeks. The elf kids are the ones who kept causing the breaches in the veil that let ferals into Luma. Did you know that? Only the elves who performed the best —who proved they had strong magic even if they were still untrained—were the ones selected for the ritual. But since Lachlan killed them all—or most of them—the tests were probably less about their ability to manipulate the veils and more about—"

"If they had enough untapped magical stores Lachlan could siphon out of them to power the portal," I finished for him.

"Exactly," Samar said, looking impressed with my superior deduction skills. Oh, if only he knew I was best friends with the draken who'd had a front-row seat to that shit show. Would he be jealous, or offended that I was playing dumb? "The VHoA logs from other hubs report that at least half of the missing fae teens are elves. Because of the whole Bliss thing, we'd been figuring that hybrids just have a preference for elves and that the missing kids were only being smuggled out for trafficking. I think that's *part* of why they're going missing, but not the whole reason. I heard Harlow rescued something like ten missing fae teens from Luma *and* got them back home. Several of them have started sharing their stories of what happened to them. Hearing their stories has really helped solidify some of my theories."

His intel was a little off again, but I couldn't correct him. "Sounds like you have a crush on this Harlow chick."

"I'd like to take her out for a beer if nothing else." Samar's cheeks went a little darker. He totally had a crush on me *twice* and didn't even know it. "So ... I got to thinking. What if the cases of missing elf teens in these other areas are because they're getting tested just like the Luma kids were? There's a theory that part of why Lachlan was able to open that portal and get out was because the Collective there was spread too thin. There have been reports from all over the country—not just in the weeks before his escape —about surges of portal magic.

"There's a Portal Relations branch of the Collective that's in charge of staying on top of closing rogue portals. Portal Relations agents were getting sent all over the place to put out those little fires. We all thought it was a distraction technique of Lachlan's, but what if it was more than that? What if his grand plan had always been for Luma, but he'd had smaller plans being executed in smaller hubs?"

My mind was spinning. I reconsidered my aversion to perusing the VHoA forum. How much of the information that had hit the organization-wide site had been input by Marisol herself? A lot of what Samar had just told me had been things Kayda and I had experienced or learned directly, which had later been shared with Marisol.

"What kind of smaller plans are you thinking?" I asked.

"You said it yourself earlier ... Lachlan chose Luma because it was a flashier, in-your-face location to open a portal. Not the smartest choice, but he's pissed at your Collective." Samar paused. "You ever been to Kensey?"

All I really knew about Kensey was that it was the hub in

Washington; it had been named after Frederica Kensey—a woman who had accidentally moved a whole island from the fae realm to the earthen realm during the Glitch—and that a pirate ship stuffed full of charmed items had been found off the coast not far from the hub city. The very same pirate ship, *Element of Surprise*, where my sword's ... grandmother? ... had been under the reluctant employ of Grayson Ipram's many-great-grandfather. It was a small, weird world.

"Haven't been to Kensey, no," I said.

"Well, Kensey's got the best libraries and museums about stuff from the fae realm," Samar said. "According to diaries I've been able to read, it sounds like it wasn't sorcerers who ruled things in the fae realm. It was dragons first and foremost, with elves as a close second. Elves with egos as big as Lachlan's probably don't appreciate the hierarchy shift.

"My guess is that Lachlan unraveled the mystery of how to reopen portals to the fae realm. I'm willing to bet the Collective would lose a *lot* of their residents if they found out they could go home. The hub system might collapse if there's a mass exodus. Sorcerers would lose their cornerstone claim about why they should be in power above all other fae. And for everyone who's left, if the doorways were back open, the Shades could make a shit-ton of money if they had a monopoly on the magic. If people are willing to pay hundreds of thousands to travel into space for ten minutes, imagine what they'd pay if entire *realms* were suddenly accessible."

I mulled that over. "It almost sounds like you're on Team Shade."

Samar wrinkled his nose. "I think getting the portals back open for the folks who feel really stuck here—like the draken who can't even shift anymore—should be able to go. That's a right and a choice they should all get since the Glitch was such a freak occurrence. Shade's just going about it all wrong. Seems like a savior shouldn't be heavily into murder, you know?"

I laughed.

"I'm worried he's going to exploit it," Samar added. "Tossing someone through a portal to an unknown world is a really good way to get rid of your enemies. If the vamps he's working with corner the market on Bliss, and Lachlan perfects not just opening portals to the fae realm but other realms more reliably, he could start an inter-realm drug and travel empire. Fae being shackled in the magic-less earthen realm will get old real quick if the Shades can offer doorways to countless worlds. The Collective would become obsolete. The *hub system* would be obsolete." Samar shrugged. "I think the guy's lawful evil. He's got a strict code he lives by, he's organized, he's got a clear vision, and he doesn't give a shit who he destroys on the path to making that vision a reality."

I grinned at him, curious what my chaotic-good buddy Welsh would think of this assessment.

"As beautiful as your smile is," Samar said, brows raised, "I'm not sure I said anything that warranted it. Unless, of course, *you're* Team Shade and you're secretly hot for evil elves."

I shook my head, still smiling. "Definitely not hot for evil elves."

I eyed the map on his screen and the colorful array of digital pushpins scattered across it. Based on the legend in the corner, he'd mapped areas that had high reports of Bliss, fae disappearances, and portal magic fluctuations—the latter of which was information gleaned from public reports filed by Portal Relations. At least according to his map, there was a definite correlation between the three. The portal magic pushpins might have been ten or twenty miles from the very tightly clustered pins marking fae disappearances and Bliss, but they were all happening in proximity to each other.

"How do you think all this is connected to his drug and travel empire?" I asked, waving vaguely at the screen.

"Ley lines," he said. "Most of those spots correspond with ley lines, or they're near ley lines. This realm had naturally occurring ley lines before the Glitch; that was the closest thing we had to magic here. Pre-Glitch, they were bands of energy that stretched across the globe that could be tapped into to fuel stronger portals. The Glitch severed some bands, creating smaller ones. Other lines were redirected. It destroyed some altogether and created new ones."

I considered the implications of this theory. Samar's line of thought led him down a path toward the hub system's eventual unraveling due to a lack of need for it. I thought about what could happen to the mundane world if suddenly beings from other realms started strolling in and out. If I thought the Collective sometimes cared little for their mundane constituents, I had no doubt Lachlan "Lawful Evil" Shade cared about my kind even less. Turning Earth into an inter-realm waystation could irreparably alter life here for the millions of people *outside* of hubs. Forget the unraveling of the hub system—this could destroy society completely.

"I've been stalling on publishing it for days," Samar said, breaking through my existential spiral. "I guess I needed to run it by someone with fresh eyes. Most people here are sick of hearing me talk about data points."

"As someone new to your data points, I think this is pretty cool," I said. "Frightening as hell, but cool."

He laughed. "That's the only problem with my conspiracy theory: I'm freaked out that I might actually be right. If Lachlan's had thirty years to plan this, and the first part already went off without a hitch—"

"He lost an arm," I blurted. When Samar merely watched me, expectant, I elaborated. "The portal opening didn't go totally without a hitch. He had to fight hard to get through that thing. It almost closed on him when he was trying to get out, and he lost part of his left arm in the process. Hopefully that'll slow his magic-wielding down."

"And how do you know that?"

"I have my own version of a VHoA message board."

His smile was slow, and his gaze raked my face once more. "It's too bad you're leaving in the morning. I like talking to you."

"There are these things known as … *cell phones*. Have you heard of them?"

He grinned. "I have."

We exchanged numbers, programming them into our respective phones. I stifled a yawn that made my eyes water.

"Alas, I've bored another beautiful woman with my love of data points …" Samar said.

I laughed. "I'm not bored, but I do need to get some sleep. Another very long drive is ahead of me tomorrow."

Samar nodded. "Can't have you turning into a fire ant."

"Exactly," I said, standing up and stretching. "Thanks for sharing your theories."

"My pleasure," he said. "Good night."

I'd only taken a few steps away from him when he asked, "Hey, Harlow?"

"Yeah?" I asked, turning, realizing my blunder a second later.

Samar was still seated, a small, tentative smile tugging up the corner of his mouth. "I really *would* like to take you out for a beer sometime. Tell me when and where, and I'll hop in a telepad."

I bit my lip. As much as I liked Samar, I was an untrusting, paranoid person. Not to mention that I still didn't know the details of where he was getting his contract work from. For all I knew, he was a Collective spy.

Samar must have sensed my trepidation because he mimed zipping his lips, locking them, and throwing away the key.

"I've got your number," I said noncommittally. "'Night."

I made my way across the warehouse toward the sleeping area. I pulled a curtain aside and was just about to slip behind it when I glanced over my shoulder. Samar was where I'd left him, watching me. He lifted a hand in parting.

He really *was* devastatingly handsome. He was a definite step up from being hit on by Cody the troll. Made even more true now that the poor bastard had been murdered via sentient sword to the gut. I hadn't let myself consider dating too much in the years since Felix. Flings, sure. Dating? No.

I wouldn't have to go through the awkwardness of explaining who I really was to Samar. He already knew. I hoped he wasn't secretly obsessed with sentient swords, because if he tried to steal mine now that he'd likely deduced it was in this warehouse some-where, I'd be very upset. His face was too pretty to end up shorn from his skull.

I waved back, sorry he and I hadn't met under different circumstances. Getting a beer with him sounded nice. Living in a world that wasn't threatened by a revenge-driven elf in cahoots with hybrid vampires sounded nice, too. But that wasn't happening anytime soon, either.

Sighing, I stepped into the sleeping area and let the curtain fall into place behind me.

That night, I didn't dream of Samar or what having a normal life would be like. I dreamed of Lachlan Shade, a man I'd never met. He stood on a hill overlooking a city below. He looked on as portal after portal opened like swirling blue eyes. Monsters roamed the streets instead of humans. Ferals galloped down empty streets in packs, like wild dogs. Humans cowered behind grimy windows in derelict buildings or peeked out from the corners of alleys. Others still were in chains, dragged behind ghastly creatures like misbehaving pets.

I woke slick with sweat, baffled about what in the hells had made Lachlan want to destroy the only world I'd ever known.

CHAPTER SIX

LACHLAN

Dressed in their forest-green ceremonial robes, Lachlan, Dusty, and Blythe sat against the back wall of the Order Hall. Children and the elderly were allowed to watch the proceedings—*not* participate—as long as they did so with an exit nearby in case something went wrong.

Lachlan tipped his head back, eyeing the deep gouge marks in the wood a few inches from the ceiling. Even in the low light, the scratches were easy to make out. Lachlan thought the repair workers should have patched the spot, or at least hung a picture over it. But his mother said the scratches were a reminder. *"One has to remember where one has been to appreciate where one is going,"* she'd said a million times.

Lachlan didn't get it. He also didn't get how his parents thought being twelve still qualified him as a child. Blythe was ten; *Blythe* was a child. Lachlan would be thirteen in a week. Thirteen was plenty old enough.

He'd witnessed this ritual—or at least the *attempted* ritual—so many times, he practically knew it all by heart. They were never going to let him help. Maybe his help was what they needed to finally succeed.

They would never see him as more than Blythe's babysitter.

He pulled the hem of his robe over his bent knees and hugged them to his chest. The ritual had been going on forever already and, as usual, nothing had happened. He could never decide if he wanted the ritual to be as disastrous as the one that had happened in the years before he was born. *That* ritual had been the one that resulted in the scratches on the walls and had killed half of the Order's members during Lachlan's maternal grandparents' early days in the organization.

At least another epic failure would be more interesting than *this.*

First, they'd lit candles. Then they'd recited the Decree of the Order—which was ten minutes too long, in Lachlan's opinion. Then they'd sung the same dumb song they always sang about the fae realm and the Goddess shining down on them, Her ever-faithful followers. And now they were in the middle of hour three *million* of chanting the portal-opening spell.

Lachlan was annoyed that the Order wouldn't use blood sacrifices like they had in the old days. His grandparents hadn't been too scared to sacrifice people. There were plenty of willing subjects in the Order who would give up their lives to get a portal door open.

"*Sacrifices might yield faster results, but they also yield more consequences,*" Mom would say.

"*The Goddess gives to those who are patient,*" Dad always added.

Blah, blah.

Were all elves as fixated on the supposed Goddess as the Order? Each group of fae marooned in the earthen realm had latched on to the idea of the Goddess being their guardian—like a patron saint of lost fae or something.

To the elves in the Order, the Goddess wasn't just protector of fae as a whole. She was the protector of nature. And since nature was integral to an elf's magic, the Order was sure that if they showed the Goddess reverence, they and they alone would be able to "go home."

Lachlan thought there must be something off in the Order's reasoning. Elves inside the hubs thought the Goddess was their patron saint, too. Those elves could live a life out in the open, unlike the Order, who took up residence in mundane forests, hiding from both fae and mundanes like scared woodland animals. The only possibilities were that the Order was made up of the chosen few—or they were all deluded.

Nothing suggested that their love of the Goddess had granted them a single boon. All it did was ensure their rituals would take an eternity to complete. He could appreciate that complicated magic took time, but this was ridiculous. His brain would surely melt and ooze out his nose due to sheer boredom.

He was in the midst of wondering what color his brain-ooze would be when a shout from the front of the room startled him back to the present. He couldn't tell if it had been an excited shout or a fearful one.

He, Blythe, and their cousin Dusty scrambled to their feet. People weren't running for the exit, so Lachlan inferred from the lack of tormented wailing that another unidentified beast twice the size and strength of a rhinoceros hadn't come through.

Boring.

A wall of people blocked Lachlan's view. They had sprung from their chairs, and now their backs were like a wall of trees before him.

An exultant cry sounded from the front of the room.

"By the Goddess, they did it!"

"Our Lady shines upon us!"

The very air crackled with energy. Lachlan pulled back the sleeve of his robe and marveled at how the fine hairs on his arm rose like the time he'd brushed a blown-up balloon along his skin. This was much more powerful than static electricity, though. The sensation filled his chest with a fluttery anticipation like he'd never felt.

Without a word to his sister or cousin, he lurched forward, hands out. He was small for his age, so it didn't take much effort for him to squeeze between people and scuttle under legs. When he reached the front row of watching patrons—many of whom were too busy crying to notice him, their faces trained skyward as they thanked the Goddess for Her bounty—Lachlan came up short. A few feet of space and three shallow steps were all that stood between him and the portal swirling on the dais.

Lachlan always thought "dais" was too grand a label for the worn wooden stage where he'd been forced to sing "Frosty the Snowman" while wearing pointy green shoes with bells on the toes during last year's Christmas pageant. Why nature-loving elves from another realm thought a Christmas pageant made a lick of sense was beyond him.

But now, staring at this churning mass of magic that literally made the air crackle, he thought the label wasn't nearly grand enough. It was like that time two summers ago when he'd taken a big swig of soda after dumping half a packet of Pop Rocks in his mouth. The concoction fizzed and sparked, then turned to foam that poured from between his lips as if he were a rabid dog. Lachlan had yelped in surprise, which caused too much of the foam to flood down his throat. He'd coughed with such force his eyes had watered, and blue foam had gushed out of his nose. Maybe *that* was the color of his brain-ooze: bright blue. Blythe had laughed so hard she'd peed her pants.

That fizzy feeling was all over Lachlan's body now. He imagined the hair on his head standing as tall as his pointed ears. He didn't check. He couldn't do anything other than goggle at the spectacle.

Standing around the portal were the Order's top six members. Lachlan's parents, Dusty's parents, and two elves who had risen through the ranks thanks to their innate abilities. They stood in a circle, their hands clasped, while the spinning vortex of energy spiraled between them a foot above the dais's wooden floor. All six had their heads thrown back. The spell that had opened the portal like a tear in the universe poured from their mouths in perfect unison. The portal itself was mostly a whirling oval of black with vibrant eddies of blue coloring the outside edge. Lachlan didn't think any of the six Order members knew how enraptured their audience was or that anyone had shouted in triumph at their success.

His parents had warned him and Blythe countless times that, if the spell worked, the spell casters might slip into a trance-like state. They'd told the Shade siblings not to worry, that it was normal.

Lachlan didn't know how long Dusty and Blythe had been standing beside him. When Blythe slid her little hand into his, he didn't flinch, nor did he snatch his hand away. Instead, he closed his fingers tightly around hers.

Craning his neck, Lachlan tried to see what lay *in* the portal. His father stood directly behind the swirling black, but Lachlan couldn't see him, other than his outstretched arms to either side and his booted feet.

Something bright yellow and vaguely elf-shaped moved from east to west inside the portal, disappearing from view almost as quickly as it had materialized. A collective gasp rippled through the room. Blythe squeezed Lachlan's hand even tighter.

This vanity-mirror-shaped hole in the world truly was a window—*a doorway*—to somewhere else.

His parents had done it!

It felt as if everyone had taken a breath and held it. The suspense was nearly a physical thing—as easily detectable as the crackling air itself.

The being moved inside the portal again, but instead of moving from one side of it to the other, it stopped in the dead center. Even though the body was elf-shaped, there were no features—a being made of sparkling, yellow light. Lachlan leaned forward an inch, as if that would make its face sharpen into something recognizable.

The image inside the portal glitched, like the picture on a TV screen distorting for a few moments when the wind buffets the antenna on the roof. When the image was solid again, a large hand three times the size of a normal elfin hand shoved its way out of the portal. The audience leaned back as one.

The members of the Order performing the spell didn't see the hand. Dusty's mom *really* didn't see it because the hand grabbed her by the torso. In two blinks, Lachlan's flesh-and-blood Aunt Lydia had turned into a being of sparkling, yellow light—just like the thing inside the portal.

It yanked Lydia in.

Pandemonium erupted. People screamed. A woman at the end of the front row fainted face first with a splat that probably broke her nose. Someone noisily threw up in the back.

Lachlan wrapped his arms around Dusty's middle to keep him from rushing forward. Tears streamed down his cousin's face as he cried for his mom over and over and over. Even though Dusty was a year younger, it took everything in Lachlan's power to keep his cousin away from the stage. Blythe clung to the front of Dusty's legs like a barnacle, her arms wrapped tight around his knees.

No one knew what to do.

But they all held too much respect for—or fear of—the Order

to rush the stage. The Order leaders had specifically told everyone not to break up the ritual for *any* reason.

It turned out that the lower-ranking members didn't have to intervene, though. Aunt Lydia getting sucked into the still-swirling portal broke the spell the Order leaders had been entranced with for what seemed like hours. The Order leaders were bleary-eyed and dazed. Their eyes squinted as if they'd just stepped into a sun-lit world after being trapped in a cave for a month. Their bumbling confusion warred with the chaotic panic of everyone else.

Dusty's dad was the first one on the stage to realize his wife was missing. The audience exclaimed, almost as one, that the monster in the portal had stolen her. Uncle Greg ran to the portal, bellowing her name as if the portal were a well and Lydia was at the bottom of it.

"Lydia!" he choked out. "Lydia, can you hear me?"

The sparkling-light being was back in an instant. It didn't turn Uncle Greg into light.

It turned him into a pile of ash.

People were really screaming now. Dusty was so upset he passed out, going limp in Lachlan's arms. Blythe hadn't seen what had happened to Uncle Greg—her back to the stage as she continued to hold tight to Dusty's legs—but she'd sensed something awful had just transpired. She started sobbing, the frenetic energy enough to tip her over the edge. When Dusty collapsed into Lachlan, Blythe disengaged from Dusty and sprinted for the stage steps.

"Blythe!" Lachlan called out, seized with a sense of panic of his own that was so all consuming he almost passed out, too. If his baby sister ended up reduced to a pile of ash, he'd never forgive himself. "Blythe, no!"

Lachlan flung the unconscious body of his cousin in the direction of the woman next to him, who was shaking so badly it was as if she were experiencing an earthquake only she could feel. She snapped out of her near hysteria and caught Dusty before he hit the floor.

Lachlan shoved past two elves, knocking a man off his feet and into a cluster of elves in the aisle. Blythe had run to their parents and had tackle-hugged their father's leg, much like she'd been doing to Dusty earlier. She was crying so hard, her face had gone splotchy, and snot ran from her nose. The points of her ears had gone red.

The leaders of the Order were huddled together a few feet from the portal. Lachlan had been moving so fast, he almost didn't stop himself in time when he reached them. The rest of the Order milled about in the main part of the room—if they hadn't already fled—as if the edge of the dais were a barrier only the members on high and their families could cross.

The portal still spun menacingly in the center of the stage, but the monster of light thankfully wasn't peering out of the portal as if it were some kind of possessed funhouse mirror. Lachlan's stomach roiled as he spotted the pile of ash on the floor. There was a footprint in the middle of it. Some part of him wanted to laugh at the fact that Dusty's dad had been turned to dust, but he knew that was because laughing was easier than dealing with the very real fact that Uncle Greg had just been murdered right before Lachlan's eyes by a being he couldn't even describe.

Chest heaving, Lachlan tried to pry Blythe away from their father's leg, but she only held on tighter.

"It's all right," his father said, wrapping a hand around Lachlan's upper arm and gently pulling him up. His father immediately returned to his conversation with the other Order members —discussing how long they had before the portal closed again— and ignoring his children.

Lachlan swallowed. "Can that thing get out?"

They paid him no heed. His baby sister continued to wail.

He clenched his jaw, then shoved his way into their cluster of four. Shooting them each a murderous look as he turned in a slow circle, he made sure they were listening before he spoke again. He was shorter than all of them. Scrawnier, too. But they needed to stop arguing about whether this was a test from the Goddess herself, or a sign, or whatever else. His uncle was dead, and his aunt must be, too. They needed to close the portal. And they needed to do it now.

He shot a finger toward the mass of black swirling on the stage. The back side of the portal was an even deeper black than the front. Lachlan somehow knew it was only traversable from one side. "Can. That thing. *Get out*?" he asked again.

"We … we don't know," his mother said. "The Goddess may—"

"No," Lachlan said, fiercely shaking his head. "You have to close it before it gets out. It can kill people just by touching them. Close it before it gets anyone else."

A roar reverberated from the vicinity of the portal. It was a deep, echoey sound. The hairs on Lachlan's arms rose for an entirely new reason. Blythe stopped sobbing and peeled herself off their dad's leg. Half the audience—who were still running around like chickens with their heads cut off—froze in their tracks.

The thunderous cry came again, louder this time.

Had the thing … heard him?

That sound was more convincing than Lachlan's little speech because the Order leaders sprang into action. With words of various spells on their lips, the four streamed past Lachlan. Blythe rushed to him, throwing her arms around his middle. Lachlan clutched her to his side, his hand on her back.

The Order leaders formed a semicircle around the portal and quickly summoned the power of the air in their lungs and the earth below their feet. They urged the Goddess to allow them to close the portal. And it *did* begin to shrink, but that only enraged the monster of light. A pair of abnormally large hands shot out of the portal, but the Order leaders knew to expect it now and avoided contact. Vines sprung from the dais and lashed at the monstrous glowing hands.

When the being's efforts were thwarted, it changed tack. Flashes of pure light shot out of the portal like miniature lightning bolts. Three audience members were struck in the chest and collapsed. The crackling air filled with the scent of seared flesh and burnt hair. That was enough to get everyone moving. As the audience members fled through the back door as fast as they could, crashing into one another to get out of the room, more were felled by lightning strikes.

Blythe yelped and buried her face in Lachlan's shirt. They stood in the safest spot in the room—on the dais but out of view of the portal. He started to tremble, feeling every bit the child his parents believed him to be.

The Order leaders had decided on a new strategy while the monster of light was busy picking off the retreating lower-tier members. Vines as thick as Lachlan's forearm burst from the dais and dove into the portal with all the force of a cobra going in for a killing strike. Lachlan's parents were flanked by the pair who had cast the vines. His parents were working on a spell of their own.

"Now!" Lachlan's mother said.

The pair controlling the vines, though their hands were empty, formed fists, braced themselves, and then yanked their fists down toward their sides, as if they held ski poles.

A great bellow sounded. A breath later, the brightly glowing torso of the monster was yanked through the portal. The being thrashed in its snare. When it opened its maw to howl in rage, blinding light poured from its mouth.

As one, Lachlan's parents thrust their arms skyward. Twin ropes of undulating water whipped around Lachlan's father's body like coiling snakes. A gale-force wind conjured by his mother swept past Lachlan, bringing with it the scent of brine. The wind formed the water into a massive scythe that swung down on the monster's neck, lopping its head clean off. The resulting cascade of sparks made Lachlan and Blythe shy away. The head of the beast had turned to something like stone by the time it hit the dais, splintering the wood where it fell. Lachlan felt the impact in the soles of his feet. He blinked away the spots pulsing in his vision.

"We have to find her," someone said. He thought it might have been his mother, but his ears rang. "She may still be alive."

"The portal will close for good soon," his father said. "We have to decide now."

"Lachlan!"

Squinting, he dragged his sister forward.

His mother dropped to a squat at their feet. She was a blur, but she was starting to take shape. Blythe frantically rubbed the heels of her palms against her eyes. His mother gently pulled one of his sister's palms from her face, then took one of Lachlan's hands. "We're going after your Aunt Lydia. Godmother Tera will take care of you both until we get back."

"What about Dusty?" Lachlan asked, wondering if his cousin was still passed out from shock.

"His grandparents will watch over him," his mother said. "They knew the risks his parents faced."

"But—" Lachlan tried.

"We quickly discovered how to kill the beast of light. We're a good team," his mother said. "We know this ritual like the back of our hands. We'll get in, find Lydia, and come back. It's a whole new *world*, Lach. The Goddess has granted us this opportunity. We can't squander it."

Lachlan wasn't sure which thing his mother wanted most: to visit a new realm or to save Aunt Lydia. Opening a stable portal was all his parents had ever really cared about, and now that they'd gotten what they wanted, they were choosing the portal over him and Blythe. Over the Order.

"Time is ticking!" his father shouted.

His mother kissed them each on the forehead. "Go straight to Tera's house."

She ran to the others.

Across the dais, his father called, "Take care of Blythe! You're the man of the house until we get back."

Oh sure, he was a man now that it suited them.

Blythe's plea of "Please don't go!" was cut off as the Order leaders flung themselves into the portal one by one.

The tear in the world snapped closed a moment after his mother, the final Order leader left, leaped through.

She hadn't looked back.

CHAPTER SEVEN

KAYDA

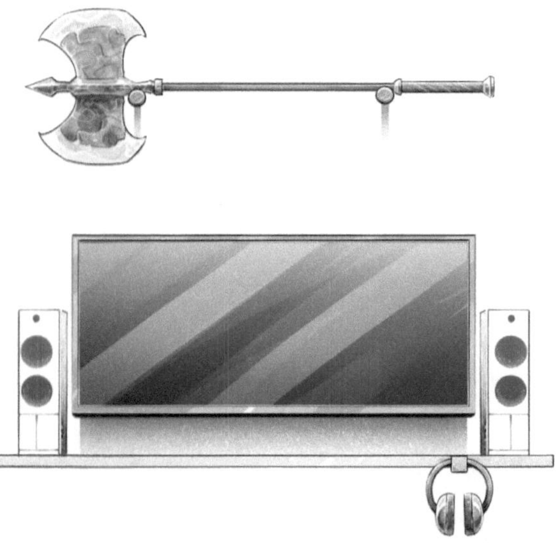

It had been four days since the feral attack in Mulgrew, Iowa. Kayda and Luma's VHoA chapter scoured the message boards constantly, but no other attacks had been reported. Speculations about why Mulgrew specifically had been targeted were as plentiful as they were varied. Conspiracy theories ran rampant in certain corners of the forum.

Marisol herself had spoken to a handful of the Mulgrew survivors, and not even they could settle on a reason why they'd been hit. Nothing had been stolen. No one had been kidnapped. No one reported having seen Lachlan Shade or hybrids in the town. It had only been ferals—who had eventually been cut down as swiftly as the residents attending that outdoor festival. A handful of ferals escaped alive, though, easily slipping through the veil with only a hiss of discomfort.

The same evening of the Mulgrew attack, just before Kayda and the rest of Marisol's crew were supposed to head out for a patrol shift, Marisol had requested a group meeting. She'd told them about a small team in Mulgrew who'd had the foresight to have travel talismans on them and had followed one of the ferals who had managed to escape. The team had run out into a clearing where they'd found a hybrid waiting for the return of his mutated charges. A trio of ferals already waited with the hybrid, the vamps crouched dutifully at the hybrid's feet. The fourth, newly arrived one had just joined the others when the VHoA team emerged. Blood had dripped from the ferals' mouths of needle teeth. Gore had coated their arms and chests.

Before the VHoA team could react, the hybrid had thrust his arms upward. Shadows stretching across the weed-choked grass of the meadow had roiled and thrashed, then pulled free from their confines. The team's own shadows broke their holds and lurched from the ground, lunging for their former owners. The VHoA team had realized soon enough, as Kayda had many nights ago, that the shadows were mere illusions meant to distract.

The shadow-being that had lumbered from between the trees surrounding the clearing had been no trick, though. It charged toward the VHoA team, its massive feet tearing up grass in its wake. It had brayed from an unseen mouth. The sound had apparently been so mind-numbingly terrifying that the team had turned tail and run, diving back through the veil. The VHoA team claimed the wall of magic rippled on their side, reminiscent of a rock thrown into a still pond. The deafening roar of the shadow monster had been so loud, the ground vibrated from the force of it. But the beast hadn't been able to get in.

Kayda knew Marisol had imparted the story as a warning that they had to be ready for anything, but it had felt like they were at summer camp being told a ghost story around the fire. A story full of boogeymen that couldn't possibly be real.

Theories were lobbed across the living room like a beach ball that night—no one holding on to an idea for long before a new one was tossed into the mix. Kayda's favorite so far was that, while the shadow beast had been crafted from shadows, what had given it life had been the hybrid's magic. And that magic, being inexorably tied to the hybrid vampire because it was *part* of the hybrid, couldn't make it past the veil any more than the vampire could.

It was comforting to think a hybrid couldn't just hang out beyond the veil in a lounge chair sipping on a strawberry daiquiri while shadow monsters did their bidding—it was bad enough they could send in ferals. What was less comforting was that the hybrid Kayda had encountered in the nature preserve hadn't been an anomaly. The one she'd interacted with had sent illusions of shadow imps at her and her friends to distract them long enough for the vamp to snatch Welsh and run off with him.

A question—well, many questions—about that night still vexed her. Had the hybrid wanted Welsh solely because he was a witch or because of Welsh's uniquely potent glamouring abilities? The hybrid had told her that hybrids could *become* what they ate. It was why the vampire had been able to cast his unnatural magic in the first place—he'd drained enough witches to alter himself. To give himself the ability to wield magic.

Jo and Welsh both claimed that the amount of blood—*fresh* blood—needed to cast shadow magic was substantial. Which would hopefully mean there wasn't an army of half-crazed, magic-wielding vampires. The ones who *could* practice the dark art were the ones who'd seen the lengthy list of requirements and had risen to the challenge.

Hybrid vampires with ambition. Ugh.

Currently, Kayda was wedged into one of the uncomfortably small desk chairs in front of a VHoA computer. She should have been in bed, snuggled up beside Henri. Sleep had eluded her since she'd watched that video of Mulgrew's attack. And now Harlow was either heading to or already in Tercla, of all places. No, Kayda would not be sleeping anytime soon.

"Hey," someone said next to her.

She started, finding a wiry guy staring at her. She'd worked alongside him dozens of times but couldn't remember his name for the life of her. Partly because Marisol had told her recently that the guy was the type of person who was unassuming when he didn't know you well, but once there was a level of familiarity, his social filter started to malfunction. Kayda maintaining her distance had kept things both professional and ... not weird.

The guy chuckled as if he instantly understood the blank look on her face. Most everyone knew by now that Kayda was terrible with names.

"Quaid," the guy said.

It was really sad that Kayda couldn't even remember a name as unique as Quaid. "What's up?" she asked, already leery.

"You see the map that went up on the forum?" Quaid asked, eyebrows rising over the rim of his circular glasses. He shoved the glasses up into his thick head of brown curls, where the glasses were practically swallowed up. With an elbow resting on the arm of his desk chair and leaning toward her, his closeness was aggravating her claustrophobia. She eased a slow breath through her nose. "It got shunted to the resources section. It's so extensive. It *deserves* to be a main thread. Not enough people are talking about it. You like a good mystery, though, yeah? You helped solve all that veil breach stuff."

"Didn't figure any of it out fast enough to stop Lachlan," she muttered bitterly before she could stop herself.

Quaid sat up straight to properly wave a dismissive hand at her. "Pah! You got there before anyone else knew what was going on. That hybrid vamp was dispatched before he or any of his kind got into the heart of the city. All your little animal friends took out a bunch of those elves. Shit, you even helped save two of the elf kids. It could have been so much worse if you hadn't shown up."

Kayda *wanted* to believe he was right, but her raging guilt said otherwise. Her thoughts strayed, not for the first time, to Snowdrop. The girl's survival guilt had to rival Kayda's complicated feelings about that night.

Instead of getting into all of that with a near stranger, though, Kayda said, "My little animal friends? I'm not exactly Snow White."

Quaid cackled. "Definitely not."

Kayda wasn't sure if she should be offended.

"Anyway, no one here wants to talk about this with me," Quaid said. "Well, Mari might, but she hits the conspiracy section a little too much as it is, you know?"

Kayda did know. "I haven't seen the map."

That was all the encouragement Quaid needed because he started in on an excited explanation about the map and how some guy named Samar maintained there was a connection between Bliss hot spots, fae disappearances, and portal magic spikes. Kayda knew her fair share about Bliss and missing fae kids thanks to Harlow, but the portal thing was new.

The idea of being able to port to the fae realm was still something that spoke to the very soul of her. She knew most people—mundane and fae alike—had felt out of place at some point in their lives. Being at a party where you didn't know anyone. Feeling left out among family or coworkers or childhood friends. Not feeling at home in one's body.

In Kayda's case, her ancestors had ended up here purely by accident. Fae weren't meant for the earthen realm. Over generations of being stuck here, fae were stripped of what made them who they were.

Kayda's ancestors could literally turn into dragons, for Goddess's sake.

She wasn't deluded enough to think she could merely pop into the fae realm and suddenly be granted all her lost Goddess-given gifts, but she could at least *see* where she'd come from. She could taste authentic draken food, hear the draken language, and visit the places her great-great-grandparents had lived—her feet treading the same paths they'd once taken.

As she studied the dozens of digital purple pushpins signifying spots of portal magic spikes on Quaid's screen, the hope that she could one day visit her ancestral home rekindled. She knew it was a foolish hope, as it was lunatic Lachlan Shade and his equally insane followers who were likely causing those spikes. She knew better than most that Lachlan wasn't trying to reopen portals for the good of faekind—to offer them a safe, no-strings-attached route home. He was doing it for his own means.

Which was cruel.

If someone like Kayda longed for a path to the fae realm, how strong must the desire be for the fae who couldn't blend in or adapt as easily here? Fauns with their bodies covered in hair and their legs ending in hooves. Draken even taller and wider than herself with skin tones in shades of red, blue, purple, and gold. Pixies who felt so out of place in Luma that many resorted to living in an abandoned zoo because it was the only place they truly felt safe. Living in the mundane world wasn't even an option for pixies. The last thing they needed was for a too-observant environmental scientist to catch one and stick it under glass.

Snowdrop and her fellow elves had been swayed to Lachlan's cause because the Shades had weaponized the teenagers' natural insecurities and vulnerabilities—then paired those with the lofty promise that the fae world would make those concerns go away. A whole other world meant *just* for them, if only they'd help Lachlan get there.

And then he'd murdered nearly all of them.

Something prodded Kayda's arm, and she glanced down at Quaid.

"Am I *that* boring?" he asked. "Maybe that's why no one wants to talk to me. It's not the subject matter but the one delivering the subject."

Kayda was only half sure he was kidding. "Sorry, no. It's not you."

"I've heard *that* one before," he muttered. "I'm starting to develop a complex."

"Cool it with the pity party. The portal thing just got me thinking is all. What's the mystery you're trying to solve?"

Quaid stared at her for a long beat, his face screwed up like he couldn't quite tell if she'd just insulted him and, if so, how he should feel about it. The desire for a conversation partner trumped all, though, because he animatedly turned his focus back to his computer. He gestured toward an area near San Diego. "The thing with the fae disappearances on this map is that these pushpins only represent recovered teens who were found during raids."

Kayda supposed that was obvious, but it was a bit shocking to realize that the abundance of blue pins only signified the kids who were found. How many had gone missing that no one knew to report? How many of them had been found deceased, or so badly injured they were unrecognizable? How many had vanished without a trace?

Since Portal Relations actively tracked down fluctuations in portal magic, did their discoveries serve as a starting point for VHoA's search for potential nests in the area?

Kayda examined the pushpins near San Diego. Quaid had been babbling for a few minutes, but she'd missed most of it. While there was a tight cluster of red pins—signifying Bliss trafficking—there was only one blue one. A knot of purple pushpins dotted the map a couple dozen miles away.

"The blue pin represents an eighteen-year-old fae kid named Kessler," Quaid said. "I've been following his vlog—those are still popular on Forage, did you know that? He must have gotten his hands on a black-market MPN to be able to tap into Forage from the mundane world."

All Kayda really knew was that Forage was the name of the corner of the internet usually only accessible in hubs. Being magic-proofed was the only reason crafty mundane hackers hadn't found a way in yet. The idea of there being MPNs—magical private networks—floating around in the mundane world was a little distressing, though. All the hubs' secrets being leaked to the mundane interwebs would in all likelihood implode the entire system even faster than whatever Lachlan Shade was cooking up.

"Anyway," Quaid said, rightly guessing that Kayda was most assuredly not up to date on vlogging trends, "Kessler got inspired by the girls here who started speaking out about what happened to them, so he's been telling his story, too."

Kayda assumed there had to be more. "*And?*" she finally asked.

Quaid grinned as if he'd just been testing how interested she really was. "I'm glad you asked!" he said, pointer finger thrust in the air. He dramatically spun his body toward his computer and hunched over the keyboard. He pulled up a tab, typed rapid-fire into the search bar, clicked around a few times, and then gestured grandly at the screen. "Behold!"

Kayda resisted the urge to palm the back of his head like a basketball and slam his face into the keyboard. Instead, she eyed the video upload page, similar to the mundanes' YouTube. There were dozens of video thumbnails on the page. As Quaid scrolled down, Kayda noted that the videos had been uploaded daily. She thought it unfathomable that anyone could have that much to say, but the time stamps in the corners were usually only between five and seven minutes.

Quaid found the video he wanted. It took up most of the screen, a play button hovering over the still frame of a young man. Kayda assumed he was of mixed parentage—he was dark-skinned, had very light-green eyes and cheekbones that could cut glass. His silky jet-black hair was pulled up in a messy man bun, which put his pointed ears on display. The tips of his ears pointed outward, rather than straight up like an elf's, and she thought they might have been covered in a light dusting of fur. Hiding his fae characteristics while living in the mundane world must have been a challenge. Were hats and long hairstyles enough, or were minor glamour tinctures and accessories imperative to blend in?

He was gorgeous, but in a confounding way—like he was too attractive to be real. She supposed that was why he'd been targeted or groomed or whatever by hybrid vamps in the first place.

Movement from the corner of her eye made her tear her gaze away from the beautiful boy on-screen.

Quaid held out two items: a pair of headphones and a napkin. "There's some drool on your chin."

Kayda was unsure if he was amused or annoyed.

She took the headphones from him but ignored the napkin. Quaid wadded it up and chucked it over his shoulder.

Pressing a finger to the corner of the computer monitor, he swiveled it her way. Kayda had to sit at an awkward angle to watch, which only made the whole interaction even more annoying than necessary. As soon as the cups were securely over her ears, the video started.

Her annoyance with Quaid faded somewhat as she listened to Kessler talk. It was a video from two weeks ago and was only about five minutes long. She did her best to ignore the fact that Quaid was just sitting there beside her, literally twiddling his thumbs. Surely there was a less convoluted way he could have shared this video with her.

Though Kessler was easy to look at and listen to—his voice was smooth and rich—he didn't say anything in the video that was particularly noteworthy, all things considered. He was the sole survivor of at least two dozen fae teenagers and young adults who'd been beguiled into joining a vampire nest in myriad ways.

Kessler had been with the vampires for an astounding three years, originally pulled in by a vampiress who had gotten him hooked on Bliss.

He and a trio of his underage friends had snuck into a mundane bar in Florida. The vampiress had been drawn to Kessler straight away—no doubt for his beauty and fae blood. The young man had had no idea vampires even existed before that night; he'd just been thrilled to gain the interest of an alluring older woman. He admitted that even without the vampiress's enthrall power lulling him into a state of utter devotion, merely being a fifteen-year-old boy being hit on by a stunning woman would have caused any number of bad decisions.

One dose of Bliss and a bite from the vampiress had been all it took to form a symbiotic bond between the two, and Kessler had left through a back door with the vamp without a word to his friends. Kessler's loved ones had spent years trying to find him, unaware that he'd been trafficked across the country.

He was currently receiving treatment at a Bliss detox facility, and while he'd been in contact with his family and friends since his escape, he was keeping his distance until he could be sure he was stable.

It was a harrowing tale, made all the more devastating when told by the person who'd lived it, but Kayda wasn't sure why Quaid had wanted her to watch it.

As it ended, she reached for the headphone cups, only to still when Quaid began rapidly scrolling through the selection of videos again, stopping at the top of the screen. He hovered the mouse cursor over the most recent video, which had been uploaded three days ago. A quick scan told her that this particular video had four times the views as the videos preceding it and at least double the number of comments.

Quaid had a mischievous glint in his eye. "Waiiiiit for it!" he said, a fist poised in the air with his pointer finger angled down. He slowly lowered his finger, then dramatically clicked a button on the mouse, as if he'd just hit the Red Button.

Kayda rolled her eyes at his theatrics and concentrated on the screen.

Kessler had bags under his eyes, and his man bun was askew. A chunk of hair had come loose from its tie and hung in a tangled snarl over one of his pointed ears. Though it felt cliché to say his eyes looked haunted, she didn't know how else to describe them.

He wore a terry-cloth tank top. The V-neck and armholes looked as if they'd been cut haphazardly with scissors—the edges jagged and uneven. It helped accentuate his toned biceps and taut torso, though, so she appreciated the wardrobe choice, even if she worried it was a sign he hadn't showered in a while.

Even though Kayda only had one video as a reference for what made for "normal" Kessler behavior, she felt her brows slam together within seconds of the video starting. He gently rocked back and forth as he talked, gesturing wildly. He'd been speaking in an even, controlled tone in the first video she'd watched; he'd clearly felt comfortable talking to the camera. It was like Kayda had been sitting across from him at a table while he told her his story.

Now? Now he was almost manic.

The difference in behavior was so dramatic, Kayda initially hadn't been able to focus on *what* Kessler was saying. She willed her brain to pay attention.

"It's not that it's not working," Kessler said, hand held up by his head, frozen in place. His pinky finger flicked up and down repeatedly as if the digit had decided it no longer wanted to be part of a unit and was trying to detach itself. "It's just that it's not working as well. Working less … less efficiently. They didn't say regress, but it feels like a regress. A regression."

He abruptly folded his arms high across his chest, his hands wedged under his armpits. He froze so completely, eyes downcast, that Kayda checked the time bar to make sure the video wasn't buffering. The time steadily ticked down.

A faint sound caused Kessler to look up sharply, staring at some point past the camera. In the case of the Mulgrew video, the person recording the event had been so physically far from the action that Kayda's heightened hearing hadn't done her any good. Yet here, given the tight quarters of Kessler's room, Kayda didn't need to adjust the dials on her hearing much to hear every word of the softly muttered "Leave no doubt."

Kayda's brows pinched further still.

Kessler pried his hands from his armpits. The rocking resumed, and he nodded to himself, muttering inaudibly. "I am … yes." He finally resumed eye contact with the camera. "I … I have regressed. I need to go back to the clinic for testing. Experiments. Experimental testing." His hand was up by his head again, this time on the left side, where the tangle of curly hair hung by his ear. He ran tweaking fingers through the mat. Kayda had no idea what it felt like to have hair so long that it tangled, but her scalp twinged in sympathy all the same as Kessler's spastic fingers attempted to untangle the hair, all while rambling about being gone for a while because he needed to start a new treatment plan.

"I'll be gone for a while," he said in such a clear, precise way, her gaze snapped back to his face. He started pointedly at the camera as he quickly lowered his hand from his head. When it was a few inches from his desk's surface, he flashed his palm to the camera, flicked his thumb across his palm, and then encased his thumb with his fingers, tucking his thumb inside. The movement happened so fast, Kayda almost missed it. The hand that had flashed the signal was below the desk now. He rocked slowly again, and his light-green eyes lost that brief glimpse of lucidity. "Don't worry about me, friends. I will be back. I need the clinic to remove the shadow … the cloud …" He angrily shook his head, as if upset with himself for lacking access to his full vocabulary. "I need to remove the pall of the poison … of the sickness that came from abusing Bliss for too long. This is why I stayed away from home." Another very pointed look at the camera. "I didn't want this to find … to affect them."

After a brief shift of eye contact from the camera to a spot just beyond it and back again, Kessler said, "Never resist getting help, friends. If the monkey is on your back, find people who can help you shake it loose." He swallowed hard and reached up to rub the back of his neck, eyes downcast.

Kayda studied the sliver of skin that was revealed on his right side. While she'd appreciated the wardrobe choice initially, as it had given her a brief glimpse of a toned stomach, now she leaned toward the screen, alarmed. Two dark black lines—like black veins—snaked across his torso. The lines weren't thick so much as unnervingly dark—with tiny tributaries of thin branches fanning away from them. It looked … infected. Was that a side effect of Bliss abuse?

Again, the glimpse was so quick, Kayda would have missed it had she blinked. She couldn't shake the feeling that he'd done the move on purpose—he wanted his audience to see what was happening to him.

Sitting up straight, Kessler smiled sadly. "Goodbye. Until next time."

The video went black.

Kayda sat in stunned silence for a moment, dismayed that she'd managed to feel so wrapped up in the life of a stranger after only two videos. When the ensuing silence *wasn't* interrupted by Quaid starting another video, Kayda removed the headphones and handed them back to Quaid.

"Well?" Quaid asked.

"Someone from his old life found him and forced him to tell his audience goodbye," Kayda said.

Quaid nodded. "He used the signal for help. Did you catch that? It's a signal used by domestic violence victims as a way to convey to a stranger that they're in danger."

Kayda had caught the hand signal, but she hadn't known what it meant—or if she'd actually seen what she thought she had.

"He's been posting a video between 8 and 8:30 a.m. like clockwork every day for four weeks," Quaid said. "The last couple videos have been a little off—where he seems less nervous than he was in this one. Someone possibly being in the room with him, like in this video, was new. On top of that, the last video was posted at 10:15—so all his fans were concerned when it was over an hour late. I don't know if that was deliberate, but it made the oddity of this one stand out even more because we were already worked up."

"Do you know if there was a wellness check done?" Kayda asked.

"The armchair detectives are putting in overtime hours on this one," Quaid said. "The vlogosphere is jam-packed with reaction videos. They found the guy's address and got the cops over there. His apartment is empty. Scrubbed clean and smelling of bleach."

Kayda sat back hard in her chair, arms crossed. "Whoever was off screen told him to 'Leave no doubt.'"

Quaid made a noncommittal noise. "Are you sure? Most people in the comments are sure the person said 'Hey, don't pout.' He looks pretty upset or maybe lost in thought when the person says that. I can't imagine this supposed new treatment is any fun. And he used the word 'experiment.' Maybe whoever came for him wasn't the vamps trying to take him back but someone from the Collective. They either want to shut him up because he was telling too many secrets, or they want to do tests on him because of the Bliss abuse. They were telling him not to pout about being kidnapped—which is a wild thing to tell a kidnapping victim. Maybe they were trying to convince him this was for his own good."

Kayda said, "I mean, maybe your theory about who was there is right, but ..." She tapped a pointer finger to the shell of one ear. "Heightened hearing. He definitely said 'Leave no doubt.' Same general vibe, but 'Leave no doubt' is a little more sinister—almost a threat. Whoever was there wanted his followers to believe he was sick and needed treatment and not to worry about him when his videos stopped. Probably because he's not coming back. And *he* knew he was in trouble, so he was trying to leave clues for his followers."

Reaching for the mouse, Kayda gently elbowed Quaid out of

the way so she could restart the video, then paused it so there was a brief, blurry view of Kessler's torso. Kayda pointed at the screen. "You know more about Bliss than I do. Are marks like that common in Bliss abuse cases?"

Quaid unearthed his glasses from where they'd been swallowed up by his hair and settled them on his face. He got so close to the screen that Kayda wondered if the addition of his glasses was hurting or helping his ability to make out the already blurry image. After a long moment, he sat back and shoved his glasses back into his hair. "Not that I know of. I've scoured the forum for that, too. No dice. Bliss just doesn't mess up fae the way it does humans. Bliss almost exclusively only affects fae mentally or neurologically. There still haven't been any fatalities, from what I've found. Commenters have been speculating that those lines on Kessler's side are everything from track marks acquired through mundane drug use to an infected scratch from a feral."

Kayda supposed a feral attack was just as probable as anything else. Most of Kessler's life—if not all of it—had been lived outside the hubs. His chance of running into a feral, especially if he'd spent three years with hybrids, was exponentially higher than her own.

"So ..." Kayda said, "what now?"

"What do you mean?" Quaid asked.

"I mean ... why did you show me that? Are you trying to reel me into the mystery and then you'll propose that we get our asses to San Diego to investigate or something? Follow the leads presented by the armchair detectives and uncover whether it was vampires who came and reclaimed Kessler, or if it was the Collective who whisked him off for their own reasons?"

Quaid shrugged. "Nah. I've just been tormented by this for the past three days, and I needed to take someone down with me."

Kayda frowned. "Seriously?"

"Seriously. Misery loves company, right?" Quaid had tried to sound flippant, but Kayda could tell the guy really was disturbed that he'd been given a window into this stranger's life and now would never know what had happened to him. "I binged *Unsolved Mysteries* for about a month a year ago. Most frustrating month of my life. Other than the month I dated Caroline, but that's another matter. All these stories with no resolutions. No closure. Now I just think about them all the time, skeptical that their cases will ever be solved. I vowed never to get sucked into true crime shit again.

"I started watching Kessler's videos from day one. Checking in on him became a daily ritual. I became pretty good friends with someone who's a frequent commenter on the videos. Then, three days ago … gone. It's like I just lost a friend. It's been eating me up. You're good at this mystery-solving shit. Maybe you'll puzzle something out. Maybe you won't. But some part of me feels like I'm doing right by Kessler by making him take root in yet another person's head. Maybe the collective hive mind will be able to rescue him if the hive mind gets big enough."

Kayda's desire to slam Quaid's face into the keyboard resurfaced.

She valiantly fought the urge again.

After Henri had fallen asleep beside her later that night, Kayda stayed up to watch all of Kessler's videos back to back, starting at the beginning. That last video, once having watched all the "normal" ones before it, made his manic behavior seem slightly less stark, but not by much. There *had* been a subtle shift from composed to anxious to flat-out erratic over those four weeks, but the changes could have been easy to miss if one wasn't actively looking for signs that something was off.

Kayda scowled at Kessler's last, final smile.

"Goodbye," he'd said. "Until next time."

Who had been in that room with him? What caused those dark lines on his torso?

And where the hells was he now, assuming he was alive? She hated that she might never know the answers to any of those questions.

Goddess dammit, Quaid.

CHAPTER EIGHT

HARLOW

Another six hours of driving brought us to our destination in California. Soren and Caspian would be staying in a motel in Fresno while Mom and I met with the leader of Tercla since we didn't know if this was going to be a trip that took hours or days. According to the instructions Vaughn had given us earlier, Caspian and Soren could drive us up an access road to one of the main gates. Mom told Soren it would be best if we were dropped off half a mile out so we could hoof it to the hidden entrance of the city, but Soren was adamant that he would deposit us at Tercla's doorstep.

Though the vamps called their home an enclave instead of a hub, Tercla had been constructed the same way as Luma. A stipulation in the Pact signed between the enclaves and the hubs was that a contingent of sorcerers would be at Tercla's beck and call to keep the enclave's veil magic intact. Veils appealed to the pure vamps because they wanted both the isolation and the privacy of running their enclaves as they saw fit, without input from outside influences. They were a nation unto themselves. And as long as they didn't violate the Pact, everyone pretended not to care what the vamps were up to behind their invisible dome.

Very few people knew the actual details of the agreement. Mom did because she'd been a bounty hunter in Luma. But because being an official Collective bounty hunter meant one had to sign a Soul NDA, Mom couldn't divulge said details. My guess was that the stipulations were awful, like they had an annual human murder quota they couldn't go over. Or they could eat a certain number of babies a month. I didn't really want to know.

Mom, about twenty minutes ago, had tried once again to dissuade Soren from driving too close to the enclave. She suggested that we drop the guys off at the motel, and then she and I could drive up to Tercla alone. One of the vamps would take care of the car, like stabling a horse, while we were in the city, and then we could drive it back to the motel where they were holed up in Fresno.

"For the last *damn* time, Camila. No," Soren had said, losing his usual loud, bubbly charm. Him calling her "Camila" instead of her alias said a lot, too. It was like a parent calling you by your full name—that was when you knew your ass was really in for it.

The car ride had been quiet after that. I had a sneaking suspicion that Soren was as uncomfortable with this "Fletcher women only" mission as Caspian was. My other sneaking suspicion was that Soren had a thing for my mom that went far beyond friendship. Perhaps Soren and Caspian would bond over a shared hatred of not being on the Terclan guest list.

Much like the location of the storage container where we'd found the missing fae girls a couple of months ago, the spot Mom directed Soren to was in the middle of nowhere. A slightly dilapidated chain-link fence ran far into the distance in either direction.

Beyond it was an overgrown field. The packed dirt road the SUV idled on sat before a padlocked gate. Chunky metal links wrapped around the gate's poles twice, looking for all the world like a coiled snake. My brain couldn't fully process what I was seeing, though. Why was this giant fence here? How did a mere padlock keep people—namely bored teenagers—out? Wouldn't the gate sag in places if it wasn't attached to a sturdier structure?

But as soon as I thought any of these things, they flew out of my head again. The longer we sat parked there, actually, the more I was sure we shouldn't be there at all.

In fact, we needed to leave.

It wasn't safe.

Soren asked, "Are you sure this is it? This can't be it. I can't let you go in there, Camila. We need to go."

His hand shot for the gear shift, ready to throw the car into reverse, but my mom put her hand over his.

"It's okay, Soren," she said in an overly calm way, like trying to coax a scared puppy out from under the bed.

The tone did nothing to soothe him.

Or me, for that matter.

"This was why I told you it was better if Harlow and I came alone," Mom said, somehow sounding annoyed and affectionate at the same time. "I told you their magic would affect you, but you didn't listen because you're a stubborn ass."

"I thought … you were … exaggerating," Soren managed.

"If anything, when it comes to vampires, I downplay. That may have been a mistake," Mom said.

Caspian let loose one of his rare semi-hysterical laughs. That wasn't a good sign.

"Harlow, you're wearing your talisman, right?" Mom asked. "Ugh. You never listen to me, either. Caspian, can you—"

I stopped listening. I couldn't listen anymore. It was as if my ears had been cemented over. No sound was getting in. Had I gone deaf?

My chest constricted, and I placed a hand over my racing

heart. It was pounding so hard, it was sure to explode out of my chest. A graphic image of a torn-open chest cavity filled my mind. Ribs cracked and broke off in large shards—large shards that then sank into the pool of blood and viscera that made up my insides, like capsized ships sinking into the ocean.

I sucked in a breath. Was I having a panic attack? Yes, I was having a panic attack.

Possibly dying.

Definitely dying.

We needed to get out of here. Now.

"Mom …" I said, voice tight, but I could barely make out my own words. "He's right. We have to go."

Caspian was beside me saying something, but I wasn't sure what. My hearing had tunneled now. That was what it sounded like—like Caspian was on the other end of a long tunnel. My lungs squeezed. My fingers inched toward the door handle. Maybe I could tuck and roll and run out of here if no one was going to turn this damn car around. My hands moved so slowly, as if they traveled through molasses instead of air.

Something thumped against my chest, and suddenly my senses snapped back to normal. I was temporarily dizzy from the force of the transition, almost nauseous. Glancing down, I found one of the talismans Vaughn had given us was now around my neck. The chain was a plain silver metal, the pendant a flat metallic disc with a swirling vortex of green energy in the hollow.

I studied Caspian. He looked more or less okay, but there was a definite sheen to his forehead. He attempted to smile, but it was closer to a wince. Mom was trying to talk Soren off the ledge I'd been on before Caspian had forced the talisman over my head. I shifted over a fraction and peered out the windshield. My mouth dropped open.

Beyond the chain-link fence—which was actually a gorgeous sandstone wall—were the tops of buildings. Stone obelisks etched with runes served as spacers in the wall. A whole town lay beyond the veiled fence. I'd grown up in a hidden hub, and yet the magic that allowed it to happen still blew my mind.

"Caspian?" my mom asked. "Can you switch places with Soren? I think he needs to lie down in the back."

"My head hurts," Soren said as if he were a little boy and not a grown-ass man. It was alarming that the big, exuberant guy could be flattened by a "keep-out" spell this effectively.

It also made me realize how many provisions had been included in the Pact for places like Tercla. What, if anything, had the pure vampires given the Collectives in exchange, other than the promise not to wantonly sink their fangs into anyone they wished?

I pulled out my phone.

HARLOW

In case I don't make it, I bequeath you my murder sword. 🧟 💀

KAYDA

😑 And here I was, for years, upset that you didn't use cell phones. Now you send me cryptic shit and ridiculous emojis.

HARLOW

Said murder sword was wedged, blade up, in the back pocket of the passenger seat in front of me. I thought of it like a joey hanging out of its mother's pouch. The sword still took great offense to being in a sheath of any kind, but the seat pocket suited it just fine.

Stowing my phone in my backpack, I checked on Caspian. He'd paled further. "Are *you* going to be able to drive?"

He smacked his lips as if he were parched. "Yes, but we should get out of here soon. The magic, I think, stimulates neurological responses that force the intruder to pass out if they don't heed its warning."

"And passing out outside a vampire enclave is not good for anyone but the vamps." I flung my door open, grabbed my backpack off the floorboard, and climbed out. "C'mon, sword."

I ran around to Caspian's side, strapping on my backpack as I went. Mom was already at Soren's door, trying to get him out of his seat. Soren had gone from little boy to semi-drunk, alternating between weeping softly and slurring his words. That was the state I'd have been in, too, had I not been wearing the talisman that negated the veil's magic. Mom's talisman hung from her neck.

Soren had his legs hanging over the side of the driver's seat, but he wasn't budging despite Mom wrapping her arms around his middle and pulling. "Oh, Cam-Cam," he said sadly.

Caspian and I froze at the nickname and swiveled toward Soren. The sword slowly floated to hover behind Mom, who had promptly let Soren go and was staring at him as if he were an exotic creature—who had just simultaneously sprouted six heads.

"I'm very scared about you going in there alone, Cam-Cam," Soren said, staring at my mom. Nope. Not staring. *Gazing.* He reached up and cupped her cheek. "So soft. You never let me get this close. Not anymore."

I quickly looked away. I rounded on Caspian, intending to drag him out by his hair if he was as drunk as Soren now. Since Caspian was magic-touched, I figured it would take longer for the veil's spell to knock him out, but the fact that it had weakened him this much already spoke to the spell's potency.

Caspian gazed at me, reaching out to cup *my* cheek. "Oh, Har-Har."

I snorted. "Don't. You. *Dare.*"

He chuckled, but it didn't sound right. I guided him out of the car, holding on to his elbow. After slinging his arm around my shoulder, we shuffle-walked to the front of the car.

Soren was on his feet now, leaning even more heavily on my mom than Caspian was on me. Mom and I got our respective charges sitting in their seats. Well, Caspian was able to sit in the driver's seat, while Soren very ungracefully flopped into the back.

By the time Mom had hefted his deadweight legs into the car and closed the door, Soren was snoring with gusto.

I propped my folded arms on the lip of the lowered driver's-side window. "You sure you're okay?"

Caspian nodded, though his face contorted. It almost looked like he was suffering through the agony of a sneeze that refused to come to fruition. "Call me or text me or … something. As often as possible. I feel like I'm dropping off a pair of lambs at the slaughterhouse."

"Eh, we'll be fine," I said, glad he couldn't tell how knotted up my stomach was. "Mom knows the head honcho. *You* text *me* when you get back to the motel, okay? Hopefully the big guy will wake up before you get there so you don't have to carry him in by yourself."

Caspian nodded tightly.

Without thinking, I leaned into the car and kissed his cheek. I hoped it grounded him the way his kiss on my temple had grounded me.

I took several steps back. "Plus, I've got Stabby. It'll keep us safe."

The sword dropped to the ground to tap once in agreement.

With a reluctant salute, Caspian put the car in reverse, made a ninety-seven-point turn in the dirt, and then headed back the way we'd come. I waved away the dust cloud. I hoped he'd actually *go* to the motel, rather than stop as soon as Soren woke up from his magic-induced nap and the fog of the "keep-out" spell lifted. The farther they were from this place, the better.

Mom and I didn't move until the taillights of the SUV were out of sight.

I turned to her. "So, Cam-Cam, what do we do now? Think that gate has a doorbell?"

"I'll call Vaughn and let him know we're here, Har-Har."

I laughed. "Soren has got it *bad* for you."

Mom winced. "I suspected, but I didn't realize he …" She puffed out her cheeks, staring into space for a long moment before noisily expelling the breath in one gust. Without further comment, she headed for the gate.

I scrambled to follow her, the sword floating alongside me. "Maybe he won't remember all the nicknames and ogling when he wakes up?"

Mom sighed. "He'll remember. Part of the 'keep-out' spell is that the person remembers this place is bad news. He'll remember enough of that interaction to make sure he wakes up embarrassed."

She placed her phone to her ear before I could reply. I heard it ring twice. "Hey, Vaughn. The Fletchers have arrived per your summons. We'll be waiting." In a tone dripping with unchecked malice, she added, "If you *ever* approach my daughter like that again, I will find a way to kill you myself, so help me."

Guess she'd been holding on to that one until she was physically close enough to make good on any threats.

Mom pocketed her phone. "Someone's coming to open the gate."

"Wanna tell me what your history with Vaughn is?" I asked, hoping she'd answer me this time. She'd grown very adept at avoiding my questions. "Did you smash—"

"No, I did not," she said, exasperated. "What's this fascination with my love life anyway? I thought hearing your mother talk about stuff like that was a no-no."

"It is. I hoped that would finally get you to answer the question. I'm just … worried, is all. If I had to make a choice for you between elder vampire Vincent Roch and Soren, though, it's Soren."

"You haven't even met Roch yet. Maybe you'll like him."

I gave her a "You're kidding, right?" look.

She sighed. "Yeah, you're not going to like him. I'm not even sure *I* like him."

I chewed on my bottom lip. The last time I'd seen her when she was truly herself had been the day she and Dad left for work six years ago. The day Dad was killed. They'd been joking and laughing in the kitchen while they'd made breakfast together. I'd been sitting at the kitchen table, watching them. They'd moved around the kitchen with ease—navigating around each other in the small space with the grace and effortlessness of dancers. They managed to touch every time they passed each other. A brush of the arm here. A light touch to the lower back there. They hadn't been a big PDA couple, but they showed how much they loved each other in those small moments. Half the time I wasn't sure if they even knew they were doing it—showing their feelings in little ways all day long.

So I knew that watching the love of her life get killed in front of her must have felt like her soul had been ripped from her body. That same day, her bosses—the Collective—had turned on her and exiled her from Luma, keeping her from coming back to her only child. I eyed her ruined left arm, the skin tight and ropy—a constant reminder that she'd tried to force her way through a veil that had been warded specifically to keep her out.

The way she'd so utterly changed in so many ways spoke to how much the losses had broken her. Maybe, when she'd needed companionship in the years since, she'd chosen partners who could never mean anything to her the way Dad had. Dad couldn't be replaced. She'd never love anyone as much as she'd loved him. But even loving someone half as much meant she could get hurt again—that they could get ripped away from her the way Dad had.

Someone like Vincent Roch was as far from safe, as far from a potential life partner, as one could get. I knew that without a doubt, despite operating on next to no details.

Soren, I wagered, was someone she *could* love half as much. And that scared the living daylights out of her.

"I'm sorry," I said, cowed by my train of thought.

"For what?" she asked.

I shrugged. "I don't know. Everything."

She nodded, grabbing hold of my hand and squeezing. Her eyes welled up. "Me too, baby girl. Me too."

The sound of metal scraping metal made us jump. A lock being disengaged? A bolt sliding free?

"You're sure the sword will be fine?" I asked hurriedly for the zillionth time.

Caspian could have cloaked it, as we often did when we went somewhere with the sword and wanted to keep it hidden. But since Caspian would be physically far from the sword, the camouflaging spell wouldn't hold long, if at all.

Mom was confident the sword would be okay, especially since Vaughn already knew I had it. He'd obviously been spying on the VHoA headquarters for a while. Still, the vamps could have something up their sleeves that could take the sword down, allowing them to steal it from me. A handful of the silver alloy powder would be enough to do it. And what was I supposed to do then? I had no recourse against a vampire as preternaturally fast as Vaughn.

Regardless of my mom's connection to this Roch guy, this had to be a terrible idea. Suicidal, even. I hoped if we got swarmed by a horde of vamps and then shredded, the sword could get away and find Caspian. Caspian wouldn't be dumb enough to try to come avenge me or anything, would he? No. He'd talk to Welsh, and Welsh would talk sense into him. Welsh would make sure Caspian got back to Luma safely.

Another bolt was scraped loose on the other side of the door. My heart rate ratcheted up. Was I having another veil-induced panic attack now that I was closer to it?

The talisman still lay against my shirt. Still swirled green at full power. So this new dip into panicked waters was all me. Cool, cool, cool.

Mom said, "The sword will be fine. Vamps rarely have an interest in weapons, sentient or not, since they're weapons themselves."

She honestly thought saying shit like that was helpful.

The sword hovered close to my shoulder in the inverted position to show it didn't come with stabby intentions. It was humming in a way that made me think it was just as nervous as I was, though, which only made my apprehension worse.

I slipped my thumbs under my backpack's straps, trying to exude a casual air while also giving my shaky hands something to do.

The door finally creaked open. Did the door not get much use, or was Tercla's online order of WD-40 delayed? Maybe the vamps kept exsanguinating the delivery drivers.

I braced myself for whatever horror had just come to greet us. I squeezed my eyes shut.

One beat. Two.

"Hi!" a chipper voice said.

I cracked open an eye. A young woman no older than twenty stood there with a bright smile on her heart-shaped face and a clipboard tucked under her arm. The toes of brown leather boots poked out from the hem of flared, dark-wash jeans. On the bright-red shirt that hugged her thin frame was a kitschy cartoon rendering of a sleepy Dracula holding a mug of coffee. "Mornings suck," the shirt said. Her pale skin was even paler thanks to her neon yellow hair, which was tied into two small buns, one on either side of her head.

"Hi," she tried again. "I'm Audrey."

Mom cleared her throat. "Uhh … I'm Camila Fletcher, and this is my daughter Harlow."

I managed a wave.

Smile never faltering, Audrey canted her head to the side and said, "And who is this?"

I aimed a thumb at the sword. "You can call it Stabby."

Audrey stood straight again, grabbing hold of her clipboard. "Excellent." She pulled a pen off the board and presumably scribbled down our names. "Personal guests of Vaughn Rosen, correct?" She glanced up, ever smiling.

"Correct," Mom said.

"Excellent," she said again. "Come with me. Vaughn will meet with you now." She stepped aside and gestured for us to enter.

Mom stepped across the threshold first. Heart hammering, I followed after her, creeping through the doorway as if I expected a bullet to the dome. Audrey smiled warmly at me as I walked past her.

I saw Audrey incline her head out of the corner of my eye. "Stabby, it's a pleasure."

The sword hummed.

"It said 'likewise,'" I translated.

"How delightful!" Audrey said. "It'll just take me a tick to lock up here …"

Three long seconds after *not* meeting my end, the intense pounding of my pulse in my temples began to abate. I let out a shuddering breath. Then I sucked one in as I finally took in the utter beauty of Tercla.

The road beneath my scuffed combat boots had the look of cobblestone but was flat, likely to prevent snapping one's ankle in half. The road led to a town square, the center of which boasted a stone statue on a raised platform. The statue was of a man in an outfit from the 1600s, complete with a ruffled collar. While most statues had serene, thoughtful expressions, this one wore a snarl, teeth bared, and fangs on display.

"Roch, I presume?" I asked Mom in a stage whisper, who stood shoulder to shoulder with me.

"That would be him," she said.

For as surreal as it was to think of her with anyone but my dad, Roch was kind of hot. Even in statue form.

Facing the statue on three sides were buildings made of stone or brick. Their front doors opened onto the flat cobblestones, which were dotted with bench seats, gas-lamp-esque lampposts, and a smattering of bright flowers planted in large ceramic pots. Narrow alleyways snaked between buildings and curved off to places unseen. Wooden signs hung above shop doors, one of them creaking on rusty hinges in the slight breeze. From where we stood, I spotted a clothier, a café, and a candlemaker.

Other than the menacing statue of Roch, the only decidedly

not-normal thing about Tercla was that no one was out other than me, Mom, and Audrey—who was coming up behind me now. It was eerily quiet.

"All right. If you would follow me," Audrey said, strolling past me on our left. She was a tiny thing at no more than five feet, but she took off at a quick clip.

We hurried after her.

Mom easily strolled along behind Audrey, whose neon-yellow hair was like a beacon, but I kept narrowly tripping over things or bumping into them. My brain couldn't process how only a small number of people were aware of an entire town that looked like it had been teleported here from another century. Part of my near-misses with everything from low-hanging signs to pots over-flowing with vibrant flowers to the corners of stone buildings was that I kept searching for some other sign of life. I gazed up at the windows on the upper floors of buildings, thinking I'd seen a shutter move or curtain rustle. I couldn't get over the fact that this quiet, beautiful place housed vampires. Vampires who preferred human blood. Vampires who had gone through no rigorous program to deem them safe to live among humans and fae alike as they had to in Luma. The Pact worked to keep the vamps in line, but that was when they were in *our* territory. Now we were in theirs. These vampires were free agents, and we'd just willingly sauntered into their lair.

Their very pretty, clean, well-tended lair, but a lair all the same.

"Are you, like, Vaughn's assistant?" I finally asked when I got a crick in my neck from gazing up the sides of stone buildings.

We were wandering down yet another cobblestone road flanked by multi-floor residences.

"Yes," Audrey said. "Well, I'm an assistant to a lot of the daywalkers, since there aren't many of them. Most vamps choose one or the other—night or day—but some, like Vaughn, have a more flexible circadian rhythm. Day vamps' rhythms often get out of whack after they've come back from their scheduled hunting, so I'm here to help them out."

I bobbed my head. Great. Chill. This was fine.

"Oh, and younger vamps are given assignments as daywalkers to test their self-control, so I deal with a lot of them, too. For their senior projects, teen vamps get sent into the mundane world to get jobs for the summer. If they can get through it without killing anyone, they graduate! They have to keep *all* biting to a minimum. Very hard to do when you have hormones driving you crazy on top of the bloodlust. Lots of students in their senior year fail because of house parties. Many, *many* students have to go into extended studies programs to get their cravings under control. Once they graduate, they choose their primary circadian rhythm and are ushered into society here."

"Did *you* pass right away?" I asked, figuring it was a question that would help determine if Audrey was a vamp herself *and* how scared of her I should be.

Audrey deftly turned and walked backward. "I failed three times. But on my third try, I accidentally turned my very human boyfriend, so they gave me a pass for adding to the population. He was the only one I bit, after all, and it was basically impossible for me to keep my fangs out of him in the heat of the moment, so it worked out for everyone." She flashed me those sharp canines, giggled, then turned to face forward.

Terrible logic. Hopefully her boyfriend had gotten a choice in the matter.

After Audrey's next turn down another alleyway, I stopped dead in my tracks. Ahead, beyond the narrow, cobblestone-lined path, was a lush park. Grounds, really. Grass, well-manicured hedges, and the edge of what looked like a stone fountain basked in the sunlight. And just beyond all the greenery was a ... cathedral. Arched doorways, a couple of towers, flying buttresses, stained-glass windows—the whole nine yards.

The sword nudged me in the back with its hilt, causing me to lurch out of the alley.

The four of us fanned out into a horizontal line once we were free of the alleyway, then paused, taking in the scene.

"Pretty, yeah?" Audrey asked, clutching her clipboard and sighing contentedly.

It was a silly question. It was like asking if a triple rainbow arching over crystal blue waters teeming with happily diving dolphins was pretty.

Audrey started off again, taking us along the curving stone path that circled the greenery. It was indeed a fountain in the middle of the grounds. Instead of the upper tier being topped by a benevolent angel replete with outstretched wings, or innocent-looking naked cherubs, this one featured Roch again. His billowing stone trench coat flapped behind him. A single curled lip revealed a fang. While the entire fountain was made of weather-worn bronze, the single visible fang glimmered a bright white in the sunlight.

The pigeon sitting atop Roch's head sort of killed the majesty of the whole thing, though.

The curving pathway led us to the arched doorway of the cathedral's main door. I shivered in the shadow of the building. The sword hummed in a disquieting, off-kilter way behind me.

Mom still didn't seem particularly freaked out by any of this. Of course, she *had* been here before. Many, *many* times. Ugh.

Audrey spun to face us. "Vaughn is waiting for you in the reception room. This is a communal residence—a den is what we call it—so be warned that there will be others inside. Pay them no mind. You're a special guest of Vaughn's, and they all know that. Your talismans are further proof. Just make sure they're prominently visible, and no one will bite you."

My talisman still had a faint wafting green mist in its hollow, but it was otherwise dormant. They'd been one-way talismans then. Hopefully Vaughn distributed "get the eff out of here" talismans just as freely as he'd given us these. I didn't want to be stuck here.

Audrey swung the door open on silent hinges, then gestured for us to enter.

"You're not coming with us?" I asked, punctuated with a squeak of alarm.

"Nope. I have to get to the eastern entrance. It's going to be busy this week! Yannick is having his annual *Are You Genetically Fit to Become a Vampire?* competition. Twenty lucky human ladies are being shipped in to participate this afternoon. I have to make sure all the ball gowns arrived on time. We had an issue last week when one of the teen trainees nearly killed a delivery driver who got too close to the gate, even though the signs make it *explicitly clear* where to park trucks." Audrey checked her watch. There was a smiling, winking unicorn on the face, its horn sparkly pink. "Oh shoot. I'm really going to have to book it if I'm going to get there in time. Can't have any of the new ladies die before the competition even starts, can I?"

Without waiting for a reply, Audrey was on the move. She turned on her vamp speed for the first time since I'd met her. I only caught a brief streak of her neon-yellow hair as she zipped down the street and beyond a tall hedge. Her girlish giggle fading on the wind made me shiver again.

Mom offered me a strained smile. "Keep your eyeballs on your shoelaces. If you hold eye contact with one of them for too long, it's like a guy buying you a drink at a bar—it's an invitation. And they don't need a lot of encouragement."

"Oh hells," I muttered.

Mom blew out a slow breath, shook out her arms as if she were about to enter a boxing ring, and then strode through the open door.

Whimpering to myself, I followed my mother into the vampire den.

CHAPTER NINE

HARLOW

Though the exterior of the cathedral looked centuries old, the interior had been converted into a modern residence. The front entryway had a series of hooks on one wall for jackets, a neat row of shoes was lined up along the other wall on a bamboo rug, and tasteful black-and-white nature photos decorated the walls.

"Are we honestly supposed to take off our shoes?" I whisper-hissed, noting the hum of voices that wafted into the foyer from an open doorway ahead.

Mom doubled back to close the door to the cathedral since I was just standing there, eyes bugged out. "No. We won't be staying long," she said. "I hope."

The sword was still humming in that off-kilter rhythm.

When Mom reached me, I repeated my earlier question that she'd avoided—again. "Is there some disturbing backstory you haven't told me about Vaughn?"

She shook her head. "There's not much to tell. He's like me—a consultant. But while I'm well versed in vampires, he's—"

"Well versed in humans," I finished for her because I'd heard that a million times already. "Aren't all vampires well versed in humans, though?"

"He's also well versed in ferals. He and I have run into each other on jobs over the years. Once he established that he could kill me but chose not to, we started sharing information when possible. Ferals are also a threat to pures."

I kept hearing that, too.

"Did he get saddled with recon on ferals because he's a speedy ninja vamp, or did he volunteer?" I asked.

"*I volunteered.*"

"Jeez-o-pete!" I screeched, flailing as if I'd just been electrocuted.

I scared the sword so badly that it shot straight into the air and got itself wedged into one of the exposed wooden beams crisscrossing the ceiling.

With a hand over my racing heart, I jabbed a finger at the newly arrived vampire. "Don't do that!" Head tipped back to address the sword high, high above me, I said, "Try not to go molten, sword! I think it's bad luck to burn down a cathedral."

The sword gave itself a few hard yanks and pulled itself free. A few bits of sawdust rained on my head. Without warning, the sword harpooned toward Vaughn, its razor-sharp tip suddenly an inch from the vampire's nose. Vaughn didn't so much as blink.

"*Jeez-o-pete?*" my mom mouthed at me, evidently having found my declaration more upsetting than anything else that had transpired so far.

"I didn't mean to frighten either of you," the vampire said coolly, despite having a sentient sword practically kissing his nose.

Did Vaughn have enhanced strength as well as speed? Could he move quickly enough that he could damage—or outright destroy—the sword before the lightning-quick thing could react?

"Sword, stand down," I said, blowing out a shaky breath.

After another moment, the sword backed away from Vaughn, then hovered in its usual inverted position by my shoulder.

Vaughn, with his hands tucked behind his back, turned toward my mom. He was dressed in loose-fitting beige linen pants and a long-sleeved white shirt. His dark hair was in a state of curly disarray that I assumed was utterly intentional. It gave him the air of someone who planned to fritter the day away while still looking polished. His feet were bare. "I'm pleased you could make it, Camila."

She scowled at him, her jaw working.

"I didn't threaten your daughter. I never laid a hand on her. When I gave her my contact information, I didn't even put the note on her person. I placed it in the pocket of her sorcerer lover."

I choked on my saliva and spluttered a cough. The sword thumped its hilt into my back a couple of times.

Vaughn arched a brow at me. "Is what I say untrue?"

"The part about not harming me is true," I said, eyes watering.

"If you are going to be cross with me, Camila," Vaughn said, "it's not my interaction with your daughter that should be the reason for your hostility."

I squinted at him. "What the hell does *that* mean?"

The sword tapped its hilt on the floor beside me in agreement.

Mom crossed her arms. "What did you do, Vaughn?"

Vaughn attempted his best approximation of looking contrite but was as successful at it as someone who'd just gotten Botox injections. "Roch has no idea you're coming. Well, he surely knows now. Rumor spreads quickly. But he didn't know until today."

"So y'all don't share a hive mind?" I asked.

Vaughn's perfectly symmetrical nostrils flared. "There's not even a mental link shared between sires and their masters. Hollywood drivel."

Mom groaned, her mind on other things. "*Dammit*, Vaughn. You told me he was expecting me and was willing to talk."

Vaughn shrugged one shoulder. "I lied. This is too important. If anyone understands the threat ferals pose, it's you. Everything I say to him falls on deaf ears. He's been so preoccupied with the change of leadership in Urcor that he's been gone for months at a time. The leadership in the Urcor enclave won't matter if Shade and his hybrids are successful. Roch might not listen to me, but he'll listen to you."

Mom looked four seconds from bolting out of here. In a pained voice, she said, "Roch hates surprises."

"I doubt he'll hate this one."

She gave him a look that articulated that she cared not a whit about Roch's affinity for her. "You'd better be right about this. Roch and I didn't exactly leave things on a positive note."

"Oh, what, you mean the part where you left an elder vampire brokenhearted because he asked you to marry him, you said you'd think about it, and then you snuck out in the middle of the night, never to speak to him again?" Vaughn asked flatly.

Mom huffed. "Yeah, that."

"*Damn*, Mom," I said.

"When I say relationships of any kind with a vampire are … complicated, that doesn't even scratch the surface." She blew out a breath that puffed out her cheeks. Addressing Vaughn, she asked, "Can we talk to him now, or do we have to wait until this evening?"

"Now is best. He'll be caught up in the spectacle that is Yannick's contest later," Vaughn said, rolling his eyes.

"Not a fan of the contest? Or Yannick?" I asked.

"Yes," Vaughn said, then turned on his heel and headed for the open doorway ahead. "I'm sure you remember the way, Camila, but I'll escort you there."

Mom gave me a stern look. "Eyeballs on your shoelaces."

"Making eye contact with Vaughn has been okay …"

"Because he knows if he tries to enthrall you he'll have to answer to me."

Tap, the sword said.

With that, Mom set off after Vaughn. Her head, I noted, was held high. I tucked my thumbs under the straps of my backpack again, said a prayer to whoever might be listening, and stared down at the floor while I hurried after her.

The sound of voices grew steadily louder the closer I got to the open doorway, but when we passed through it, all talking ceased. I almost tripped over my own feet, but I kept my focus locked on the heels of my mom's shoes ahead of me. What little I saw of the living room was dotted with modern furniture. On a giant sectional couch to one side of me, I saw the tops of a few vampire heads—or maybe ones belonging to their humans. Bare feet were crossed at the ankles and propped on ottomans. A man sat with his arms folded over the back of the couch. I had to walk right past him to stay on the path my mother carved through the maze of furniture.

"Mmm, fresh meat," the man whispered, his words like a caress on my arm, my neck, my cheek. He reached out a finger, his fingertip grazing along my forearm before I could course correct and get out of touching range.

My instinct to tell him to keep his undead hands to himself had only taken hold for a nanosecond, my gaze defiantly snapping in his direction. He had his head angled so we'd make eye contact as soon as I turned my head a fraction of an inch. I halted instantly. Like the brakes put on shopping carts if they leave their designated parking lots. The sword bumped into my backpack. I idly wondered if it had sliced the bag open, but the man watching me was more important. The very plain man—no, handsome. No, *gorgeous.* Goddess above, I'd never seen anyone so breathtaking in all my life.

"Are you new here, pet?" he asked.

"Uh-huh," I said huskily, twirling a curl around my finger. My thighs pressed into the back of the couch while I practically shoved my chest in the man's face. He didn't seem to mind. I was glad. He deserved everything he wanted. Everything and more. Everything I had to give. He could use me and discard me, and I would revel in it.

In one fluid motion, he was sitting on the back of the couch and my hips were wedged between his knees. His breath was dank and stale … no, it smelled of mint and chocolate. Of promise and need.

I was yanked back so hard by my backpack that I almost lost my footing. Shaking my head, a fog lifting, I glanced at the couch long enough to see the man's feet flip over his head. I supposed he could have just lost his balance, but that was like a cat losing its balance—unlikely. When the man righted himself, he was glaring daggers at Vaughn, who stood several feet away beside my mom. Vaughn had a hand wrapped around Mom's forearm, and she looked even more murderous than the vampire Vaughn had just upended.

Since the vamp's ire was squarely directed at Vaughn, I took in what the guy actually looked like. Mid to late fifties, receding hairline, dad bod. None of which was bad, but he shouldn't have been hitting on a woman my age regardless of whether he was mundane *or* a vamp.

Damn, that enthrall power was something else.

My stomach roiled. It had happened so mind-numbingly fast.

When Dad Bod made eye contact, I quickly looked away.

"As I have already made *explicitly* clear, these two are my personal guests," Vaughn said, and while his tone was calm, even I could feel the undercurrent of literal power in his words. The air crackled with it. "You, especially, knew that, Yannick. You have your bevy of ladies being shipped in *today*. Surely you can control yourself. Try that shit again, and your guests are going to be greeted by a headless corpse swinging from the bell tower. Understand?"

"What am I going to hang from if I don't have a head?" Yannick muttered, his voice whiny and nasally.

Vaughn didn't dignify that with a response. No one did.

The longer the silence stretched on, the eerier the air felt. The hair on my arms rose.

"Understood," Yannick finally said.

The tension in the room popped like a balloon. Mom and Vaughn started moving in my peripheral vision again, so I started after them, almost crashing into a chair in my haste to get the hell away from Yannick.

"Find me on the second floor tonight, the last door at the end of the hall, if you want an evening you'll never forget," came his whispered words, coating my skin like oil.

I shuddered. This was already a *day* I wouldn't forget. I didn't need to add nighttime horrors, too.

I peeked up at my mom, who was glaring over her shoulder. She looked enraged with both me *and* Yannick.

Jaw tight, she pointed her first and middle fingers at her eyes, then down at her shoes.

Eyeballs on shoelaces. Yeah, yeah.

I couldn't sense the sword and peeked behind me as quickly as I could.

The sword was still in the inverted position but was hovering where I'd last been standing. I stopped. It vibrated with barely controlled rage, its blade cherry red. I realized then that the sword hadn't reacted earlier because, while my actions had been out of character, Yannick's enthrall power was so strong that even the sword hadn't been able to tell if I'd been in actual distress or not. Now it could, and it wanted Yannick's head on the floor.

"Sword," I hissed at it, then dropped my eyeballs back to my shoelaces. Face flaming, knowing no matter how much I lowered my voice, all the vamps could still hear me, I said, "Don't. Guests or not, if we piss one of them off enough, we're in trouble. Unfixable kind of trouble."

The sword issued a drawn-out hum that somehow sounded

frustrated. But the vibrating had stilled. A quick glimpse confirmed the blade had cooled.

"*Interesting,*" someone muttered.

"*Curious indeed,*" said another.

Yannick's rich-as-honey, slimy-as-motor-oil voice whispered over my skin and across my neck. "*A mundane who controls one of the fabled sentient weapons. You're as intriguing as your blood. We could make so many glorious mistakes together. Look at me, pet. Loooook at me.*"

It took everything in me not to turn my head in his direction. My neck ached with the force of *not* looking. I clenched my jaw so hard it hurt.

I dug my fingernails into my palms, concentrating on the sharp pinpricks of pain. Then I took a step—away from Yannick and toward my mother and Vaughn. The loops of my shoelaces flopped with every deliberate step.

Yannick's deliciously awful laugh slithered through my head. Out loud, he said, "I suppose I shouldn't be surprised your daughter is as stubborn as you are, Camila!"

When I finally reached my mom, she grabbed hold of my forearm. "You all right?"

I nodded tightly. "I'm good."

We kept moving. I felt as if I was wading through molasses again. Yannick kept calling to me mentally. I felt horrible for the busload of women showing up for whatever this vampire version of *The Bachelor* was. I hoped they knew what they were getting into because I was sure, once they signed whatever contract Yannick drafted for them, they weren't getting out of here without being severely changed. Or dead. Or worse.

I hated this place.

Absolutely fucking hated it.

It wasn't until we'd made it across the reception area and into an adjoining hallway that Yannick finally released his mental hooks. I desperately hoped it was because he could only mess with me when I was in visual range, not just because he'd lost interest. If proximity *wasn't* a factor, it meant vampires like him could manipulate me from anywhere.

I was paranoid on the best of days without adding that shit to the mix, thanks.

I listed to the side now that I was no longer weighed down by Yannick. My shoulder thudded into the wall. Mom was in my face in an instant, hands on my arms and gaze searching my face.

The sword hovered behind my mom, buzzing angrily, like a possessed hummingbird. Its blade pulsed red.

Giving my head a shake, I said, "I'm okay. Holy shit, that's terrible. *Please* tell me they don't all have enthrall powers that strong."

"Most of them have to work harder at it than Yannick does," Mom said, and I almost burst into tears from relief.

"Another survivor of magical malaria?" I asked.

She nodded. "Most of the vamps who live in the cathedral are the really old-school ones. They've lived through centuries of wars and plagues and great social shifts. Some, like Yannick, get bored easily. Give them an inch, and they'll take your life."

"I'm so glad we took this mother-daughter trip," I said. "So glad."

The sword, glowing like an ember, tapped the tile floor once. It glowed even brighter, then tapped the floor again harder.

I wished then that it was a little fluffier, that it had fewer sharp edges, because I wanted to hug it for being so concerned. As much as having Caspian's steady presence beside me would have been nice, the last thing any of us needed was him getting so mad at Yannick that he blasted him across the room with one of his signature concussive air blasts. Yannick probably would have enthralled him to walk into the kitchen and impale himself on a butcher knife.

Rolling my shoulders, I stood straight. "I'm good. Let's go talk to Roch. I'm not dreading this at all. Not one bit."

Mom forced the fakest smile I'd ever seen. "Me either. It'll be great to see my elder vampire ex-lover who I walked out on two years ago and who didn't know I was crashing his den until today."

I looped my arm through hers and led her toward where Vaughn waited semi-patiently at the base of a stone staircase. "Look at it this way: This has gotta hold the record for one of the most uncomfortable reunions ever. You're practically an award winner!"

Mom barked a laugh, some of the tension lines in her forehead smoothing out. In a quiet, sad tone, she said, "You remind me so much of your dad sometimes, it's like getting kicked in the stomach."

I swallowed down the lump in my throat. "Pro tip: If you're trying to get into the good graces of your ex, it's best not to be reminiscing about the lost love of your life."

Mom nodded, her mask of cool impassivity settling into place again. "Solid advice."

"Anything in particular I need to know about Roch?" I asked as we slowly walked toward Vaughn. The sword floated in the inverted position by my shoulder. I had a feeling it was watching me—waiting for a sign that I really *wasn't* okay, so it had an excuse to zip back out into the common area and lop off Yannick's extremities. "I feel like you're spoon-feeding me little details about this place as necessary, and I can't decide if I appreciate that or not."

"If I'd told you everything upfront, you wouldn't have come. Vaughn thinks having you here will help our case." Louder, to ensure Vaughn heard, she said, "As *furious* as I am with Vaughn—"

His flat expression asked, *"Do you really think I care about something as insignificant as your feelings?"*

"As mad as I am," Mom said, softer now, "calling in my favor to Roch *is* a good idea. He's got a research facility here that's been studying ferals since they became a problem a few years after the Glitch. Very few non-vampires have access to that kind of information. Even though Tercla and other vamp enclaves honor the

Pact with the Collectives, cooperation between hubs and enclaves doesn't stretch far beyond what the Pact explicitly dictates."

We stopped in front of Vaughn, where he still loitered at the bottom of the steps.

"Do people like Sorceress Rhiannon know about your connection to Tercla—specifically to Roch?" I asked. "Is that why *our* Collective wants you back—because they somehow know you have access to this research intel and want to truth serum it out of your brain like the manipulative monsters they are? I mean, I'm sure they're totally just going to nicely ask questions and diligently take notes. I absolutely take them at their word that they want you back in Luma simply so they can ask you stuff."

Mom pursed her lips. Apparently, this possibility hadn't crossed her mind. I knew my mom was an expert on bloodsuckers, so it made *some* sense the Collective would want to consult with someone they'd worked with previously—especially one locked into their Soul NDA. They wouldn't have to worry about Mom leaking any of their secrets since she was soul-bound to keep them. But I'd had a long time to think about Rhiannon's offer while waiting for my mom to stop dragging her feet on leaving the VHoA warehouse. Plus, I'd developed a healthy habit of assuming the Collective always had ulterior motives. Expert or not, there had to be a reason why they specifically wanted my mom back. They'd exiled her. They'd turned me, the sword, and Caspian into fugitives. They'd need a damn good reason to reverse all that beyond needing a vampire history lesson that otherwise could be given over the phone or in an email.

"It *is* an interesting question," Vaughn said thoughtfully.

The sword tapped once on the floor.

I eyed the vampire. "*You're* the one who set up this meeting. You're a free agent, right? No allegiance to a hub or enclave? Are you the middle-vamp between my mom, Roch, and the Collective? Sounds like you're pretty worked up about what Lachlan and his hybrids are up to. Worked up enough that you're pulling puppet strings behind the scenes to get people to act?"

Vaughn, staring at my mom, tilted his head in my direction. "Is she always this distrusting?"

Mom's arm was still linked with mine. "Is she *right* to be this distrusting?"

Vaughn didn't answer right away.

Mom groaned. "*Dammit,* Vaughn."

He lifted his hands in placation, palms up. "My allegiance is to Roch. But, as you say, I'm an old-school vampire. I've got the benefits of having lived a long time and possessing an excellent memory. I don't know if Roch's lack of concern over Shade is hubris or complacency. The others only grow twitchy when Roch does. Not even the Vampire Council can be persuaded to care … though Roch isn't on speaking terms with them anyway.

"So while war is brewing, Yannick is hosting another of his asinine competitions. Roch is busying himself with political infighting among enclaves. The others are consumed by planning out their next hunting excursion, like middle-aged mundanes whose lives revolve around what to eat for dinner."

I jutted my chin at him. "You still didn't answer my question."

Vaughn sighed. "While my allegiance is to Roch, I have acquaintances outside of Tercla." He gestured to my mom as an example. "Bounty hunters. The occasional VHoA member. And yes, a couple of Collective sorcerers. But I assure you there is nothing duplicitous going on here. I'm facilitating meetings between like-minded individuals, nothing more. I cannot control what happens in these meetings once they begin. That part is up to you." He paused. "You know what it feels like to be enthralled now. I'm not employing my power. I haven't used it once in your presence."

My gut told me to believe him, but the concept of a truthful vampire felt as probable as a passive car salesman. "It's cute you think I don't know that you can use your enthrall power like a slow-drip IV, so by the time I'm doing your bidding, I'd think it's what I wanted to do all along."

I didn't actually know that was how enthrall worked, but I

had my suspicions. If most vamps had to "work harder at it" than Yannick did, who seemed to use his power with all the subtlety of a fire hose, I figured the ability usually took more finesse.

Vaughn shot my mom a long-suffering look. "Congratulations. Your spawn is even more exhausting than you are."

The sword dropped to the floor to tap once.

I glared at it. The sword glowed blue. Just my luck to end up with a sword with a sarcastic sense of humor. I pondered who I might have ticked off in a past life.

Vaughn lightly shook his head in disgust. "Great. Now I'm in agreement with a sentient weapon."

In a stage whisper, I asked my mom, "Is he always this grumpy?"

"Always."

Without a word, Vaughn turned on his heel and headed up the stone steps.

CHAPTER TEN

HARLOW

After traveling up too many steep stairs and down two hallways, Vaughn led us to an ornate double door. The wood was a deep blood red, reminiscent of the resin used to make Chinese figurines. Carved into the right door was a tangle of limbs, teeth, and necks. It was impossible to tell where one being began and another one ended. A human elbow here, the pointed ear of a goblin or orc there. Elfin fingers stretched out, splayed, like the branches of a barren tree. Wide faces alongside thin ones. Veins bulged beneath skin like rope. Eyes of all sizes were trained in the same direction, though—toward the figure on the left door.

Etched into the red-hued wood stood Vincent Roch, one arm tucked behind his cape-draped back, while his other hand grasped the haft of a staff nearly as tall as himself. A roaring lion's head topped the staff. Roch's countenance was serene compared to the roiling mass of bodies beside him. A mischievous smirk drew up Roch's top lip, revealing a needle-sharp fang. I didn't know if the tangle of creatures was straining to reach Roch in a fit of all-consuming loathing or lust.

Either way, Roch's message was clear: Let them come, friend or foe, as no one is a match for me.

The sword hummed softly by my shoulder. If I hadn't known any better, I would have said the thing was shivering. Was there some trauma in its past connected to vampires? Whatever the sword had seen when Oliver Randal had held it during the auction where Haskins eventually bought it had upset the sword so much that it had gone off on its own to kill Randal. Randal had a connection to vampires—however loosely—because his addiction to Bliss had led to his involvement in fae trafficking. The sword had some shit it was still working through, but unfortunately there was no such thing as therapy for sentient weapons.

Its brand of therapy was murder, which was problematic for all involved.

Hopefully the sword wouldn't wig out in Roch's presence. Maybe I should have left it with Caspian …

After staring at the door for a few more beats, I whispered to my mom, "I can't decide if I'm terrified or proud that you landed Roch."

"*Yeahhh*," Mom said, staring at the doors with the same sense of awe as myself, though she'd presumably seen them many times over.

After allowing us to gawk for a little while longer, Vaughn took hold of the right doorknob—which looked unsettlingly like one of the scene's bulging eyeballs—and opened the door. I had a feeling the leftmost door didn't actually open; Roch was immovable, even in his artistic renderings.

I followed Mom over the threshold into the room, my pulse pounding in my ears. Once we were inside, Vaughn closed the door behind us. He stood just to the side of the door, his stance wide and his hands folded in front of him, like a bodyguard. Mom stood to my left, while the sword hovered on my right as we took in Roch's living quarters.

While Audrey had been the antithesis of what I'd associate with vampiric, well, anything—Roch's den was exactly what I'd expected. Despite the sunlight cascading into the room from the trio of arched, floor-to-ceiling windows on the wall opposite the door, the room was dark. The top two-thirds of three of the walls was painted a deep red—reminding me of a freshly poured glass of wine—while the bottom third was lined in cherrywood. The fourth wall had been covered in maroon wallpaper decorated with tan damask.

The side of the room to the right of the windows was set up like a study or office. An elegant jet-black wooden desk was oriented toward the windows, the sunlight bathing its surface giving it a shiny sheen, as if it were made of marble or ebony. Tall vintage bookcases lined two walls, stuffed with leather-bound books standing resolute behind glass doors. Wingback chairs, settees, and vintage round-arm sofas upholstered in dark red velvet or leather were scattered around the large space, creating reading and lounging nooks. A few feet from me, a table lacquered in black stood on a damask-patterned rug that matched the wallpaper. Somehow, the oddest thing about the table was the fluffy, pure-white cat that dozed atop it.

A large swath of the left side of the room was taken up by a massive four-poster bed whose legs were so thick they reminded me of tree trunks. It was as if the bed had grown straight out of the wood flooring. The bed was topped with a blood-red comforter and was piled high with black-and-white pillows. The sheets that lay beneath the comforter were undoubtedly made of silk. Remembering how much time my mother had spent *in* that bed, my attention didn't linger there for long.

And then there was Roch himself. In true dramatic vampire fashion, he stood before one of the windows opposite the door, his hands clasped behind his back as he surveyed the grounds of the cathedral. His expression was sure to be pensive and world-weary.

When he finally turned around after what felt like half a century, his black cape swished about his calves. From across the expanse of this large, dimly lit room, I could tell he was even more gorgeous than his depictions.

This was what I'd expected when I'd first met Caspian.

I was glad now that my assessment of him had been unequivocally wrong.

It took Roch another half a century to finally start walking toward us. I could feel the tension pouring off my mom. I hooked my arm around hers again, to give her something solid to hold on to.

I blinked, and then Roch was there before us. This lightning-quick movement thing was going to put me in the hospital due to heart failure.

Up close, I couldn't tell what ethnicity Roch was. The guy was old as shit, and my cursory internet search on his last name had told me it was French in origin. His skin was light brown, but it was hard to know how much of his original color had been bleached away by his vampirism. Hell, maybe he was normally pale as a ghost, but he got a lot of sun, and this was him with a tan. He had the bone structure of a model or Hollywood star and piercing light-blue eyes. His brown beard was kept short, and his brown hair was up in a messy man bun that absolutely shouldn't have worked for him, but of course it did.

He wore black slacks and a white shirt that was unbuttoned to his pecs. His feet were bare. Maybe vampires just hated shoes. The strings holding his cape in place formed a perfect bow at the hollow of his neck. The outfit shouldn't have worked, either.

I'd never seen anyone like him before. Even if relationships with vampires were as complicated as my mom claimed, I wasn't sure I'd kick the guy out of bed. My face bunched up when I recalled that this guy had shagged my mom. I shuddered. *No sloppy seconds with your mother, Harlow. That's gross.*

It *was* gross, wasn't it?

Yes, definitely gross.

I bit my lip. Probably.

Mom had told me that vampires essentially had magic-enhanced pheromones that oozed off them like a fog, helping to lure in victims. Was that what was happening now? Because I couldn't possibly be attracted to a guy who had hooked up with my mother—repeatedly.

He studied Mom as if she were one of the great wonders of the world. Even if Mom had considered this smoking-hot man to be nothing more than a fling, Roch had seen it as more than that. His throat bobbed as he swallowed, his piercing gaze roving her face as if committing every line and curve to memory.

"We have much to talk about, Cammie." His voice was velvet smooth.

"I didn't come here to talk about us, Vince." A hint of affection laced her tone. "There are much more important things to discuss."

Her grasp on me tightened, whether to keep me there or to ground herself further, I couldn't be sure. As he glowered at our intertwined arms, a lock of his hair slipped free from its elastic binding and fell over one eye.

My fingers itched to tuck it behind his ear as if I were a lovesick heroine in a rom-com. I squeezed my free hand into a fist. His beauty was so otherworldly that it was breaking down rational thought.

He was enchanting. Beguiling. Arresting.

His attention suddenly snapped to me, his lip curling minutely as if I were something foul and sticky he'd stepped in. His blue irises turned a distressing shade of red. I was unable to blink, to look away. A feeling similar to the one I'd felt outside Tercla before Caspian forced the talisman over my head slammed into my chest. *Get out*, it said. *You're unwelcome.*

My instincts forced me to take a step back. My heart thundered so hard, I was sure my chest would bruise. Mom grasped my arm tighter.

The sword glowed bright red in my peripheral vision. It quaked. Anger and frustration pulsed from it in time to my thrashing heartbeat, but the sword made no move toward Roch. Was it restraining itself out of fear?

An alarming thought hit me: Was this vampire's enthrall power strong enough to keep the sword from acting?

"Knock it off, Roch," Mom snapped.

A basketball-sized force hit me center mass. It wasn't a physical assault so much as a war on my nervous system. My brain was doing its damnedest to convince my body that we needed to get the fuck out of here. We were under attack. Fleeing was the only way to survive. My heart thudded, my throat closed up, my palms sweated. I wanted to blink, my eyes itchy, but I couldn't. The fear was so all-encompassing now that my vital organs were sure to shut down entirely, dropping me to the floor like a sack of potatoes.

The sword flew away from me, the thunk of its blade sinking into a wall behind me causing me to flinch.

Out.

That time, the feeling had a voice—and it was *in* my head.

Leave.

I shied away, my head pulling toward my shoulder like a turtle trying to pull into its shell. Yet I still couldn't look away from him. If he released his hold, how fast could I bolt? I was willing to risk another interaction with Yannick if it meant I could get out of here. Away from Roch. Away from Tercla.

Could Roch cause someone to have a heart attack just by dumping fear into them, overwhelming their senses until the person drowned?

Mom shoved the heel of her free hand into Roch's chest. He'd been so preoccupied with using his enthrall on me, that the shove caught him off guard. He stumbled back half a step. It was enough to break the eye contact. I heaved out a breath. I yanked my arm away from my mom's so I could prop both hands on my knees. I sucked in great pulls of air, as if I'd just broken the surface of a dark lake that had been trying to swallow me. Tears welled in my eyes.

This was a mistake.

Mom rubbed a hand on my sweaty back. She was saying something to Roch, but I couldn't hear it over the ringing in my ears. The pulse in my temples sounded like the whoosh of a rushing river now. Saliva flooded my mouth.

"Sword?" I croaked out.

I heard it pulling itself free from the wall, and then it was hovering between my feet and my face.

"You okay?" I asked.

A brief flash of blue.

Once my breathing had calmed, Mom helped me stand to full height. The sword hovered by my side again, but a little behind my shoulder instead of directly beside it. I made the briefest of eye contact with Roch when I stood, and Roch growled with all the menace of a wild wolf. I had the good sense to drop my gaze to the floor.

Eyeballs on shoelaces. Eyeballs on shoelaces. It would be my mantra.

"At least she's a quick study," Roch said, his voice still as smooth as caramel. "You may be Camila's daughter, girl, but you haven't earned the right to look upon me yet."

I wanted to roll my eyes, but if I did that while my head was down, I'd pass out.

"Well, it's good to know you're still a dick, Vincent. Any lingering guilt I had about how things ended with us is gone now, so thanks for that," Mom said. "Let's go, Harlow."

She hooked her arm around mine again and managed to angle us toward the door. I got the spins. The sword beelined for the exit, as desperate to get out of here as I was. But Mom and I had only taken a single step when the toes of Roch's bare feet entered the edge of my limited view of Roch's floor.

"Don't be dramatic, Cammie," Roch said.

"Don't call me that."

Roch sighed. "Don't be dramatic, *Camila*."

From the direction of the door, I heard, "He may be acting rashly because he doesn't know how to deal with the very human emotions of heartbreak, jealousy, or envy. His enthrall power is tied to emotion, and his own emotions are currently spinning out of his control."

I didn't think Vaughn should be goading the guy, but I kept my mouth shut. If I remained meek and uninteresting, maybe Roch wouldn't short-circuit my nervous system.

"I don't remember asking for your opinion on the matter," Roch said. "Besides, it's *your* fault I was thrown off-kilter by her … unexpected visit."

"Hear that, Camila?" Vaughn said. "He almost admitted that he missed you deeply and that's why he's being less than welcoming to your beloved daughter."

Roch grumbled something I didn't catch.

"What was that?" Mom asked.

Roch sighed. "It *is* good to see you." Softer, he added, "I feared you'd never grace this room again."

"Apologize to Harlow and keep your grubby fingers out of her head or this *is* the last time you'll ever see me," Mom said.

Nothing happened for long enough that I worried Roch had begun waging a mental war with my mom now. Vaughn said himself that his loyalties lay with Roch. If Vaughn's plan to force my mom and Roch into the same room backfired and Roch turned on my mom, I was toast. Neither vampire gave a shit about me. I had nothing to offer other than the blood in my veins—and that wouldn't be offered willingly.

"I apologize, Harlow," Roch finally said. It sounded like every word hurt, as if they scoured his throat on the way out. "As a daughter of Camila, you will always be welcome here."

I said nothing, keeping my eyeballs on my shoelaces. My breath expelled in a rush when the sight of his bare feet finally left my view. My eyes flicked up to the door. Vaughn still stood there in his bodyguard stance. The sword floated beside him, the blade pulsing red again. Vaughn cocked a brow at me as if he could read my escape plans and was silently advising me against them. He whispered something to the sword.

The blade cooled and the sword slowly, reluctantly, joined me.

"Which one of you is going to tell me the reason for this ambush?" Roch asked from somewhere behind me.

Mom leaned toward me. "I trust him to keep his word to leave you alone, but keep your eyes diverted anyway."

"I've never been more willing to act submissive in my life," I muttered.

The sword hummed.

She huffed a laugh, then turned us toward Roch again. She deposited me and the sword in front of the windows that over-looked the cathedral grounds, then let me go. I had a clear view of the fountain we'd passed on the way in. The pigeon that had been resting on Roch's stone head had flown off, but not before leaving a deposit that was now sliding down Roch's forehead. I smiled softly.

I listened as Vaughn and my mom told Roch their concerns—about Lachlan Shade's success at opening portals, the feral activity in Mulgrew, and the fear that both pure vampires and the people who called hubs home were under threat from whatever Lachlan was cooking up. I got the impression that Roch had heard a lot of this already, but he more or less stayed quiet as the other two spoke.

I was eventually asked to tell them what Domino the orc and the elf in his employ had said before they'd been killed on the Winchells' lawn. Both Domino and the elf had said they wouldn't rely on an unrealistic pipe dream to save them—they would save themselves. Their salvation, they said, lay in The Restoration, not with Lachlan Shade. I still had no idea what The Restoration entailed.

I then relayed what I could from Kayda's tale of Lachlan's escape from banishment.

"Oh, do stop looking at your feet," Roch finally said, exasperated. "I'd rather speak to your face than the crown of your head."

"You haven't exactly instilled me with trust in your word," I blurted, then winced at the floor.

Roch's laugh was pleasant, like a caress. It slithered around my neck, easing the tension there before traveling up the back of my head like strong, confident fingers threading through my hair.

I glared at him, jaw tight. "*Stop it.*"

He grinned. My traitorous stomach flipped.

"Using your mojo to make me compliant is just as bad as using it to scare me shitless," I said. "*Stop it.*"

Roch laughed again, but the tingle of his magic slipped away from me like a shawl slowly being pulled from my shoulders. "She's as headstrong as you, I'll give you that much, Cammie." Though his magic remained at bay, the way he scanned me from head to toe made my skin flush. It was the look of a man sizing up a woman he found intriguing. "She looks like you, too. An even younger version of the woman who spent so many nights in my—"

"Nope! No. Nuh uh. Whatever you're going to say—no. I want no details. *And* I'm not interested," I said. "Get all thoughts of … *whatever* … out of your head right now. I don't care how hot you are." I winced again.

Roch's smile was disarming. It was little wonder my mom had fallen under his spell, especially when she'd already been so vulnerable.

Vaughn spoke up, doubtless wanting to get the conversation back on track. "The elves have always been an insular group. They keep to themselves—"

Mom scoffed. "Pot meet kettle."

"The difference," Vaughn said, barreling past her interruption, "is that, despite the vampire community's secrecy, when it comes down to it, what we want is well known. Hells, it's well documented. We want freedom to hunt within reason. We want our privacy. We need to drink blood, preferably from the veins of a warm, living body. We're that simple. You're privy to the details of the Pact, Camila. There might be stipulations that rankle your mundane morals, but there's nothing particularly surprising in that agreement. Can you say you know the elves' desires to that same degree? Their ability to manipulate veils and their extensive command of nature magic were both details that had been kept close to the vest until recently. Those are two bits of information you have now solely because the elves are willing to show a few of their cards."

I frowned, thinking back to that fateful night in the secret club in Luma. The night where I'd gotten drunk on elfin wine and inadvertently offended Haskins because I'd caught the eye of a sexy, mischievous elf. I'd snubbed Haskins. And because I'd snubbed him, he no would longer give me the time of day once everyone was sober and thinking clearly. Because he refused to acknowledge me, I'd had to sneak into his basement to check out his collection of charmed goods for myself.

If that stupid elf hadn't been loitering in the dark corners of that bar, whispering promises of a night of ravishing if and only if I climbed into the rafters and proved to him that I could fly, I wouldn't be standing in a vampire den right now.

A few steps were missing from A to B, sure, but that was the gist of it. In my mind, elves were in the same category as house cats—they could pull off world domination if they really wanted to, but they'd rather cause a bit of self-indulgent mischief before taking a long nap. They played pranks because they were too unambitious for anything on a large scale.

I'd been more wrong about them than I had been about Caspian.

They weren't lazy. They'd been biding their time, plotting and scheming while pretending to do the exact opposite. Samar had dubbed Lachlan "lawful evil"—someone organized and calculating to a ruthless degree and who lived by a meticulously constructed code of conduct. Those were not characteristics of a lazy individual.

I thought back to the mundane who had wandered into Luma, dazed and confused, begging me to explain how he'd ended up in a city he hadn't known existed. The guy's car had broken down on the side of the road in the middle of summer. The elf had shown up with water and instructions on how to find a nearby gas station that was so new that it wasn't even on maps yet. I'd accepted that there had been some elfin nonsense afoot and that the water had been laced with something strong enough to override the veil magic keeping mundanes out. If their wine could convince me I could fly, who was to say they couldn't craft or buy something powerful enough to mimic the magic in a travel talisman?

I was realizing now that the water had been part of the misdirection. Elves were mischievous, and like the fae of lore, you were taking your life into your own hands if you accepted food or drink from one. What had actually been going on that day?

The elf in question might have torn open a curtain in the veil for the discombobulated mundane, allowing him to slip into Luma unharmed. I hadn't known then that anyone other than a sorcerer could manipulate veil magic, so the possibility hadn't even occurred to me. Had the stunt not been a prank on the elf's part, but a way to test the strength of the veil in a section of the city that wasn't a dedicated entrance? The human had likely been used as a guinea pig. If the elf had failed and the veil magic killed him, at least the elf would have a new data point.

I wished I could talk to that guy again. But I'd dropped him off at a Visitor's Center and left him in the hands of people whose job description included wiping the memories of the few stragglers who got into Luma by accident. Even if I somehow tracked him down, he wouldn't remember anything about the encounter anyway. Which the elf had probably banked on.

"Harlow?"

I snapped out of my wandering thoughts and found my mom and two vampires studying me curiously.

"Care to share with the class?" Roch asked.

I told them about the random interaction from months ago.

"Curious," Vaughn said. "It does speak to a larger plan, one that was happening here in the earthen realm *and* whatever world Lachlan was stuck in for decades."

I said, "Domino's elf lackey said that the goal of the movement is in the name. What would the elves want to restore?"

My mom said what I'd already been thinking, which lined up with the conclusion Samar had come to via his extensive research. "The path home. It's what Lachlan claimed he wanted three decades ago."

"That doesn't explain why the Shades are in league with hybrids, though," I said. "It doesn't explain why they want to disrupt the veils."

Vaughn asked, "Could it be as simple as Lachlan wanting to inflict as much destruction as possible against the people who wronged him? Who knows what kind of realm he's been in all this time? He could have been driven mad. One cannot find reason in the plans made by someone who has lost all grasp on reality."

Mom and I both shook our heads, not buying that theory.

"I haven't met the guy, and even I think there's gotta be more to it than that," I said.

"My other thought," Vaughn said, "is what if this supposed Restoration and whatever Shade has planned are one and the same. The elf you spoke to, Harlow, made it sound as if they were different causes. One side maintains that the elves' future resides in their own hands, while the other believes it lies within Lachlan's. Lachlan, as you say, is a planner. Shade may be pumping out dual messages, managing to appeal to both sides of the elfin cause without them realizing it, resulting in him having the entire base behind him, now that he's accomplished the impossible."

Roch scrutinized Vaughn. "All I'm really hearing here is that the elves are trying to get home. Good riddance to the lot of them. Since when are elfin concerns *our* concerns?"

A bright flash of red sparked in Vaughn's eyes. It was there and gone in an instant, but it was eerily similar to the way Roch's eyes had looked when he'd tried to enthrall me and the sword out of here. I couldn't be sure if Vaughn was turning his enthrall powers on Roch or if he was just pissed at his boss. During our first meeting, Vaughn had referred to Roch as a "stubborn mule." I still couldn't tell if this was a leader and bold subordinate dynamic or a brotherly one.

In a measured tone, Vaughn said, "For whatever reason, the elves have allied with the hybrids. My best guess is that they plan to eventually break through the veils in places like Tercla and let ferals into the city just as they did with Luma and Mulgrew. That would make this a *vampire* concern."

Roch considered this.

After a moment of hesitation, Vaughn said, "You wouldn't want your work for the Council to go to waste, would you?"

Roch's perfectly chiseled jaw clenched. Instead of addressing Vaughn, he turned to my mom. "Vaughn has always been one for conspiracy theories. I'd expect more from you, though, Camila. Does Vaughn's latest *hunch* have merit?" He said "hunch" as if it were something offensive. "You met Lachlan Shade yourself. Is this something he's capable of—petty, bloody revenge?"

I glanced at my mom, who had been relatively silent for most of this conversation. She was much quieter than I remembered. Not reserved so much as broody.

"He sacrificed sixteen teenagers in Luma to get himself through that portal," Mom said. "He tried to sacrifice one thirty years ago, too. He's of a single mind now, and his mission—whatever it is—is his priority, to the detriment of everything else. He doesn't seem like he's got anyone or anything he truly cares about beyond seeing this through. So, yes, I think he's capable of this. His alliance with hybrids *should* worry you, Vincent."

Roch stared at my mom for a beat. "Then I have something to show you."

Vaughn took this as his cue; he turned on his heel and headed back in the direction of the door. I didn't miss the tiny triumphant smile on Vaughn's face just before he turned away. Instead of leaving Roch's den, Vaughn skirted the table still topped by the dozing white cat and headed for a corner of the room. He pushed an unseen button on the wood paneling and the outline of a hidden door materialized. Pulling it open, he slipped inside, followed closely by Roch.

Mom and I eyed each other warily before trailing after the vampires.

CHAPTER ELEVEN

HARLOW

I stepped into the hidden hallway first, my curiosity getting the better of me. The narrow space was stark white and devoid of decoration. The ceiling was lower here than I would have expected—only a couple of inches above Roch's head, who I guessed clocked in at six feet.

At the end of the hall was another door controlled by an unassuming button embedded in the wall. Vaughn pressed it, and the door eased open. I bit my lip as I crossed over the threshold, unsure what Roch could possibly want to show us. Probably a torture room where he'd string me up and bleed me dry.

I soon found myself in a mundane-looking three-story laboratory. The ground floor took up most of the space, while the top two floors were more akin to lofts. The center of the ground floor was dotted with long, stainless-steel tables. The farthest wall was lined with shelves. Some held books, while others held thick binders. Glass beakers and flasks sat alongside dozens of test-tube racks. Others still had shiny equipment lined up in neat rows—microscopes, scales, what looked like tiny glass-fronted refrigerators, and dozens of other contraptions I had no names for.

A handful of people were milling about the space wearing white lab coats. I had no idea if they were vampires or mundanes. If they'd sensed our arrival, they didn't show it.

Mom and I crept farther into the room while Vaughn set off at a quick clip, weaving around tables and disappearing up a small set of steps that led to the second floor of the lab. I inspected the balcony straight ahead where it hung a few inches over the book-shelves, but I was only able to see a few other shelving units and not much else.

Turning toward the wall shared with the secret door we'd just stepped through, my breath hitched. Here, there were three seven-foot-tall glass enclosures, each occupied by a single feral. Two of the monsters were either asleep or dead, slumped on the floor of the small space, their heads lolling toward their chests. The third one, in the enclosure closest to me, was very much awake. The tube couldn't have been wider than five feet deep. The feral—male from what I could tell—had been standing with his necrotic hands on the glass, peering out at the world beyond his prison. When he sensed me looking at him, his behavior went from curious observation to unchecked ferocity in an instant. He lunged at the glass. Goose bumps rose on my arms as his body thudded against the enclosure over and over. He bared his yellowed teeth. There was nothing sapient left in his wall-to-wall-black eyes. He was hunger and rage personified.

I'd seen enough horror movies in my day to know that wild beasts trapped in a lab never stayed locked up for long. "You don't worry about them being able to get out?" I asked no one in particular.

The sword hovered by my shoulder, still buzzing like an anxious bumble-bee.

"We've had a few breaches," Roch said, suddenly by my side, though he only had eyes for the feral still doing what he could to bodily slam his way through the thick walls of his enclosure. "We've suffered casualties, both while capturing the monsters and during experiments in the lab. But every mistake made and life lost has gotten us closer to finding a cure."

I glanced up at him. "A cure for what? Turning them back from being feral?"

I thought of the cab driver I'd ridden with what felt like years ago now—the one who had driven me to Haskins's place back when I'd first seen the Code 154 violation on my pocket mirror that had resulted in this whole adventure. The cabbie's eyes had been wall-to-wall black too, but her arms had been covered in runes that quashed her addiction to fae blood.

Hybrid vamps who had slipped too far into feral territory and wanted to claw their way back to sanity could go through an elaborate process to heal themselves. The cabbie had seemed sane enough and had obviously passed the rigorous vetting process to be allowed into Luma as a citizen, so I knew it was possible to be saved from fully succumbing to their addiction. I just didn't know if there was a threshold that, once crossed, couldn't be corrected. Maybe that cabbie had merely flirted with going feral before realizing she'd gone too far.

I apprehensively watched the snarling man in his glass prison, still relentlessly slamming against the wall. This guy had done much more than flirt with the dark side.

"A cure for *us* if we're bitten," Roch said, reminding me that I'd asked him a question. "For pure vampires, a bite from a feral can kill us in minutes. We're trying to craft something that works almost like an EpiPen—something that we can inject post-bite that will stave off death."

"Any luck yet?"

"Not yet." Roch sighed. "During our last … mishap, a feral

that *had been* unconscious and strapped to one of the exam tables here … woke up. It had been given enough tranquilizers to take down an elephant. It woke in the middle of being cut open, managed to snap its bindings, and bit the five scientists working in the lab that day. Four had been bitten only once and were dead —a bite meant to neutralize threats. The monster had been found while it was in the process of draining the fifth and was thankfully killed immediately upon discovery. In that scenario, this EpiPen cure idea might not be enough. I don't know. But it's foolish to not at least try. A breach here in Tercla, as Camila and Vaughn suggest, would result in wholesale slaughter."

His tone told me he was finally taking the threat seriously. Vaughn ostensibly had been right to trick my mom and Roch into this impromptu tête-à-tête; Roch had clearly been in denial all this time, and seeing my mom had dispelled any notions that this matter was merely another of Vaughn's "hunches." There was a haunted look in the vampire's eyes now.

I asked, "How are you able to capture them alive if they're such a threat to you?"

"We've found that if they're in a feeding frenzy they're distracted. It results in a hyper-focus that we've learned to exploit," Roch said. "We either construct a scenario to coax them into a preferred location, or we have to get lucky."

"Do you venture out of Tercla often?" I asked, not sure why I pictured Roch as an immortal homebody.

"Of course. I'm quite well traveled and there are numerous ways out of the city," Roch said. "Pure vampires wander your mundane streets more than you know. You only know we're there when we want you to."

Wonderful.

I thought of Welsh then. What kind of mischief could he get into if he were both a glamourer *and* a vampire? He could hide so well in plain sight that no one would know he was a vampire until they were already bitten. "At least you can't change forms, I guess."

Roch studied me curiously. "What, like a flea-bitten werecat? I should think not."

"Odd thing for a Cat Dad to say," I said. "But I meant a glamourer."

He fully turned toward me, his cape swishing about his calves. "And where did you hear such a term? Glamourers are as rare as they come."

"A friend of mine is a glamourer. He's a rare bird, that's for sure." And a perpetually grouchy jerk.

I actually kind of missed him.

A mischievous glint flickered in Roch's eyes. "Have you seen his ability at work? In Luma?"

"Oh, sure. He can shift from a young human male to an elderly female gnome to a sore-encrusted zombie lord in a blink. He can even make tinctures to do the same thing. It's really incredible, honestly. I tell him all the time that I'm glad he's using his powers for good, because if he switched his ethical alliance, he could wreak some serious havoc." I cocked my head, curious why he'd care. "Why?"

"This is what suitors do with their lovers' offspring, isn't it? Ask questions? I'm trying to make conversation about your interests or what-have-you to help butter up your mother."

My face scrunched up as my dumb brain conjured a very disturbing image of Roch, my mother, and a tub of margarine. I desperately needed to talk about something else. I gave the guy a once-over as his gaze returned to the captured feral. "What's with the cape?"

He peered down at me. "First of all, this is a cloak, not a cape. Beyond that, I suppose it's a holdover from my early days in Europe. It gets drafty in the cathedral, and my kind tends to run cold. A cloak is much more convenient than wearing a coat, and it also leaves my arms free. As an added bonus, they're excellent for hiding weapons."

I decided Roch and Caspian might actually like each other. That was a Caspian-level answer.

The sword tapped the ground once as if it had heard my thoughts. I presumed it was actually voicing its approval of a garment that would help keep something like itself hidden.

"I'm not going to wear a cape *or* a cloak, sword," I said.

The sword's blade flashed red.

Roch chuckled. "I did not extend my full apology to you as well, sword," he said, addressing the floating weapon on my other side. "I enthralled you when it was uncalled for."

The sword offered one quick hum.

"I think it just said 'okay.' Not accepting your apology, but not outright rejecting it, either."

Tap.

"I suppose that will do," Roch said.

The smile he sent me was almost … friendly. When he acted normal, he wasn't so bad. As long as I didn't think about the fact that he possessed the power to shut down my nervous system without laying a hand on me, everything was fine. Sort of.

"What was it you wanted to show us, Vince?" Mom asked.

We all turned, finding her with a hip resting against a lab table, her arms crossed, and her lips pressed into a thin line.

Somehow Roch and I both understood her expression. As much as the vampire freaked me and the sword out, it felt like we'd reached an impasse. I was happy to chat with the blood-sucking weirdo as long as he kept that enthrall power to himself.

"You wanted us to get along, didn't you?" Roch asked. "I can be quite agreeable when I want to be."

Mom sighed. "I'm well aware."

Roch grinned that disarming smile and I could tell Mom was trying very hard not to react to it. "Right this way." He started for the steps Vaughn had gone up earlier.

After a quick walk across a short landing, Roch led us into a sterile room that reminded me of something out of a cop drama. The space was narrow and dimly lit, comfortably fitting the six of us—Mom, me, the sword, Roch, Vaughn, and a woman in a lab coat. I didn't think any more than five additional people could squeeze into the rectangular space without it feeling cramped, though. The woman in the lab coat was positioned near the front corner of the room opposite the door. Beside her stood a desk covered in electronics.

Three walls were paneled in some kind of dark metal, while the fourth—one of the long arms of the rectangle—was made almost exclusively of dark glass.

Roch closed the door behind us, and once it had snicked shut, the woman in the lab coat pressed a button on the wall that illuminated the space on the other side of the glass. A trio of ferals hissed and shielded their eyes against the harsh light. Their metal room was twice the size of this one, and it was empty save for the ferals. I couldn't even make out the outline of a door. The ferals didn't appear interested in each other; they coexisted. One sat huddled against the wall directly across from me, rocking back and forth. Its head moved in quick, jerky movements—like a bird or a lizard. I couldn't tell if it was a tic or if it was some kind of instinctual behavior, like a prey animal always on the alert for any new noise. The other two—both formerly women, I guessed—prowled around on all fours, but there didn't seem to be much thought behind it. Were they pacing? Searching for a way out?

I was about to ask why we were watching this when the woman in the lab coat turned to a computer on the desk and began clicking away on the keyboard. She typed something onto a page already lined with text. When a prompt box popped up, she selected YES.

The sound of hissing drew my attention back to the glass wall. All three ferals looked up, their wall-to-wall-black eyes homed in on a spot above the feral still seated on the floor. What looked like a sprinkler head descended from the ceiling and doused the still-seated feral in a clear liquid. He spluttered and coughed. Whatever had poured from the ceiling had gotten into his nose and mouth. While he was distracted by that, swiping at his face with his necrotic hands, the pair of female ferals stilled.

Though the glass separating them from us was thick, I could

still hear the way the pair chittered to each other. Maybe there was a hidden speaker and intercom system. While the male continued to cough and swipe at his face, the female pair jerkily tilted their heads at unnatural angles as they observed him. Their shoulder blades were too far apart, as if all the bones in their backs had been broken and then mended in a haphazard alignment that looked wrong beneath their human skin.

My sixth sense blared a warning, yet I took several quick steps toward the two-way mirror. I pressed a hand flat to the glass, somehow as intrigued as I was wary about what was sure to happen next.

One feral angled her face toward the ceiling and made a great show of sniffing the air. She snarled. The other one let out two quick barks. The hair on my arms rose.

The female ferals charged.

In two bounds, the pair closed the distance between them and the still-seated feral. They shredded him with ruthless efficiency. A circle of condensation bloomed on the glass as my breath expelled in a whoosh. Spatters of blackened blood coated the wall and floor where the feral had been sitting mere moments before.

Yet the death of the feral hadn't stopped whatever had been triggered in the other two. They continued to sniff at the air. One leaned forward and sniffed at the other. That one unleashed a series of barks. Unnaturally configured bones shifted under too-tight skin as the pair squared off, slowly circling each other as they tracked through the blood of their victim.

One breath. Two.

The women collided a foot in the air as they launched at each other at the same time. They savagely tore into flesh with teeth and necrotic claws until they both collapsed from their fatal injuries.

They were both dead seconds later.

My stomach roiled. The sword was humming that off-kilter sound again. Mom was muttering obscenities under her breath.

Black blood oozed across the floor in an ever-widening circle.

Gore dripped down the walls. A chunk of chewed-up flesh had hit the window I stood in front of. It slid down the glass like a viscous raindrop.

From the time the sprinkler had emerged, the attack had started and ended in a matter of a minute.

I whirled on Roch, jabbing a thumb in the direction of the carnage. "What in the hells was that?"

"That was what I wanted to show you," Roch said.

The woman in the lab coat flipped a switch on the wall, throwing the room full of dead ferals into darkness.

"You finally perfected the attractant ..." Mom said.

I couldn't tell if she sounded impressed or horrified.

Roch nodded. "The dose we used here was overkill on purpose, ensuring the attractant would get onto the others as well." He gave me a considering look. "Remember what I told you about the feeding frenzy? Well, we took that and weaponized it."

My stomach still churned. There was no love lost between me and the ferals, but that had been ... brutal.

"We're working to manufacture as much of it as we can," Roch said. "We've found that the most successful attractant is one with a strong faun blood base. Goblin blood, surprisingly, is the second most effective."

"Do I want to know where and how you're getting a stable supply of faun and goblin blood?" I asked.

"No," Mom and Roch said in unison.

Roch grinned. Mom did not.

Speaking for the first time since we'd stepped into the room, Vaughn said, "The attractant can be used both offensively and defensively. Dropping a concentration of the stuff could pull ferals *away* from an area. Once the ferals are drawn to a more neutral location—preferably one with VHoA or werecats lying in wait nearby—the ferals can be dispatched more easily."

"Like shooting fish in a barrel," Roch said, looking quite pleased with himself. "And, as you've just seen, it can be used to turn the monsters on themselves. It could even be used to take out hybrids if we got creative enough. I do think it would be fitting for those abominations to be eviscerated by their mutated pets.

"We're in the process of not only crafting as much of the attractant as possible but finding ways to aerosolize it. We're also working to create vessels that can safely hold the concoction while being handled or transported, but that will shatter on impact if thrown."

I tried not to imagine what would happen if I had a bottle of the stuff in my purse, like pepper spray, only to have the "vessel" break prematurely. It would be a horrific way to go. But I could already see ways that the attractant could help—especially if there was an insurmountable swarm of the monsters. If all ferals got as singularly fixated on the kill as Roch had just demonstrated, the attractant could help level the playing field.

"My proposal …" Vaughn said slowly, "is that, instead of only Tercla and anti-Council pures getting access to the attractant, a mutually beneficial deal be struck between Roch and the Luma Collective."

"This again?" Roch muttered.

Vaughn worked his jaw. "You call Lachlan Shade petty, yet you're willing to hoard the attractant as a political statement."

Roch waved a dismissive hand. "The Council is full of narrow-minded elitist pricks, and you know it."

Vaughn gave a little shrug as if saying, *"Well, yes, but that's beside the point."*

Mom huffed a frustrated sigh. "What kind of deal, Vaughn?"

"Our veil has been weakening in spots for some time," Vaughn said, studying Roch as if he expected the other vampire to shut him up. Roch stayed quiet, though, so Vaughn soldiered on. "It's part of the reason we use the tunnels as often as we do. Collectives everywhere are stretched thin. Buffing up the veil in Tercla isn't on any of their priority lists. But if veils in general are under threat, we need ours to be reinforced, priority or not. We have a supply of elf and hybrid blood that could be used to craft more specific 'keep-out' spells to be added to our obelisks. And we're isolated out here, which until now has been a blessing. But if our walls are stormed, we'll be sitting ducks. In exchange, Roch could be talked into donating a generous amount of the attractant. I'm sure the Collective could find some creative uses for it."

Mom and I studied Roch. I was mostly curious how the vampire felt about Vaughn speaking on his behalf.

Roch didn't say anything for a while. He merely stared at the dark glass. Did his heightened vampire sight allow him to see what lay in the room beyond, or was he staring off into some place only he could see? "Fine," he finally said and then strode for the door.

I couldn't tell if that was a "I wholeheartedly agree" kind of fine, or a "Once our guests leave, Vaughn, I'm going to have you assassinated for speaking out of turn in front of my former lover" kind of fine.

After pulling the door open and letting in a flood of light, Roch said, "Have the specimens dissected and stored."

"It's already under way," the woman in the lab coat said.

Without looking back, Roch headed not for the stairs that led back to the ground floor, but up two more steps that led to the landing that hung over the bookshelves I'd been eyeing earlier. The sword followed me out, but rather than floating along behind me, it drifted to the middle of the lab, high above the tables. I guessed it was trying to take in the full scope of the place, but maybe it was experiencing some form of claustrophobia and needed the metaphorical breathing room.

The landing Mom, Vaughn, and I followed Roch to wasn't very wide. The back wall was lined with what looked like refrigerator doors, while the two shorter sides had shelving units pressed against them, crammed with books, binders, and lab equipment. Roch walked to the first door, grabbed hold of the handle, and gave it a forceful yank down. The door issued a hiss, and as Roch pulled it open, a gust of cold air swept past me. Inside, lined up on the metal shelves, were rows and rows of test tubes. From what I could see, most of them were filled with blood. Labels along the shelves bore the names of the species the blood had come from. On the topmost shelf, though, were small vials of clear liquid. The blood-filled vials were unnerving—mostly because there were so damn many of them—but it was likely the innocuous-looking black-capped vials were the ones to be worried about. Roch removed four of them before closing the door.

Bracing a vial between finger and thumb, he held it in Mom's direction. He tipped the vial back and forth, revealing that the liquid wasn't wholly clear. Tendrils of a silvery substance wafted through it, like translucent worms. "This is a sample of the most potent mixture. You only need a third of this to attract them. If they're within a five-mile radius, they'll smell it and come running within twenty minutes or so. The more you use, the faster they'll come. Pouring it onto something that would already smell enticing to them—like a rotting carcass—is a surefire way to lure them in."

I supposed Roch and I lived in very different worlds if he thought having a rotting carcass handy wasn't unusual. Or gross. "How much was used on the poor bastards in the kill room?"

"About twenty vials' worth. Like I said, it was overkill on purpose," Roch said.

Mom took the vials from him. "Does the attractant have a scent humans can detect?"

Vaughn chuckled. "It smells like pungent garbage inside in a floral-scented trash bag that's been left out to bake in the heart of summer."

My nose wrinkled. At least we'd have an olfactory warning if one of the vials broke. "Do we need to keep them chilled?"

"No," Roch said. "We try to keep the attractant in a location that has the least chance of causing a problem should one of the vials break. They have a shelf life of about six months, chilled or not. This batch was created just a few weeks ago. As long as they don't shatter on your way back to Luma, you have nothing to worry about. I'll send you off with a carrying case."

Mom and Roch gazed at each other. I couldn't tell what was going on in either of their expressions.

"Uhhh … Vaughn?" I asked. "Can you walk me to the nearest restroom?"

He was clearly about to ask why I needed such a thing when he caught sight of the charged looks, too. "Of course. I'll wait with her in Roch's chambers until you're ready to leave, Camila. Then I'll escort you out of town myself."

Mom arched a brow at me, but I nodded once, letting her know I was okay.

I followed Vaughn back down the two sets of stairs and toward the still-open secret door. The feral who had been pounding relentlessly against his glass tube earlier spotted me as I walked past. He resumed his manic, hopefully fruitless, attack. When Vaughn dipped into the hidden hallway ahead of me, the sword rocketed past him and out of sight. The sword was definitely not a fan of vamps—or maybe specifically not a fan of Roch.

Stopping at the threshold of the hallway, I hazarded a glance over my shoulder. I could only see my mom and Roch from the chest up. They stood a foot apart. Mom was speaking. Roch, now that they were mostly alone, watched my mom with such undisguised longing that I didn't know what to make of it. When he reached out to cup her face and Mom didn't shrug off his touch, I turned my back on the scene to give them their privacy. It was hard to see anyone do that to Mom who wasn't my dad. But Dad wouldn't have wanted her to be alone forever, right? I couldn't say he'd be pleased that the person she'd made a connection with was the kind of monster he and Mom had spent their lives hunting, though.

Sighing, I headed down the hallway after my sword.

CHAPTER TWELVE

LACHLAN

A knock on the door severed Lachlan's immersion in his work. He unceremoniously dropped his pen on his notebook and turned in his chair, an arm thrown over the back. "What?"

The door swung open with such force the doorknob thunked

into the already-existing divot in the plaster. Blythe laughed sheepishly, as usual.

The *unusual* thing was what was in her hands—a messily decorated cake atop a chipped ceramic plate. It was held out toward him like the offering it was. The dim lighting of the hallway made the flickering flames of the eighteen candles stuck haphazardly into the chocolate frosting cast deep shadows across her smiling face. It somehow made the points of her ears appear even sharper.

He chuckled softly, despite his irritation at being interrupted. "I told you I didn't want a cake."

"And you *knew* I wouldn't listen. Eighteen is a milestone," Blythe said. "Mom and Dad would be very disappointed if I skipped this one."

His chest twinged. Blythe winced, and Lachlan knew she was mentally kicking herself for bringing them up.

Lachlan regarded the cake. He appreciated the work that must have gone into making it. Their godmother, Tera, wasn't strict, exactly, but she also didn't keep sweets in the house. Blythe must have used her babysitting money to pay for the ingredients and candles. Tera was out for the night with the rest of the family, having already prepared a small birthday dinner for the Shade siblings. Tera, a widow when she'd first taken the Shades in, had remarried a couple of years ago. Her new husband had two kids of his own. The small house felt more crowded by the day.

There had been no dessert or presents from Tera or her family because Lachlan had insisted he didn't want any. Blythe knew him better.

He asked, "You just going to stand there all night, or are we going to eat cake until we want to throw up?"

Blythe grinned and hurried to Lachlan's desk. He shoved aside his notes and books to make room for the cake. The wafting smoke from the candles tickled his nose. Blythe dashed out of the room long enough to grab plates and utensils from the kitchen.

Blythe sang the customary "Happy Birthday," but she did so

as if she were an opera singer. Lachlan resisted the urge to laugh —if only because that was what Blythe wanted, and Lachlan was nothing if not stubborn. She was making it very hard for him to stay grouchy, though.

He wasn't rankled because she'd interrupted his work. It was that the interruption had thrust him back into reality—a reality where his parents were missing yet another birthday. In the years since they'd vanished into the portal to worlds unknown, he'd thought Mother's and Father's Days would be the hardest. Or the big family holidays like Thanksgiving—the elfin version of it, anyway. Those he could handle. It was birthdays that made the grief and anger well up. His parents had always harbored an unhealthy preoccupation with portals and the quest to find the home realm—their current absence being the stark truth of that. They were notorious for missing school events and forgetting to prepare holiday meals, leaving Lachlan and Blythe on their own to figure out how to cook the traditional goose with sage-mint jelly for Yuletide. But birthdays? Birthdays they remembered.

Despite being an adult now—at least according to earthen laws—Lachlan tapped into his childhood self, made a wish, and blew out his candles in one breath. Blythe clapped with more enthusiasm than necessary, and Lachlan did laugh then. Blythe beamed.

Tera had been good to them as far as necessities went. The Shade siblings had a roof over their heads, food in their bellies, and allowances in their piggy banks. But Lachlan had always felt like a burden to Tera, even more so when her stepchildren joined the household. Now he felt like a secondary child—an obligation —not a cherished member of the family.

He studied his sister. Blythe fit in well. Then again, Blythe fit in most places.

Perhaps it wasn't Tera who made him feel a step removed from the family. Maybe that had been his doing.

He sighed. This was why he needed a task. If he was busy with a project, it kept the bitterness and melancholy at bay.

He and Blythe had three slices each. The third slice was very much a mistake, but it was so good, he happily risked the food coma and inevitable sugar crash later.

They talked about the crush Blythe had on a boy in her class. Blythe harassed Lachlan about asking Annalise out before "the girl gets sick of waiting and settles for someone else." Lachlan wasn't sure Annalise even knew his name.

Their cousin Dusty, who had just graduated from a tiny school in a Wyoming hub, was their main topic of conversation, though. He'd just gotten back into town a couple of days ago. The school was a strict correctional organization for wayward fae youth. Dusty had not handled the disappearance of his mother and the death of his father well. After six months of the twelve-year-old starting fights, finishing fights, and committing acts of petty theft, he'd been shipped away by his grandparents. The school had successfully squashed the rebelliousness in Dusty, but it had squashed everything else about him, too. He was subdued now. Lachlan would have been comforted to see a quiet rage in his cousin's eyes, if only because it would mean Dusty was still in there somewhere.

The urge to return to his project tugged at Lachlan. The sugar had given him a jolt of renewed energy. His project had been growing more urgent with every passing birthday, but especially with this one. Not because it was a milestone birthday, but because Dusty was back. Dusty needed Lachlan to succeed even more than Lachlan did.

Blythe sighed dramatically. "Okay, you wacko, you can return to your work *on your birthday*. You look at those notes with more longing than you do Annalise, which is saying something, let me tell you." She collected the plates and utensils.

Lachlan, feeling mildly guilty, picked up the larger plate that held the meager remains of the cake. He'd only taken one step toward the kitchen, following after Blythe, when the hairs on his arms rose. The air crackled with electricity. It was so strong and so sudden, his breath hitched.

He'd felt this before. Blythe whirled in the doorway, her eyes wide. She'd felt it, too, then.

Her wide gaze slid away from Lachlan and to his right, toward his closet doors. The plates in her hands dropped with a clatter. They shattered into large shards. A fork—its tines coated in a fine layer of chocolate frosting—skittered to a stop when it hit his big toe. He still clutched the plate holding the remains of his birthday cake, the lip digging into his stomach. He focused on the pressure against his abdomen and the small mound of blown-out candles lying beside the cake. He wasn't sure what he wanted more—to see nothing or to lock eyes with what he was almost positive was there.

Blythe tiptoed around small globs of frosting, fallen silverware, and broken porcelain pieces. She cowered in front of him, keeping him between herself and the source of the crackling energy.

Releasing a slow breath, he turned his head. He gasped, almost losing his hold on the plate.

A swirling vortex of energy hovered at about chest height. It was roughly the size of a basketball but oval-shaped. It had the usual vanity-mirror-like appearance. He thought of those metal-handled hand mirrors from fairy tales—the ones where villains sought the location of their enemies. Yet even after what had to be several minutes of Lachlan and Blythe diligently watching the portal, it never grew larger.

"Should we get closer?" Blythe asked.

Lachlan stalled. It didn't appear to be big enough for a monster to stick its hand through, but that was what the monster on the other side would *want* him to think.

Wordlessly, they crept forward together. Lachlan had yet to relinquish his vise grip on the plate. Perhaps he could chuck it like a frisbee if something tried to crawl its way out of the inter-realm doorway.

When the Shade siblings were a foot from the portal, Lachlan crouched slightly to be at eye level with the spinning void ringed with crackling blue energy. He couldn't see anything inside it but endless black.

The electricity in the air suddenly grew more frenetic, making Lachlan and Blythe stutter back a couple of steps. The portal started to shrink. Tightness squeezed Lachlan's chest. Disappointment settled over him, as thick as the frosting on his birthday cake. He dropped his chin. It was stupid of him to get his hopes up.

"Wait, what's that?"

His head snapped back up.

Something was pushing its way out of the portal. It made vague shapes in the blackness, like something trying to punch its way through plastic wrap the color of tar. A flat edge here. A sharp point there. Lachlan's pulse thundered in his ears.

A bright burst of blue light shot out from the outer ring of the portal. Lachlan shied away, squeezing his eyes shut. Blythe buried her face in Lachlan's side.

In the same instant that the crackling energy abruptly vanished, something hit the floor. Lachlan flinched, his eyes still screwed shut. If one of those murderous light-beings had just teleported itself into his bedroom as the most fucked-up birthday present from the universe ever, he wasn't ready to see it.

Blythe, as usual, was braver. "It's a ... book."

Lachlan's eyes flew open. Sure enough, lying on the floor below where the portal had been, was a leather-bound book. A *journal*, possibly.

Lachlan extricated himself from his sister's grasp, deposited the plate of cake on his desk, and snatched the book off the floor. He only allowed himself a moment to appreciate the feel of the soft, supple leather before he undid the clasp holding it closed and flipped open the cover. A folded piece of paper slipped out and fluttered to the floor.

Blythe snatched it up before Lachlan could react. She unfolded it, intently inspecting the words.

The seconds ticked by in mind-numbing silence.

"*Well?*" Lachlan asked.

Without looking up, she read: "*What the Order thought it knew about portals is laughable. The Order has barely scratched the surface. Compiled here is the next tier in portal magic understanding.*"

Doing his best not to tear the note from her hands, he took it so he could read it for himself. If the familiar handwriting hadn't been enough to deliver a sucker punch, the end of the note did.

"*Happy birthday, Lach. We're so close to finding our way back. Perhaps we'll be celebrating your 19th in person. Don't give up hope, sweet boy. Mom, Dad & Aunt Lydia.*"

Lachlan's wide eyes met his sister's watery ones.

"Somehow I knew they wouldn't miss this one," Blythe said. There was something so childlike in the joy he saw in her smile. She looked every bit of her sixteen years then—showing him a hint of the carefree girl she would have been had their parents still been here. "I told you eighteen was a milestone."

Lachlan blew out a long breath. His parents were alive. His *aunt* was alive. He just had to get to them. Should he tell Dusty? Would that knowledge unearth the buried part of his cousin that Lachlan desperately hoped still resided somewhere beyond the deadened shell?

The journal in Lachlan's hands suddenly felt heavier, as if the weight of his task had taken on physical form. If his parents and aunt were holding steadfast to the hope that they could one day return to this realm, then Lachlan vowed not to give up, either. They needed him.

He contemplated his workspace in a new light, filled with a renewed sense of purpose that crowded out the last dregs of his melancholy and bitterness.

He had work to do.

CHAPTER THIRTEEN

KAYDA

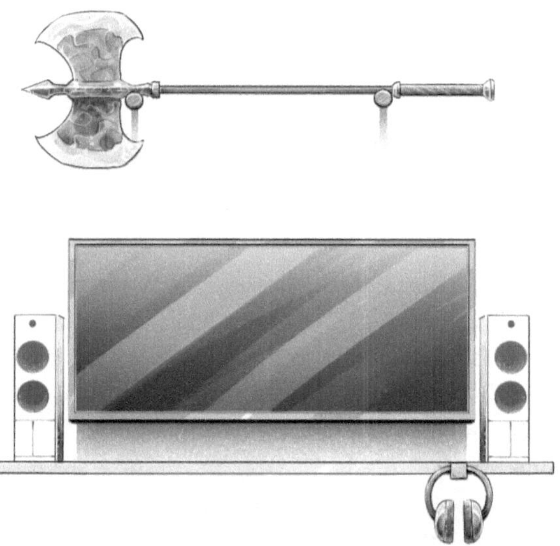

K ayda pushed open the door to Yogurt Town, enjoying the frigid blast of cold air that swept over her skin. She'd worked up a bit of a sweat walking across town to get here. She'd told herself she needed the long walk to help her work out what she wanted to say. In reality, she'd hoped she'd change her mind along the way or that Marisol would call her with some urgent VHoA business and she could turn back.

No such luck.

The attack on Mulgrew had gotten all of VHoA riled up, sure this was the start of Lachlan's nefarious plan, but nothing else had happened since. Life had gone back to scouring the forums during the day and mostly uneventful patrols at night. No new videos from Kessler had popped up, either. She knew because she checked every morning. Kayda felt stuck, like an insect forever trapped in amber.

The young girl at the counter had been idly tapping at her phone. "Welcome to Yogurt Town," she said flatly, wrapping up whatever she'd been doing on her phone before Kayda had walked in. "Can I help you find your perfect flavor—"

The girl froze when she made eye contact with Kayda.

"Hi, Snowdrop," Kayda said.

The girl swallowed hard. Kayda could hear how hard her heart thumped. She didn't think the young elf was scared of her so much as the sight of Kayda triggered some kind of PTSD response. Snowdrop's equally young coworker, who had been wiping down surfaces, watched them warily from the corner of his eye but otherwise kept to himself.

"Hi," Snowdrop managed. "How um … how are you?"

"Do you have a lunch break soon?" Kayda asked. "We could get a pizza or something."

Snowdrop audibly swallowed again, but her stomach betrayed her by rumbling a millisecond later. It was usually a sure bet that a teenager wouldn't turn down free food. "My break is in about fifteen minutes."

"I'll wait," Kayda said.

Snowdrop offered a shaky smile. "Great."

Kayda had never been much of a sweets girl, but she got a cup of frozen yogurt and piled it with a random assortment of toppings to help kill time. She wedged herself into a too-small pastel-yellow chair beside a bubblegum-pink table and idly picked at her dessert. The shop was fairly dead at this hour, so Snowdrop spent a lot of her time behind the counter pointedly *not* looking at Kayda. Snowdrop's coworker tried to discreetly ask if they needed to "call security about the creepy draken lady" a couple of times, but Snowdrop waved him off.

A cursory glance at the kid told Kayda he was the same young man who had been working the last time Kayda was here. Granted, that day she'd been with Henri and Welsh. Welsh had been glamoured to look like a wealthy elfin businessman, and Kayda and Henri had been his stoic bodyguards. If Kayda remembered correctly, Welsh had lightly threatened the kid. Kayda imagined that when Snowdrop had come hustling back inside after her altercation with the menacing trio she'd looked no less than freaked out.

Kayda didn't blame the boy for being leery now, and she appreciated that he kept trying to make sure Snowdrop was okay.

When Snowdrop's fifteen minutes were up, she grabbed her purse from under the counter, left the main floor to presumably tell her boss in the back room that she was leaving for lunch, then waved meekly to her coworker who had taken up Snowdrop's vacated spot.

"I promise to bring her back in one piece," Kayda said as she held the door open for Snowdrop.

The boy only offered a tight nod in response.

Kayda dropped her half-eaten yogurt in a trash can as they left, and then she and Snowdrop walked the five minutes to the pizza place in silence. It was the same restaurant Kayda had gone to with the guys after they'd interrogated Snowdrop about her role in manipulating the veils in the Industrial District, thereby letting in three ferals.

Kayda was fairly certain she knew why Snowdrop was so nervous around her.

On the night of Lachlan Shade's escape, when the werecats had finally arrived on the scene, the room had been filled with dead bodies of elves and woodland creatures. Of the eighteen elfin teenagers who had been coerced into participating in the ritual that had freed Lachlan from exile, only two had survived. One was a young girl who had fled before Lachlan crawled out of the portal, and the other was Snowdrop.

The same Snowdrop who had used a charmed ring against Kayda, resulting in Kayda having several broken ribs. Snowdrop had let ferals into Luma at least once. She'd potentially murdered innocent mundane animals, too, like the coyote Kayda had found, as part of her training.

By all accounts, the young girl should have been in Collective custody. Maybe she *should* have even been tried and sent off to the Antarctic hub. But when the werecats had interviewed Kayda, Kayda had told them that the elfin teens had been gaslit in the worst way. She adamantly argued that the Shades possessed manipulative powers beyond anything she'd ever seen. Snowdrop, she said, was not only a victim but was now living with the reality that over a dozen of her peers had just been murdered. That was punishment enough.

Henri, Erik, Jo, and Welsh had reiterated Kayda's sugarcoated truth without hesitation. Even the pixies had come to Snowdrop's defense.

Kayda hadn't mentioned the other escaped elfin girl to the werecats, and they hadn't asked. Kayda didn't know the girl's name anyway.

Snowdrop had sobbed openly while the survivors of the attack professed her innocence. Kayda knew the outpouring of emotion was part grief over being betrayed so badly by someone she'd truly thought was her savior and part relief that this gaggle of strangers who had every reason to rat her out, hadn't.

Snowdrop's evident nervousness *and* her willingness to join Kayda for lunch were no doubt tied to the girl's worry that Kayda had changed her mind. Or that Kayda was now going to black-mail her in exchange for keeping Snowdrop's involvement in the Shades' schemes a secret.

After ordering two pizzas—meat lovers for Kayda and a plain cheese for Snowdrop—Kayda finally broke the silence.

"How are you?" she asked.

Snowdrop looked up sharply from the sugar container she'd been fussing with, rearranging the packets by color. "Fine."

Kayda blew a raspberry. "I don't want a bullshit answer. How are you, really?"

Color rose in Snowdrop's cheeks. The tips of her pointed ears were hidden by her Yogurt Town ball cap, but Kayda suspected they'd gone pink. She shoved the sugar away and folded her arms on the table. "Not great."

Kayda tilted her head back and forth. "That's a little better. Your heart is racing, though. That fear or something else?"

"Seriously?" Snowdrop asked. "You know you're kinda scary, right?" She bit her bottom lip. "Sorry. You and your friends saved me, and I appreciate that and everything, but—"

"But what?"

Snowdrop clenched her jaw.

Kayda listened to the way the girl clicked her teeth together.

Huh. The girl wasn't scared. She was … pissed.

"Who are you mad at?" Kayda asked. "Lachlan Shade for lying? The pixies for not letting you die with the others? Me for choosing to save Grayson over you when Lachlan forced me to choose? Yourself for getting duped?"

Snowdrop started to say something, but then her mouth snapped shut. "Wait. You *didn't* choose to save me?"

"Nope," Kayda said. "Lachlan gave me a choice and I had to make a split-second decision. I chose a friend I'd known longer than you. I had no idea the pixies were going to try to save you."

After a long pause, the girl softly jasked, "Is … is it messed up that that kind of makes me feel better?"

The waiter appeared with their drinks, a basket of bread, and two small plates. "Your pizzas are almost ready, ladies."

After he'd vacated the table, Snowdrop grabbed a piece of

bread, but she just tore it into small pieces that she then dropped onto her plate.

"I'm not going to lie," Kayda said, making Snowdrop look up from her bread massacre, "but I wanted to see you mostly out of guilt. I feel like it's my fault that psychotic elf got loose. It's my fault all those kids died. Sure, I can say *you* survived, but like I said, that wasn't my doing. Some part of me wanted to make sure you were okay to somehow make me feel less terrible about all this."

"Kinda egotistical to make it all about you, isn't it?" Snowdrop asked in a snotty tone that somehow brightened Kayda's mood.

The kid had some claws after all.

Snowdrop went to town ripping up another piece of bread. Without looking at Kayda, she said, "There's a therapist I've been seeing. He's assigned to the group home where I live. It's sort of hard talking to him. I mean, I feel like he's just there for the money anyway, but I can't tell him what *really* happened that night. There's doctor-patient confidentiality or whatever, but he doesn't really seem like the kinda guy who would stick to that if it would help him somehow. The Collective wouldn't care all that much about my privacy if it meant they could truth serum me to learn about …" She worked her jaw. "All the stuff I did."

"You could talk to me," Kayda said.

Snowdrop barely avoided rolling her eyes. "Why? To make *yourself* feel better?"

Kayda knew a defense mechanism when she saw one. She had been Snowdrop, in a way, once. Kayda knew all too well what it was like to be a confused, scared teen with next to no support. She knew the Shades had been selecting fae kids not just for their magical prowess but because of their home lives. The neglected, the homeless, the lost—those were the ones who had a better chance of not being missed when they disappeared or their absence not being noticed until it was too late.

Kayda could have easily ended up in a bad situation if the wrong person had found her at the right time, promising a family and a way home to the fae realm where she "belonged." As much as Kayda had hated her father for exploiting her natural fighting ability and forcing her into the cage fighting circuit, the sport had given Kayda discipline and confidence. Confidence she'd then used to extricate herself from her abusive father. At the ripe old age of fifteen, she'd gotten herself through a series of telepads and come to Luma, ready to beg her ailing grandmother to take her in if that was what it took. Thankfully, her grandmother had greeted her with open arms.

As much of a bully as Kayda's father was, deep down he was a coward. She'd known if she could just get herself out, he'd leave her alone. He hadn't believed she'd do it. Yet the confidence he'd forced her to acquire ensured that she did.

Kayda's grandmother knew downplaying her son's behavior wouldn't help anyone. So she told Kayda the truth: Kayda's father was a little man who had been raised by an even littler one. Nothing Kayda could have said or done would have changed him. The man would have to change himself, and it wasn't worth Kayda's effort to keep trying to prove herself to someone whose self-esteem was so low that he tore others down to make himself feel better—including his daughter.

"You'll never be enough for him," her grandmother had told her, even as tears streamed down Kayda's face. "It's not your fault. You're just an easy target for his self-loathing. He doesn't deserve you. You have to take care of *yourself* first."

The fact that even his own mother had said such things about him had helped Kayda immeasurably. It still took her a long time to get his voice out of her head, the one that constantly told her everything she did was wrong, abnormal, unworthy. But it would have taken a lot longer had her grandmother not been honest with her. Positive outlooks on life were all well and good, but the Kumbaya method didn't work on everyone. Sometimes the best way through the hard shit was to barrel into it headlong, as messy and painful as it was.

"I don't see you as a charity case," Kayda finally said. "I

already told you this whole situation makes me feel guilty as hells. And while I do have people I can talk to about that night, no one other than Grayson—"

"The guy you saved instead of me," Snowdrop said.

"Yeah, him. Other than him and Aster, you're the only other person I know who was actually *in* that room when shit went down," Kayda said. "So, yeah, talking to you about it will help me feel better, but it could help you, too. What's wrong with that? Most people do nice stuff for others because they get something out of it. I'm just being honest about it."

Snowdrop pursed her lips. "You're not gonna use all this to turn me in or something, are you?"

"Nope," Kayda said. "I don't blame you for being suspicious. A whole bunch of people who were supposed to be acting in your best interest did you dirty. I'd be paranoid, too. All I can do is keep telling you I don't have an ulterior motive. It's up to you to decide whether or not you think I'm bullshitting you."

Snowdrop finally stopped shredding bread into bird food and sat back in the booth, her hands in her lap. "I have the same nightmare almost every night," she finally said.

"About what?"

"Umm …" She took a deep breath. "When I was in that trance —when I was in that floating orb of light, you know?"

Kayda nodded.

"I wasn't *totally* in a trance," Snowdrop said. "You know, like when you're asleep, but only kinda? Like you're aware of stuff, but you can't really do anything? And everything is kinda fuzzy?" She chewed her lip. "It was like that. Like my body was doing one thing, but my brain was bouncing between the spell and what was going on in the room. In the nightmare, my friends … my friends are calling for me to help them, and I can't do anything. I just watch them die, one by one. Lachlan laughs the whole time."

"Grade-A asshole, that guy," Kayda said.

Snowdrop laughed awkwardly, almost guiltily, as if, even after everything, she didn't want to actively disparage a man who had indirectly promised to rescue her. Maybe some part of her still hoped he'd prove her wrong and redeem himself.

Kayda had held on to that same shameful, false hope about her own father for years after she'd fled his abuse. His continued absence—not even showing up to his mother's funeral—proved she'd been right about the guy all along. Only time had let her see the truth of him; she knew nothing she said to Snowdrop would pry her fingers loose from the tight hold she had on that hope, no matter how small the kernel.

"Has your therapist talked to you at all about survivor's guilt?" Kayda asked.

"Not really," Snowdrop said. "He mostly just makes me talk about the group home and how I feel about losing my parents. They died in a car accident when I was seven, by the way, in case you want to psychoanalyze me, too."

Kayda ignored the sarcasm.

She hadn't seen a therapist in a while, but the one she'd gone to as a teenager at her grandmother's behest sounded better than this appointed one. "Want help finding someone better to talk to?"

Snowdrop cocked a brow. "I thought that was what *you* were for."

Kayda held up her hands in placation. "I'm looking for a friend, not a full-time job."

Eyes narrowed, Snowdrop said, "I can't tell if that was mean or not."

Their pizzas arrived then, and they slipped into a comfortable silence as they wolfed down three pieces each. Kayda wondered if the girl was hungry all the time—because teenager—or if she skipped out on meals occasionally so she could save her pennies. Maybe she was building a nest egg so she'd have funds when she aged out of the group home.

Snowdrop spent an inordinate length of time wiping grease from her fingers on a napkin. Kayda figured she was working up to something, so she waited the girl out.

"What you asked me before …" she finally said, "about who I'm mad at? I'm kinda just mad, period. It sort of scares me sometimes—how mad I am."

Kayda understood that. She'd been mad a lot as a kid, too. It was why she'd had such a love-hate relationship with fighting. It was both a source of and a cure for how angry she was. Kayda wasn't about to suggest cage fighting to this slight, sometimes meek girl. Even if Kayda felt like she understood her on a fundamental level, it didn't mean they were wired the same.

"What makes the anger go away?" Kayda asked.

"That's part of the problem." Snowdrop shrugged one shoulder dismissively, like what she planned to say next didn't matter. Which told Kayda it meant a lot. "I really loved practicing my magic. That ring you and your friends took from me?"

"The magic-enhancing one?" Kayda asked.

"Yeah." She coughed awkwardly. "When I bought it, it was a Level 1."

Kayda whistled. "You got it up to a Level 4 on your own?"

Snowdrop nodded vigorously, eyes wide. She sat up a little straighter. "I'm not really great with runes—I can copy them, but I can't craft rune arrays on my own. Like … I can mimic the art of it, but I don't understand the language."

Kayda was clueless about all of it.

"But I understand elfin and witch magic—that's more about connecting to energy in the world and manipulating it. It's like … it's like molding things out of clay," Snowdrop said, more animated than Kayda had ever seen her. "It's hard to explain, but it's like magic is a physical thing I can interact with. *That*—communicating with magic—is when I don't feel angry. It makes me feel like, I don't know, like I have a purpose or something. It just feels right, like that's what I'm supposed to be doing. That's why I like the idea of the fae realm so much. That realm is *made* of magic. Sometimes I feel like a plant drying out in the sun—like my magic is shriveling up. I thought the fae realm would make that feeling go away."

How much of that feeling—like life was sucking Snowdrop dry—was literal, and how much was figurative? Kayda knew better than to suggest that Snowdrop's very heightened emotions about life and belonging could just be a normal part of being a teenager. Everything had felt bigger when she was a teen.

Still, she didn't want to belittle the girl's feelings—those feelings were very real to Snowdrop, even if they were slightly melodramatic. Not to mention that Kayda didn't know how it felt to have a connection to magic like Snowdrop did. Maybe magical people really *did* dry out, in a way, the longer they were in a realm with next to no magic. Hells, Kayda's people had lost the ability to shift into dragons after only a handful of generations.

Kayda asked, "Were you increasing the magic in the ring for any specific purpose, or were you just testing your limits?"

"Both, I guess," Snowdrop said. "My dream is to work in a talisman shop—you know, to make stuff with enhanced properties?"

Kayda instantly thought of Josephine. Perhaps the woman would consider taking on another apprentice. She must have her hands full with Erik, though. Even if Jo wasn't willing to take Snowdrop on, Jo might have a recommendation she could pass along to the elf. Kayda vowed to text the witch later.

"Have you looked into it at all?" Kayda asked.

Snowdrop's shoulders rounded, making her smaller—like a turtle retreating into its shell. "Not really. You need certifications and stuff to even get interviews. I can't afford anything like that yet. I work at Yogurt Town as much as I can, and I pick up courier jobs, too. I don't really like courier jobs 'cause we get robbed so often. That was part of why I made that ring—if I could tell someone was coming after me, I could turn my weak wind power into a tornado and blow them away. Literally." Her cheeks flushed, as if realizing she shouldn't have admitted that.

Kayda nodded. "Smart."

A small smile graced Snowdrop's face. "Thanks. I'm saving up as much as I can so I can get my own place in a year—that's when I have to leave the group home. A friend might be able to move in with me so we can share rent, but she and her boyfriend break up and get back together every other week, so I don't want to have to rely on her."

"Also smart," Kayda said.

"Umm … any way I can get that ring back?" Snowdrop asked. "I promise not to use it for evil."

Kayda laughed. "I can talk to Welsh about it. Can't guarantee he hasn't already sold it off, but I'll see what I can do."

Snowdrop paled a bit at the idea of her beloved ring being gone forever. A blaring chime sounded from the purse on the seat beside her and she jumped. She hurriedly pulled out her phone and tapped at the screen. "I have to be back at work in ten minutes."

Kayda hailed the waiter to get the check. After paying and boxing up their leftovers, the pair left the restaurant. Kayda hadn't been sure what her plan was when she came to talk to Snowdrop, but she did feel better. Maybe the kid would avoid Kayda at all costs now, but Kayda was relieved that the elf, despite everything, seemed to be faring okay.

"Hey, uh …" Snowdrop said, the edge of the pizza box pressed into her stomach. She stared down at the parlor's logo. "Could I get your number?" She cautiously peeked at Kayda from under the low brim of her ball cap.

"To harass me about getting your ring back?" Kayda asked.

Snowdrop chuckled softly. "Well, obviously. But … also to just, you know, talk? I won't blow up your phone or anything, but maybe if—"

"Of course," Kayda said, cutting off the girl's rambling and pulling her phone out of her pocket.

After the two swapped numbers, Snowdrop cursed. "Sorry, I really gotta book it if I want to get back in time. I'll talk to you later though, okay?" She walked backward. "And thanks for the pizza."

"Any time," Kayda said, smiling to herself as she watched the young elf in her too-big uniform hustle down the sidewalk.

As Kayda headed in the opposite direction, she texted Henri.

KAYDA

Have you left for work yet?

HENRI

Nah. My shift doesn't start for another two hours

KAYDA

I have leftover pizza. I also was very selfless earlier and you need to reward me accordingly

HENRI

I don't think you're supposed to request prizes for doing nice things

KAYDA

Do you want pizza or not?

HENRI

My door is unlocked

CHAPTER FOURTEEN

HARLOW

While I waited for Mom to get back from her one-on-one with Roch, I received an unexpected text.

SAMAR

Hey.

HARLOW

Hi.

SAMAR

Make it back to Luma in one piece?

HARLOW

We'll get there later today. Made a pitstop.
How'd the launch of your super nerdy map go?

SAMAR

Decent. Folks aren't nearly as excited about it as I expected. Maybe I didn't post it in the best place on the forum. It got shunted into the resources section because of lack of engagement.

HARLOW

I'm sorry you didn't get your bevy of data point groupies. Give it time. I have faith you'll be drowning in spreadsheets soon

SAMAR

There was only one data point groupie I was really interested in…

I smiled down at the screen.

SAMAR

Just say the word and I'll be in a telepad

HARLOW

Give me a few days. Things might get hectic in Luma when we get there. When the dust settles, though, I could be persuaded to grab a beer

SAMAR

It's a date. Safe travels!

A FEW MINUTES LATER, MOM WALKED BACK INTO THE ROOM VIA THE hidden tunnel. I tried to get a read on her. Roch didn't look overly pleased with himself, so I didn't think Mom had agreed to get back together with him or anything. Which was fine by me; I wasn't sure I could handle an ancient vampire for a stepdad.

Mom, however, looked even more troubled than she had when I'd left her alone with Roch on the laboratory landing.

The sword had been flitting around the room while we waited, as if it were committing every inch of the place to memory. It had even played with the white Persian cat for a while. The cat had spotted a circle of light on the floor—a reflection off the sword's blade. When the cat spotted the shimmering light, it offered that odd, chittering "ekekek!" noise cats made upon locating potential prey. It had quickly given chase. The sword had darted about once it realized what was happening, happily turning itself into a laser toy.

But when it realized that Roch was trailing after my mom back into the room, the sword quickly abandoned the game so it could hover by me instead. The cat sat on her haunches in the middle of a maroon-colored rug, her pupils blown wide as she tried to ascertain how her prey had disappeared so suddenly.

I really needed to determine where the sword's vampire aversion stemmed from.

When we all met in the middle of the room, I expected the cat to scamper off. Instead, Roch patted his thighs twice, prompting the cat to mew and then launch straight up. Roch caught her easily. The cat draped herself on his forearm, her legs hanging off either side, as if his arm were a branch, and she a jaguar lounging in a tree. The name etched on the heart-shaped charm hanging from her gold-colored collar said DUCHESS.

Roch idly stroked Duchess's head, in the way of all good villains. Though it was hard to take him too seriously with cat hair dusting his black slacks. The cat purred loudly, her eyes squinted in contentment.

"Vaughn will escort you back out," Roch said now. "We'll get to work producing more of the feral attractant on the assumption your Collective will agree to the terms. One of our human runners will make the drop when the time comes."

Mom nodded once.

Roch turned to me. "It was a pleasure to finally meet you, Harlow."

"We both know that's a lie," I said. "But likewise."

Roch flashed me a pearly white smile.

The sword hovered just behind me, humming in that off-kilter way again. The sound made my teeth ache.

I studied the ancient vampire. "Before we go ... a few of your vamps downstairs knew about my sword. One of them said, '*A mundane who controls one of the fabled sentient weapons.*'"

"Is there a question in there somewhere?" Roch asked, though he only had eyes for Duchess. If you've never seen a vampire fuss over a fluffy cat, just know it's a sight to behold.

Domino had been as tuned in to the black-market scene as anyone outside the hub system could have been. It was all but confirmed that Domino's people—or his connections—were the ones who had raided the *Element of Surprise* when she'd first been exhumed from her watery grave at the bottom of the ocean. Domino's minions snatched items like Margaret Fengast's treasure chest right out from under the Collective's nose. And yet, even Domino had been astonished by the existence of sentient weapons. The vampires, however, hadn't been floored that the sword existed, just that I could "control" it.

"How fabled *are* these weapons?" I asked.

Roch's gaze slid to a spot beyond my shoulder. The sword's humming became even more erratic.

"Vaughn mentioned that you and your sorcerer lover visited a forge once owned by a Margaret Fengast, correct?" Roch asked.

I shot Vaughn a look that I hoped conveyed that I didn't appreciate his spying on me. He was unmoved.

"That area ... what was that odd-sounding name ... Klickitat County?" Roch asked, which earned a nod from Vaughn. He scratched the side of Duchess's face as he spoke, the charm on her collar softly jangling. "There were rumors back in the '50s or '60s that there were several weapons like your sword. The weapons were tasked with asinine, mundane things like housework and yard duty.

"There was a hybrid vampire who lived in that territory. He had, by all accounts, found a balance between consuming fae blood and human blood, but he was starting to suffer the ill effects of his growing addiction. There aren't enclaves for hybrids like there are for pure vampires, and many of them end up as nomads.

"This nomadic vampire had set up shop in Klickitat because of its thriving gnome population. Gnomes gave him enough fae blood to keep the addiction at bay without tipping him over the edge into madness since the little beasts are no bigger than toddlers. Subsisting on toddlers, however, is not sustainable."

I resisted the urge to ask him how he knew that.

"The vampire had committed what essentially amounted to Gnomish genocide in that region. While planning where to head next, he heard rumors about a family crafting sentient weapons. He saw it as a potential way to make some good money. Humans pay exorbitant sums for items of dubious value, so he surmised the weapons would more than secure the funds needed to aid in his relocation. Which is what led him to Fengast's forge. The property of Fengast and her son had been heavily fortified with wards that prevented him from stealing their sentient weapon. It was an ax, if I recall. Eavesdropping on the family, however, eventually provided him with the locations of the properties where the four other weapons resided. The vampire stole each one while the mundanes slept."

Shane Winchell and his wife, Alice, lived on Margaret's property now. Shane was convinced that the weapons had been stolen by a wind elemental—someone who could float alloy powder on the wind and subdue the weapons before they sensed they were under threat. But a hybrid vampire who could skulk about in the dark would have been even stealthier than a fox.

I remembered Roch's earlier confession that he'd been using his powers on the sword as well as myself. Someone like this gnome-murdering vampire wouldn't have needed alloy powder to steal the weapons. "With your powers, can you enthrall someone *not* to do something?"

Roch's grin was as alluring as it was chilling. "Yes. He simply enthralled the weapons not to resist their own theft."

The sword's odd hum hadn't let up behind me.

"And how do you know all this?" I asked.

"The hybrid, Likho, developed quite the reputation in vampire circles decades ago," Roch said. Duchess continued to purr loudly from her perch on his forearm. "He proposed a great number of intriguing uses for weapons like your sword. They weren't the kind of thing that appeals to pure vampires on principle—we value the old ways. We like to stalk our meals ourselves. Using a magic-fueled weapon to do it would cheapen the whole experience. But we humored him. Honestly, we put up with him as much as we did because he'd once been in line to join the Council —before his addiction took hold, anyway. There was a slight chance, no matter how slim, that he could have cleaned himself up, but he was so far down the line of succession, no one tried that hard to help him. It would be like a distant cousin in a royal line winding up on the throne if and only if his entire family perished at once.

"Anyway, he was something of a traveling magician who we allowed to entertain us on occasion back before Tercla became our home base. He had the weapons under his complete command like trained dogs. It was quite remarkable." He eyed my sword. "I'm not sure if yours was with him, though. Hard to tell. Swords all look the same. At any rate, I don't remember any of them showing such signs of wanton free will. This one *may* have been in Likho's possession. Maybe he'd stowed it elsewhere to ensure it didn't misbehave. My enthrall doesn't work on it as well as I'd anticipated; it puts up quite a bit of resistance."

Roch's ridiculously powerful enthrall was no doubt his gift from surviving magical malaria. I supposed I should have felt grateful that the sword obeyed me as much as it did, considering that I had no magical way to keep it in line and it was apparently strong enough to fend off the mental attacks of an elder vampire.

The sword's humming had shifted back to a more familiar hum of contempt.

"Any idea where Likho is now? Do you think he still has any of the others?" I asked.

Roch waved his free hand. "Likho is quite dead. *Dead*, dead."

Vaughn added, "His death has been an ongoing mystery for years, particularly for a few prominent Council members. Our best guess is that he showed his two-bit magician act to the wrong person, and someone decided they wanted the items for themselves. That, or a pure vampire took him out solely for being a hybrid abomination. He was found decapitated in 1985. The handle of an industrial broom had been shoved into the neck hole, and the broom was left in a closet. Overkill and flashy, which isn't our way either. That's why we suspect it was a murder fueled by emotion rather than necessity. The killer likely removed his head so the discovery of Likho's fangs wouldn't muddy the waters of the investigation by adding Satanic panic into the mix, or whatever other nonsense was going on in the '80s. The officer who found the body ran outside to retch in the bushes." He smiled softly. "It was all quite gruesome."

Roch nodded, idly scratching Duchess under the chin now. "Likho's headless body was found by mundane police during a cocaine drug bust in New York. Whoever killed him wanted it to appear that he'd died as a result of mundane quibbles. Likho had acquired quite the collection of charmed weapons, as you mundanes call them, by the time of his death. Either the majority of the collection remains hidden, or someone cleaned out his stash and then his body was dumped later. Rumors spread in the vampire community just like any other. Speculation ran rampant about who had killed him and where his loot had ended up."

I turned to face the sword. "Any of this sound familiar?"

Tap … tap.

Maybe. Its blade burned cherry red. A *frustrated* maybe.

If the sword had been enthralled by Likho enough times, maybe the sword had eventually gotten fed up and retaliated against the vampire when the opportunity presented itself.

"Did *you* decapitate Likho?" I asked it.

Tap-tap.

Well, there went that theory.

If the sword *had* been enthralled by Likho, it might explain some of its rage issues—and its aversion to vampires. Maybe it didn't remember all the details, but a psyche internalized trauma and buried it deep. Some part of the sword's soul could recognize the inherent danger in a vampire's presence without specifically knowing why.

Once silence had settled over us for several seconds, Vaughn said, "If you ladies are ready, I'll escort you to the access road. Your men can pick you up there." He headed for the door.

"I'll be back in touch after I speak to the Collective," Mom told Roch, then moved past him.

"Cam—"

She turned and walked backward. "Business only, Vince."

He sighed, continuing to pet Duchess. The cat was lucky that a vampire's arms never tired. Petting could last an eternity.

I scooted past the vampire and out the door. The sword harpooned past me with such speed I felt the wind of it whiz by my head.

I'd just taken a few steps out of Roch's lair when I glanced back. The gorgeous vampire wore a purely mundane look—devastation. He shuttered it an eye-blink later, but I'd seen it. In another blink, he was at the door, rather than in the middle of the room. He closed the door in my face.

I stared up at the rendering of Roch on the left door. His mischievous smirk drew up his top lip, revealing a needle-sharp fang. When I'd seen this door before meeting the vampire himself, I'd thought the message behind his depiction was clear: *Let them come, friend or foe, as no one is a match for me.*

As I headed down the stone steps, I knew that assessment wasn't true. My mother was a match for him, and she'd won —again.

I hoped that fact wouldn't come back to bite us later.

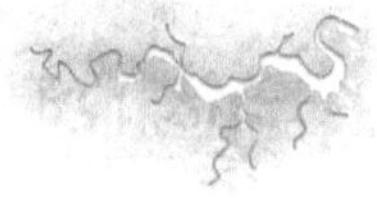

Vaughn led Mom and me through one of Tercla's many underground tunnels. It was cold and dark, save for a few electric lights embedded in the walls, but it was pristine, as far as tunnels went. Not a rat or cockroach in sight. Did pure vampires drain rats as a snack? Maybe they were the equivalent of popcorn. I shuddered.

Shortly before Mom had come back into the room after her private chat with Roch, I'd texted Caspian to ask—*beg*—him to come get us. It was late afternoon now, the air still warm despite the sun being on its descent.

The end of the tunnel was lined with metal rungs, reminding me of the ladder I'd used to access Haskins's basement the day I'd stolen the sword. The same sword that was hovering alongside me, no longer issuing that discordant hum.

The ladder led to a hatch that opened into a small copse of trees that sat alongside one of Tercla's access roads. After depositing us outside and vowing to keep in touch, Vaughn disappeared back into the tunnel like an undead mole. Foliage covered the hatch, the metal painted to seamlessly blend in with the ground. We were thankfully out of range of the potent "keep-out" spell woven into Tercla's veil.

Mom and I had only been waiting for a few minutes before the guys showed up. While waiting, we'd discussed in great detail the potential uses of the feral attractant tucked into the front pocket of my backpack. We'd expertly avoided the topic of Roch altogether. Her tormented expression said she was working through some shit; she'd let me in on it if and when she wanted to. Thinking about my mom's love life was complicated even under the best of circumstances. Throwing an ancient vampire into the mix knocked the circumstances firmly out of the "best" category.

It wasn't until we were all in the car—the sword tucked into the pocket in the back of the front passenger seat again—and Soren was hightailing it away from Tercla that I felt the tension in my shoulders finally ease.

Kayda would be so disappointed that I hadn't brought back a shot glass from one of Tercla's shops. Seeing as I was never going back, my bestie was SOL on that front.

Luma was only twenty miles away from Tercla, so it was still early evening as Soren drove into the tucked-away mundane neighborhood that served as a front for the main entrance. All the houses in the neighborhood were lived in, lest Luma have a squatter problem, but the houses were all occupied by people who worked in the city. Mostly folks like draken, werecats, and elemental witches who could help defend one of Luma's main entrances in case someone sketchy tried to get in without the proper clearance or travel talisman.

Soren cruised through the picturesque neighborhood, driving deeper and deeper until the sounds of traffic disappeared. The closer we got to Luma's entrance, the twitchier Caspian got. He wasn't showing his unease in a manner so gratuitous as a bouncing knee or chewing on his cuticles, but I could tell something was bothering him.

"You okay?" I whispered.

He flinched minutely. "Sure."

I narrowed my eyes. Vague answers weren't Caspian's style. His earlier texts had suggested he'd spent most of his time in the motel doing research, but he'd been "doing research" for days now. If he'd somehow found something I needed to know, he'd tell me. At least I hoped he would.

Soren pulled onto a short, paved road. To the right stood a row of towering Italian cypress trees that blocked the view of anything beyond them. The eight-foot wall with an imposing yet elegant black gate helped obscure everything else. To the left, marking the turnoff onto this small road, was a stone sign, the background of which was layered in emerald-colored tiles. In looping white script, the sign informed us that we'd arrived at MORNING

MEADOWS. The sign stood on a bed of bright-green grass surrounded by colorful flowers being visited regularly by butter-flies and bees getting their last bit of nectar and pollen before settling in for the night. A large guard booth was erected between the sign and the gated entrance, adding an extra layer of "this place might be pretty to look at, but you aren't getting in."

One of the three guards inside the booth ambled out as Soren eased the car forward. The guard was a jovial, plump man in his fifties. A sheen of sweat glistened at his temples. "What can I help you folks with today?"

Though Soren was a professional vampire hunter who'd decapitated more undead than I could probably count, his outward appearance suggested he was nothing more than a goofy kid trapped in a man's body. His hair was shorn close to his head and dyed platinum blond. Today, in lieu of one of his signature "silly ties," he wore a shirt that said "It's not a dad bod. It's a father figure."

The guard eyed him dubiously.

In Soren's usual overly loud, happy tone, he said, "I'm Soren Larsen escorting Camila Fletcher, Harlow Fletcher, Caspian Black-thorn, and a murder sword back to Luma, sir."

The color drained from the guard's face. He regarded my mom for a long moment, then craned his neck to peer through the dark glass of the SUV's tinted passenger windows. Caspian lowered the window to give the guard a good view of our faces.

His eyes widened to the size of dinner plates when they landed on me. I gave him a finger wave. The sword pulled itself out of the seat pocket and floated between me and Caspian. The sword tilted its blade back and forth as if it were waving, too.

"Goddess above," the guard muttered. Beads of sweat dripped down the sides of his face now. "One moment," he said, and I got the distinct impression that he'd just narrowly avoided an urge to curtsy.

He darted away, then practically dove into the guard booth. The heads of the two other guards poked out of the doorway a moment later. The two women goggled at us. Soren saluted them. They ducked back inside.

"Is this what it feels like to be a celebrity?" Caspian asked, pulling up on the power button for his window to close it. "I don't think I like it."

I snorted. "Liar. You love being a household name. You just don't like being a *recognizable* celebrity."

He considered that. "Accurate."

The sweaty gate attendant finally emerged from the guard booth. He must have put in a call to Collective Headquarters, or at least someone higher up on the food chain than himself, to get confirmation that we were allowed to drive through the gate like any other resident. All but one of us was a fugitive or supposed to be in exile, after all. Perhaps he wanted to make sure that a pack of werecats wasn't supposed to meet us on the other side of the shiny black gate.

He held a square device in his hand, roughly the size of a cell phone. It looked like plastic, but there was a shimmery, iridescent sheen to it that quickly distinguished it as anything but mundane. "This will get the car and all of its passengers through the veil," he said a bit robotically, slapping the box to the driver's-side door. "It'll dissolve or drop off after five minutes. But, uh, keep the windows up … just in case."

"In case of *what*?" I asked, leaning forward to poke my head between the two front seats.

The guard visibly swallowed when we made eye contact. The sword hummed menacingly by my head.

I thought of Mom's left arm and how it was awash in mangled skin thanks to her attempt to enter Luma without a travel talisman post exile. She was lucky she'd only passed out after sustaining the burns, rather than the veil magic outright killing her. If Sorceress Rhiannon had lied about my mom getting taken off the exile list and something happened to her when we passed through the veil, the sword's murder ban would be lifted effective immediately.

"*Uhh …*" the guard said, hands up, glancing between me, Soren, and Mom as he spoke. "I didn't mean … it's just that the veil's been a little … twitchy lately. Someone drove through earlier with their windows down. They had a kid in the backseat. Real little kid—four years old, maybe. The kid conjured a small fireball by accident, as elemental toddlers do, and flung it out the window as the car was passing through the veil. The fire hit the barrier, and I swear a half-mile stretch of the veil winked out for nearly half a minute! It's a miracle no mundanes were driving by when it happened." He swallowed hard, gaze flitting to my sword for a moment, then to me. "I don't know what kind of magic lives in that sword of yours, ma'am, but it might be enough to set the veil off again, is all. Better safe than sorry, right?" His laugh was forced and awkward.

I feared the poor guy was about to pass out.

"Suggestion duly noted," Soren said, giving the man a hearty salute before rolling up the window.

I sat back properly in my seat, and the sword wedged itself back into the seat pocket.

I'm not saying I held my breath as Soren eased the car through the now-open gate, but I didn't *not* hold it, either. The entire SUV gave a shudder, like an airplane buffeted by turbulence, as the device on the car door reacted to the veil's magic. I imagined the car surrounded by a sphere of protection.

Then suddenly we were through, no worse for wear. I turned in my seat, peering out the dark glass as I searched for any sign that the veil had malfunctioned. But I couldn't even see the guard booth anymore, just the glowing wall of magic that marked the border of Luma.

I was home.

The reality didn't fill me with the sense of comfort I thought it would. I no longer had a physical home in Luma that was mine. Kayda was here, but I'd be lying if I said going to see her didn't still scare me. If something ever happened to her because of me, I'd never forgive myself.

Mom was in Luma, finally, but I didn't know how long she'd stay.

I felt Caspian watching me. His expression was pensive, like he wanted to say something, but what was there to say? We were supposed to head to the Collective's Tower. That was the main condition of us being allowed back—we all needed to share everything we knew about Lachlan, vampires, and anything gleaned from Domino's operation. Sorcerer Sweeney undoubtedly was in Collective custody by now and had been truth-serumed within an inch of his life, which meant the Collective would know Caspian and I had fled with Margaret Fengast's treasure chest and the secrets inside.

In the Tower, we'd be surrounded by sorcerers who blew up all our lives one way or another. I didn't know much about Soren's history, but I knew enough: He chose to live outside the hubs because he didn't trust the people who ran them.

"I have a proposition," Caspian suddenly blurted. "Camila, do you think we could get away with delaying our visit to the Tower?"

Mom and Soren had a very intense silent conversation. Without a word, Soren drove another half a mile and then parked at the curb in front of a small cottage with a robust garden.

Mom sharply turned in her seat to face the back seat. "Why?"

Caspian shot me a nervous look, as if seeking reassurance, but I had nothing to offer him. I didn't know what he had in mind either.

Swallowing, he returned his attention to my mom. Soren was eyeing him curiously in the rearview mirror. "I've been doing a lot of research—"

Soren chuckled. "Is this state-the-obvious day?"

Mom lightly smacked his arm.

"I mean, the guy was even researching while we were in the motel," Soren said. "Books and notes were all over the bed. He paid for access to Wi-Fi and was hunched in front of his laptop chewing on the end of his pen while whispering, 'Curious indeed!' to himself."

"I was exceedingly more productive than you bellyaching over your weepy display of affection toward Camila earlier," Caspian snapped. He was definitely worked up if he was taking potshots.

Soren laughed nervously and rubbed the back of his head. "I wasn't bellyaching …"

Mom huffed a breath out of her nose. "Researching what, Caspian?"

He offered Mom a short, grateful nod. "Mostly about the runes on the cutlass. I think—and I can't be certain—but there might be something in the spell for sentience that is connected to an anchor."

No one replied.

I sighed. "Cas, you gotta talk to us like we're idiots. None of us have any idea what the hell you're trying to say."

The sword pulled itself free from the seat pocket so it could offer a muted tap on the upholstery.

"The cutlass's sentience may be tied to an energy source from the fae world," Caspian said. "It's fairly evident that the cutlass has its own personality and memories, but I've been curious if somehow its existence is powered by a puppet master, so to speak."

The sword's blade flared red, deeply offended.

Caspian ignored it. "At least part of the Collective's goal in allowing our return is to study the cutlass and Harlow's connection to it. If I could prove there was an entity somewhere holding the reins, it could help further clear Harlow's name as far as being the supposed master of the weapon."

I flushed a bit, having been unaware that at least part of Caspian's late-night study sessions had been to help me. "So *is* there a puppet master?"

The sword forcibly tapped twice on the seat between Caspian and me.

"I don't think so," Caspian said, echoing the sword's

adamant reply. The blade flashed blue in response to Caspian's answer. "I do believe the cutlass exists entirely on its own. As did the ax we met. Even though the cutlass and ax were crafted by the same person, they have personalities and memories independent of each other. And yet, the cutlass and the ax in part gained their sentience from a source—like children who are their own person but who wouldn't exist without their original source."

Soren whimpered dramatically from the driver's seat. "Clear as mud, dude. So you're saying you found the sword's parents?"

Caspian sighed in frustration. "Sort of. The cutlass's sentience is connected to magic harnessed from the scales on its hilt, in addition to the runes on its blade. But there's something in the runes—if I'm interpreting them correctly—that speaks to an anchor. A parent, as you say."

A sudden bolt of worry made my brows smash together. "If this source, whatever it is, is destroyed, would it kill the sword?"

Caspian said, "If the parent analogy is correct, then no. The death of a parent doesn't result in the immediate death of their child. At any rate, we may need that source, whatever it is, to wake up the one in the trunk. Almost like a battery that needs a life-starting jolt before it can run on its own."

The group fell silent.

"As interesting as the sword's history is," Mom said slowly, "why is this something that needs to derail the current plan to visit the Tower? Staying off their Most Wanted list is contingent on us meeting with Rhiannon. She's granting us this because she expects something in return."

I still wondered if there was anything to *my* theory that the Collective didn't want my mom back just because she was a walking encyclopedia of vampires but because of her connection to Roch and Tercla. Roch's feral attractant was something he was purposely denying the Vampire Council, if I was gleaning the details from Vaughn's comments correctly. Were the Vampire Council and the Collective in contact because of the Pact? And if so, did both groups want access to the attractant Roch was squirreling away for a select few?

Even if Mom trusted Rhiannon—as much as one *could* trust a Collective sorcerer—Rhiannon still had her own agenda. Mom wouldn't blindly walk back into Luma without promises from Rhiannon that ensured our safety. I knew that. But since so much of what sorcerers told Mom was locked behind a Soul NDA, she couldn't share details with us. We all trusted Mom, so I supposed we were deciding to trust Rhiannon by association.

"Have you looked at the VHoA forum lately?" Caspian asked, breaking me out of my musings.

Soren turned in his seat to look at me directly. "Does he always talk in questions? This is exhausting."

"Cas has a unique way of getting to the point." I knew Caspian had to be going somewhere significant with this, but he was visibly having a hard time getting his thoughts in the right order. "No, I haven't looked at the forum lately."

Mom and Soren echoed me, though Mom sounded like she was running out of patience.

"Harlow's new friend Samar published a map on the forum that tracks what looks to be a correlation between Bliss hotspots, vampire nest locations, and areas of heightened portal activity," Caspian said. "On *every* place on the map, those three things are clustered relatively close together. The only place where there is an anomaly is near a reservoir in Paso Robles. Namely, near Lake Nacimiento."

"As in the lake featured on the map we found with the second sword?" I asked.

"One and the same," Caspian said.

Soren sighed again. "Can someone please explain?"

I quickly pulled out my phone and searched for Lake Nacimiento. I angled my phone toward him and Mom, who turned in their seats to study the aerial view of the lake nicknamed "the dragon."

The aerial view of the lake looked as if a dragon had been cut into the earth. Creeks formed what looked like a swooping tail and back. Another pair of large creeks made up the dragon's pair of hanging arms, and a lake, dam, and marina that all bore the Nacimiento name made up the dragon's curved head.

I remembered that, on the map found with the second sword, near the start of the dragon's tail, was a large red question mark near "Oak Shores." I asked Caspian if that was where this anomaly was reported.

Caspian shook his head. "They've all been in a section of the lake known as Christmas Cove."

"What kind of anomaly are we talking about?" I asked.

"Much like Margaret's map, there's a question mark over the cove," Caspian said. "An info box pops up when you hover over it that says there have been five reports of portal fluctuations in that location, all within the past few years. I looked up the reports in the Portal Relations archive, and all five say the same thing: Magic-touched residents in the area reported seeing a small portal opening near the shore of the small cove. The portals don't grow larger than a basketball, and they only last roughly two minutes before disappearing again. Portal Relations officially deemed the site as an anomaly, as the reports are too similar to discount, and yet, by the time anyone from the department arrives on scene, they can't find any traces of the portal. Not being able to pick up portal traces is allegedly unheard of."

I asked, "So there are credible sources for the reports, but Portal Relations can't confirm nor deny the portals actually existed?"

"Correct," Caspian said.

Curious.

Caspian barreled ahead. "We know that Bliss and hybrid vampire nests are linked because vampires are making Bliss. We know whatever Lachlan is planning is also connected to hybrids. In addition to that, we know that thirty years ago Lachlan was trying to open portals. It stands to reason that he's still trying. I'm willing to bet that all these clusters of events on Samar's map are directly tied to the Shades."

At least it felt like we were getting closer to what Caspian was trying to explain. "You're thinking that the anomalous portal activity at Lake Nacimiento is somehow related to all the other cases on Samar's map?" I asked. "What if it really *is* just an unexplained anomaly—an outlier, as far as data points go?"

"I considered that," Caspian said. "Yet the very rare sentient weapons have a connection to this lake, too. At the very least, Margaret and her son had an interest in the place; hence, the map in the box with the second cutlass."

"What if …" Mom said slowly, thinking it through, "this place has an abnormal amount of portal activity and is also *not* related to the Shades?"

I frowned at the back of her seat, concerned that passing through the veil had affected her after all. "Didn't I just say that?"

"What I mean is," Mom said, with an edge to her voice that said she didn't appreciate my tone, "what if the portal activity there is natural, like, I don't know, an erupting geyser, and not that the portals are being manually opened by the Shades?"

Caspian lapsed into thoughtful silence.

I voiced something that had been niggling at me for a few minutes now. "Do … do you think this could be the start of another Glitch somehow? Or someone from the fae realm trying to get in contact with us here? Maybe there's something about that specific spot that's like Sedona or Stonehenge—a power vortex or whatever."

Mom and Soren went thoughtfully quiet, too. I supposed no one liked the idea of another Glitch happening in our lifetimes.

Mom spoke up first. "Can I assume that you're mentioning this, Caspian, because you want to investigate this potential power vortex?"

"I can't shake the feeling that the Collective went through an astronomical, unjustified amount of fuss to turn the entire city against Harlow over this cutlass," Caspian said. "While I'm sure they *were* apprehensive about the danger the cutlass potentially posed—especially since it *did* kill several shifters—the lengths they went to suggest a fear of the cutlass that goes beyond public safety. Margaret Fengast as much as said the early version of the Collective were the ones funding the exploits of pirates. Those early sorcerers encouraged the death and poaching of fae animals; the fruits of those labors provided the magic that now animates the cutlass and its brethren. There's something beyond the weapons' sentience that frightened our Collective. I question the wisdom of walking into the Tower with Harlow and the cutlass without knowing more about why they staged a city-wide hunt for her."

Mom grumbled. "You couldn't have mentioned this sooner?"

"The delay was twofold," Caspian said. "The logical part of me knew that, if Harlow and I were to slip away, there needed to be people in my house for the Collective's cats to spy on. I have a few plans in mind that even mundanes can pull off to make the cats believe there's more than just two of you there." He sighed softly and sneaked a quick look at me. "The less logical part of me hesitated to mention any of this, as I've spent a great deal of time convincing myself I was being paranoid.

"Seeing that guard's reaction to us only solidified my fears, though. He looked at Harlow as if she were the boogeyman who'd crawled out from under his bed. What exactly has the Collective been telling their employees about her and the cutlass? It's unnerving to think that the only safe place for her in Luma is the Collective's Tower. I don't know what assurances Rhiannon gave you, Camila, but I'd hoped they'd at least walked back some of their claims in our absence. The reactions of those guards say otherwise. If these people—who are more in the know than the average citizen—are *still* this fearful of her, can you imagine the reaction of the general public? There must be a countless number of residents who would report her return either out of fear or in hope of the reward money."

"There's *still* an active reward for my arrest?" I asked. "Even after Rhiannon promised our records would be scrubbed?"

"According to the Luma Police Department website, yes."

Mom gusted a long sigh. "Shit. Okay, one sec."

My stomach was in knots. Was coming back a mistake? Were packs of werecats galloping toward us now, ready to arrest half of us and slaughter the rest?

"Hello, Camila," came a tinny voice from the front seat.

Mom had put her phone call on speaker.

"Hi, Rhiannon," Mom said, sounding inexplicably pained. "We made it inside the city safely, but we've all contracted food poisoning." Soren provided an incredibly convincing retching noise right on cue. "Would postponing our meeting for a couple of days be all right?"

Rhiannon was quiet for a beat. "Should I be concerned this is part of a ploy to wreak havoc in my city after I put my neck on the line to get your resident status reinstated?"

Soren noisily mimicked retching once more and my stomach heaved in sympathy. What a bizarre skill to have in one's back pocket to pull out at a moment's notice.

"We have a long history, Rhiannon," Mom said slowly, as if every word cost a great effort. "Remember the Dwyer case?"

Rhiannon gave a short, incredulous chuckle. "I still have the occasional nightmare about that one."

"I ask for the same trust now that you granted me then," Mom said. "And also trust in Caspian's instincts."

His brows shot toward his hairline. Was he more surprised about my mom dropping his name or that Mom thought such an addition would aid significantly in the negotiation?

The silence stretched on for ages.

"You and I are bound by a Soul NDA," Rhiannon finally said, but in an odd, measured tone. "Anything I tell you now is not something you can repeat to your travel companions. And you, of course, would never let them overhear, would you?"

"I most definitely didn't put the call on speaker before you answered," Mom said.

"Oh, well that is a relief," Rhiannon said. "Because what I'm mentioning to you now *is* in confidence. It may be fortuitous that Caspian's inklings have caused you to second-guess this meeting."

"Oh, no, it was definitely the food poisoning," Mom said.

Soren provided yet another noisy approximation of losing his lunch.

"There may be something akin to a faction war erupting here at the Tower," Rhiannon said softly. "Some of my colleagues are resolute in their belief that this business with Lachlan Shade would have been stopped in its tracks had the Collective been more unified in their priorities. A faction—*my* faction—keeps proposing ideas and paths for the Collective that run counter to the notion that sorcerers and sorcerers alone are the ones who should hold power in Luma."

My head reared back in surprise. The admission, though, further confirmed why Mom had a relationship with Rhiannon. They were on the same page.

"I can buy you three days," Rhiannon said. "There's enough infighting going on that the Collective at large will be distracted, but you all have to be smart about how you use the freedom. If you start frequenting any of your old haunts, Camila, and the wrong person sees you, I'll get more than a slap on the wrist for granting you lenience. It wouldn't be the first time I was accused of playing favorites with you. Then you'll be forcibly hauled in instead of being allowed to walk in of your own accord." She paused. "That goes double for that sword of yours, Harlow. Keep out of trouble, or the entirety of the werecat force will be on you. I won't be able to stop them. They are, to put it mildly, quite miffed with you."

Caspian said, "We'll be staying at my home the Collective raided months ago. I'm sure the cats will have *no problem* finding it again."

I eyed him curiously. He was testy today.

"Whatever happened at your home was not the result of an order from me, I assure you," Rhiannon said. "The cats are beginning to choose sides in this brewing war. Some of them grow more willful by the day."

The sorcerers losing control of their trained cats didn't bode well.

Mom said, "Thank you for this, Rhiannon. I know you circumvent rules to the best of your ability. I appreciated you then, and I appreciate you now. You're a hidden gem. Truly."

A touch of emotion colored Rhiannon's voice when she said, "You know how I feel about compliments."

Mom laughed. "We'll see you in three days."

The sorceress huffed a little sigh. "Don't make me regret this."

As Mom ended the call, Soren—sounding quite chipper now that we *weren't* going to the Tower just yet—said, "Woo! Going off script. Where to, Caspian?"

Caspian called out directions to his house as Soren drove. Soren turned on the radio and settled on a pop station. He bobbed his head, tapped fingers on the steering wheel, and softly sang off key. At least half the words were wrong. He playfully swatted Mom's hand away both times she tried to sneakily change the station.

Movement shifted in the corner of my eye. Caspian had his phone out with a text thread pulled up. When he noticed me looking, he turned the screen toward me.

There were a few texts from what looked like an earlier conversation, given the time stamps.

CASPIAN

If he doesn't stop bemoaning how he embarrassed himself in front of Harlow's mother, I will brain him to death with this book

WELSH

I can't blame him for being worried when the ladies are alone in Tercla. Pure vampires are just as bad as the rest of them. Maybe worse.

CASPIAN

Wanna talk about it?

WELSH

The answer is still no.

I reached out to swipe up on the screen and get to the more recent part of the conversation.

CASPIAN

We're back. Get to my house ASAP. We need your best disguises.

WELSH

Hello to you, too.

CASPIAN

Don't be dramatic. You're welcome to join us. We're going portal hunting.

WELSH

Will it be sunny where we're going? The change in climate might be good for my constitution.

Turning the phone back toward him and staring pensively at the screen, Caspian said, "I was ninety-nine percent sure he'd say no. He doesn't like to be too far from his clientele."

From the front seat, over the sound of Soren loudly singing along to a Katy Perry song, Mom said, "Wouldn't it be nice to listen to a little Ira Glass?"

"If Ira isn't belting his heart out about fireworks, I don't want it," Soren said, before resuming his horrendous ballad.

Mom muttered, "You're ridiculous," but there was a hint of a laugh as she said it.

Caspian began typing a reply, evidenced by how he softly

spoke the words as he typed them. His fingers stilled mid-type. He shot a wide-eyed look at me then gaped at the phone.

"What?" I hissed.

Without a word, he turned the screen back to me.

Welsh had sent a picture. He wasn't the kind of guy I'd peg as a proponent of selfies. The picture, though, wasn't of him throwing a peace sign outside Al's Burgers but a close-up of his neck marred by two dark puncture marks. The skin around the marks had tendrils of black spiderwebbing away, like tiny streaks of lightning.

Another message came in as I stared, horrified, at the picture.

WELSH

I don't have a hankering for blood yet, but shadows whisper to me now, which I can't imagine is a good thing.

Kayda had told me that Lachlan Shade's vampire friend had bitten Welsh and run off with him and that Erik had killed the vampire for his efforts. But it didn't seem like even Kayda knew more than that.

"I … I thought …" I said, voice low enough that I hoped Mom and Soren couldn't hear me. Welsh probably didn't even want *me* to know about this latest development. My heart thumped hard as I tore my gaze away from Caspian's phone and toward his shell-shocked face. "I thought fae couldn't be affected … like … *that*," I said, gesturing at the picture.

"Lady, you're a firewooork!"

Caspian visibly swallowed. When his words reached me, they were whispered so softly I could barely hear them. I suspected he'd somehow used his magic to send them on the gentlest of air currents. "Welsh said the vampire had been a practitioner of shadow magic—a vamp who's been mutated into something else … something whose bite alters his victims, regardless of race or species."

"C'mon let the ooooothers wooork!"

"What does that mean for Welsh?" I asked, my stomach pitching as if I really *were* suffering from food poisoning. "Is he turning, or is he … dying?"

It took Caspian a long time to reply, and when he did, his voice was small and quiet. "I don't know."

CHAPTER FIFTEEN

LACHLAN

Lachlan had been deep in the throes of grief when Teo Santoro strolled into his life. It was highly probable that he never would have befriended the vampire otherwise. Lachlan had also been drunk, which hadn't helped his decision-making.

In true cliché fashion, he'd been drinking away his sorrows in a back corner of a dark, mundane bar. He'd been in some nameless small town in Indiana. Or maybe it had been Ohio. Either way, it was a forgotten, run-down place where no one would give him shit as long as he kept his pointed ears tucked under his worn ball cap. If he didn't hold prolonged eye contact or cause a disorderly, drunken fuss, people usually left him alone.

He knew getting blitzed would have been safer in a hub, but he wasn't in the mood for all the hoop jumping necessary to secure a travel talisman. They were getting harder to come by, mostly because the gatekeepers had grown increasingly elitist in the past few years. He wasn't sure if he was on some master hub-system-wide blacklist, but his name was certainly making the rounds.

His money was as green as anyone else's but the Collective's asinine, draconian rules evidently meant more than his patronage.

He wasn't sure he was blameless in the matter. He might have finally burned too many bridges—last night especially. Last night, he'd managed to make enemies of friend *and* foe. That was a record, even for him.

Blythe wasn't taking his calls or replying to his messages. She'd gotten mad at him before, as was customary for siblings, but last night? Last night had been different.

He picked up his bottle and knocked it back, only to find it empty. He grumbled to himself. He would have peeled himself off the cracked leather booth seat to get another if he trusted his legs to stay underneath him.

Clunk.

He flinched, suddenly finding a frosted dark bottle of beer on the table, and a strikingly handsome man seated in the booth opposite. The man raised a single brow in question.

"Look, I'm flattered," Lachlan started, noting that his words were a bit slurred as he held up a hand to ward off his potential suitor.

The handsome man rolled his eyes. His very … peculiar eyes.

Lachlan hinged forward, the lip of the sticky table pressing into his chest and further wrinkling his already rumpled T-shirt.

He wasn't sure if he was so drunk that he was hallucinating or if it was a trick of the dim lighting, but he could have sworn there were swirls of black dancing in the whites of the man's eyes.

"What I want isn't in your pants," the man said. "It's in your veins. I could smell you before I even walked in the door. Which is saying something, as the stench of this place is foul."

Lachlan scolded his alcohol-soaked brain into catching up. A word finally came to him, and it hissed between his teeth like an expletive. *"Hybrid?"* He sat back hard, as if that few inches of distance would protect him.

The man nodded once, then held out a hand above the table. "Teo Santoro."

Lachlan shook it. "Lachlan Shade."

The black in Teo's eyes seemed to undulate wildly in response, like an excited goldfish thrilled by the promise of food.

Lachlan realized later that offering any part of himself, no matter how innocent the gesture, to an admittedly hungry vampire had been stupid indeed. All Teo would have needed to do was flip over Lachlan's wrist and sink in his fangs.

Hybrids balanced on the precarious edge of insanity—*of going feral*—didn't they? Shaking the hand of a hybrid was like depositing a recovering alcoholic on day one of sobriety at an event with an open bar. Sitting across from a full-blooded fae without taking at least a nibble showed more restraint than Lachlan realized hybrids possessed.

Teo had simply shaken Lachlan's hand and then let it go before sitting back in the booth, fingers idly drumming the table's worn wood.

"That's it, then?" Lachlan finally asked. "If I give you some of my blood, you'll leave me alone?"

Teo glanced to the left at the sparsely populated bar. A couple stood at the ancient jukebox in the corner, quietly discussing which song to play next. A woman nearby played darts, the needle-sharp tips plunging into the surrounding wood far more often than the thick foam of the target. Everyone else quietly nursed their beers or stared fixedly up at the TV that hung above the wall of liquor bottles behind the bar. The Cincinnati Reds were getting their asses handed to them.

Teo swung his focus back to Lachlan. "Consider the beer both a gesture of greeting and a gift from a fan. It has been a treat to follow your work in discovering … *travel alternatives*."

Lachlan wasn't drunk enough to let a statement like that go without comment. "Why the fuck would a vampire care about portals?"

He was, however, drunk enough to casually mention portals in a mundane bar. He mentally winced.

Teo's small smug smile said he was amused by Lachlan's loose tongue. "I wasn't sure it was you at first, but rumor spreads fast in our circles, and those rumors led me here. Word about the Shades has been gaining in frequency for months. The power your last attempt gave off was felt for miles. You've got the Collective quaking in their boots. They've propagated the bullshit lie since day one of the Glitch that the ability to control portals was near impossible. Your work with the Shades proves otherwise."

Lachlan's thoughts pinballed, his heartbeat quickening at such bold declarations from someone who thought the same way he did. "You still haven't answered my question. Vampires originated in the earthen realm. There are other species like you in other realms, but your people were here well before the Glitch. Why do you care about portals? Want all the magic-touched to leave so you're the only supernaturals left—especially since the werewolves are already wiped out?"

"For an elf who can open doorways to other worlds, your lack of imagination is disappointing," Teo said.

Lachlan bristled, possibly more so than he would have had he not been twenty beers deep. A heightened metabolism made getting drunk both expensive and a lot of work. He leaned forward again, the lip of the table pressing into his chest. Jabbing his pointer finger against the table, he snapped, "I can do more than open doorways. I possess power you could only *dream* of."

Teo remained impassive—his posture and features relaxed. It only annoyed Lachlan more. Partly because he sounded like a petulant child even to *his* ears—as if he were twelve again, being told by his parents that he could only watch the Order's rituals instead of leading them … because he was too young, too unskilled, too reckless.

Blythe had roared that last one in his face the night before.

"When will it be enough?" she'd screamed, tears streaming down her dirt-streaked face. *"You're all I have left, Lach. Doesn't that mean anything to you? Don't I? Your recklessness is going to get you killed one day. I refuse to be here when it happens."*

"What is it you want?" Teo asked.

Lachlan snapped from his melancholy. He turned his bleary, fuzzy gaze toward the vampire. Pair of vampires. Wait, no. Just one.

What *did* he want? He wanted another beer. He eyeballed the sweating bottle on the table that he'd yet to drink. Teo slid it away, then folded his hands on the table.

"I don't mean right this instant," Teo said. "Think bigger."

Lachlan bristled again, scowling at the vampire.

"What do you want beyond freeing your parents from whatever realm they're trapped in?" Teo asked, piquing Lachlan's curiosity about just how much of his personal story had made the rounds in the supernatural rumor mill. He supposed Teo could be a stalker of sorts, obsessed with the elf who could tear holes in the world.

"Do you really want to bring them back just so you can be lorded over again?" Teo continued. "They'd become instant celebrities. You know that, right? Even though you'd be the one who allowed them to return, *they'd* be the ones who had survived for years in another realm and lived to tell the tale. They're softer, more palatable people." He smiled, presumably amused with his own choice of words. "You and your Shades are too wild. You'd be old news within twenty-four hours of their return."

Lachlan couldn't tell if Teo was goading him, baiting him, or if he'd somehow seen into his very soul and plucked free his most shameful, niggling fear.

"The Order lies dormant, hoping for your parents to come home—as the Goddess supposedly wills it," Teo said, rolling his unnatural eyes. "Yet the Order outnumbers the Shades by a wide margin. The Order has been running scared since your parents' departure. Scared of history repeating itself, scared of pushing the boundaries, scared of *you*. The Order doesn't see the scope of your abilities. The Shades don't. Hells, *you* don't. But I do."

"How do you know so much about me?" Lachlan had always hoped that when he finally gained a following, he'd also gain at least a few beautiful fans to fawn over him.

An unhinged vampire hadn't been what he'd meant.

Teo's fingers resumed their incessant drumming as he quietly contemplated Lachlan in that unreadable, infuriating way. Half an eternity later, the drumming stopped, and the vampire lifted his hand. With an uttered phrase and a flick of his wrist, the light in the already dim bar winked out.

Shouts of alarm filled the room. A few curses went up from the guys at the bar who'd been watching the Reds.

Lachlan had inadvertently grabbed the lip of the table for stability. His well of knowledge about vampire lore was admittedly low, but knowing vampires didn't possess the ability to wield magic was as commonplace as knowing that whales couldn't fly. Stranger even than Teo's constant stream of uttered spells was that, once the initial shock wore off, Lachlan finally saw what had snuffed out the light. It wasn't that Teo's magic had short-circuited the bar's mundane electricity. It was that the bar was overrun with shadows—much like the shadows that swam in the vampire's eyes.

Lachlan canted his head. Correction—shadows that had *once* swum in Teo's eyes. It was as if whatever unholy change the vampire had undergone had taken physical form. The shadows hovered on the TV, clung to light fixtures, and wafted across the blinking, garish displays on the jukebox. They engulfed people's faces like opaque shrouds.

Shadow magic.

The kind of magic that tempted the hearts and minds of disturbed people in stories, turning them into dastardly villains.

He felt even more foolish now for his childish outburst earlier. He must have sounded like a toddler throwing a tantrum. But it begged the question all over again: What did this powerful vampire want with *him*?

With another flick of his wrist, the shadows peeled away, slithering out doors and windows, between slats in floorboards, into Teo's eyes. The patrons of the bar looked about in confusion, shaking their heads as if waking from a dream.

"Must be something with the breaker," the bartender announced to no one in particular. He tossed a towel over his shoulder and strode off to investigate the cause of a problem he'd never find.

Everyone else returned to their previous activities, though the trio watching the game were fuming: The Reds had managed to score two runs during the blackout, and the disgruntled patrons had missed it.

Folding his arms on the table, Teo said, "My question for you is simple: Why are you seeking out people who abandoned you for their own ambitions?"

Because they're family felt like too trite a sentiment for a vampire to understand. Hells, not even Lachlan was sure he understood this burning desire anymore. The fruitless endeavor was costing him more than it gained.

Now his sister—his rock—wouldn't even speak to him. Were his parents and aunt worth all this fuss? Or was he doing this solely to prove he could?

Teo said, "Surely you have ambitions of your own. What will you do if you succeed? Find a nice woman to turn into a housewife, pop out a few kids, and live the mundane American dream?"

The vampire couldn't have sounded more mocking if he tried.

Lachlan's lips compressed into a thin line. "What bigger picture do you think I'm too simpleminded to see? That's why you're here, isn't it? You want to expand my horizons?"

Teo's smile was a flash of white. "Take a cue from the Collective—the global one. Sorcerers found themselves marooned in a world without magic, so they created magical pockets where they could thrive. And, more importantly, they placed themselves at the top of the food chain. The newly arrived fae were too shell-shocked or homesick or whatever drivel to realize the sorcerers saw an opportunity to erect an oligarchy—and they took it. Now they decide who stays and who goes. If they deem a fae, magic-touched, or native supernatural as unfit for their vision of what their society should look like, they cast them out. They've put up walls to exclude the unworthy. But the unworthy, nine times out of ten, are those of us brave enough to question them.

"Why do only sorcerers get to dictate the rules and laws of the hubs? There're no checks and balances. Everything they decree might be for the so-called good of us all, but that *us* sure as hells doesn't include you and me. At the end of the day, they make decisions based on the best interests of sorcerers first and the rest of us last. And my kind might not be on that list at all."

It took Lachlan a minute to reply. His mind still wasn't firing on all cylinders. "No offense, but it's hard to side with someone who's kept out of hubs because too much blood from my kind turns your lot into raging lunatics."

"Ouch, Shade." Teo dramatically slapped a hand over his heart. "*No offense*, but your assessment is borne from propaganda straight out of the Collective. They find our lifestyle distasteful, *and* they're in bed with the elitist, so-called *pure* vampires, so of course they make us out to be the bad guys. We've tried countless times to get an audience with representatives from the Collective to broker a pact like the pures did. They got places like Tercla and Urcor. Hybrids get nothing. No one will even talk to us. Our entire *race* has been blacklisted."

Hadn't Lachlan been thinking something similar about the Collective earlier? That even getting a travel talisman into a hub was becoming more and more of a chore? His name surely *did* grace some master blacklist. His parents and the Order had all been anti-hub, but he'd always thought that had been a personal choice. It was conceivable that, much like Teo, they'd been cast out for posing a threat to the Collective's cornerstone claim: that their ability to craft and maintain veils—allowing fae and magic-touched to live life openly in this magic-less realm—was why they were crucial to the continued existence of the hub system. And the hub system was vital because the portals home were closed for good. The earthen realm was the fae's permanent home now, and only the Collective could guarantee a safe life for fae in this foreign land.

The Collective was the ultimate power because they were the *only* power.

Lachlan's jaw clenched.

"You can keep opening doors to worlds when you don't know what awaits you on the other side," Teo said, smug smile tugging at his mouth again, as if he knew he'd just succeeded in reeling Lachlan in, "or you can learn to tear open holes in the small worlds that already exist *here.*"

Lachlan gaped at Teo, his eyes wide, as he suddenly grasped his meaning—suddenly saw the bigger picture. "Elves possess veil magic?" he asked, sounding once more like an unskilled child.

Teo reached into his inside jacket pocket and produced a small notebook. He slid it across the wood.

Lachlan slowly flipped through the book, whose thin pages were crowded with tiny, neat script and detailed sketches. There weren't rune arrays here, but theories about how the various subsets of nature magics could each potentially hold the key to unlocking veil magic.

"It's all still theoretical, but I believe elves specifically, with their unique connection to nature and their proclivity toward illusion-based skills, have the potential to craft veils even more powerful than the ones created by sorcerers," Teo said, gesturing to the book. "Several of us have been researching this since the early days of the Glitch. We've postulated that the groundwork for veil-creating rune arrays is elfin in origin. The running theory is that sorcerers in the fae realm had always been on the cusp of holding positions of power, but it was beings like dragons and elves who were revered. Sorcerers, who wound up here in greater numbers than dragons *or* elves, seized their chance at a power that had eluded them for countless generations.

"The sorcerers in the earthen realm don't want to give that up. So people like you, people like me, we get the short end of the stick. If those of us on the outside tore down their lies, if we showed everyone that they're not as powerful as they claim, the whole system would fall like a house of cards. We could restore balance. We could reshape the world."

Lachlan felt like the very blood in his veins was humming. *This* was the kind of challenge he craved. The rush he got from facing down an insurmountable obstacle and finding a way around it was even more intoxicating than the alcohol in his long-forgotten beer.

Blythe didn't get it. She didn't get that, as much as he cared for her, *this* was what made him get out of bed in the morning.

He wasn't reckless.

He was bored. Unchallenged.

But perhaps Teo was right. Lachan's boredom might have simply been a symptom of being plagued with the dangerous affliction of too-narrow thinking. His horizons *had* been expanded. He didn't need to find his parents to prove that he was just as skilled as them. He didn't need to show them that they might not have been lost all these years if they'd utilized his skills instead of relegating him to babysitting duty.

No, what he *needed* was to topple the hub system.

Expectantly, excitedly, Lachlan asked, "Where do we start?"

CHAPTER SIXTEEN

HARLOW

Caspian's supposed mansion was in the western section of the Ardmore neighborhood, near the border with uptown Luma. From the outside, the house looked strikingly similar to that of its neighbors. As in no gold-plated columns, ten-foot fences patrolled by ravens or gargoyles, or tall spires sporting black pennants. The house was in a section of the city that was well out of my price range, and likely always would be, but it wasn't so posh—like certain areas of uptown—where the police might be called on me for looking suspicious merely for gracing the neighborhood with my presence.

Just another way my assumptions about Caspian had been wrong. I was a little disappointed he didn't live in the McMansion in the Warehouse District. The Warehouse District was a bold place for a sprawling estate like the McMansion, too, because it was sort of in the middle of nowhere. People that filthy rich usually liked scenic views to gaze upon while they sipped imported gourmet coffee out of their solid-gold mugs or whatever.

Now it begged the question of who lived *there* if it wasn't Luma's most notorious supervillain.

Soren pulled the SUV up to a closed gate being manned by a keypad sitting atop a shiny black pole. "What's the code?"

"I'll have to do it," Caspian said, unfastening his seat belt. "The letters are Goblish, and the buttons are bespelled to only recognize the fingerprints of a select few."

The whole of that list was likely Caspian and Welsh.

I scanned the quiet street. A pair of kids rode by on bikes, so lost in their conversation they didn't even glance Caspian's way. Which suggested that the zany shit Caspian experimented on here happened well behind closed doors.

The keypad issued a series of beeps at Caspian's ministrations. The gate's lock disengaged a few moments later and then began its inward swing. His smile was strained as he climbed back in and closed the door. Around the same time that the Collective had put a bounty on my head, they'd also placed one on his. Felix had said werecats and bounty hunters alike had raided the place searching for Caspian. Maybe he was worried his house had been wrecked.

The yard to the left of the driveway that sat before a three-car garage was modest. Given how long we'd been gone, Caspian must have a gardener who kept the lawn trim and the smattering of flowers in pots watered.

"The garage is … uhh … full, so you can just park in the drive," Caspian said.

As I climbed out of the back seat, I was delighted by the possibility of meticulous Caspian being a secret hoarder. Maybe there were old magazines twice as old as himself stacked in piles taller than a draken. I grinned at the idea of his garage being stuffed to the brim with sagging cardboard boxes filled with useless junk.

The sword and I rounded the back of the SUV so I could help grab my stuff out of the back. Mom and Soren joined me. Caspian, however, was trudging toward his lawn, his gait sluggish and shoulders slumped.

"Oh no," Soren whispered. "What if one of the werecats left a 'gift' on his lawn—you know, like when a cat brings you a decapitated bird carcass? But in this case, it's his housekeeper."

Mom and I swung bewildered expressions at him that I was sure were nearly identical.

"Maybe his prized begonias died," Mom said slowly. "Why do you always think the bad news is a corpse?"

He shrugged. "In my defense, in our line of work, it usually *is* a corpse."

Now Caspian stood at the edge of the lawn, his head bowed and his hands shoved deep into the pockets of his khakis.

Frowning, I said, "I'll go see what's going on."

The sword and I slowly approached the crestfallen Caspian. If this really was about the loss of his begonias, I didn't know how I could comfort him. I wasn't even sure what a begonia looked like.

As we got closer, though, I realized Caspian was being berated mercilessly by a swarm of green-hued pixies. I couldn't make out most of what they were screeching at him, as they were all talking over each other a mile a minute, but I got the gist: They were livid he hadn't warned them he'd be leaving.

At first, I was sure they were mad that his absence meant they weren't paid for services rendered to keep his garden in tip-top shape, but it sounded as if they were mostly mad because they'd been concerned for him.

I crept toward them, not wanting to startle anyone. One did not startle a swarm of irate pixies if one didn't want to be bitten by hundreds of very tiny human-like teeth. It was equal parts disturbing and painful. And, no, I didn't want to talk about it.

"You could have at least warned us! The werecats trampled all over your poppies in the back. We only just got them replanted," one pixie said.

"I'm sorry, Julip," Caspian said in a rush, finally getting a word in. "I had to leave in a hurry. They placed a bounty on me."

All twenty-plus of the pixies issued a noise of utter disgust and spit toward their feet. I tried not to recoil as a slight breeze kicked up and sent a fine mist across my face and arms.

The sword had been hovering by my shoulder and also got an impromptu shower. It lacked tact, though, unleashed a high-pitched shriek, and flung itself into the grass where it rolled around like a dog after a bath. Half the pixies offered shrieks of their own and buzzed over to the sword, yelling at it to stop ruining their grass. There *was* a rather impressive bald spot in the middle of the lawn where the sword had shorn off a wide circle of grass down to the soil.

The pixies were either brave or stupid to go off on a sentient sword with such gusto. I was *relatively* sure the sword wouldn't get so mad that it turned the pixies into bloody mulch to shut them up—which would probably help with the lawn's bald spot, but not so much with pixie morale.

Before I could think of something to say to defuse the situation, Caspian dramatically cleared his throat. "Cutlass? I have a rage room in my basement!"

The sword stilled in midair in the inverted position. A pixie clung to the hilt, arms and legs wrapped around it in a bear hug. He repeatedly punched his little fist into one of the dragon scales, wailing about the sanctity of lawn care.

Caspian said, "If you leave the pixies alone, you can smash my last shipment of ceramic plates until they're reduced to powder."

The sword shook the pixie loose, who, in a streak of green, went flying into a potted rhododendron. Several of his comrades dove in to save him, seeing as the torpedoed pixie had acciden-tally disturbed a small swarm of bees who were now waging war. Unbothered, the sword took off like a shot toward the house.

I winced at the small-scale chaos. "I apologize on the sword's behalf."

"I'm honestly surprised the first words out of your mouth weren't about my rage room."

"Oh, don't worry," I said. "I expect details and full access. Though that might have to wait until we get back."

A hissing buzz reverberated by my ear, and I flinched back a fraction upon finding half a dozen pixies glaring at me. While their skin tones varied from pale to dark, they all had green hair of one hue or another.

I was fairly certain that the lightly tanned one with a high ponytail of forest-green hair was the one Caspian had referred to as Julip earlier.

Julip zipped in front of Caspian's face, leaving the others to hover menacingly near me. "You're leaving *again*?"

"Only for a couple of days this time," Caspian said gently. "Can I count on you all to keep the rookery informed about anything amiss while we're gone?"

"Don't insult me," Julip snapped.

The other five near me muttered tiny indignant curses.

Caspian held up his hands in placation. "All I meant was that I'd understand if you're upset with me and don't want to add anything else to your plates."

Julip's wings flashed red for a moment. "You know how I worry."

Caspian nodded. "I know. And I apologize again for not informing you that I'd be leaving. I also knew deep down how resourceful you are and that you'd keep an eye on things for me."

Julip's wings pulsed blue before going translucent again. "You know we're loyal to the bitter end. Though we should charge double after all the times we've had to deal with Welsh."

"Without Welsh, you wouldn't be living here," Caspian said in a tone that suggested he'd had to remind the pixie of this in the past.

Julip bunched up her tiny nose. "He's been even worse than

usual the last few days. At first I thought it was because he was even more worried about you than we were, even though *he* was worthy of regular updates while we were not. I think it might be something else, though."

I recalled that picture Welsh had sent. "Does he seem sick?" I asked, only realizing I'd asked that out loud when Julip was suddenly back in *my* face.

The pixie looked pensive, at least, and not outraged. "Maybe. A bit pale. A little sweaty. But he's always been a bit off. Shows up here all the time sweaty or filthy or outrunning ticked-off bears."

"The bear thing was only once." Caspian leaned toward me. "He was helping a lady shifter skip town, and her abusive bear-shifter husband found out and gave chase."

The pixies near me laughed. One smugly commented, "Nothing stops a bear in his tracks faster than a pixie in his ear!"

Once the dust finally settled in Luma, I was going to make Welsh and Caspian join me and Kayda so we could swap stories over drinks. An overwhelming feeling of defeat washed over me at the realization that we might never get the chance—either because of Lachlan Shade succeeding in whatever he had planned or because of Welsh potentially being on borrowed time.

"Oi, chin up," a tiny voice said. I found Julip watching me closely. "The lady bear got out of Luma safe and sound, and the brute was hauled off to jail."

"Happy to hear it," I managed, my smile strained.

Caspian eyed me pensively but refocused on the pixies. "Welsh is on his way here now. We also expect that a few werecats are going to show up to surveil the house soon, so keep a watchful eye. When Harlow and I leave, Camila and Soren will be staying behind."

We all turned to look at Mom and Soren, who were talking quietly on the other side of the driveway. Soren leaned against the driver's-side door listening to Mom, who was talking animatedly. They sensed us looking and glanced over, each raising a hand in acknowledgment and clearly unsure if they were being summoned to join us.

"I'll go over everything with you and them before we go," Caspian told the pixies. "I'll replenish your acorn stores on the way out, too."

The promise of acorns was apparently enough to assuage the pixies' remaining concerns because, without another word, they flitted away.

When it was just us, Caspian asked, "You all right?"

I considered dragging him down with me into my anxiety spiral. "I'll be a hell of a lot better after you show me this rage room."

He laughed easily.

The four of us unloaded the car, save for the second sword. It was back in the original metal box we'd found it in. I wasn't sure when Caspian had moved it out of the treasure chest, but this Lake Nacimiento plan had obviously been cooking in his head for a while.

Caspian and Soren, weighed down by the treasure chest, hustled toward the stairs that led to the upraised porch and the front door. Mom and I grabbed all the duffels and backpacks. Mom also shouldered her bow and quiver of arrows.

The guys struggled to get the treasure chest up the half-dozen wooden porch steps. I kept expecting the sword to materialize to help them, as it had when Caspian and I had needed to get the chest from the car into the motel room, but the damn thing was nowhere to be seen. It couldn't have been in the house already, as I assumed the house was locked and warded.

The wide porch was tastefully decorated with boring yet expensive-looking outdoor furniture. A round glass table with a closed umbrella resting in the hole in the middle was ringed by four chairs. The fabric of the umbrella and the chair cushions was beige. An enclosed fire pit sat on the other end of the porch, surrounded by more beige-cushioned chairs. I tried to picture Caspian out here, sitting around a fire with friends. He had friends other than Welsh, didn't he? Not that I was one to talk. Other than Kayda, the rest of my "friends" were clients. Making friends as an adult was hard.

When I was a kid, a mutual love of the same color was enough to form the foundation of a lifelong friendship. Now ingrained quirks, caution born out of experience, and a deep-seated paranoia about the magical government being out to get me got in the way.

"What's that smell?" Soren asked.

Everyone's noses pointed skyward as they sniffed.

I didn't smell anything at first, but then the wind shifted. My face screwed up. "Cat pee."

Caspian moved to the wall just before his recessed doorway. He touched a finger to one of four long claw marks that raked across the brick. The scratches were around knee level, so I hadn't seen them earlier.

I stepped further out onto the porch and looked around more closely. Scratch marks on the steps, a bite taken out of a railing on the far end of the porch, past the table. A piece of fluff poked out from the corner of one of the chair's white accent pillows. I grabbed the pillow and flipped it over. Stuffing spilled from a diagonal slash in the pillow, like a sliced-open baked potato. *This*—rather than Soren's theory about a proffered corpse—was the cats' "gift" to Caspian: a pungent message that they were pissy because Caspian had slipped away.

Caspian gusted a sigh. "Welsh said he'd cleaned up what he could. He rearmed the house a week or so after we went into hiding."

A sad, tight-lipped smile that I couldn't quite read graced Mom's face. Maybe she was just quietly grateful I was still in one piece.

Caspian went through a disarming sequence on another box by the front door, this one's buttons graced by Gnomish numbers. After a series of beeps, Caspian placed his hand, fingers splayed, in the middle of the simple black door. A rune array fanned out from beneath his palm, the nested circles glowing blue. A pulse of power that I saw more than felt skittered across the whole door—and then the walls and floor.

"What the heck was that?" I asked, inspecting my person, half expecting to find myself crackling with blue magic. It was mostly a rhetorical question; undoubtedly, he'd just deactivated a doozy of a ward.

If *Welsh* had rearmed the wards, they'd been tweaked to recognize him. I didn't need to know much about magic to know how complicated all this runework was—made even more complicated by the need to allow a non-sorcerer like Welsh to manipulate them. The more I learned about the scope of Caspian's abilities, the more I saw why Caspian's teachers *and* parents had blown a gasket over him abruptly giving up his schooling during his final year. He'd been a prodigy who'd quit to become a recluse who dabbled in light to medium criminal activity. They felt that he'd squandered his potential.

I didn't know much about the circumstances that had led to his friend Marcus's death, but they'd been bad enough that Caspian had washed his hands of being part of the Collective despite years of schooling and thousands of dollars in tuition. It was one of the few topics I didn't try to push him on. Even the news that he hadn't actually graduated from the academy hadn't been something he'd told me directly. Sorcerer Albert Sweeney had goaded the information out of him. Caspian had been so furious with Sweeney, he'd almost roasted him *and* the entire motel—with us in it—before I'd managed to convince him not to.

What Felix had said about Caspian evading authorities popped into my head. *"I don't know if he's got a bounty mirror too or what, but a full team raided his place early this morning. When we got there, the gate to the property was open, and the wards were down. He'd known we were coming and took off well before we got there."*

"Felix told me you left your wards down. You trusted the cats with whatever you've got inside?" I asked.

"I let them have access to the yard and *part* of the house. I might not have had time to warn the pixies, but I made sure the wards were up on the garage and basement. There was no way I was letting them in there," Caspian said. "On my basement door, above an array very similar to this one, is an independent rune phrase. The runic language isn't really constructed for communication, but any sorcerer worth their salt who had the skill set needed to break my wards would have been able to read it. It roughly translates to 'You break. You explode.' I banked on them leaving the important rooms alone if they knew there was a possibility that if they triggered an explosion it would also take out my neighbors in a three-mile radius."

His almost flat affect made him sound a tick above a psychopath.

Soren laughed awkwardly. "You're kind of scary, kid."

Caspian waved the comment away. "If I didn't give them at least partial access, the cats would still be sleeping on my porch. I gave them enough so they could feel proud of themselves for violating my space but also let them know there were consequences if they pushed too hard. I genuinely believe their assumption that Harlow and I were masterminding some elaborate plan—with the sentient cutlass as the cornerstone—was what kept them from breaching my wards. They worried something much worse was hidden inside." He fell silent for a long moment. "As I said, their fear of the cutlass and its origins is so potent, I'm very reluctant to allow either one into the Tower before we know more."

A silent war waged behind Mom's eyes. "Despite my very tumultuous past with the Collective, my trust in Rhiannon still runs deep. Her power is both formidable and unique. Unique enough that it trumped my usual paranoia. I'm sure you're right to be cautious, Caspian. Maybe I've just gotten tired of running. I don't know."

"We're all just guessing at what we should do, Mom. None of us knows the right decision to make."

Her jaw was tight as she stared at me. "I should be better at it when it comes to you."

I didn't know how to respond to that. She looked equal parts hopping mad and devastated. Maybe being trapped in Caspian's heavily warded house for a couple of days would do her some good. She needed forty-eight hours of sleep at a minimum.

Soren started to reach for her again but stopped just short of touching her shoulder, letting his arm fall back to his side.

Caspian awkwardly cleared his throat, dispelling the tense silence. He pulled an unlocking talisman necklace out from under his shirt as he walked to the recessed front doorway. "Welsh said the smell inside is worse," was all he said as he swung the door open.

The ammonia smell hit us full in the face, like a slap. We all gagged as we hustled inside and dropped everything in the foyer. From what I could see of the open-plan living room, it didn't *look* like the place had been ransacked. There weren't chunks of broken furniture, shards of smashed glass, or shreds of clothing scattered everywhere. There certainly weren't any obvious puddles of cat urine, despite the stink of the place. But there also wasn't much in the way of furniture, period. Maybe, instead of a hoarder, Caspian was a minimalist.

With a heavy sigh, Caspian said, "Welsh seems to have downplayed the situation. Perhaps I can shop for a new living room set while we're on the road. Camila, Soren, I can show you to your rooms. I have a few guest rooms always primed and ready."

He set off across the foyer and then made a right out of view. Soren grabbed their bags, then followed after him, asking if air fresheners were one of the complimentary amenities.

Mom stopped just before she reached the corner and turned back. "You all right?"

I nodded tightly. "I gotta go find where that fool sword disappeared to."

She looked like she wanted to say something more but instead offered me another small, sad smile, then set off after the men.

I surveyed the flotsam in the hallway and briefly considered asking Caspian if we had time to do a quick load of laundry before we left.

Instead, I headed for the living room. "Sword?" I called, hands on hips.

The only furniture in the space were bookshelves—and those looked built-in. A gently curving staircase to my left led to a second floor. I couldn't see much from my vantage point, other than what might have been a mezzanine that overlooked the living room I stood in now. Across from the front door were large floor-to-ceiling windows that looked out on another patio area. The balcony from the floor above, held up by thick, dark wooden beams, hung over the patio. The yard beyond appeared to be full of native California plants, including a wealth of bright orange poppies. While the garden wasn't exactly an overgrown jungle, the plants had been allowed to flourish with wild abandon. There were a few benches scattered around, as well as a curving walking path made of sandstone pavers. A fountain burbled just off the path, but it was tucked away among the wildflowers as if the man-made structure had sprung from the soil just as the sage bushes dotted with blue-purple flowers had. Colorful songbirds splashed about in the water.

I supposed this was the type of garden one got when its keepers were earth pixies.

The front door to the house opened, and I whirled away from the window, heart racing, as I chastised myself for getting lost in the view. Another call for the sword was on the tip of my tongue, just in case the person letting themselves in was a werecat who had gotten past the gate and the pixies, but it was only Welsh.

The memory of the texted picture flashed in my mind, and I was across the living room and back in the foyer in record time. I knew it was impossible to use sight to assess how Welsh was doing, seeing as I still didn't know what his natural face looked like. He was using his glamour magic to mask the marks on his neck, as there was no sign of them now above the collar of his black T-shirt. I got on my tiptoes to try to see them anyway. He gently smacked my hand away when I reached toward his throat.

Though he could easily sidestep me, he allowed me to corral him before the closed front door. He crossed his arms and scowled at me. I wasn't sure if I was alarmed or relieved that he wasn't currently sporting his signature trench coat, the inside pockets filled with weapons and tinctures, and instead wore a simple outfit of T-shirt and dark jeans.

"Caspian already told you about my ... affliction, then?" he asked.

"I saw your text *and* picture," I said, then quickly shot a look behind me to make sure we were still alone. "How are you feeling?"

"Cornered," he said.

I lightly smacked his chest with the back of my hand. "I'm serious. You said shadows are *speaking* to you? That sounds demonic. Is it demonic? Can you understand them, or are they speaking in tongues? And are they talking about normal things, like the weather, or evil things, like demanding you to push the elderly into traffic or encouraging you to wear socks with sandals?"

Welsh was silent for a long beat. "I must be getting worse, because I almost think I missed you."

"Aww!" I said and flung my arms around his middle.

He grumbled something unintelligible, then awkwardly patted my back.

Keeping my arms around him, I peered up. "Honestly, are you okay? On a scale of one to ten, how worried should I be?"

His glamour flickered. It reminded me of a horror movie where someone is possessed and the two entities are at war for control of the body. Instinct told me to let go and put distance between us in case the demon got a firm hold of the reins. But my gut told me whatever was happening to Welsh was merely affecting his ability to keep his glamour in place.

The blackened puncture wounds on his neck popped into

view, as well as the thin snaking black lines that radiated away from them. Was it poisoning his bloodstream?

"Oh, Welsh …" I murmured.

"An eight on the worry scale," he said in the softest, most vulnerable tone I'd ever heard from him. And if that hadn't been enough to scare me, the way he sucked in a few shaky breaths, like he was warding off the urge to cry or shucking off the hold of an approaching panic attack, surely did.

I fully wrapped my arms around his middle again, noting that the back of his shirt was slightly damp. Maybe he wasn't wearing the trench coat because he was running a mild fever. I pressed my cheek to his chest.

Reluctantly, he hugged me back.

Knowing he wouldn't want me to fuss too much, I only held the hug for a little longer before I loosened my hold to look up at him again.

His glamour was back in place.

"We'll figure this out, okay?" I said quietly, searching his gaze for any sign that he knew it was a promise and not a meaningless platitude.

He nodded once, visibly swallowing.

"Harlow?" Caspian called from down the hall. "Did you find the cutlass? Those plates aren't going to smash themselves."

I let Welsh go and took a few steps back. Louder than necessary, I said, "Get your shit together, Zander. Your dramatic emotional display is frankly embarrassing."

Caspian, Mom, and Soren—sans belongings—stopped at the mouth of the foyer.

"*My* emotional display?" Welsh asked, sounding disgusted.

"Yes, you," I said, shooting a glance over my shoulder at Caspian. "Welsh said he *missed* me."

"Don't put words in my mouth, woman. I merely said I didn't hate seeing your face as much as I thought I would."

Soren barked a laugh. "Ouch!"

Welsh strolled past me, nearly bumping into me, and held

out a hand to my mom. He turned on his charm full blast. "You must be Camila. I'm Zander Welsh, but everyone calls me Welsh. We spoke briefly on the phone the evening of Lachlan's escape."

Mom shook his hand. "Oh, that's right. It's nice to meet you, Welsh. I know you and Caspian both went out of your way to keep Harlow safe when she had to go into hiding. Thank you for that."

Welsh bobbed his head. "You're welcome."

"Oh sure, *now* you're pleasant," I said, sidling up next to him.

"I'm always pleasant," Welsh said. "There are just some people who can even try the patience of a saint." He smiled warmly down at me, and I considered punching him in his perfectly constructed nose.

I tried to remember that only a minute ago Welsh had given me a glimpse into the real him. The real him who was possibly in dire straits.

He was just so good at being a jackhole that it was easy to forget that a vulnerable human lived behind that unnaturally pleasing face. He was like the annoying little brother I never wanted. Or was he older? For all I still knew, Welsh could actually be a geriatric goblin woman in his true form.

"*Oookay,*" Caspian said, stopping Welsh and I from bickering further. "We need to come up with a game plan so we can get out of here safely while Camila and Soren hold down the fort."

"I'll make dinner," Welsh said, striding down the hallway in the opposite direction that Caspian and the others had gone earlier. "I went shopping yesterday."

We all followed Welsh toward the kitchen.

Soren leaned down to whisper to my mom, but we all still heard him. "I thought Caspian had his sights on Harlow, but now it seems like he's married to the pretty guy."

I winced. When I'd first met the pair, I'd voiced something similar. In response, Welsh had donned his sore-encrusted zombie lord persona solely to scare the bejesus out of me. The move hadn't been borne from homophobia but rather annoyance at my assumption.

Welsh sighed deeply. He rested his hip on the kitchen island, arms crossed, and waited for us to file in. "I'm clarifying this solely for Camila's sake, as I want her mind at ease about my intentions for her daughter."

My lip curled at his formal tone. The look he shot me implied this clarification was very much for my sake, too. *Mostly* for my sake? Had he read too much into my affectionate display when he arrived?

"When it comes to the subject of dating, I … don't have a pref-erence," Welsh said, sounding supremely uncomfortable. "As in I don't have a preference for anyone of any stripe and never have."

Oh.

"I find romantic entanglements both confusing and the cause of unnecessary complications," Welsh said.

"Amen," Soren muttered.

"Complete and *utter* waste of time," Welsh added.

Kayda *had* said that Welsh grew extra grouchy any time she and Henri were flirting, or, in one case, sucking face in the park. I supposed it wasn't the existence of their "romantic entanglement" that bothered Welsh, only that said entanglement kept encroaching on their task at hand.

"Can we *please* move on now?" Welsh asked. "The dish I want to make is labor intensive."

"Please do," Mom said.

Welsh happily beelined for the fridge.

CHAPTER SEVENTEEN

HARLOW

While everyone got Welsh up to speed, my concern about the sword finally caught up to me. I skirted the island and peeked around one length of the L-shaped kitchen, finding a dining table nestled in an alcove made by three walls. One of the walls had a door that led to the back yard. I pulled aside the cream-colored curtain hanging over the window and immediately sighed.

Yanking the door open, I marched out onto the back deck and stood at the railing. A gaggle of green-hued pixies and my sword hovered near a manzanita sapling. Several pixies sat or stood on a long reddish branch, like so many pigeons huddled together on a power line.

Dozens of tiny voices cheered in unison. "Daphne! Daphne! Daphne!"

In the center of a ring of hovering pixies was my sword, seesawing and spinning like a whirling dervish. A pixie, her long, lime-green curly hair flapping behind her like a banner, had one little fist in the air while her other hand held on to the sword's guard. The sword had turned itself into a bucking bronco, and Daphne, presumably, had taken on the challenge of seeing how long she could hang on. The sword could move ten times faster than it currently was, so it was humoring the pixies. I didn't have the first clue how this scenario had started.

Daphne lasted ten more seconds before being pitched ass over teakettle when the sword increased its speed. The watching pixies cheered, semi-discreet bets were paid out, and then enthusiastic requests for a new competitor rose in a tiny swell.

"Sword!" I shouted, hands up in the silent equivalent of "what the hell are you doing?"

It stilled, swiveled to me, and its blade went a vibrant shade of pink. It harpooned toward me and then through the open door into the kitchen in a blink.

A tidal wave of tiny boos followed me into the house.

After making sure the patio door was firmly shut behind me, I rejoined the others. "How many pixies live here?"

The sword was buzzing around Welsh's head as the witch busied himself at the cutting board chopping onions and garlic. Its blade cycled through a rainbow of colors. It prodded its hilt into the back of Welsh's thigh half a dozen times before the witch finally slammed down his knife and whirled to the sword.

"*What?*"

Now that it had gained Welsh's notice, it zipped backward, got into the inverted position, and conjured an illusory body around itself. This time it was in the form of Caspian. A wide goofy grin spread across Fake Caspian's face, and with its free hand not holding the sword, Fake Caspian waved at Welsh with all the exuberance of a child who'd just spotted his best friend across the playground.

The tension leaked out of Welsh like a dam bursting, and he huffed a laugh. "Hi, sword. It's good to see you, too."

The illusion dissolved and the sword's blade glowed a brilliant blue. It then darted directly into Caspian's face, where he, Mom, and Soren stood at the opposite end of the kitchen island from where Welsh had resumed his vegetable chopping.

Caspian reared back, going a little cross-eyed from the proximity of the sword to his nose. "You know, cutlass, I really should make you wait to use the rage room. You missed the tour when you decided to gallivant with the staff." He leaned away from the sword to address me. "There are roughly eighty pixies in residence at the moment. Three are pregnant, though."

Without looking up from his work, Welsh added, "And the Wisterias are having twins. The father wouldn't shut up about it when I got here just after the cats tore up the place. It's very hard to patch drywall when you have a pixie buzzing in your ear about the joys of fatherhood."

There was a lot to unpack there, but I was mostly lost in imagining how positively tiny a pixie newborn must be.

"I'm still working on an alchemical solution for the smell, by the way," Welsh said, scooting aside the pile of chopped garlic on the cutting board to make room for a bell pepper. "The last one got rid of the odor from a patch of the floor, but it also burned the wood to ash, so I'm calling it a wash."

"Personally, I'd call that a fail," I said.

The sword tapped its hilt once on the counter, momentarily forgetting about its promised access to the rage room.

"Yeaugh!" Caspian yelped eloquently, and we all started, turning to him in surprise. "Julip! Goddess above, we've talked about this."

The pixie was floating in the same spot the sword had been moments before.

"Sorry!" she said, but it came out sharp, like a curse. "Just thought you'd want to know there are two cats outside. One tried to jump the gate, but the ward zapped her good." Cheerfully, she added, "Smells like burnt fur out there."

"Dammit. They got here even quicker than I expected," Caspian said. "Thanks for the heads up, Julip. Any around back yet?"

"Don't think so, but I'll check," Julip said. "We got the back tunnel exit cleared away, just in case. The blackberry brambles had gotten a bit out of control since you haven't needed that route in a while."

The pixie zipped away in a streak of green.

It was silent save for Welsh's lightning-fast dicing of several stalks of green onions.

"Harlow," Mom said. "Can we talk?"

She abruptly left the kitchen. I shot a questioning glance at Soren, but all he gave me was a shrug.

I found Mom in the furniture-less living room, standing before the windows overlooking the garden. My stomach knotted up, and I inexplicably felt like a kid again, on the verge of being grounded for sneaking out with Kayda to a party in the Necropolis.

When she turned at my approach, her expression was grim, and the bags under her eyes somehow appeared darker. I really hoped she'd let herself get some sleep soon. Was my leaving again going to make that impossible for her? I would have thought by now that she knew I was safe with the guys, especially with the sword traveling with us, too. Unless she wanted to come with us. Oh jeez, what if she needed help convincing Soren to leave Luma because she didn't want to be stuck with him alone here? I hadn't even considered that.

"Was Welsh bitten by a hybrid?"

My bouncing thoughts slammed headlong into a wall. "What?" I asked dumbly.

"I couldn't hear much over Soren's terrible singing in the car, but I heard parts of it," Mom said. "And even though Welsh's glamour is in place, it's glitched a couple of times. I'm not sure if he's even aware of it. Had I not been staring at him when it happened the last time, I would have missed it."

I chewed on my bottom lip, desperately wanting to talk to my very own vampire expert about this, but not wanting to violate Welsh's trust. Especially since, if it was up to Welsh, I probably wouldn't know what little I currently did.

Mom must have sensed my reluctance because she said, "There have been a few cases of this happening—of a fae suffering the ill effects of a hybrid bite. From what I've heard, it's only affecting witches so far."

"Really?" I asked, unable to help myself. "Is it fatal?"

"There's not enough data to pinpoint any kind of pattern," she said. "It *was* fatal in one case."

I blew out a shaky breath.

"In another case, the witch turned. He essentially became a hybrid who could wield magic," Mom said. "It's believed he was a fire witch before he turned, but afterward, he could also control shadows. And, possibly most upsetting, despite being a hybrid, the turned witch didn't *need* blood to fuel his newfound ability. Meaning his very powerful shadow magic *wasn't* limited by how much blood he could consume. His magical ability mutated, yet its method of use was the same as before he turned. It was tied to his skill level."

Kayda had once explained skill level as being some nebulous thing determined by innate ability combined with practice and training, just like with any mundane skill. Kayda didn't have magic, per se, but even her heightened senses could be honed like a muscle. Just because someone had a natural aptitude for kicking ass and taking names in the cage fighting ring, if she didn't put in the hours needed to improve, someone with less innate skill but more drive and determination was more likely to succeed.

"So the more powerful they are as a witch, the more powerful they'll be at shadow magic if they're turned?" I thought about how many times I'd heard that Welsh's glamourer abilities were so strong, they were nearly off the charts.

"That's right," Mom said.

Had that vampire bitten Welsh specifically in hopes that he'd turn and join the vampire's unholy ranks? The vampire, according to Kayda, had been powerful in his own right, as far as shadow-wielding went.

He could have exsanguinated Welsh rather than just biting him. He could have fled from Luma with Welsh as his prisoner, keeping Welsh doped up on a steady drip of mind-numbing serotonin so Welsh remained his "willing" blood bag indefinitely. Instead, he'd chosen to bite him. Mom had said that in order to complete a vampire transformation the victim needed to consume some of their sire's blood. I had no idea if that had happened in the window between Welsh getting grabbed and bitten, and the vampire being divested of his head by Erik.

All of this was mere speculation. No one had seemed willing to supply Kayda with details of that night, either—not even Henri. That stuttering draken teddy bear of a man had stronger will power than I'd given him credit for.

Maybe I could finally get the full story out of Welsh once we were all trapped in the car together. I could be relentless when needed. And if this really *was* turning out to be a life-or-death situation, my relentlessness was imperative.

"My concern," Mom said in her Mom Voice, causing my gaze to instinctively meet hers, "is that we don't know how long the incubation period is for fae in general, or witches in particular. In mundanes, a successful turning takes place roughly two weeks after infection. Anecdotal evidence suggests the virus needs longer to cook in fae. My guess is he's got a month to either turn or—"

"Die?"

"Well, that's the other problem," Mom said, her tone more soothing now that she knew she had my full attention. "The virus itself doesn't seem to be fatal, but the complications caused by it are. Even though these infected fae don't *need* fae blood to survive —or any blood for that matter—the virus does. If the virus isn't fed fae blood, the virus eats away at the brain, often resulting in erratic behavior. The witch I mentioned who died? Well, he stepped out of an eighteen-story window just after telling the confused office workers in a building where he didn't work that he'd found the burning rainbow bridge and was going to walk to Asgard."

"Oof," I muttered.

"The best-case scenario for Welsh—a miracle cure notwithstanding—is that he's genetically predisposed to turn, becomes a hybrid vampire, and can maintain a steady enough supplemental diet of fae blood so he doesn't go mad but not so much that he becomes addicted and goes feral."

Mom knew that honesty and information were what ultimately kept me from being eaten alive by anxiety—which was why her disappearing on me six years ago was even more devastating than the situation would have been otherwise. I *needed* to know what was going on; otherwise, my overactive imagination conjured up the wildest of possibilities, and I wound up with ulcers and insomnia.

It was why I'd made that rule with Felix—if either one of us asked if everything was okay, the other was required to answer truthfully, no matter what. At least I knew now that a combination of Mom's Soul NDA and her bosses unexpectedly exiling her had been the reason for the radio silence.

So while this current deluge of very honest information about Welsh was enough to weaken my knees, I appreciated her telling me. I pulled her into a hug. She shuddered slightly before hugging me back.

"I'm sorry, baby girl," she said softly. "Caspian has given me full permission to raid his library. I have contacts all over the world who know even more about vamps than I do. I've got the VHoA forum. We'll figure this out, okay?"

My throat tightened at hearing my words to Welsh repeated back to me. "Thanks," I choked out.

When we pulled apart, she swiped her thumbs under my eyes. Apparently I'd started crying. She held my face in her hands.

The gesture was only comforting for a few moments. She got that look in her eye that told me more unpleasant truths were coming, and she needed to be sure I heard them.

"If he turns, he's more of a danger to Caspian than you," she said, then let my face go. "He'll need fae blood. It's very possible, given how powerful Welsh already is, that he'll need a substantial amount of blood to stave off insanity. I recommend getting a supply of it, rather than him getting it directly from the source. An especially hungry vampire who hasn't developed self-control yet can easily drain a victim by accident. Those two are ride-or-die, just like you and Kay. Don't let Caspian's love for his friend get in the way of his safety. I don't want you to lose either one of them."

My stomach pitched. "Should I keep the two of them apart until we know what's going on with Welsh? Welsh would never forgive himself if he hurt Cas."

"If anything," Mom said, "this scenario might be ideal. Welsh's willpower to war against his baser instincts if he turns will be strengthened all the faster if you two are with him. Not going to lie—I'm going to be sick with worry the whole time because there are so many ways this could go bad." She sighed deeply. "Talk to them both. Let them know I'll do whatever I can to help. Based on how private Welsh wants to keep this, I can loop Soren in, or give him minimal details, or I can leave him out of it. Same goes with my contacts—both mundane and vampiric."

A voice sounded from the foyer. "As long as you don't divulge too much of my personal information, I'm well past secrecy."

I sucked in breath at the sight of Welsh standing on the other end of the living room. A thin, swirling cloud of black fog wafted about his feet. The puncture wounds on his neck were visible, and while the spiderwebbing lines radiating out from them hadn't grown longer, they were definitely darker.

Soren and Caspian stood in the hallway off the kitchen, wearing twin expressions of unease. The sword hovered behind Caspian's shoulder.

"The shadows are … whispering," Welsh said softly, his head titled toward his shoulder and eyes closed, as if that would help him hear better. "I can't understand them. I truly don't know if that's because they're mumbling or because it's in a language I don't speak. They go away when I'm glamoured, almost like I'm banishing them because the glamour I'm wearing doesn't use whispering shadows as an accessory. But it's getting harder to hold the glamour."

When he finally opened his eyes, it wasn't me or Caspian he settled on for answers. It was my mom. He looked so much like a little boy then, I almost rushed across the living room to hug him again. "What do I do?" he asked.

"Eating helps, right?" Mom asked. "Builds up your strength?"

Welsh nodded.

"Then we'll eat first, you'll get a glamour back up to dispel the shadows, and then we'll talk once your head is clearer," Mom said authoritatively but without sounding demanding.

Without a word, Welsh turned for the kitchen, wispy black mist wafting about his feet as he walked. Soren, Caspian, and the sword hustled back down the hallway as if they were kids caught eavesdropping.

I stopped just inside the doorway to the kitchen, where Mom had started helping Welsh with meal prep while Caspian filled Soren in on Welsh's attack the night Lachlan escaped.

I pulled out my phone.

HARLOW

Welsh is in trouble. Possibly the fatal kind. We don't know all the details yet, but that vamp bite isn't agreeing with him. I still don't know what the hell happened that night!

KAYDA

What can I do?

HARLOW

Nothing yet. We need to keep him away from fae other than Cas right now. We're leaving Luma again to follow one of Cas's leads. It'll only be a few days. I'll call you later to tell you everything we know.

KAYDA

I'll try again to pry info out of Henri. I'm planning to visit Jo today, so maybe I can squeeze her for details, too. We aren't losing Welsh, Low. He might be an asshole, but he's our asshole

HARLOW

Gross

KAYDA

I regretted it as soon as I hit send

HARLOW

Oh! You know that massive estate in the Warehouse District? Not Caspian's! He lives in a relatively normal house in Ardmore

KAYDA

Who the hells lives in the McMansion then??

HARLOW

A question for the ages

I worried at my bottom lip as I contemplated my screen.

HARLOW

I love you, you know

KAYDA

Damn. If you're getting sappy on me, it really IS bad. Love you, too. Chin up and shit

HARLOW

I would have thought that finally going to Funky Town with Henri would have improved your emotional vocabulary

KAYDA

Happy to disappoint

HARLOW

KAYDA

CHAPTER EIGHTEEN

KAYDA

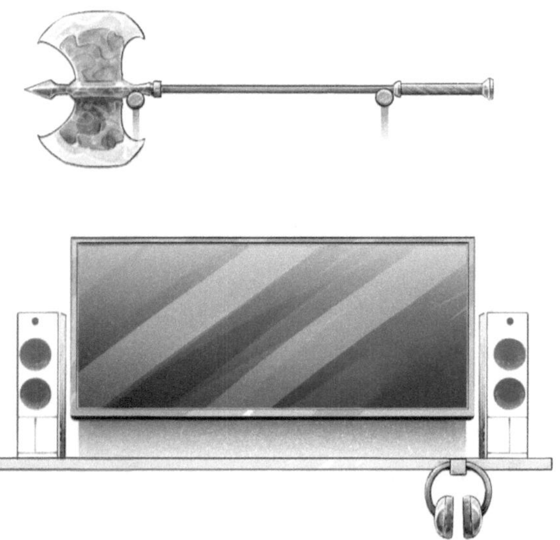

Jo's Apothecary was busy—so busy that Jo herself was behind the counter helping Erik ring up customers. Three other employees were flitting around the store. Kayda had always semi-dreaded coming here as it was, since the place triggered her mild claustrophobia. It being clogged with people only made the feeling worse. There were shelves along the walls as well as free-standing ones scattered around in a haphazard configuration. Tall wooden barrels whose previous lives had probably been spent in factories or shipyards were now used as display stands for soaps and bundles of herbs. The only good thing about the shop's crowded interior was that it was infinitely more open than the stuffy little area in back that served as both storage and Jo's office. Kayda hated the office. She was too big, and the space was entirely too small.

Kayda remained resting against a pillar for a solid twenty minutes before Jo and Erik got a break in the crush of customers, then she wove through the maze to the counter.

"Kayda," Erik said flatly, then abruptly turned around to restock items in the apothecary wall behind the cash register, as if he couldn't stand the sight of her.

His offbeat behavior had never bothered her that much anyway, but at least now she knew the guy was more than just a rude jackwagon. He was a bit "touched in the head," as her grandma used to say. Kayda could only imagine just how off he'd been *before* he'd started his apprenticeship with Jo to help get himself under control.

"Hey, Kayda," Jo said, huffing out an exhausted breath that sent a loose strand of black hair flapping. "This isn't about my two-for-one special on mood-sensing candles, is it?" She aimed a dark thumb behind her.

A row of colorful candles were lined up along the back wall, complete with a sign about the one-day sale. Kayda was almost tempted to ask how a mood-sensing candle worked, but she resisted the urge.

"Nope," Kayda said. "I wanted to talk to you about Snowdrop."

Jo's shoulders sagged. "How is that poor girl?"

"Doing better than I expected, honestly," Kayda said. "She's tougher than she looks."

Turning to Erik, who was now ripping open a cardboard box

with his bare hands, Jo asked, "Are you going to be okay up here by yourself for a few minutes while I speak to Kayda?"

Erik shot a death glare over his shoulder at Kayda. If it wasn't for Welsh's declaration that beneath that petulant little boy personality, Erik was a ruthless fighter, Kayda would have laughed at his over-the-top aggression. Instead, she only felt mildly discomfited.

His gaze shifted to Jo then and his face softened, like a parent gazing at their precious sleeping child—who he would slaughter entire villages of babies and puppies to protect. "I am at your command, Lady Josephine. I will not let you down."

Jo patted him gently on the shoulder. "It's okay, Erik. Feeling overwhelmed when we're this busy is normal. Remember your breathing exercises. I'll be back shortly."

Kayda remembered Harlow's comment about Kayda's lacking emotional vocabulary. She supposed there could be some merit to the claim. Jo said things like "Remember your breathing exercises," and Kayda's first reaction had been to say, "It's not that serious, bro."

"I will await your return," Erik said and bowed over the mangled box in his arms. He lifted his head, and when he found that Jo had already retreated, he shot another venomous glare at Kayda. "Do not keep her long. You distract her from her work."

Kayda rolled her eyes then. She couldn't help it. She'd always be grateful to him for helping Welsh and disposing of the vampire, but the guy was fruit loops.

A minute later, Kayda was once again walking down the cramped hallway of the storage area. Without even looking at her, Jo said, "Get your shoulders away from your ears."

Grumbling, Kayda rolled her neck a few times and relaxed her shoulders.

Once they were standing in the slightly more open area where Jo's desk was wedged into an alcove, Kayda relaxed a bit more. Though it seemed as if the area was even more cluttered than it had been the last time Kayda was here. The map Jo had bespelled to track Harlow's movements was still tacked to the wall opposite Jo's desk, but there were no dots scooting around the thin lines marking highways and even thinner streets, the magic having run out. At least Kayda knew where Harlow was now, even if she hadn't physically seen her yet. And given the news about Welsh, it still might be a while before that happened.

Jo's long hair was tied back in a single braid today, which she draped over her shoulder now so she wouldn't sit on it when she perched her backside on a corner of her desk. She tucked a wispy flyaway behind an ear and placed her hands in her lap, her feet crossed at the ankles. Jo always looked a bit ethereal. She wore one of her signature long, flowing dresses—this one patterned in a wild knot of leaves and vines—and her wrists were adorned with stacks of mismatched bangles. Rings graced nearly every finger. The sharp intelligence in her dark eyes always reminded Kayda that, no matter how soft Jo looked on the outside, she wasn't a witch to trifle with.

"So, Kayda," Jo said patiently, "what can I help you with today?"

"Two things, actually," Kayda said. "First, are you in the market for another apprentice?"

"What kind of apprentice?" Jo asked, head cocked. The weak fluorescent lights winked off her large gold hoop earrings.

Kayda relayed what Snowdrop had told her over pizza. "I admit I don't understand magic like you two do, but the magic in that ring was enough to lift me, Welsh, and Henri off our feet. The wind spell was so strong, it wrapped *me* around a tree. The three of us were no match for the magic that little elf threw at us. Increasing the ring's magic from Level 1 to 4 seems pretty impressive."

Jo was quiet as she stared off into space, thinking. "She might actually be good for Erik. He's got a soft spot for the girl, I think. He knows what it's like to be a child with powerful magic, only to be exploited by those he trusted the most."

Kayda could practically hear Harlow in her head. "*Ask her*

what the hell that means! Get details!" But she kept her mouth shut; Erik's past wasn't any of her business. She wouldn't want anyone prying into *her* life.

"If you give me her information," Jo said, "I'd be happy to chat with her. If nothing else, I'd like further reassurance that she's okay."

Kayda understood that. "I was going to warn you that she's prickly and defensive, but you handle Erik with all the patience of a saint, so I'm not worried."

Jo laughed, light and sweet. "And what was the second thing you wanted to talk about?"

Wrinkling her nose at how hypocritical she was about to be, Kayda said, "Welsh isn't doing well. Harlow said the bite he sustained might be fatal."

Jo's hand went to her throat. *"Really?* What terrible news. I thought fae were immune to such effects."

Kayda wanted to respect Welsh's and even Henri's privacy about something they were both reluctant to discuss, but Harlow was more than concerned—Kayda could tell that through text messages alone. "Can you give me any insight into what happened that night? It could help Welsh."

A troubled look crossed Jo's face and she tightly folded her arms, her bangles jangling softly. "Has Henri not said anything?"

"He clams up, which isn't really like him," Kayda said. "I mean, *mostly* isn't like him. I think. Rules kind of change once you start dating someone, you know? It's all the same and totally different at the same time. Good different—*really* good—but still different. We're adjusting still. Is adjusting normal? I would think so. I woulda thought it would be *easier* to talk about stuff, but it's somehow harder."

Jo's smashed-together brows implied she'd expected a response more along the lines of "No."

It took Jo long enough to speak that Kayda had been sure she wasn't going to. Maybe the rambling had put Jo off, and she was contemplating a polite way of kicking Kayda out of her office.

"After incapacitating Welsh," Jo finally said, "the vampire used his shadows to shield both himself and Welsh, then took off through the zoo. That was when we separated from you and Grayson."

Kayda obviously knew that part, as she'd been there, but Jo must have needed time to get acclimated to the memory.

"Erik is … Erik is of an unknown mixed parentage. Not even he knows who his father was—or *is*, I suppose; we also don't know if he's alive or dead—but Erik is magic-touched. His supernatural speed saved Welsh's bacon more than once that night. It was that speed that allowed Erik to catch up to the vampire, and in the process of the two of them battling, the vampire dropped Welsh.

"The vampire used his shadow magic so effectively that he was able to shroud himself *and* Welsh in darkness while also casting shadow clones of himself. The forested area outside the zoo was already full of natural shadows, so we were constantly struggling to work out which shadows were the vampire and which ones were a distraction. While we were trying to find Welsh, that's when he was bitten.

"Henri *heard* the attack—as both the vampire and Welsh were, uhh … moaning. Henri followed the sound—we were nowhere close, by the way—and found them. Without Henri's heightened hearing, I'm not sure we would have found Welsh in time. The vampire was so enraptured by the meal, he didn't sense Henri until he whacked the vampire in the skull with that damned flashlight.

"That disoriented the vampire enough that Erik was able to hit him with his fire whip. The fire whip is Erik's weapon of choice." Jo offered a pained smile then—like a parent proud that their child was passionate about a hobby but being less than thrilled about the hobby itself. "The whip lashed the vampire's back and set his suit on fire. That helped dispel most of his shadows, but he was raving mad. He tore off his jacket, bellowed like a troll, and turned his sights on Erik and me. Henri dragged Welsh out of the way while Erik and I threw everything we had at the vampire, but the blood the vampire had just consumed made his magic even stronger. He could essentially teleport with the shadows—popping in and out of view in a blink. He lashed at me with shadows that somehow had enough mass to cut, in addition to the pair of physical daggers he had. One noise of pain from me, and Erik went on the defensive, more concerned with protecting me than killing the vampire."

The more Kayda heard about shadow magic, the less she liked it.

She was also suddenly distraught that what had happened to Kessler—the fae boy who still haunted her thoughts, just as Quaid had intended—was also happening to Welsh. Had Kessler been bitten by a hybrid who had then tried to turn Kessler? Would that explain the black vein-like marks on Kessler's side, his pallor, his manic behavior?

It would also potentially explain why either the vampires wanted him back or the Collective was invested in getting him into custody. If Kessler was turning, he was neither a pure vampire who could live in a place like Tercla nor a "normal" hybrid. A fae going feral was a wild card—one that grew wilder depending on who was bitten.

Kayda had been comforted unknowingly by the fact that fae couldn't turn. The idea of a feral draken, orc, or troll was petrifying. She had to hope that what was affecting Welsh, and possibly Kessler, was an anomaly and not a new, disturbing trend.

"When the vampire realized Erik had switched to defending me," Jo said, reeling Kayda back in, "he teleported to Henri and Welsh. The vampire was absolutely crazed by then, like a wild, starving dog ready to fight to the death for his hard-won meal. He'd set his sights on Henri as a rival animal he needed to put down. The vampire had Henri caught in a tangle of shadow vines he was using to pin him in place. He kept shouting that he was going to break Henri's neck for stealing his property. Erik reached him before the vampire made good on his threat."

If this vampire wasn't already dead, Kayda would have torn his head off with her bare hands. She knew her face had flushed green. She ground her teeth so hard, her jaw ached.

A gentle hand landed on Kayda's arm, and she flinched so hard, she bumped into a stack of cardboard boxes. The women only narrowly prevented the tower from crashing to the floor.

"He's fine, Kayda," Jo said, having taken several steps away now that the possibility of an avalanche had passed. "You *know* Henri is okay. You *know* the vampire is dead. Breathe."

Kayda let out a long exhale, aware that Jo had told Erik something similar earlier. Jo spent a lot of her time telling other people to cool their jets.

After resuming her perch on her desk's edge, Jo continued. "While the vampire was lost in his blood lust, I used earth to cement his feet in place. Erik lassoed the vampire's neck with his fire whip and tugged, and both the vampire's headless body and Henri hit the ground."

After allowing herself a few moments to process the story, Kayda asked, "How long did the vampire have Welsh shrouded before Henri heard them?"

"A minimum of thirty seconds," Jo said slowly, "and potentially as long as two minutes." She fell silent, chewing on her bottom lip.

"What is it?" Kayda asked, not liking Jo's pensive expression.

"I didn't think about it much then, but I remember that when the vampire died, Welsh sat bolt upright, as if the vampire's death snapped their connection," Jo said. "Blood had been trickling from Welsh's neck wound, but I also saw him wipe the back of his hand across his mouth. The back of his hand was streaked in reddish black, and his teeth were stained red. I just assumed he'd split his lip or bit his tongue during the fight, but now ... Goddess, I don't know why I didn't even consider it. I thought the vamp had merely been taking advantage of an unexpected opportunity when he'd grabbed Welsh—since witches were his favorite food. I wonder now if the vampire forced his blood into Welsh's mouth."

Kayda's lip curled. *"Why?"*

"That's one of the key steps in turning a vampire—consuming blood of the sire," Jo said, contemplative.

"You think the vamp tried turning him?" Kayda asked, confused. "Vamps don't drink from each other, do they? If the creep was addicted to witch blood specifically, why would he want to turn Welsh and lose him as a food source?"

"That I can't answer," Jo said. "The very obvious jolt in power he got from feeding off Welsh was undeniable. One would think that boost would have made him want to keep Welsh around, but Welsh's sheer power also might have convinced the vamp that Welsh would be better turned than merely used as food. The vamp might have voiced his intentions to Welsh during the attack; he's the only one left alive who may know the answer."

"It's honestly incredible you all survived." In the days since, Kayda had tried damn hard not to think about that too much. Thinking about it stressed her out, destroyed her digestive system, and disrupted her sleep. Dwelling on what could have been didn't help anything.

Granted, instead, she beat herself up for not being able to stop a psychotic elf who out-powered her on so many levels that a fair fight hadn't even been in the realm of possibility.

"Do you see why we signed up for those training sessions?" Jo asked. "We were out of our depth, even three against one. Henri, I think, was a little embarrassed that the vampire bested him so easily. Not to mention he was terrified about how you were faring. I suspect he's not talking about any of it partly because he simply doesn't want to think about it. Does he usually avoid talking about difficult topics?"

Kayda thought about the fact that Henri hadn't been able to tell Kayda how he felt about her until she'd been glamoured to look like someone else.

Maybe he was worried she'd think less of him if she knew the details of what had happened that night, but it wasn't as if Kayda expected *anyone* to know how to ward off a vampire at full power. Not many people had fighting experience like she did—and even then, fighting in a controlled environment like a ring was nothing compared to the free-for-all chaos of fighting ferals, or hybrids doped up on fae blood.

Any time Kayda asked how he was doing, he said he was fine. He was dialed in when they were together in any capacity, and he was always quick with a joke to make her laugh or to offer a shoulder to cry on.

But then she'd taken the job with Marisol, and though Kayda and Henri still spent time together, it wasn't consistent. She'd believed he was okay simply because he hadn't told her otherwise.

"I'm going to, once again, suggest my mood-sensing candles," Jo said.

Kayda's eyes refocused as her gaze shifted to the witch.

"The smoke will change depending on the mood of the person closest to it," Jo said. "It could be a way for you or Henri to be prompted to start up a conversation when the smoke gives either of you a hint."

Kayda squinted at Jo. "Are you implying I'm *also* bad at discussing feelings?"

Jo chuckled heartily, but sobered quickly when Kayda didn't join in. "Oh, for Goddess's sake, that wasn't a joke?"

Kayda frowned.

Jo stood and straightened her skirts. She gave Kayda's arm a pat as she headed for the hallway. "I'll throw in a third one for free."

The shop was still bustling when the pair emerged from the back room, but it wasn't nearly as packed as when Kayda had first arrived. Jo joined her in line behind three waiting customers. While they waited for Kayda's turn, Jo programmed Snowdrop's number into a phone that she'd pulled from an unseen pocket, promising to get in contact with the elfin girl in the next few days. To pass the time, Jo explained what each hue of smoke meant, mood-wise, even though she assured Kayda that the candles came with a color map.

Kayda tried not to feel offended by how desperately Jo seemed to think Kayda needed these damn candles.

Erik sneered at Kayda when she reached the counter. She'd show Jo she could talk about feelings just fine, thank you very much.

"Thank you for not only saving Welsh, but Henri," Kayda said without preamble. "I'm deeply grateful you were there when I couldn't be."

The weaselly little man spluttered. "You're, uh, you're welcome," he managed, taking time with each word, as if he'd never spoken them before.

Kayda thought it was a good sign that the disturbed man could wrangle his warring emotions enough to sound normal even when his instincts clearly tried guiding him in a different direction.

"I put the vampire's head in my fridge so it'll dry out," Erik said cheerfully. "I want to mount it on my wall."

So much for that.

"We talked about this, Erik," Jo said. "You're going to have a hard time dating if you keep displaying troublesome trophies."

Erik muttered *"dammit, dammit"* and knocked himself in the temple with his knuckles a few times.

Kayda had no idea how to process any of this, so she didn't. "I'll take two mood-sensing candles."

"Ocean breeze, nocturnal forest, lightning storm, or wildflower meadow?" Erik asked flatly.

"Uhh ... the middle two?" Kayda asked.

"Throw in a second lightning storm for free, Erik."

Once she'd paid and her candles were bagged up, Kayda thanked Jo and headed for the exit. She'd only made it a few steps outside when someone aggressively hollered her name. She considered feigning deafness and sprinting down the sidewalk but told herself to pull up her big girl panties. She moved closer to the wall so she wouldn't block the entrance to the apothecary.

Reluctantly, she turned and looked down at Erik's upturned, pinched face. "Yes?"

"Can you put in a good word for me with Marisol Ortiz?" Erik asked in a rush.

Kayda blinked. "Uhh … why? You want to go on patrol?"

"Yes. Yes, very much. I need to learn how to be more of a … team player. I become too preoccupied with Lady Josephine's well-being. If she had not instructed me to help Henri that night, I might not have gotten to him in time," Erik said, in a halting tone that somehow sounded genuine *and* too forceful. When he was hostile, his speech pattern was even and natural. Being pleasant wasn't his forte. "I would have felt very bad about that. Henri is a good guy. You would have pulverized me into paste had I let him die."

If that last sentence had come out of Harlow's mouth, it would have had a sarcastic, funny edge. Erik's intense sincerity made Kayda deeply uneasy.

"I want to be useful," Erik said. "But I know I am … odd. But you are also odd, yet Marisol likes you. You convinced a nice, normal guy like Henri to sleep with you. Can you talk to her for me?"

Kayda said, "I'll … uhh … see what I can do."

Erik turned on his heel and sprinted back inside without a word. Kayda shook off the chill that ran down her spine. What if the bizarre little man had been a serial killer as a child or something and now was trying to rehabilitate himself?

She clutched her bag of candles to herself as she hurried away from the storefront, sure that if the wicks were lit the smoke would be red, signifying fear.

It took until she was a mere block from her apartment for her unease to dissipate. She'd only glanced behind her seven times on the walk home, half expecting to see the weasel man charging down the sidewalk after her, fire whip flicking about behind him. She considered what "mixed parentage" the strange man might have. Was it nature or nurture that was most responsible for what he was today?

The sound of pounding paws on cement made Kayda hit the brakes. Had it not been for that bizarre interaction half an hour earlier, she might not have been so jumpy. When the sound not only persisted but got closer, she darted into an alley. This one ended at one of her neighborhood's local bars. The last time she'd slipped into this alley, it had been Felix Turner who had been trailing her.

She stopped halfway between the bar and the mouth of the alley, heart thrashing and candle bag hugged to her chest.

Get it together, Kayda! she chastised herself.

It was likely just a pack of werecats—not an unusual sight *or* sound in Luma. Mundane cities had sirens. Luma had thundering cat paws.

Her mystifying interaction with Erik was throwing her off her game. It wasn't like whatever this was could be any weirder than that. And, honestly, how egotistical was it of her to think that whatever the origin of the sound, it had anything to do with her?

Blowing out a calming breath, she dialed up her hearing and closed her eyes, attempting to pinpoint not only where the creatures were coming from but who the paws belonged to. As she relaxed, she decided the thuds weren't loud enough to be coming from werecat paws after all; as quiet as the massive beasts could be, a pack of charging werecats would have been as loud as gong beats to Kayda's ears. No, these stampeding animals were smaller. But there were a *lot* of them.

Her eyes snapped open, and she stared down the length of the alley. Three seconds later, the first of them rounded the corner. Kayda sucked in a breath, holding tight to her bag and marveling that the glass jars hadn't yet shattered under the pressure. A dozen more animals followed the first. And then a dozen more after that. The creatures were small and low to the ground, their snouts slightly elongated. The animals moved so quickly that the muscles undulating under their thick coats reminded Kayda of rippling water. The click of their large claws sounded like a discordant tap dancing troupe where everyone was off beat.

White and black stripes streaked across their cheeks. Her mind yelled *"Skunks!"* but she instantly knew that was wrong.

This was so much worse than skunks.

Kayda pressed herself against the cold brick wall, seized with fear for the second time today. In her defense, the sight of dozens of badgers would scare most people. Apparently, she hadn't been egotistical after all. The badgers weren't headed for the Blind Wildebeest; they were headed for *her*.

Within moments, the badgers had formed a semicircle around her. There was a foot of space between the snout of the lead badger and the toes of Kayda's combat boots. It was enough clearance to punt the thing down the alley, but it wouldn't buy her the time needed to escape should the rest of them choose to shred her to ribbons.

Kayda gawked at the badger standing closest to her, its beady black eyes boring into hers. *All* the badgers studied her intently— as if they expected her to do something. What could *anyone* do when surrounded by this many badgers? In a blink, the badger shifter's eye level went from Kayda's boot laces to her nose.

She heaved a relieved breath. *"Fabian?"*

Kayda hadn't seen the gorgeous lunatic in over a year, when she and Harlow had been at an auction that had gotten raided by werecats. Even though Fabian had invited Harlow there, as soon as the event went sideways, he'd ditched them. Kayda couldn't even be mad at the guy. Badger shifters were bonkers at the best of times; they couldn't help it. They operated under clan rules that no one understood but them.

Fabian's wavy brown locks were in artful disarray around his shoulders. His tanned skin—most of it exposed—was covered in a fine layer of sweat ... or maybe that was baby oil. He wore only a loincloth. A very *short* loincloth. His feet were bare, the nails neat and trimmed.

She had to admit that the muscles of his rock-hard thighs were a sight to behold. Her tongue involuntarily skated across her bottom lip as she took in every inch of his toned physique. Goddess help her, being that captivating should be a crime.

She desperately hoped badgers gave off mind-melting pheromones and that was why she had an instant reaction to him. She mentally apologized to Henri for having her hormones hijacked.

Thankfully, Fabian usually broke his own spell the moment he opened his luscious mouth.

"Mmm. Hello, Kayda." He scanned her from head to toe, idly fiddling with one of his nipples. The guy had a deep affinity for his nipples; that much she remembered. "I've never ridden a dragon before. I have a pair of leather wings you can wear, and I have a mini blowtorch I've been *dying* to try."

For what? she wanted to ask, but decided she didn't want the answer.

His loincloth swung up like an old-fashioned garage door.

Oh for Goddess's sake!

The paper bag she held like a life raft crinkled loudly.

Before Kayda could voice that, no, she did not want part of … *any* of this … the badger nearest to him waddled forward an inch and bit him squarely in the calf. Hard. The surrounding badgers sucked in a collective gasp. Fabian squawked in surprise and whirled around, but his protest was short-lived. Kayda was temporarily distracted by an eyeful of sculpted butt cheeks.

The offending badger stood on its hind legs, crossed its forelegs, and tapped a foot. Kayda could have sworn one of its brows arched.

Fabian bowed deeply, and Kayda hastily scooted to the side to keep his bare ass from making contact with her. "My love, I apologize. You know what this human form does to me."

The badger snorted, shaking its head. It jerked its head in Kayda's direction.

"She *is* fetching, yes," Fabian said, winking at Kayda over his shoulder. To the badger, he said, "I will do my best to behave, my love."

The badger must have been satisfied with the apology because it dropped back to all fours.

Fabian turned to address Kayda again. The loincloth wasn't standing at attention anymore, at least. "This is my wife," he said, gesturing to the badger who looked nearly identical to all the others.

"Does she, uh, not shift?" Kayda asked.

"No. She is my one and only badger lover. We have an open marriage. She's smashed her way through most of those in attendance here, actually. But we have a rule not to openly flirt or partake in carnal pleasures in front of each other—unless group lovemaking is on the agenda, of course. It's just that sometimes I can't help my flirtations when the specimen before me is as tantalizing as yourself." He scanned Kayda again. "She's willing to have a threesome, if you're down."

Kayda shot a horrified look at his wife. The badger winked.

"This *can't* be the reason you ambushed me," Kayda said, her voice shrill, as she tried to get the idea of being ravaged by badgers out of her head.

Fabian chuckled, the sound smooth and rich. "No, no. It would be a bonus, is all. I wanted to officially offer you the assistance of the badger clans. News of your alliance with the pixies, and how you and your water elemental fought to save the preserve, has reached all facets of the so-called *lesser* fae community. We are so often ignored. It is an honor to be recognized by a draken."

Kayda most assuredly didn't have an alliance with the pixies, but this wasn't the time to argue.

All at once, the badgers stood on their hind legs and bowed their black-and-white striped heads. Kayda noted then that some had grayish-white backs, the color also reaching over their heads like a cap, while the bodies of others were covered in black fur stippled with white. They all had wicked-sharp claws that looked better suited to a bear than animals this small. Kayda was just glad they were allies and not enemies. Not even she would stand a chance against this many of them.

"Should danger breach our veil and threaten our city again," Fabian said, standing to full height, "the badgers will fight tooth and claw by your side, Kayda Verdan."

The badgers all dipped their heads in respect once more. With that, the group behind him dropped to their paws and reversed course to run back out of the alley toward the street. Shrieks of alarm told Kayda she wasn't the only one terrified by the sight of a sea of badgers. Only Fabian remained, though his wife—Kayda guessed—waited for him at the mouth of the alley.

"My other offer still stands," Fabian said, his voice taking on that intoxicating purr. "The lesser fae are underestimated as lovers, too. Don't let our small stature dissuade you. We're excep-tionally good at digging holes and tunnels—but we're even better at finding them. Give us the word and we'll find every one of your pleasure tunnels ..." He took two swift steps forward, the heat of him radiating against Kayda's arms. She was so thankful that the bag of candles provided a barrier. "And we'll thoroughly excavate every. single. one. Simultaneously."

Kayda swallowed.

He reached behind him and produced a business card with his name and number on it. Kayda had no idea where the hells the thing had come from. Since she had a death grip on her bag, he wedged a corner of the card between two of her fingers. The thick white paper was warm. She didn't want to know where he kept his cell phone, either. "Call me any time, for any reason. We're always down for anything." He ran his tongue over his teeth. "And I do mean *anything*."

An instant later, Fabian was a badger again and had scam-pered off to join his wife. They disappeared around the corner, punctuated by another startled cry from someone on the sidewalk.

Kayda slumped against the wall, heaving out a long breath. She supposed it was her fault for thinking she couldn't possibly have a weirder interaction than the one she'd had with Erik …

CHAPTER NINETEEN

HARLOW

We sat around the dining room table in quiet shock. Nothing like this had ever happened while I'd been holed up in Caspian's second house in the Necropolis.

"Let's just clear the air, okay?" Welsh asked. "No, I didn't go to culinary school. No, I don't have aspirations to be a chef. I cook for me and the people I care about. Everyone needs an outlet. Cooking is mine."

Mom elbowed Soren in the side. He was nose-deep in a small dish that had already been scraped clean. I couldn't blame him; the sauce was incredible.

"There's alchemical *something* going on, right?" I asked, jabbing at my spotless plate. That would make me feel better. I'd made at least one very private noise that I hadn't needed my mother, of all people, to hear.

"A little bit," Welsh said. "But there's a science and art to cooking in the mundane way, just like there is in crafting tinctures."

Soren finally put the dish down. I refrained from informing him that the tip of his nose was shiny with sauce. He leaned toward Caspian on his other side and very loudly whispered, "I know we already covered this topic, but if *you* aren't going to marry him, *I* will."

I snorted.

"Well, thank you," Welsh said amiably, noticeably getting great pleasure from us experiencing his food, even if he didn't outright say it.

He'd made enough to easily feed the five of us, and I realized he must have shopped accordingly, knowing my mom and Soren were going to be here. The warm fuzzies I felt for the guy were only outmatched by my burning desire to know what had happened in his past to turn him into such a prickly curmudgeon. Was there an abusive family member I needed to track down so the sword could gut them in retaliation for hurting my friend?

Now that he'd eaten, Welsh looked better—both his pallor and his ability to bring his glamour back to full power. I didn't think Welsh had lost his hold on his magic so thoroughly that his glamour had outright failed, revealing his true self to us, but his hold had been tenuous. The wispy shadows had retreated, and the bite marks on his neck had disappeared, as if covered by a layer of concealer.

Caspian and I cleared the table, then tag-teamed washing the dishes. The one downside to Welsh's amazing cooking was that he left the kitchen looking as if a bomb had gone off. While we did that, Mom rehashed with the guys what she'd told me earlier about cases involving witches infected with corrupted magic. I kept a watchful eye on Caspian, figuring he hadn't heard everything while the boys had been eavesdropping. When I caught him staring off into space, water running endlessly over the bowl he clutched in his hands, I suggested he take the trash out instead. The dishes were promptly abandoned, and he all but sprinted out the door, full bag in hand. The sword zipped out the kitchen doorway after him, but I suspected it was more interested in cavorting with the pixies again than keeping Caspian company.

By the time I was done cleaning up, Soren was outside on the back deck, a phone pressed to his ear as he talked to a contact in Illinois who worked at a fae morgue. If a fae died of something freakier than usual, that guy was often the one cutting them open. Soren was sure that, if there was anyone who had seen corrupted magic poisoning, it was him.

Mom sat close to Welsh, a hand on his upper back, and was talking quietly enough that I couldn't hear. Welsh's head was bowed, and though there was evident tension in his shoulders—whether from being touched or whatever Mom was telling him, I wasn't sure—he was also listening intently.

Caspian still hadn't come in from outside, so I slipped out of the kitchen. I found Caspian leaning against the railing of the porch peering out at the sword, who was indeed cavorting with the pixies again. If nothing else, the werecats currently spying on Caspian's house would have the amusing task of explaining what fresh horrors they'd observed the murderous dragon sword performing.

A pixie was bucked off the sword's hilt and was flung, shrieking, into a hedge. Her high-pitched "eee!" was drowned out by the rest of the pixies cheering on the next competitor. The sword, in the inverted position, pumped itself into the air repeatedly, the undefeated champion.

"The sword keeps getting stranger, doesn't it?" I asked, sidling up next to Caspian. "Is that my fault, or is it thriving now that it's being allowed to let its freak flag fly?"

"What if there's no cure?" Caspian asked softly, not looking at me.

I knew he meant for Welsh, not the sword's strangeness.

Whether Caspian personally identified as such or not, he was a sorcerer through and through. They were practical, they didn't appreciate wasted effort, and they preferred actionable goals over lofty promises not backed up by evidence. "If somehow this takes Welsh down, and I'm not saying it will, then we'll keep at it as long as we can until we find the cure so we can help save others in the same boat."

Caspian nodded tightly.

"Eeee!" went another pixie scream. This pixie pitched over the side of the sword's hilt and fell in a pinwheeling flail of limbs before crashing into the lawn. It apparently had forgotten to use its wings. The group, sword included, stilled as they waited for signs of life. I supposed, for a creature so small, a fall from that height could have broken its neck. I was too far away and too high up to spot the pixie; it had been thoroughly camouflaged by the grass.

The pixie shot up from the lawn, and the crowd cheered, the sound like distant wind chimes.

Caspian turned his back on the display and rested an elbow on the railing behind him. He shot a thumb over his shoulder. "That's definitely your fault."

My nose wrinkled. That the sword was only *sometimes* murderous seemed like a positive development, even if it was hard to know at any given time what new bizarre thing would intrigue it.

I said, "I know we agreed we'd take tonics since our friend is a bit under the weather. You know, even more than we are?" I wrapped my arms around my stomach and tried to moan pitifully. "Do you think he's too sick to even do that much? What if it drains him of his energy even further?"

I hoped Caspian understood that I didn't think we should openly discuss pending plans when there were at least two were-cats watching the place. Who knew what resources they had to grant them even better hearing.

"Tonic craft is similar to his cooking skills," Caspian said. "It's more a mundane skill than a magical one. His, uh, illness means he might be a bit slower, but it won't affect him more than anything else he's doing. After a good night's sleep, he'll be in even better shape."

I scanned the edges of Caspian's property—from the driveway to the left, to the closed metal gate directly across from us, to the lawn where the sword and pixies still created a ruckus. The fence attached to the gate circled the entire property, and while visible magic didn't waft off it like steam—at least not to me—I knew it crackled there all the same. I didn't doubt that, if the Collective issued a magical warrant of sorts, they'd have a sorcerer on hand who could cut the magical cords of the ward and let themselves in.

"And you think waiting until morning isn't too long to, uh, wait?" I asked.

"Wait for what?" he asked, but in his scholarly tone—the one where he knew the answer to the question already but wanted his intrepid student to find her own conclusions.

"I don't know. I was so anxious to get back to Luma, and now I'm even antsier being here."

"Remember, only half an hour ago you were ready to stroll into the Tower until you—um, until you began vomiting voluminously."

I shot him a look that I hoped silently conveyed my disappointment in his attempted save.

"I'm just saying your current anxiety is fueled solely by new information," Caspian said. "Our pending research is still about the cutlass, not Welsh's … illness. He's here because he's feeling scared and vulnerable, which are his two least favorite emotions. Our objective is to unearth more about the cutlass and its origins as well as how the results of that research directly affect *you*. Welsh is just along for the ride."

I heaved a slow breath out my nose, realizing that was it. I fled from danger. Welsh's condition sent panic coursing through my nervous system, telling my body that we needed to *move*. Where it wanted me to go was irrelevant; it just wanted to run away from the thing that made me feel this way. But I couldn't very well run away from it if Welsh was coming with us. I needed to calm down, or I wasn't going to be of use to anyone, including the sword.

I'd come out here to try to comfort Caspian, and instead he was the one attempting to soothe *me*.

"Oh," Caspian said, standing straight instead of leaning on the railing. "I wanted to run something by you. It's inside, though. I just needed a breather after—"

"Your own voluminous vomiting after eating Welsh's cooking? I told you that food was too rich for your delicate digestive system," I said, giving his stomach a little pat.

He narrowed his eyes. "You're one to talk, given your debilitating diarr—"

"*All right*," I said, waving my hand dismissively. "Enough with the gross symptom alliterations. What did you want to show me?"

I followed Caspian inside, not bothering to call the sword back in. I was sure Caspian's rage room was suitably outfitted to deal with magical assaults, but I'd rather have the sword spend its time entertaining pixies than potentially going ham in the basement and destroying the house's foundation or something.

The curving staircase in the nearly empty living room led us to a second-floor mezzanine area. I personally would have turned the space into a loft-style bedroom, but Caspian, naturally, had gone with a library. A pair of plush black recliners sat in the middle of the space, facing the wrought-iron railing that looked over the living room and the backyard beyond. Between the two recliners stood a round wooden table stacked high with books. Like the living room below, three walls were covered in built-in bookshelves. The only breaks in the walls of books were a half-open door in the back that led to a bathroom, and an open doorway to the right that revealed a hallway.

Caspian walked to the stack of books on the table and placed his fingertips on them. "This was my maybe-pile when I was fleeing the house. I regret not taking them now."

"You had enough wherewithal to sort books into a maybe pile, but you didn't have time to inform your pixies?"

"Is this the part where you lecture me on my misaligned priorities?"

"I wouldn't dream of it," I said, punctuating my sarcasm with a sweet smile.

He picked up the topmost book, which had a hard, dark-brown leather cover and no adornment other than an oval that took up almost the entire space. It, and the wavy line around it, were reminiscent of a kid's interpretation of the sun's rays, with the lines embossed in gold.

A series of multicolored tabs poked from the pages, suggesting he'd read the book many times over.

"This is a rather rudimentary tome on the basics of portals," Caspian said. "It's more theory than a guide on construction; understanding portal construction is far above my pay grade. I won't bore you with the minutiae, but—"

"Never stopped you before," I muttered.

He ignored me. "It covers theoretical postulations rather than anything backed up by scientific absolutes, which is why I left it behind. But other than a few niche experts, most of what is known about portals is nebulous at best anyway."

I crossed my arms and idly tapped a foot.

He cleared his throat. "Sorry. Okay, so the earthen realm is always classified as magic-less, yes? But according to this book in particular," he said, tapping the still closed cover of the book he cradled in one arm, "there has to be *some* magic here in order for portals to open in the first place. You yourself mentioned a very common theory—that portals are potentially more likely to open near power vortices, like the ones reported in places like Sedona."

I puffed up a little, like a proud peacock.

Caspian tamped down a soft smile. "There are also similar theories concerning ley lines. Regardless of whether it's power vortices or ley lines or something else entirely, the cornerstone of the theory is that there needs to be an energy source *here* that the traveler on the other end can tap into. There's a lengthy chapter at the end of the book on *intra*-realm portals versus *inter*-realm portals that adds a whole layer to this that I can't even begin to process. And frankly, what we know about intra-realm travel comes almost exclusively from lessons learned via maintaining the telepad system. I fear the more complex theories about intra-realm portals died with Frederica Kensey."

I'd researched the mother of teleportation travel a few times during my bouts of insomnia at the Washington VHoA headquarters. What little I could find had suggested that the magical expenditure needed to move an entire island had fried something in the brilliant woman's brain. Granted, Kensey hadn't meant to move the island from the fae realm to this one, but the Glitch had impeccable timing.

Perhaps Kensey's mind and magic could have been healed had she found a way back to her realm where there would have been potent magic-based medicines available to her, but instead she, according to rumor, had gone a bit mad in the years after the Glitch. She'd kept it together long enough to see the first set of successful telepads go online, but after that, she'd disappeared into obscurity. So much so that I hadn't even known Kensey was the mastermind behind the telepad and telepost systems I'd used on a nearly daily basis for most of my life. Her name certainly had never come up in any significant way in high school.

"Anyway," Caspian said, wresting my thoughts away from my idle musings. "Beyond the power-source component, the only other semi-concrete thing we know about portals is that there are five types, from least powerful to most. The lowest ranked type is an echo. Echoes are analogous to residual ghost hauntings, or the sensation left by a phantom limb. The portal is merely a memory of one that once existed, and the heightened energy of the location allows the echo to pop in and out of existence. It can't be used for travel. It can't be manipulated into becoming solid."

"The reports you found about the portal near Lake Nacimiento didn't label them as echoes, did they?" I asked.

Caspian shook his head. "They were labeled as '*potential* tears.' Minor and major tears are theorized to be places where portals had been stuck open the longest during the Glitch. Portals aren't meant to stay open longer than an hour at maximum, and ideally, they're only open for a handful of minutes. During the Glitch, some stayed open as long as forty-eight hours. Even though all the portals eventually closed, minor and major tears continue to leak magic. They're also the places where random, short-lived portals have the best chance to pop into existence. These portals *are* solid, and occasionally something from the other side can cross through, and vice versa. Usually insects, small animals, or lesser fae, given that the portals are rarely very large."

I asked, "Since the portals seen near the lake are solid, is that why the Portal Relations report said it was odd there wasn't some kind of magical signature left behind after the portal closed again?"

"I presume so," Caspian said. "The locations of the major tears are mapped out more thoroughly than minor ones, as there were more eyewitnesses and data for those. Conversely, a few new minor tears are discovered every year. This book was published five years ago, and as of its publication, no new major tears had been found in over six decades."

I pondered that. "So are the ones near the lake 'tears' or something else?"

"That's where your assessment comes in. Echoes and tears are considered natural portals, as they form on their own, triggered by fluctuations in magical power. Your mother comparing them to the natural eruptions of a geyser wasn't far off.

"The last two types of portals are man-made, for lack of a better term, and are either 'unstable' or 'stable.' Unstable portals snap closed without warning. Sometimes they give off great bursts of magic before they close. Sometimes they wink out as if they'd never been there. Supposedly there's still some detectable trace left behind, as unstable portals are almost exclusively the result of a portal being opened incorrectly, too forcefully, or in an area that doesn't have an energy source sufficient enough to sustain it. It's even possible that an unstable portal snapping closed forcefully could cause a minor tear."

I asked, "So I'm guessing a stable portal is one opened in perfect conditions?"

Caspian nodded. "Those are exceedingly rare, at least in this realm. Intra-realm portals—portals opened to traverse from one point in a realm to another—have a better chance of being stable than an inter-realm one. But you've seen how complicated telepads are and how often they need maintenance. Telepads exist in a manufactured, highly concentrated energy pocket in an environment with very little of its own. Given the difficulties with intra-realm travel, it's honestly incredible that travel between realms is possible at all."

I nodded absently at that, trying to keep everything straight.

"Given everything I've told you, do you think the reports from near the lake are tears or unstable portals?" Caspian asked.

"They all pop up in the same general location, don't last longer than five minutes each, but leaves behind no magical trace?" I asked.

"Correct."

"Unstable portal," I said with little hesitation. "Portal Relations classifies those portals as an anomaly, so they're not quite natural portals, but not quite man-made ones, either. I think the fact that this particular spot is also getting an honorable mention by Samar as potentially connected to the Shades makes it less likely that these are naturally occurring portals."

Caspian's expression was pinched, almost disappointed, as if he'd hoped I'd say something else. "That was my assessment as well. I reckon our best bet is to talk to the witnesses of these portal fluctuations and get a firsthand account. Such accounts may prove more thorough than the watered-down versions in public Portal Relations reports."

I cocked my head. "Specific names of witnesses were given?"

Caspian sighed deeply. "At least two reports state that witnesses include … sirens."

"As in beautiful maidens with haunting voices who lure sailors to their death?"

"There are male sirens as well, though they faded from stories around the fifth century," Caspian said. "The two mentioned in the reports were male."

The silence ticked on as I waited for him to say more. He minutely shifted his weight from foot to foot.

I crossed my arms and jutted my chin at him. "All right, out with it. You're being cagey."

He rubbed the back of his neck. "Okay, concern number one is that, if these are indeed unstable portals, it means either someone in this realm is repeatedly opening portals in a specific location, or there's someone on the other side who keeps trying to get in. Maybe it's like Earth sending messages out into the vastness of space hoping we get a reply—to get proof that there are other intelligent life-forms in the universe."

"Or it's a Shade from another realm trying to find a chink in the earthen realm's armor."

"Precisely," Caspian said. "Concern two is that sirens are incapable of lying while simultaneously being grouchier than Welsh when he's hungry—and has been denied food for a week."

I winced.

"They're also less motivated by murder and more by … uhh, lust."

"So they use their siren powers to lure people into bed rather than their watery graves?"

Color rose in Caspian's cheeks, and the tips of his ears went red. It was kind of cute how easy it was to embarrass him. I was desperate to know the details of his booty-call relationship with the sorceress from the academy. Was it strictly a missionary-only, no-kissing kind of deal, or did things get wild when they both let loose to burn off the stress of their lunatic schooling?

Caspian cleared his throat awkwardly, and I snapped out of thoughts that were inching toward lurid, thankful my dark skin would mask most of my own blush.

"The sirens in this realm aren't exactly the same as ones from earthen myth, but the label is as close as I've been able to find." Caspian rubbed the back of his neck again. "There's an article in the *San Luis Obispo Tribune* about a local who lives in a home overlooking the lake. This particular local has a tendency to get into bar brawls on a nearly weekly basis, once got so upset about the price of apples that he smashed his fists through the windows of a grocery store, and has also broken up at least three marriages in the last year. I suspect the bar brawls are started by the cuckolded husbands."

"Oh boy …"

"To make matters worse, if the siren uses his abilities on someone, he can convince them that they aren't actually upset with him, and the victim will eventually go on their merry way."

"Uhh … I thought they couldn't lie."

"They can't. But if they have their siren powers turned up, they can tell someone an awful truth, their siren power soothes the victim, and the victim hears whatever they *want* to hear."

I wanted to chat with these sirens less and less by the second.

Caspian said, "Male sirens have an affinity for three things: deep secrets freely shared, rare magical items, and human women."

I scrunched up my nose. "Human women who are susceptible to their horny siren powers."

"Right," he said. "I'd been considering sending in Welsh wearing a human woman glamour, as Welsh would probably be immune to the siren's seduction tactics, given that he's not attracted to *anyone*. But with his current precarious hold on his magic, that seems ill-advised. He undersold his condition."

Caspian had uttered that last sentence with complete disdain.

"How rare is rare, when it comes to the magical items they fancy?" I asked.

"I honestly don't know. What I've told you is the extent of my siren knowledge. I would imagine the rarity preference depends on the siren in question and what mood he or she is in." Caspian tapped his chin thoughtfully. "Some of the items in the treasure chest might be of interest, but I don't know if offering him such trinkets would make him feel as if we've reduced his whims to that of a mundane crow easily swayed by the promise of a shiny bauble."

"So you're saying our best means of enticing this grouchy-as-hell-slash-womanizing siren into talking to us is … me."

Caspian offered me a smile that was all teeth.

I sighed. "I can't tell if I'm more or less worried that you think I'd be safer in the company of a siren than the Collective."

"We'll be there with you the whole time—the cutlass as well," Caspian said. "But you … uhh … might consider keeping a closely held secret in your back pocket to share, just in case."

This would no doubt be a disaster.

CHAPTER TWENTY

LACHLAN

Lachlan woke with a splitting headache and the grit of sand in his mouth. It felt like he'd been hit by a bus, backed over, and then hit again. He struggled to sit up. Every joint and muscle ached, though the center of his chest hurt the most. He pressed a palm to his torso, expecting to feel the sharp bite of pain from palpating a bruise, and the pressure of his hand stole the breath from his lungs—breath that wheezed and whistled on the way out.

He surveyed the landscape to the left, then right, trying to get his bearings. Even his eyes hurt.

The world around him was bleak—expansive stretches of coarse sand decorated only by the occasional boulder. No trees. No distant call of a bird. No insects buzzing around his head. Sand fleas didn't hop around his outstretched legs. The sky was a milky baby blue, as if the color was slowly being leached away. The sand beneath him wasn't as hot as he would have expected, nor did he feel as if he were roasting alive in unrelenting heat. Not even the sun wanted to waste its time with this place.

It took a minute or two of sitting there—listening to his whistling breaths and waiting for the pain needling his entire body to settle into a persistent, manageable ache—for his memories to resurface. Hewitt was the reason he was here instead of in that clearing, waiting for the last of Kira Alpin's blood to hit the bowl. The last drops of blood that would have opened the portal to his parents, aunt, and the small contingent of acolytes they'd amassed to join Lachlan's cause.

Because even his parents had accepted that he'd exceeded their skill sets. In their monthly handwritten correspondence delivered via small, short-lived portals, he'd told them about his work, about the growing number of Shades, about Teo and his vampires who had joined his ranks. They, in turn, told him about the flora and fauna of their realm, and how the principles of magic were much the same there, though it manifested in myriad different ways. Ways that they could potentially exploit. Over time, he'd made it clear to his parents and aunt that he didn't just want to get them back to the earthen realm for a heartfelt family reunion—his plans had grown exponentially.

But it had all gone wrong.

Now Blythe had been abandoned by her entire immediate family. There was no way for Lachlan to tell her where he was because not even *he* knew.

Hewitt claimed he and his precious Portal Relations knew more about portals than Lachlan did. Those Collective sorcerers didn't know shit. That last interaction had been eye-opening, at least. It proved the sorcerers knew even less than Lachlan imagined. He had to ascertain where he was so he could relay his location to his parents, to Blythe, to Teo. The Shades needed to know they were on the right track.

"You act as if you know more about portals than I do," Hewitt had said. *"The Collective has been studying portals and portal magic for decades, elf. You're not the first overzealous idiot who has tried to reopen the portals, and you won't be the last. Portal magic is unstable. Any portal opened using blood magic is even more so—especially blood not willingly given. You don't even know what world is beyond that door."*

Hewitt had made it sound as if Lachlan were testing theories with all the finesse of throwing spaghetti at the wall and hoping something stuck. No, Lachlan had known exactly what he was doing.

He also knew now that, despite being smarter than Hewitt by a mile, Lachlan had made a stupid mistake.

An image of that woman sprang up in his mind then—the pregnant one. Camila Fletcher. He'd been too curious about her—her *and* her husband—when Teo had mentioned them in casual conversation months ago. Teo made a point to keep apprised of vampire hunters, especially ones who had become household names among his kind. Rumors about the Fletchers had been circulating for years: a pair of fully human private investigators who had an uncanny knack for solving missing persons cases involving fae.

Lachlan had chosen a residential neighborhood in Northern California as his snatching ground in part because it was in the Fletchers' territory. Blythe had thought it was yet another of Lachlan's unnecessary side quests. Worse still, she was adamant that Teo was poisoning his mind and that he'd planted the Fletcher seed knowing it would grow into something covered in thorns that would snag relentlessly at Lachlan's curiosity. The truth was,

Lachlan knew Teo didn't use his enthrall abilities on him. Teo didn't need to. They were on the same page. They shared the same vision.

Lachlan had explained to Blythe on countless occasions that he'd grown addicted to challenging himself and others. The more difficult the problem, the more satisfying it was when he succeeded. Challenge built character. Made him stronger. Made him resilient. Made him the kind of leader people wanted to follow.

The growing roster of devotees he'd collected over the years was proof he was right. His vision drew like-minded people to him, like moths to a flame—people who didn't see his stumbles as failures, but rather steppingstones to something that could alter the earthen realm even more than the Glitch had.

He had not just elves in his party, but vampires, trolls, orcs, and other cast-outs from the hub system. If Lachlan had been able to pull this off under the noses of the Fletchers, he and Teo were confident it would help persuade some of the leerier hybrids.

Lachlan just hadn't anticipated that the Fletchers had gotten so good at their job that they'd garnered the notice of the Collective. He hadn't believed Camila when she claimed to have a connection to the organization of elitist sorcerers. He'd wanted to watch her and her mundane husband chase the clues to the invisible magical barrier Kira Alpin was trapped behind—and then be unable to find the girl. He'd known the Alpins would follow the Fletchers, once they discerned where Lachlan's breadcrumbs led. He'd wanted to be hiding in plain sight as he watched the dawning horror cross Camila's face—as it crossed Kira's family's faces.

Because that was the final key to unlocking the world of his choice. He'd needed the energy borne from anguish to give his spell that last final jolt of power. It had to be a level of anguish that matched his own when his uncle was killed and his parents and aunt wound up in a different realm. He'd needed a beloved member of a family as his sacrifice. The Alpins not only had fae blood, but they'd deeply loved their youngest daughter. They'd been the perfect family to target. The fact that the Fletchers were nearby had only sweetened the deal.

It was just his luck that the sorcerer the Fletchers had on speed dial was Hewitt. The same lead sorcerer who had disrupted the Order's portal-opening attempt eight years ago. The five-horned monster that had charged out of the portal and gored three sorcerers to death had been worth the price of admission, though.

The Order had kicked him and Blythe out after that. But it had been a long time coming. The Order had gone as soft as old cheese in the years since his parents had disappeared. They were too cautious now. Too scared. They didn't understand how revolutionary his parents' ideas truly were. Dusty understood. He was the only one Lachlan and Blythe had taken with them when they set out to create their new order—the Shades.

An involuntary breath wheezed out of Lachlan's taxed lungs at the thought of his cousin.

Dusty was dead now. It had been the grief of his loss that had resulted in Lachlan being drunk in a mundane bar the day Teo Santoro had slid into the booth across from him. A vampire, of all people, who had opened Lachlan's eyes and broadened his horizons.

Dusty's death had been a tragic loss, but his cousin had known the risks. He'd known better than anyone that sometimes the best way to gain great knowledge was at the expense of others. Lachlan had learned a lot from Dusty's death.

The memory of the portal's magic flickering as Dusty stepped into the vortex of energy flashed through Lachlan's mind. He recalled the way the magic had abruptly snapped off like a switch being thrown. Dusty had been reduced to a pile of body parts on the wet leaf litter. There'd been no blood to mix with the remnants of the previous night's rain. Every cut sustained by Dusty's body had been instantly cauterized.

By the Goddess, the *smell*, though …

Blythe had bawled for what had felt like hours. The Shades—

his new Order—couldn't kick him out that time, as he *was* the Order. It wouldn't exist without him. A lot of his supposed followers left that day, though. Blythe did too, for a while, but she came back, just like Lachlan knew she would.

Hewitt had been there in an attempt to stop Lachlan last year, too, but he and Blythe had escaped before Hewitt found them, all thanks to Teo. Having vampires as allies had proven useful count-less times over. They were adept at slinking around undetected and were blessed with heightened senses that put even Lachlan's and his fellow elves' to shame. Teo's shadow magic helped, too.

Lachlan hadn't been so lucky this time. Now Blythe was alone, Teo couldn't reach him, and Lachlan was … here. Wherever here was. All because he'd gotten bored and restless again and called the bluff of a mundane woman.

If he ever got out of here, he was going to wring Camila Fletcher's neck.

He grabbed a fistful of coarse sand and threw it. All he got for his efforts were stabs of pain in his chest and dust in his face.

His chin quivered at the thought of the pile of dust his uncle had been reduced to. The way Dusty had sobbed, throwing himself forward as if he thought, if he were quick enough, he could put his father back together. Lachlan swallowed the lump in his throat.

Fucking. *Hewitt.*

Hewitt had cast an air spell at Lachlan, the magic hitting him center mass and flinging him through the portal and into this Goddess-forsaken world. Kira had surely awoken the instant the portal snapped closed—woozy from blood loss but probably alive. Such a waste.

Due to the way Hewitt had disrupted this specific spell, the portal's destination had been randomized.

The Shades had been instructed to descend on the sacrifice location after sundown to clear away the altar and Kira's body. Lachlan had planned on being too busy welcoming his family back to this realm to be bothered with the asinine task of cleanup.

The presence of his Shades any earlier than sundown could have easily thrown off the spell, but now Lachlan wished he'd had backup. He wished he and Blythe hadn't recently fought so bitterly over Teo's role in The Restoration. She and his Shades would have torn Hewitt and the Fletchers to pieces had they been waiting nearby.

They'd deduce what happened eventually, even if it would be impossible for them to track down which realm he sat in now. Perhaps he'd become a martyr for the cause, spurring them into action. His misfortune, much like Dusty's demise, might serve as the conduit for great knowledge. Maybe it would finally make Blythe and Teo see eye to eye.

His fate might teach her that he and Teo had been right all along: That the Collective knew Lachlan had tapped into a power the sorcerers had been selfishly keeping to themselves since the Glitch.

Hewitt knew how skilled Lachlan had become and wanted to stop him for good. Sure, death and destruction usually poured forth from the torn-open doorways between realms, but that only meant they hadn't opened the right ones yet. If the Collective weren't so elitist, so overbearing, so scared to be unseated, he wouldn't be here.

Blythe wouldn't hate him more often than not.

The Order wouldn't have turned their back on him.

His parents and aunt wouldn't be lost.

His uncle wouldn't have been reduced to ash.

Lachlan tightened his jaw to stop his chin from quivering again. Grit crunched between his teeth.

If the Collective was cooperative instead of punitive, Dusty would still be alive.

Enough wallowing, Lachlan chastised himself in a voice that sounded suspiciously like Teo's. *Get up.*

Groaning like a wounded bear, Lachlan staggered to his feet. His boots sank half an inch into the sand. He cast another wary glance around his desolate surroundings, unsure which direction to head in first. It all looked the same. Something like hysteria fluttered behind his rib cage like a trapped beetle. What if this was the entirety of the world and he eventually walked into a wall that had only been painted to *resemble* a desert landscape? Had he been deposited into a terrarium belonging to a bored god who'd wanted a new pet?

A glint of light flashed in his periphery, and he whirled toward it.

Still nothing but sand and scattered boulders. There weren't even cacti here.

The glint came again. He squinted, unsure if he really *did* see a shifting shadow stretching out from behind a nearby boulder.

A moment after a humanoid figure scuttled atop the boulder in question, a dart was sticking out of Lachlan's shoulder. The bright blue fletching of the dart was such a pop of color in this bleak landscape, it almost hurt to look at it.

For the span of a breath, he appreciated the efficiency of the full-body paralytic that stole his pain away. In the next breath, panic took flight anew as he pitched backward, stiff as a board, slamming into the sand. Blessedly, he didn't feel it. The only parts of him he could control were his eyes, which rolled about wildly in his skull as he frantically scanned for his attacker.

His brain told his body to flinch when a face swam into view. Lachlan's body did not move.

He tried to determine whether the being was more human-like than reptile-like and decided it was a sixty-forty split, heavy on the reptile. It had scaly skin, feather-like sideburns, and yellow, slitted eyes that were positioned too far apart for a human face. A forked tongue slithered between thin lips as the thing spoke to Lachlan. He assumed it was speech, anyway.

When all Lachlan did in response was widen his eyes in terror, the creature huffed an annoyed-sounding breath that smelled of sage. Its feather sideburns fluttered.

The creature lifted a six-fingered hand into Lachlan's range of sight, its fingers dancing at dizzying speed. A yellow mist, reminding Lachlan of poisonous gas, materialized out of nothing, traveling from scaled elbow to fingertip. The mist coalesced and solidified, forming a circular shape between the reptilian's face and Lachlan's frozen one.

While Lachlan didn't understand the words flowing from the reptilian's mouth, he recognized the hovering shape for what it was: a rune array. With a quick thrust of the creature's palm, the array flew straight for Lachlan's nose.

It hit him so hard, it was a wonder all the bones in his face didn't shatter. Something in his brain … *ripped*. It wasn't a painful sensation so much as a foreign one. Pressure built in his temples with such sudden force he was sure his skull would explode like a melon. He would have screamed if his mouth worked. His back would have arched had his spine not felt as if it were made of concrete.

The pressure dissipated just as quickly. He knew tears leaked from his eyes, but he couldn't feel their slow slide down his skin and into his hair.

Welcome, traveler, a gravelly voice said in his mind. The reptilian's lips didn't move, yet Lachlan knew that was who spoke. *You will be given the same conditions as those who came before you. You have three cycles to impart your knowledge of interworld travel. If you wound up here because you are a fool like all the others, you will be fed to the virna. It is worse than a thousand simultaneous deaths.*

Lachlan's heart thrashed as he was suddenly airborne. His view went from pale blue sky to a bouncing, sandy terrain. The creature had flung him over its shoulder and was carting him off like a sack of potatoes.

After only a couple of minutes into his bumpy ride, a roar sounded in the distance—a raspy, fear-inducing rumble that must have come from a monster the size of a 747. The reptilian stopped short.

That … is not a virna. That one is worse. A second ticked by. Two. The ground beneath them began to quake. Lachlan heard it more than felt it, which was somehow worse. The creature holding Lachlan's paralyzed body broke into a run.

Lachlan bounced violently on the creature's shoulder, his stomach pitching as if he were on a ship being tossed about by a choppy sea. His vision blackened at the edges. The paralytic was going to overwhelm his entire system.

When the heart-stopping roar boomed again, though, he thought the paralytic might be a blessing.

I suggest you think quickly, traveler, the voice continued in his head. *We want to flee this place even more than you do.*

Lachlan managed to curse Hewitt one last time before the poison in his body won and everything went black.

CHAPTER TWENTY-ONE

HARLOW

The morning after arriving at Caspian's, I sat on the back patio at a too-early hour, thanks to another bout of insomnia, listening to the gentle rustle of leaves as a warm breeze swept through the garden, the burbling water in the fountain, and the soft chatter of pixies hard at work. The sword lay on the bench seat next to me like a worn-out dog taking a nap. On my other side lay my cell phone.

I'd just finished catching Kayda up on everything about Welsh's condition, giving her permission to share the information with anyone she trusted in VHoA. Even though I'd interacted with Marisol a few times, Kayda knew her better, especially now that Kayda was on her payroll. It sounded like Welsh was, too, but on an as-needed basis.

Even though Caspian kept assuring me that glamour tincture crafting wasn't strenuous enough magic-wise to affect Welsh's ability to keep the shadows at bay, I couldn't help but worry. What if shutting out the shadows was akin to stopping up a leak with a wad of chewing gum, and it was only a matter of time before the dam burst? What if Welsh went from staying one step ahead of the corrupted magic to, a breath later, wholly succumbing to it?

I'd voiced all of this to Kayda too. She hadn't been able to offer me more than a sympathetic ear, but I'd needed that even more than a miracle solution.

There was still the added wrinkle of how the three of us—glamoured or not—would be able to leave Caspian's property without arousing suspicion. Just before my call with Kayda, the pixies had let us know there were now eight werecats keeping an eye on the place. Four were prowling around the front entrance, while the other four were last seen skulking by a back gate.

Last night, Caspian and Welsh told me that our best bet for getting off the property without tipping off the cats would mean going underground. From the basement, we could access a tunnel that led to the garage of the house across the street. Caspian owned that house, too.

My bland supervillain had a bat cave!

Problem was, the family who rented the house was out of town *and* not answering their phones. Caspian would be unable to sneak his car into their garage without first knowing whether or not it was empty. The family was used to Caspian—their odd, beige-bedecked landlord—occasionally asking for access to their garage. They didn't ask questions, largely because they had their own secrets to keep.

The Duns were a family of four: a mundane woman, her draken husband, and their two kids. The draken's immediate family was involved in "criminal activity," according to Welsh, who'd refused to elaborate no matter how many times I'd asked. Any time I'd asked Caspian for details, he'd feigned hearing loss.

In addition to Coaldon Dun being part of a shady crime family, Coaldon's family was personally affronted that he'd married a human. They'd threatened to kill Susan if she ever bore Coaldon's children. The Duns had fled their home in Nevada the same night Susan had found out she was pregnant with their first child. Somehow or other, they'd gotten into contact with Welsh, who'd procured them new identities, and eventually into a rental agreement with Caspian.

Normally, Caspian would call one of them, ask for access to their garage, don a disguise, and then mosey off undetected to one of his auctions. The Duns' family car needed to be moved every time, as it was purposefully kept parked on top of the rune array that would activate once the array's counterpart in Caspian's basement was turned on.

Since the Duns were on vacation, the spot *could* be empty. Or the foursome could have rented a car. Or used a rideshare to get to an airport.

Last night I'd asked, "Can't Cas just flip the magical switch to fire up the arrays, and if the magic doesn't work the way it's supposed to, that'll mean the path isn't clear?"

Caspian's small smile politely said my lack of knowledge about the intricacies of magic was showing—again.

"The array on their end turns the concrete into something similar to mercury," Welsh had explained. "The floor literally liquefies and floats into the air so the elevator can get Caspian's car into place. Once his car is pulled forward, the concrete reforms. The spell has a five-minute limit, so there's very little room for mistakes."

"So if you turn everything on and their car *is* parked there, does that mean it falls through the hole left behind and crushes anything beneath it?" I asked.

Welsh had made a noncommittal gesture, absently scratching at the spot where his bite marks were, even though his glamour shielded them from view. "That's what *I* expected to happen. There was a lot of trial and error with this whole system. Turns out that the car *also* liquefies. When everything reforms, the concrete has a mangled car trapped inside."

Caspian had sighed heavily. "Ask me how we know."

Chuckling, Welsh had said, "It wasn't that bad. We're quick learners! We only destroyed two of their cars."

"That's easy for you to say. You weren't the one who had to buy them a new one every time it happened."

"We got pretty good at DIY projects." Welsh had addressed me. "It's hard to hire someone to re-pave your secret lair entrance who is trustworthy enough *not* to blab about it."

"At least all your new DIY skills helped when you needed to patch up the house after it was ransacked by pissy cats," I'd said.

Welsh's smug grin had filled me with the warm fuzzies again. "See! What's the price of a couple of cars when it gained us so much valuable life experience?"

"The first time was admittedly my fault," Caspian had said, though he'd sounded grouchy about it. "That dwarf was a liar and a swindler, and he deserved to lose his ear. But the second time? If you listened to me even *thirty* percent of the time, we would have been in the clear." Caspian's ticked-off tone suggested this was an old argument whose wounds had been torn open. That, or he was still in denial about the reality of his friend's condition and was lashing out because of it.

Welsh had waved Caspian's comment away. "You know I can't be held responsible for what happens when you go off on a tangent about rune theory. If you bore me, you're taking your life, and the fate of heavy machinery, into your own hands."

Caspian had shot me an exasperated look, as if I could have remotely added anything to the conversation. I hadn't even followed most of it. That was when I'd decided it was the perfect time to take a shower and go to bed, leaving the two to bicker. Mom and Soren had been deep in research mode, so it meant the boys could have a quiet moment to talk privately. I knew it would be an awkward conversation neither one of them wanted to have, because neither was great at talking about their feelings. They were like brothers, though. They'd have to talk candidly about Welsh's situation eventually.

I only hoped they'd both gotten some sleep last night. They'd both desperately needed it. Welsh's room was on the first floor, but mine and Caspian's were both upstairs. We shared a wall. After a brief period of sleep, I'd gotten up around three a.m. to use the restroom and thought I'd heard him moving around. Maybe I could get the sword to knock Caspian out if the bags under his eyes still looked too pronounced.

I replayed my conversation with Kayda. We'd brainstormed ways the boys and I could check the status of the garage without it tipping off the cats. We both pegged the sword as the best spy, assuming it was trustworthy enough to stay on task and not go off script and start murdering more shifters. Welsh was too ill to risk glamouring the sword or any of the pixies with invisibility. Not to mention that the glamour was sure to break once any of our spies were out of Welsh's range.

An hour later, the murmur of soft voices coming from the kitchen made me venture back inside. Welsh had slept, if the less-pronounced bags under his eyes were any indication, *and* had completed our glamour tonics. Mom was just setting a steaming mug of coffee in front of a wrecked-looking Caspian as the sword and I entered the kitchen. There was no sign of Soren; he must still be asleep. Which was the state any sane person should be in at six in the morning.

Mom and I made a simple breakfast of bacon, eggs, and toast. The smell of bacon roused Soren, though he didn't seem particularly happy about it. The jolly man was most definitely not a morning person.

We were just wrapping up breakfast when Julip came hurtling into the kitchen, scaring the daylights out of Caspian again.

"We're up to ten cats!" Julip said, ignoring Caspian's pleas to take her screeching down a level. "One of them is a giant tiger with a messed up right eye—like he got into a fight with a rabid raccoon and lost."

Caspian aimed an exhausted frown at me. "O'Neill?"

"Sounds like it."

I explained to the others that O'Neill had been one of the were-cats in my apartment the day the Collective had tried to have me arrested for murder. The sword had killed O'Neill's partner as well as maiming O'Neill. I couldn't imagine I was high on that guy's list of favorite people. Kayda had suspected he was trailing her for a while, too—especially in the days after Caspian and I had fled Luma.

If even a *whiff* of funny business was detected around this house, I had no doubt O'Neill would be the first one to report it to his bosses. Which could in turn get Sorceress Rhiannon into hot water with her colleagues.

Mom and Soren helped poke holes in every plan we came up with. Unfortunately, we all kept circling back to sending the unreliable sword on a reconnaissance mission. The sword was not helping its case whatsoever, as it had donned my likeness and was darting about the kitchen in what I presumed were supposed to be spy moves. It was currently ducked behind one of the dining room chairs, periodically peeking both my head and the tip of the sword over the chair's back in an effort to show how stealthy it could be.

I startled when my phone chimed in my back pocket. It was a message from Kayda.

KAYDA

You still trapped in the house?

HARLOW

Yep. Up to ten cats now. We're considering sending the sword and pixies out in a trench coat. Hopefully none of the cats will think it's unusual that the person strolling out of the gate doesn't have legs. Or a body. Or a face.

KAYDA

Be ready to go in five minutes.

HARLOW

What do you mean?

KAYDA

The garage is empty. You owe me. Aster is an absolute pain in the ass.

HARLOW

Like calls to like.

KAYDA

YOU owe me, too.

HARLOW

I still don't know what you're talking about!

KAYDA

That unidentifiable taste on your tongue? That's karma.

KAYDA

I'm assuming kickoff time will be marked by screaming.

HARLOW

I don't like being on the other side of this! A vague and mildly threatening aura is my MO, not yours.

KAYDA

Four minutes.

I cursed and shoved my phone in my pocket. "New plan! We have to be ready to go in four minutes. The garage across the street is empty. Kayda is doing … something. There's supposed to be screaming."

Welsh shrugged. "I'm into it." Turning to me, he said, "For your glamour, I strongly suggest a loose tank top and shorts. I'd rather not slather you in mayonnaise again to get you out of your pants."

"*Again?*" Soren asked at the same time my mom went, "Excuse me, what?"

Without replying, I ran upstairs to my temporary bedroom, quickly changed, shoved my toiletries and remaining clean clothes into my backpack, then hurried back out. Caspian and I almost collided in the hallway. He wore jeans, which was already odd for a guy who preferred bland khakis—especially since these were *skinny* jeans—but what was even more confusing was the floral-patterned silk blouse.

"Umm ..." was all I managed to get out.

The tips of his ears had gone pink—which complemented the blouse, honestly. "I have a closet full of clothes for glamours. Welsh can craft the tinctures faster if there aren't clothes built into the disguise, too."

I had a lot of questions—like where a person's clothes went when one used a tincture with built-in clothing—but we didn't have much time, and Caspian was already hot-footing it down the hallway toward the stairs. I scurried after him.

The six of us—sword included—huddled in a back hallway in front of the basement door.

Welsh addressed my mom and Soren. "All the tinctures you need are in the fridge and are labeled. Rotate through them as you wish. Maybe switch up who you are when you go outside so the cats don't get suspicious that they only see the same two people milling around. The duration on the labels isn't shelf life, but how long the glamour lasts. Don't take one before the previous one wears off; otherwise, you'll get stuck as a subject from a Picasso painting."

Soren paled.

"He's kidding," I said.

"Am I, though?" Welsh asked.

I honestly wasn't sure. Giving my head a clearing shake, I gave Mom a hug. "We'll be fine. Two days tops. If something goes sideways here, we'll come right back."

She sighed, squeezing me extra hard before letting go. "We'll keep up the research here, Welsh. If there's any change in your condition, let us know."

"Becoming a shadow wielder who needs to consume blood for any reason isn't a life I want," Welsh said. "If I become a legitimate threat to either one of them, I'm not going to waste time calling in my symptoms. I'm going to pursue a life in the woods." He employed an overly thoughtful air as he said, "I should research the price of yurts."

Caspian and I shared a pinched expression. We both knew that, despite the sarcasm, Welsh meant every word of that—well, maybe not the yurt part. We had to reverse or curb the effects of the corrupted magic poisoning him, because even if it didn't kill him, we could still lose him.

My phone chimed. I yanked it out of my pocket.

KAYDA

One minute.

"We gotta go," I said.

After another hurried round of goodbyes, Caspian deactivated the rune array on the basement door. A pulse of blue raced across the surface, revealing the hidden intricate designs. Caspian placed a palm flat on the door. Something deep within the metal door slid free. After a few creaks and groans, the door gave a hiss, then popped ajar. Caspian hefted it open, then took off at a jog across a short landing and down a set of dimly lit stairs. The sword shot past him into the unknown. Welsh went next, and I brought up the rear.

Just as I was wondering how Caspian felt about keeping the door to the basement unlocked and unwarded, a rune array the size of a saucer—glowing gold—zipped over my head. I didn't hear the array make contact, but I flinched hard and almost tumbled down the stairs when the door behind me slammed shut and the locks began to re-secure themselves.

The stairs led to a cavernous underground space that seemed as wide as the house above. While the basement didn't telegraph hoarder, it was heavily suggesting mad scientist. Two dozen steel worktables were arranged in neat rows—most topped by half-finished projects. The walls, unsurprisingly, were lined with crowded bookshelves. Since we were currently pelting down an aisle made by two rows of tables, I didn't have time to investigate what on earth went on down here. I saw more than a few half-formed weapons—though I couldn't tell if they were in the process of being constructed or dismantled.

Past the tables was a small fleet of vehicles arranged in a neat line, reminding me of the VHoA headquarters. There were no flashy neon-yellow Lamborghinis or fire-red mustang convertibles. They were all sensible, forgettable cars in white, black, and gray. Caspian beelined for a black minivan with a slightly dented passenger door.

Welsh produced a vial from each front pocket of his jeans. He handed the one with swirling green liquid to me. Caspian's was a translucent white.

"Throw your stuff in the back seat," Welsh said. "When the glamour is on, Harlow, you'll drive. We need Caspian in the passenger seat so his hands are free to craft arrays on the fly in case this doesn't work."

I had a lot of questions again, but I just placed my bag on the back seat, uncorked the vial, hoisted it toward the guys, and knocked it back. I had a sneaking suspicion of what this glamour was already, but I still braced myself.

I yelped when my eye-line went from level with the top of the minivan's windows to a foot over the vehicle's roof. I peered down at a Caspian who was now a pretty blond woman who had her hair styled in two French braids. Freckles dotted her cheeks and nose.

An older feminine voice to my other side pulled my gaze to a plumper, shorter version of the blond woman. "Meet Mr. and Mrs. Dun and Sue's mother."

I noted that Welsh's glamour had come with high-waisted jeans and a blouse covered in flamingos. I once again resisted the urge to ask where his clothing had gone while he was wearing something else.

My phone chimed, and I pulled it out of my shorts pocket. I was glad I'd opted to wear the elastic-waisted basketball shorts I typically only reserved for period days. They were so old, the elastic no longer had any stretch. Even still, they were tight around this draken man's thighs. My phone looked tiny in his large brown hand. The latest text wasn't from Kayda this time, but my mom.

MOM

The screaming has started.

That was it. That was her whole message.

"Time to go!" My eyes widened at the depth of my new voice.

I scrambled to the driver's side, noting that the seat was already shoved back as far as it would go. I climbed in, my head pressed against the ceiling. The keys hung in the ignition, so I cranked the engine over.

The sword zipped in through Caspian's open passenger door and tossed itself on the dashboard. I winced as its blade clacked against the windshield.

I stared blankly at it. "You can't possibly think that's a good idea. Sunlight will glint off your blade like a neon sign."

Caspian closed his door. In his high, light voice, he said, "We won't be outside for at least ten minutes. The cutlass can stow itself in a seat pocket once we reach the Duns' garage."

The blade pulsed blue, and it wiggled its entire being as if snuggling in further.

Welsh fussed in the back seat, muttering obscenities under his breath because he'd sat on an errant LEGO. He was fishing around between the seats looking for his seat-belt buckle but was only finding desiccated french fries. "This isn't *actually* the Duns' car. Why are there LEGOs and old food?" Welsh asked, though the words lost some bite due to his matronly voice.

"I believe in authenticity," Caspian said. "Children are messy."

I eyed the back seat in the rearview mirror, curious whether the car seat beside Welsh had been bought used or if Caspian had added what looked like dried jelly to various places himself.

Shaking my head, I took in the plain cement wall before us. Before I could ask, Caspian pulled open the glove box and produced what looked like a mundane garage door opener. He hit the single button. Nothing happened. The longer nothing happened, the harder my heart thudded in my too-big chest. I swore I could hear it echoing in there.

I couldn't imagine what would happen to any of us—not to mention Mom and Soren—if this little escape plan didn't work. If the cats suspected anything, they'd call the Collective. Sorceress Rhiannon had said, *"Keep out of trouble, or the entirety of the werecat force will be on you. I won't be able to stop them."*

Rhiannon may have expected that at least a few of us were planning to sneak around Luma—or leave it completely. "Keep out of trouble" meant don't get caught. Werecats surrounding the house meant the cats, the Collective, or both were hoping we'd try to wriggle away again, giving them an excuse to bring us in, even if we were technically no longer fugitives or exiled.

If this didn't work, Mom could be in a serious bind; she had legitimate enemies in the Collective. They just found me annoying.

Out of all of us, Welsh might be under the most threat if we were caught. If the Collective discovered he was on the verge of turning vamp, there was no telling what might happen to him.

I supposed I should have been happy that, despite all that, Welsh's present concern was why his fingers were sticky and smelled of apricots.

A thick dark line formed in the wall, snapping me out of my panicked thoughts. The line created three sides of a square, with the floor marking the bottom. Within a handful of seconds, the massive chunk of cement trundled up into the ceiling, revealing a tunnel that curved to the left.

Okay, maybe all the supervillain talk hadn't been totally unwarranted.

"Just follow the tunnel, love," Welsh said from the back. "It's literally impossible to get lost. Ouch. What is that?" Rustling. "*Another* LEGO?"

Said LEGO bounced off Caspian's ear.

"Ow!" He whirled to glare at the middle-aged woman in the back.

"If you kids don't knock it off, I'm turning this car around!" I bellowed.

A LEGO pinged off the back of *my* skull.

I shot a silent "Can we leave him here?" plea at the blond in the passenger seat, but Caspian was already facing forward again, working on an array. Namely the one that would activate the array on the floor of the Duns' garage. I remembered then that the floor-liquefying spell had a five-minute limit, so I hit the gas. The minivan's tires squealed on the smooth concrete.

"Easy, Furiosa!" Welsh shouted from the back.

I eased up on the accelerator and managed to make the turn ahead without shearing off a side mirror. The sword slid along the dashboard, its blade thunking into the side pillar. It pulled itself free, humming happily.

"This draken foot is made of lead." I felt like an adult behind the helm of a kid's Power Wheels. At least I didn't need to operate the car by pedaling my massive feet.

After a short distance, the tunnel curved again before leveling out.

"It's a straight shot from here," Welsh said.

Heart in my throat, I drove into the dimly lit tunnel, hoping our escape plan would work and that Sorceress Rhiannon wouldn't be forced to call in the rest of the cavalry to come after us.

Geraldine Stone's warning from what felt like a century ago replayed in my head. *"All I know is that you can't trust what the Collective says. Don't turn yourself in, all right? You run and you don't look back. If you go into a precinct, you won't come back out. I'm sure of it."*

That went double if we were dragged in, fighting tooth and nail.

I drove a little faster.

CHAPTER TWENTY-TWO

HARLOW

Logically, I knew another car wouldn't come barreling toward us from the other direction of the tunnel, but it was a really tight fit. The headlights illuminating my path provided more than enough light to see by, and yet it still felt too dark. Probably because of the whole underground thing. I'd obviously watched too many horror movies. My shoulders were tense, constantly bracing for impact with the zombie horde that had doubtless invaded the tunnel.

I cast a quick glance upward, as if I could see through the minivan's roof to the road above us. Had "the screaming" stopped? Not that I knew who had been doing the screaming to begin with. Kayda had mentioned Aster. Had Kayda recruited an additional set of pixies, with both swarms then attacking the cats like weaponized mosquitoes?

"Nothing stops a bear in his tracks faster than a pixie in his ear!" one of the pixies had said earlier. I supposed the same would be true of a werecat.

Caspian abruptly thrust both hands out in front of him, the fingernails of his slender hands painted a glittery shade of pink. The tunnel's lights winked off the diamond in his wedding ring. Magic pulsed away from his hand in the form of a disc that passed harmlessly through the windshield and zipped down the tunnel. That extra bit of light confirmed there were not, in fact, any zombies shuffling in an undead mass impeding our exit.

The tunnel abruptly ended, but thankfully I was tipped off by the painted stop sign on the wall. That, and the massive metal platform with a series of cables sprouting from each corner. The cables connected to a pulley system above the platform. I cautiously pulled the minivan onto it, warily eyeing the cables, sure they wouldn't be able to hold the weight of the car and three passengers. The platform rattled and clanked.

I craned my neck to peer out the windshield. At first I thought my vision had gone fuzzy. I realized a moment later that there was an undulating mass high above me—the liquefied concrete floor of the garage.

Caspian was in rune array construction mode again, and I watched his hands and fingers flitting through their latest dance. This array he flung upward. It flew through the roof of the car and out of sight. The platform gave a great jolt. I grasped the steering wheel in a vise grip as the minivan rocked, as if it bobbed in the sea.

As we rose, more and more of a mundane—albeit overly large —garage came into view. Metal shelves lined the walls and were stuffed with random odds and ends—paint cans, toolboxes, cleaning supplies. Large plastic tubs with labels like "Christmas stuff" and "Bronwyn's dolls" were stacked in neat columns. The garage was big enough for two cars, but the other half was taken up by an absurd amount of gym equipment.

The platform rattled into place, then rotated one hundred eighty degrees.

"Pull forward," Caspian said in his high, light voice.

I did so, clenching my teeth the whole time. Even after the back tires had cleared the platform and I watched it begin its descent in the rearview mirror, I didn't quite trust we were in the clear. As the platform descended, so too did the liquefied concrete.

The boys climbed out of the vehicle, so I reluctantly followed. In a matter of thirty seconds, the platform was back below ground, and the concrete had reformed. I tapped the smooth floor with my foot. No seams marred the floor, and the etched rune array was visible, but only just. I noticed then that my giant feet were wedged into the largest pair of high-tops I'd ever seen. Were my trusty combat boots currently floating in some interdimensional pocket?

I snapped back to the present and scanned the garage, finding Welsh and Caspian both rummaging around in bins in different areas. How often had they done this? Did the Duns find their landlord's antics to be a necessary evil they had to endure in exchange for Welsh helping them start a new life, or were they unbothered by the whole thing? Welsh hustled back to the car with a black zippered bag under his arm and a pair of tennis shoes dangling from two fingers.

"Toiletries," he said in his matronly voice before getting into the back seat again.

Caspian pulled out a black zippered bag of his own, though this one looked like a leather case an artist might keep supplies in. He hurried over to the array behind the minivan, then dropped to his knees. I lumbered over to stand beside him.

Inside the case were what looked like artist's tools—brushes, pencils, charcoal sticks, several long-stemmed matches, nail files. As mundane as they looked, even I could feel the faint aura of magic wafting off them. I watched as Caspian deftly retouched the runes, crossing from one end of the two-foot diameter circle to the other, spotting flaws and cracks that I never would have been able to find, let alone fix. After a few minutes, he stood and backed away from the array to stand beside me. The array emitted a bright burst of gold for a breath, then the light winked out. The entire array darkened, as if scoured into the concrete. Then it disappeared altogether.

He nodded once. "Ready when you are."

I looked at the floor where the array had been, then at him, then back at the floor. I honestly didn't know what to say—mostly because I suddenly felt bummed that I didn't have the discipline necessary to accomplish what he did so casually. The same went for Welsh, though at least with him, he'd had a massive head start by being born some kind of prodigy. An annoying wave of inadequacy swept over me like a tide. Here were these two powerful people going through all this fuss for magic-less, kleptomaniac me.

We were sneaking into someone else's garage to evade werecats who worked for sorcerers who never would have issued that bounty on Caspian had I not stolen the sword. All because the Collective feared my sentient, murdering sword was one of Caspian's creations.

Sure, Caspian and Welsh had had the magical Batcave set up well before me, but they were using it now to find information that could help *me*. Even with Welsh on the brink of turning into a shadow vampire, the guys were going out of their way to go on a research mission to help the sword and me be more prepared when we met with the Collective.

Caspian placed a hand on my massive elbow and craned his neck to force me to acknowledge him. I got distracted by the top of Mrs. Dun's head, hoping one day she could give me a tutorial on French braiding my hair.

He shook my arm. When I finally looked at him, he said, "If you're beating yourself up about something, stop. Whatever it is, it's unfounded. You got that same look on your face the day the three of us started plotting to uncover what was going on at the Ghost Lily. We're all in this together, all right?"

If anything, this was further proof that my poker face wasn't nearly as good as I thought it was if Caspian could still read me even while wearing someone *else's* face. I nodded tightly.

We got back into the minivan.

I went to restart the car, only to still at the sight of the empty dashboard. "Uhh ... sword?"

My seat vibrated softly.

"It's sticking out of the pocket of your seat," Welsh said. "It decapitated a Barbie as it got situated. Someone needs to take away your credit cards, Caspian."

"Says the man who spent nearly two thousand dollars on a handmade chef knife from Thailand," Caspian said as he rummaged through the glove box again.

"As if the pattern of the Merovingian-twist Damascus didn't make you weep with envy," Welsh said.

Caspian held another boxy garage door opener aloft in triumph. I had no idea if all of Caspian's glove boxes were organized by chaos or if the chaos was to keep the vehicle's interior authentic to the Duns. This was like method acting—but somehow weirder. He shot me a conspiratorial glance. "The knife is absolutely breathtaking."

"I have no clue what either of you are talking about, but given Welsh's culinary skills, I say he should have whatever overpriced gadget he wants if it keeps him cooking," I said.

Welsh's rant—about how calling the knife "overpriced" and "a gadget" was an insult to him *and* the bladesmith who created the masterpiece—was cut off by the rattle of the garage door beginning its ascent. Caspian's manicured thumb was still resting against the clicker's button.

I'd only inched halfway onto the driveway when I suddenly hit the brakes. A werecat was galloping down the middle of the street. It didn't pay us any heed, as it was currently preoccupied by the half-dozen badgers clinging to its coat. A large pack of the black-and-white beasts—at least twenty strong—went sprinting the other direction, streaming around the badger-adorned cat like water around a boulder. The pack passed the mouth of the driveway in a matter of moments, then disappeared around the low hedge that ringed the Duns' lawn. I cranked my window down.

"Ah," I said after a beat. "*There's* the screaming."

"Yes," Caspian said slowly. "But are those the battle cries of the badgers or the terror-stricken screams of the cats?"

Another shriek sounded.

"Definitely both," Welsh said.

I eased the minivan to the edge of the driveway. A few of Caspian's neighbors were standing on their porches or peering through windows at the ruckus. The number of cats had jumped to at least a dozen. The badgers numbered at least fifty and had been joined by a half-dozen raccoons and at least one opossum.

Caspian hit the garage door button again and then stowed the clicker back in the glove box. Once the door behind me was closed, I pulled onto the street, driving at a snail's pace, as giant rodents were galloping across the street and down the sidewalks. I'd gotten past two houses, and thought we were in the clear when a black jaguar darted in front of the minivan and stood its ground, head bowed. I hit the brakes yet again.

Once it had apparently decided I wasn't going to turn it into roadkill, the jaguar seamlessly shifted from cat to human. The guy wasn't anyone I recognized. He held up a hand in the universal sign of "don't move," then strolled to the driver's-side window. I rolled it back down.

"Good morning, sir," the werecat said to me. He was fair-skinned, blond, and his icy blue eyes swept over me not with suspicion, necessarily, but curiosity. Welsh couldn't roll down the window in the sliding door of the minivan, so he wedged his rosy-cheeked face between the front seats. "Ladies," the officer added, addressing the guys.

Though the officer had the same feline confidence as all werecats I'd met, he'd developed a twitching-eye tic that flared every time there was a high-pitched shriek in the distance. Which was … often. He flinched minutely then, looking toward his feet, like a swimmer who'd just felt the unsettling sensation of seaweed tickling an ankle. He'd undoubtedly have badger-themed nightmares for a while.

"Did you just leave 9621, sir?" the officer asked, watching me again.

I had no idea if that was the address.

"Yes, officer," Caspian said, leaning toward me and the cat, and putting Mrs. Dun's pearly whites to good use. "What's all the commotion about?"

A primal roar sounded, and I glanced at the rearview mirror just in time to see a puma go racing up the trunk of a tree with frightening speed, followed quickly by a raccoon shooting out of the canopy like a T-shirt shot from a cannon. Hopefully the offending raccoon hadn't broken too many bones on the way down. I got the sense that the cats had lost most of their professionalism by now.

When I returned my focus to the werecat loitering by the window, I noted that he'd produced a cell phone–like device from a pocket on his utility belt. He tapped away at the screen, giving me another flashback of O'Neill and his now dead partner. I really hoped the murder weapon stayed snuggled into its seat pouch and didn't draw the cat's scrutiny toward the *inside* of the car.

The officer looked up, making eye contact with each of us in turn. "Coaldon Dun, Susan Dun, and Julie Farr?"

"That's us," Caspian said cheerfully.

"And where are you three headed this morning?"

Welsh asked, "Is it customary for werecat guards to ask residents of their own neighborhoods about their personal traveling habits?"

"As you can see, *ma'am*," the officer said, gesturing to the continuing pandemonium behind us, "tensions are high, and we're making sure everyone stays safe."

"With all due respect, *sir*," Welsh said, "you didn't ask if we felt safe. You asked where we were going."

His eyes squinted in a vaguely feline way before craning his neck to presumably peer past Welsh's head and into the back seat. His gaze cut sharply to Caspian. "You have two children, is that right?" He consulted his device briefly. "Bronwyn and Tanner?"

"That's correct," Caspian said, expertly employing a tone that implied this mother did not appreciate her children's names coming out of his mouth.

"Where are they so early in the morning during summer break, if not with their parents and grandmother?" the officer asked.

"Fishing at Sycamore Island with my husband," Welsh said without hesitation. "It's a public mundane park in Madera County. We go every summer."

"*We?*" the officer asked.

"My father takes them for a few days so my husband and I can get a break, and then we join them later," Caspian said.

"Is that where you're headed now?" the officer asked me.

"Preparatory shopping," I said.

From the back, Welsh asked, "Do you need our shopping itinerary, too?"

I must have made a "Yikes!" face because the officer winced at me minutely, as if to say "I'm sorry you're stuck in the car with her." My expression had more to do with wondering if Welsh was getting mouthy because his mask emboldened him or if he was mirroring the real Julie Farr's personality.

Going on a hunch, I slightly gestured my head toward the back seat and then very dramatically rolled my eyes.

The officer tamped down a smile. He mulled something over, then shot me a conspiratorial look. A "just between us guys" look. "How well do you know your landlord?"

"Mr. Waterstone?" Caspian asked—his question a little too loud and with an edge to it—before I could get a word out, which was just as well, because I'd almost used Caspian's real name.

The officer worked his jaw.

"He's a pretty quiet guy," Caspian said. I leaned back a bit, and he leaned forward so he could better offer a sweet smile to the testy cat. "Keeps to himself. But he's a good landlord. Things get fixed in a timely manner. As long as we pay on time, we hardly hear from him."

The cat pointedly looked at me. "Has he ever used another name?"

"Other than Waterstone?" I asked. "No, sir. He's a formal guy. Not really one for casual chit-chat."

Welsh chimed in, his head still hovering between the front seats. "No matter how many times I've asked him to call me Julie, he insists on calling me Mrs. Farr," he said. "Is all this hullabaloo because of Mr. Waterstone somehow?"

The cat leveled a flat-lipped stare at Welsh, then went back to tapping at his screen. When he flipped it around to me, my picture glared back. It was a still from that newscast ages ago, when it was broadcast to all of Luma that the magic in the stolen dragon sword had turned me into a werecat-murdering lunatic with an unquenchable taste for vengeance—or something equally dramatic. "Have you seen this woman at your landlord's home or seen the two of them together? Or that sword she's holding in the picture?"

"Oh my!" Welsh said. "Isn't that Harlow Fletcher? She's the one who helped free those kidnapped fae teens, isn't she? Can't say I agree with how she went about it, but those girls are home now because of her. My friend's daughter's niece is best pals with one of the kidnapped girl's little sister's best friends. They sure are glad she's home."

I developed an eye tic of my own trying to follow the family tree of Welsh's made-up acquaintance.

The werecat didn't look remotely pleased with Welsh's admiration. "Be that as it may, Harlow Fletcher is still under investigation for the murder of *four* shifters. Hero of kidnapped teens or not, she's a mass murderer. She's also a reported confidant of your landlord."

Caspian giggled delicately. "Mr. Waterstone? Are you sure? He brought over a piece of our mail that he'd opened by accident. He told me he wouldn't hold it against me if I reported him for mail tampering. I don't even think that law applies in hubs, but he was steadfast in his conviction that it was within my rights to report him for the felony. Does that really sound like someone who would associate with a so-called serial killer?"

The werecat's nostrils flared as he regarded Caspian, but then his focus resettled on me. "And what about you, Mr. Dun? Have you seen Harlow Fletcher at your landlord's residence? Has he ever mentioned her?"

"He—" Caspian started.

A growl reverberated from the werecat. "I was not addressing *you*, Mrs. Dun. You've hardly let your husband get a word in edgewise."

I leaned toward the cat and cupped my mouth to whisper, "I said something similar a few days ago and spent a week on the couch. Maybe they'll let me talk if an officer gives me permission." I used my free hand to mimic a yapping mouth.

The werecat chuckled good-naturedly. He lowered his voice, resting an elbow on the windowsill and shielding himself behind my massive shoulders. "You seen any weird shit go down across the street? Especially today?"

"Honestly, no," I rumbled. "Other than the weird shit happening right now." Another screech sounded behind us. "I truly wish I had something to tell you. The guy is ... abnormal. But he's either straight-laced to the point of being duller than watching paint dry, or he hides his extracurriculars well. He's always really nice to the ladies but acts like I'm not even there, you know? I'm the one who's paying the rent, but I might as well be the hired help."

The werecat nodded sagely, as if his estimation of Caspian's/Mr. Waterstone's personality had just been confirmed.

"So, uhh …" I said, employing a similar conspiratorial tone, "what's going on out here? Were the badgers causing problems and the werecats were called in to break up their party? Or were you all here first and the badgers attacked? I know they're unhinged by nature, but attacking law enforcement for shits and giggles seems loopy, even for them."

The cycle of emotions that flitted across the man's face said he didn't know whether or not to be affronted by my veiled accusation that the cats were the aggressors in this situation, what with us being united in our mutual distaste of chatty women. Maybe he was just trying to decide whether he wanted to lie to his new friend.

Eventually he schooled his features back to a more neutral countenance. "Let's just say your landlord isn't who you think he is. If you hear or see anything odd in the next few days—doesn't matter if it's extreme or mild—please let me know." He stood to full height and produced a business card from his breast pocket.

I took the card, cataloging that the guy's name was Derrick Andover, and then passed it to Caspian. Derrick watched the card uneasily, as if his newborn babe had just been sent downriver into shark-infested waters.

"This will be announced soon enough," Derrick said, still keeping his tone low, "but there'll be a reissue of the reward for any information about Harlow that leads to an arrest. You see anything, call that number and extension. The call will go right to me. You've got one of the best vantage points of anyone in the city to help us catch her. Your tip pays off …" He shrugged as if his next statement meant little. "Then I get a bonus by way of a finder's fee. Not to mention extra cash for us both if Mr. Waterstone is involved."

"What kind of money we talking here?"

A light hand landed on my arm. "Oh, honey. I can't imagine Mr. Waterstone—"

I turned to Caspian so forcibly, the minivan rocked. "How about *I* hang on to that card, babe."

"But—"

I thrust out a large hand, palm up. When Caspian merely pouted at me, I curled and uncurled my fingers in rapid succession.

Huffing, Caspian plucked the card from where he'd placed it under the sun visor and placed it in my waiting palm.

Card held between two giant fingers, I returned my attention to the officer. "Safer with me." I chuckled. "Maybe when we get back, I'll post up in the bedroom with my binoculars."

The officer looked like he wanted to hug me.

"Assuming I can get them away from the shopping center before noon," I muttered. "And with any money left. Spend it faster than I can make it!"

Caspian whirled in his seat to face his "mother." He and Welsh both started up a tirade, talking over each other as they ranted about my disrespect. Honestly most of it was incomprehensible, but the vibe was enough to make Derrick back up several steps until he was on the curb.

"Goddess speed, Mr. Dun," the officer said. "Hope to hear from you soon."

"Thanks," I said, sighing deeply. "I'm gonna need it." With another epic eye roll as the volume of the bickering women increased, I waved at Derrick in parting, then headed down the street.

Caspian and Welsh instantly stopped fake raging.

The battle between badger and cat had mostly moved down the street—past Caspian's front gate—so I was able to speed away at a reasonable pace without worrying about running over a shifter or rodent.

After a full minute passed without incident, Caspian gusted a sigh. "I feel a little bad. Sue's not like that at all. Julie isn't, either, though she has her moments."

I said, "I guarantee you, even if you were acting overly rational, that guy would have still said you two were acting hysterical."

"I was doing a little back-seat detective work," Welsh said, waving his phone in the air for a moment, "and Officer Andover is currently going through a contentious divorce. He cheated on his wife, his mistress found out he was married and informed the wife, and now the wife's trying to get full custody of the kids. He reportedly said she can keep the kids as long as he doesn't have to pay for them. He's clearly very bitter."

"Maybe a badger will bite him," I suggested hopefully.

My seat vibrated softly. I decided that was sword-speak for "Ditto."

In addition to multiple garage clickers, the chaotic glove box also housed a travel talisman. Once we were in the clear as far as being chased down by werecats, Caspian rolled down his window and clapped the magnetized device on the car door.

"Wake me up when we get there," Welsh said once we'd made it out of Luma. "Sleep, uhhh … can help just as much as food as far as replenishing my magical energy goes. But, uhh, it usually results in pretty horrific nightmares, so if I wake up thrashing, I'm not turning shadow vamp. I'm just being mentally shredded by the possibilities of what I'll become *should* I turn."

As much as I wanted to slap Welsh for being an asshole most of the time, these fleeting glimpses of his vulnerability scared the crap out of me.

"It's your fault for having such a fucked-up imagination," I said.

Welsh chuckled.

I hazarded a glance at Caspian. This face wore worry more plainly than Caspian's natural one, and that made the pit in my stomach drop even further.

I knew there was nothing we could do for Welsh yet. We needed more information. Mom's, Soren's, and VHoA's contacts and resources had to hold the answer. Hopefully getting Welsh out of Luma would calm his anxiety, at least a little bit.

My anxiety shifted priorities as we drove. I worried less about my mom and Kayda after Caspian read me texts from them both.

The badgers, led by my old client Fabian, had all either scattered or been arrested. Kayda assured me that even the ones who'd been thrown in jail cells had been delighted by the outcome of their assault on the unsuspecting werecats.

Mom and Soren had each been out front on the porch, in clear view of the pandemonium on the street, while wearing my and Caspian's likenesses. The pixies had reported back that a werecat had made a phone call post-mass-badger-arrest and told one of his superiors that "Harlow and Caspian were watching the whole thing, ma'am. If they orchestrated the attack, I don't know why. No one has been seen leaving the house last night or this morning. We've been watching it from all sides. If they were going to bolt, it would have been overnight. No one has visited the house, either —not even delivery drivers. Maybe this was all just a distraction or a precursor for something else, but for now, we think the badgers were just bored, ma'am. This isn't the first time they've done this."

At least for now, we were in the clear in Luma.

Now my anxieties transferred to what lay ahead at Lake Nacimiento. I had to somehow be bait for and not be baited *by* a grouchy siren with an appetite for human women.

When I'd changed into loose shorts and a tank top at Welsh's behest earlier, I should have changed undergarments, too. If our ability to get useful information out of this siren involved seduction, I feared my current pair of granny panties could very well ruin our chances.

CHAPTER TWENTY-THREE

KAYDA

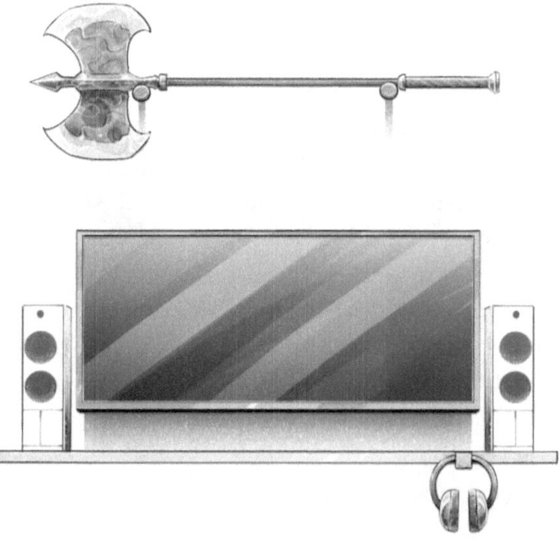

Kayda smiled to herself as Quaid nearly fell out of his chair as she dramatically plopped her large frame into the seat beside him. He jumped again when Marisol took up a seat on his other side, perched on the desk with her arms crossed and a Cheshire Cat grin aimed his way.

Quaid shoved his glasses into his hair, then rolled his chair away from the desk until he had a clear view of Kayda and Marisol both. "As much as I've dreamed about two women coming at me at once, I have a feeling this isn't my fantasy come true." His gaze flicked between the two women.

Kayda asked, "You still interested in finding out what happened to Kessler?"

He sat bolt upright. "Did you crack the case?"

Kayda regarded Marisol, who shrugged. Marisol was up to speed on it all now. Shortly after talking to Harlow this morning, and getting a heavy dose of reality about Welsh, Kayda had phoned Marisol. Kayda didn't know the nature of Marisol's friendship with Welsh, but the other woman had burst into tears at the news that Welsh was sick. It took a *lot* to make Marisol cry.

Kayda had given her the rundown on Kessler, Welsh, and what little she could cobble together about shadow vampires, as Harlow had taken to calling them. Kayda knew if anyone could track down all the related conspiracy theories with the accuracy and speed of a bloodhound, it was Marisol. Because that's all they had at the moment—theories and anecdotal stories. But they needed all hands on deck if Welsh's—and possibly Kessler's— days were numbered.

Marisol, naturally, dove into the story headfirst, and in a matter of twelve hours had become even more obsessed with what fate had befallen Kessler than Kayda and Quaid combined. That was when the women had hatched their plan. They still hadn't decided who should divulge said plan to Quaid, though they *had* agreed to mess with the guy as much as possible along the way.

Kayda thought it said a lot about Quaid that when Kayda had suggested an ambush, Marisol had readily agreed, saying, "It'll be nice to turn the tables for once."

Marisol addressed Quaid now. "On one of the San Diego subthreads on the forum, there're a few pictures of Kessler from two years ago. They aren't the clearest shots and are more paparazzi-like since the VHoA member who took them was just gathering info from afar. Looks like they were trying to photograph the hybrids at a bar and caught Kessler in the background. He went through a lot of changes during the years he was with the vamps, so it took some digging to track down all the posts potentially connected to him.

"It looks like he wound up in San Diego within a week of being enthralled and hooked on Bliss. We got lucky that so many of Luma's kidnapped girls—at least the batch we found—were kept close to home and hadn't been trafficked across the country like Kessler was," Marisol said. "Anyway, he never divulges his parentage in his videos, but based on the photos and posts I could find, I think he's half nyad. Not a super accurate label, since fae-realm-born water nymphs have their own culture and lore, of course, but that's the closest term we have for it."

Marisol hadn't mentioned anything about Kessler's heritage when they'd talked this morning. "Did you figure all that out this afternoon?" Kayda asked.

Marisol's cheeks went rosy. "I did a *lot* of digging after we talked. His username is 'biologically_framed_echoes.' *Bioframe* is a popular RPG game, and the water elemental character is named Echo. In one of Kessler's earlier videos, he talked about how gaming was his go-to coping mechanism because it was the only thing he could find that turned off his brain when his PTSD kicked in. He has a throwaway line about *Bioframe* in video seven, but his handle would suggest he's a big fan of the game. He said, 'Playing Echo feels so meta because his struggle to escape in the end game isn't the only thing I'm echoing when I play him.'"

"What the hell does *that* mean?" Quaid asked.

But Kayda got it, and she was a little embarrassed that she hadn't caught it, too. In her defense, she hadn't played *Bioframe*. Single-player games weren't her first choice lately; she was in her MMORPG era, and her heart belonged to *Mangrin's Gate*. "What made you jump to nyad over a water witch, though?"

"His ears," Marisol said. "The ridiculously gorgeous face."

"Ugh, you too?" Quaid muttered.

Marisol ignored him. "A deep dive into the *Bioframe* wiki revealed Echo was a nyad when the game launched. Early access players discovered that maxing out the skill tree in one particular path basically made him a god."

"They nerfed him?" Kayda asked.

"Yep. Within a month of launch. They turned him into a generic water elemental. The early artwork for Echo, though, looked so strikingly like Kessler, I honestly wouldn't be surprised if he was somehow the inspiration."

"This conversation both confuses and arouses me," Quaid said.

Kayda shot Marisol a look. "We don't *have* to take him with us. The only argument for telling him the plan was that he's the one who told us about Kessler in the first place. You're a hells of a lot more loyal than me."

Marisol snorted. "You're more loyal than a golden retriever, and you know it."

Kayda scowled at her. "Did you just call me a dog?"

"I find myself aroused again."

Marisol abruptly stood. "Yeah, fuck it. He stays here."

Kayda made to move, but Quaid shot to his feet, hands out in placation.

"I'm sorry! I want in, whatever this is," Quaid said. "Y'all are just saying so much without saying anything. It's really stressing me out."

Marisol nodded to herself and sat on the corner of the desk again. "Huh. You were right, Kay. That actually worked."

Kayda didn't know what Marisol was talking about, but she rolled with it anyway. "Told you." She leaned toward the nearest computer screen to make a dramatic show of checking the time. "Happened five minutes ahead of schedule, too."

"Ugh," Marisol said and stood up long enough to fish something out of her back pocket.

Kayda reached out a palm just in time for Marisol to slap a

five-dollar bill into it. "Pleasure doing business with you," Kayda said with a nod.

"Yeah, yeah," Marisol muttered as she sat back down. "I'll get it back on the next one."

Quaid tightly crossed his arms, offended by the nonexistent slight.

Kayda asked, "How does the nyad thing factor into this?"

"It'll be easier to show you," Marisol said, hunching over Quaid's keyboard since his chair was still scooted several feet away.

Kayda watched as Marisol expertly clicked through the forum and pulled up a post from last year. A quick skim of the text above the video told Kayda that a VHoA member had been experimenting with using a body-cam during a raid. Kayda knew some chapters were adamant about their use, while others argued they were too expensive—especially given how often they were destroyed.

After Marisol hit play, Kayda had her own doubts about the body-cam's effectiveness. The footage was choppy, as the wearer of the cam was running into a building behind a single-file line of black-clad people charging ahead of him. While Kayda usually associated vampires with opulent settings and wealth, the warehouse the VHoA members ran into was squalid. Dilapidated factory equipment hulking below smashed-up windows, towering stacks of broken pallets, sagging piles of cardboard boxes, and rows of dirty mattresses lying flat on the stained and moss-encrusted cement floor. Signs of human habitation were scattered in places—heaps of clothes, snuffed-out cooking pits, a few freestanding dirt-smeared bathtubs half full of stopped-up murky water. The humans in question didn't lurch to their feet from those filthy mattresses like one would expect when their makeshift home was raided by men and women in tactical gear and armed with magic-infused weapons. But Kayda knew they were all enthralled and/or hopped up on Bliss. She didn't spot hybrids anywhere, and neither did the VHoA team; they scattered from their tight line and fanned out around the warehouse. They shouted to each other, searching for the vampires. In the periphery of the camera's limited view, the occasional VHoA member dropped to the side of a comatose victim, either trying to rouse them from their stupor or merely checking vitals.

Kayda saw the incoming threat even before the man wearing the body-cam did. A dark shape dropped from the ceiling of the warehouse and seamlessly blended in with the shadows of the already dark building. Ahead, the body of a VHoA member—marked by the golden glow of their machete's blade—was hurled across the camera's view. A clamor sounded to the right. The camera's wearer whipped that way. A yelp sounded to the left. Skittering shapes crawled down walls, launched off stacked pallets, and flung themselves out of the shadows onto unsuspecting VHoA members.

The scene descended into chaos, the feeling amplified by the erratic movements of the body-cam as the wearer fought for his life. He eventually was hurled across the warehouse where his fall was broken by the unmoving body of one of his colleagues. The impact shattered the camera, abruptly cutting off the cacophony of screams, feral chittering, and people's dying breaths.

Kayda shuddered and sat back.

"Did you miss it?" Marisol asked, gaze flicking back and forth between Kayda and Quaid.

"Miss what? Who I was five minutes ago before I saw that?" Quaid asked. "Because yes."

"Same," Kayda muttered.

Marisol returned to the video, scrolled back half a minute, and then hit play again. Kayda reluctantly leaned forward.

"Watch in the background this time," Marisol said. "It's coming up on the right side, in the back ... wait for it ... there!" She hit pause.

Kayda scanned the slightly blurry still image, wishing her heightened sight could somehow work to make the picture clearer. But as her vision adjusted, she saw it: Kessler, partly obscured behind a bulky, broken-down machine, standing behind a crouching feral who appeared to be protecting Kessler from an oncoming trio of sword-wielding VHoA members. Kessler, who had his arm outstretched, his head thrown back, and a veritable tsunami rising behind him. The towering wave was cresting a few feet above Kessler's head. At first blush, the whitish markings on the wave could have been confused for moonlight cascading in from the various broken windows, but the longer Kayda looked at the image, the more she was sure it was froth from churning water.

Churning water that looked to be made of ink—or, she supposed, shadows.

Marisol started and stopped the video in quick succession, moving the image by only a frame at a time. Now Kessler's hand was thrust in front of him and the shadow wave had shot forward *and* had shifted to the right, the charging team of VHoA members directly in its path now. A frame later, the trio was engulfed by the shadow wave.

Marisol unpaused the video, and the remaining two seconds played out. Kayda still got the shivers as the camera abruptly and violently met its end. She opted not to ask Marisol if she knew the fate of the camera's wearer.

"So we're thinking," Kayda said slowly, "that the fae who are turned end up with a magical skill that's some combination of their innate skill and whatever the blood-poison does to them? Assuming it doesn't kill them outright."

Marisol nodded. "I'm guessing the weaker the fae—as far as magic goes—the less likely they are to turn. Nyads are rare, but they're also inherently powerful, especially when they have access to water. All this time, I thought hybrids didn't turn their fae victims simply because they couldn't. Plus, why turn them and then lose them as a food source? Undiluted bloodlines must appeal to hybrids the most, as there's more magic in the blood. But maybe there's a fine line where the sheer power in some of their victims is too great to pass up the chance to turn one of them to their side. Especially if it's a hybrid in league with the Shades—Goddess only knows what those lunatics are up to."

Two things kept cycling through Kayda's head. One was that Welsh's power getting a shadow revamp—pun *sort of* intended—could be terrifying. Kayda thought of the shadow imps that she and her friends had fought off that night in the zoo. Those hadn't been able to physically hurt anyone, and yet Jo had said that after getting a jolt of power from Welsh's blood, the vamp *could* inflict damage with his shadows. She recalled Marisol's story about the shadow monster that had pounded its fists against a veil, and while it couldn't get through, it still had enough of a physical presence to ripple the magic and shake the earth. What unholy twist would shadow magic give Welsh's unprecedented ability?

The other thought was far more hopeful. In that video, Kessler had been under the thrall of the vampires, and his water-based magic had been twisted to be used against the very people who had been there to save him. Yet, two years later, Kessler had been back to "normal." Black hadn't swirled in the whites of his eyes. Shadows hadn't crept from him like a fog. Which meant that, even if the blood poisoning turned Welsh into a vamp, there was a way back.

Of course that didn't account for the possibility of Welsh not surviving turning at all, but Kayda wouldn't allow herself to dwell on that. They weren't losing Welsh. Period. End of story.

"This doesn't change anything for me," Marisol said, snapping Kayda out of her bouncing thoughts. "Whatever happened to Kessler could hold a key to figuring out how to help Welsh. We need to go to San Diego and meet up with the chapter there. They've got some good leads."

"I'm still in," Quaid said. "All the way. I don't know who this Welsh guy is, but I'm still in."

Kayda nodded once. "We'll take a telepad from here to a piano store near downtown San Diego. The average mundane never goes into a piano store, so it's a good front for hiding a telepad station."

Marisol added, "We'll rent a car and stay in the VHoA headquarters there. Fingers crossed that we'll only be gone for a couple of days, but the gang can hold down the fort here while I'm gone. Hopefully things stay quiet on the feral front here until then. Pack a go-bag, Quaid. We leave in an hour."

The guy was out of his chair and darting out of the War Room as soon as Marisol finished speaking.

Marisol laughed, watching Quaid go, but she sobered quickly. "Am I a terrible friend that I'm more worried that what's happening to Welsh and Kessler is a new phase of something we won't understand in time to stop it than I am about Welsh himself?"

Kayda shook her head. "That stubborn bastard won't die on us. Knowing our luck, he'll become even more of a threat than Lachlan and his Shades. He'll be fine either way. We won't be."

Marisol sighed deeply. "You really *do* suck at pep talks."

"Consistency is a positive trait, right?"

Without a word, Marisol walked out of the room.

"Guess not," Kayda muttered.

CHAPTER TWENTY-FOUR

HARLOW

Caspian had been calling out directions while I drove, but now that we were closer to the lake, I finally asked, "Where exactly are we going? I'm assuming the reports didn't include addresses for the witnesses."

"First, we're going to drop our stuff off at the vacation rental Welsh got," Caspian said.

"You'd better appreciate the digs, too. It's only five minutes from the lake," Welsh said from the back, his matronly voice still in place. "I had to do a whole lot of sweet-talking over the phone with the Airbnb host to get her to let us book so last minute. You know how I feel about sweet-talking."

The fact that we were traveling on a weekday helped, too. I'd assume lakeside rentals on the weekends during the summer were booked out weeks, if not months, in advance. I'd also never say as much out loud, but I knew Welsh could be sweet as pie when he wanted something.

"Well, thank you," I rumbled from the driver's seat.

"You're welcome," Welsh said. "I get the master."

Caspian laughed, his voice light and pleasant. "I'm sure everyone will be comfortable. The place sleeps six, right? Even the cutlass can have its own room."

My seat vibrated.

After an hour and a half, Caspian directed me to turn onto a street off the freeway. We cruised up a two-lane road lined on each side by pale yellow grasses and dark-green shrubs and trees. Low wire fencing separated the road from the expanse of dried-out fields and small rolling hills. Cows lounged in the shade beside creeks or lazily grazed along the hillside.

Switchbacks and rutted roads with a few low blind drops carried us farther and farther from the highway. Empty expanses of untamed wilderness abruptly gave way to sprawling vineyard estates tucked behind elegant black gates adorned with artfully rendered logos featuring grapevines or leaping horses.

We turned onto G14, the two-lane road now lined with Spanish moss–laden trees. An abandoned barn hulked in a field, its doors missing, reminiscent of a monster's gaping mouth. Bee boxes dotted an empty field. Horses stood by a fence along the road, watching the world pass them by.

The road was often deserted in both directions, which was good, as our glamours were due to wear off before we reached the lake. New and old pickups passed us in equal measure, some hauling boats. Welsh warned us when the change was imminent, so I was able to pull over before it happened. After I was suddenly a foot shorter, I adjusted the seat and the rearview and side mirrors, and then I was off again. Thankfully the change hadn't happened while another car was passing us, or the shock of seeing people shifting forms could have sent a rubbernecker into a ditch.

Unfortunately for Caspian, he was still clad in skinny jeans and a floral top since his glamour hadn't come with built-in clothes. I didn't pretend to understand it.

"I didn't consider what would happen when the glamour wore off," Caspian said, tugging morosely at a tassel that hung from his blouse. "You suggested which roles we'd play and what we should wear for exactly this reason, didn't you?"

Welsh snickered on and off for a good ten minutes.

When we reached a fork in the road—one direction leading toward the lake entrance itself and the other to a dam road, Caspian directed me to the right. The lake glittered like a smattering of diamonds to my left. I'd never seen anything like it in real life—only in movies and TV shows. The silver screen hadn't done it any justice. I was suddenly desperate to see the ocean. I didn't even care *which* ocean.

"Eyes on the road, please!" came Welsh's familiar grumpy voice from the back.

I swerved back into my lane. The curving road inching up the hillside eventually led us to a narrow road to the left marked by a sign that announced "Vacation Rentals!" A plastic box was attached to one of the posts and packed with flyers. Welsh instructed me to turn onto the road, though after only a few feet, the path was blocked by a closed metal gate.

"One sec …" Welsh said and let himself out the sliding door of the minivan.

He walked a few feet ahead of the idling car's bumper to a pole with a keypad attached—much like the one outside Caspian's gate. Welsh consulted his phone before tapping in a code.

The gate gave a groan, then started its slow swing inward.

After Welsh was situated in the back again, I crept forward, easing down the curving, well-paved path. If the gate and "Private Property" signs hadn't already been a clue, the gorgeous view told me that the rentals on this side of the lake weren't cheap.

The house in question was a one-story farm-style home. The

exterior was lined with wooden siding, and the windows were strikingly accented by large round stones that seemed affixed by magic. I pulled the car into a small parking lot near the house and climbed out, gaping as I turned in a slow circle. Massive trees dotted the property, the lake glittered in the distance, and I couldn't hear a car, siren, or airplane. It was so peaceful, it was as if we'd been transported to another planet.

The sword zipped out of the still-open door of the minivan and took off like a shot around the side of the house and out of view. Hopefully the mundane owner of the rental didn't have security cameras that she checked often. Could we claim the sword was a really unique, high-tech drone?

I turned to Welsh, who had a small smile on his otherwise usually impassive face. "I appreciate the digs. I haven't even seen the inside and I already appreciate it. Hell, I think there's a wrap-around porch. I'd be happy sleeping out there, even."

His smile went full-watt, and my stomach flipped a little. It was nice to see him happy. "There are wild pigs out here. Some are rumored to be puakas. They're pig-like demons who wander near bodies of water at night. They have acidic saliva, and if they catch you, they can literally lick your skin from your bones."

I swallowed hard. "You're joking."

"I never joke about pig demons," Welsh said cheerfully.

I squinted at Caspian over the hood of the car. "Is he joking?"

"About pig demons?" Caspian asked, the slight breeze tousling the ruffles of his collar. "No, never."

"I hate you both," I declared and then set about getting my stuff out of the car as fast as possible, even though we were hours away from nightfall.

As I passed behind the minivan, whose door Caspian had just pulled open, I eyed the small stockpile of electronics. I wondered if such a setup was always back there and if similar sets of equipment were in the trunks of *all* the gassed-up cars in Caspian's Batcave. The second sword's box, coated in a thick patina, looked even older lying next to the gleaming black gadgets.

There was also a pair of coolers in the back. One of the boys must have been loading up the car in the middle of the night. My bets were on Caspian.

Welsh keyed a code into the front door and gestured us in. It was a lovely, tidy house with a full kitchen, three bathrooms, six bedrooms, living room, den, sunroom, and wraparound deck. The décor was some combination of cozy dated farmhouse and simple modern design. The color scheme favored black, white, and beige, with bright pops of red, green, or yellow by way of throw pillows, vases, and oversize pots brimming with wide-leafed plants.

I picked a bedroom with a pair of doors that opened onto the deck. Aerial photographs of the lake hung on two of the walls, one from last year, and a black-and-white one from the seventies. After tossing my bag onto the fluffy white comforter on the queen-size bed, I fired off a text to my mom, letting her know we'd made it safely.

MOM

Glad to hear it. Let Caspian know it's been quiet here, though there are still at least five cats loitering outside at any given time.

HARLOW

Anything illuminating in the research?

MOM

Not yet.

The sword zipped into the room then, flipped itself into the inverted position, and tapped the comforter with its hilt. I thought it was trying to communicate with me, but when it bounced higher, did a flip in midair, and then landed on its hilt again, I realized it was just hopping on the bed like an excited kid on Christmas morning.

"Don't shred the bedding, okay? Welsh will make *me* pay for the damages," I said.

The blade glowed blue as the sword performed a complicated whirling spin before landing hilt-first on the bed again.

Rolling my eyes, I returned to my texts.

HARLOW

Have you heard of a puaka?

MOM

Sure. Nocturnal, flesh-eating pig demons.
They're from earthen lore, though, not fae.

I heaved a breath. A lot of what mundanes labeled as demonic were often just spirits or poltergeists, not beings who'd slipped into this realm from a hellscape dimension. Rumor had it that creatures who wound up in this realm due to the Glitch and who fit the description of demons, found they could live in relative peace in places like abandoned mundane buildings and old growth forests. Interaction with mundanes was rare, and if the creatures *did* cross paths with a human, they really leaned into the demonic persona to make sure the curious humans didn't come back.

Though some, of course, returned with film crews. Only the most stubborn stuck around when high-tech equipment was erected in their territory; most simply relocated.

MOM

There might be fae-born wild boar out there, though. They don't eat flesh but they ARE extremely territorial and have stealth power. A vampire enclave in Georgia thought they were under assault by a rival clan until they realized it was actually a band of vengeful pigs. They were pretty embarrassed but at least they solved the mystery before they went to war. Keep your eyes peeled. You won't know you're being gored by a wild boar until there's a tusk through your thigh.

HARLOW

I love these sweet mother/daughter chats. What do normal moms and daughters talk about?

MOM

I don't know. Planning brunch trips followed by getting mani pedis?

HARLOW

...that sounds amazing.

MOM

I'd commit a heinous crime for a pedicure. I have the feet of a gargoyle

HARLOW

Is Soren a foot guy? If so, we need to remedy the feet problem ASAP.

MOM

You blame me for being the reason for our weird conversations but you're at least 60% of the problem, child.

HARLOW

The disrespect!

MOM

Check the local shops there. It's not common to sell pig repellent, so if you see any, grab some. It means the locals know their pig population is aggressive, even if they don't understand why

HARLOW

Copy that. Thanks, Mom.

MOM

Stay safe

HARLOW

You too

I fired off a "We made it!" text to Kayda too, but after five minutes, she still hadn't replied. I only had one person left on my list.

HARLOW

So things got weird when we got to Luma so I left again. But just for a little bit! I'll let you know when this Tower meeting actually happens

FELIX

I'm honestly relieved to hear your meeting was postponed. Tensions are thick here. I'm not even sure what the hell is going on. There's infighting among the sorcerers. There's infighting among the cats. I've been avoiding the office as much as I can.

HARLOW

Here's to hoping it gets canceled altogether

FELIX

BTW, did you have anything to do with a pack of werecats being attacked by badger shifters?

HARLOW

Sorry, I gotta go! The reception is really bad. Crackle, crackle!

FELIX

I hastily pocketed my phone and wandered out of my claimed room toward the sound of voices, leaving the sword to its own devices. I passed through the open-plan living room into the dining room, where Welsh and Caspian were setting up that impressive array of electronics on the long wooden table. Caspian had since changed back into one of his signature outfits of khaki pants and a button-up shirt—today's a wild shade of eggshell.

There were two giant monitors, a computer tower, a laptop, and several football-sized black boxes that pulsed with dark blue magic even I could see. I came to a stop at the head of the table and crossed my arms, waiting for one of them to pause in their nerdy chat long enough to notice me.

I caught things like "MPN" and "magical signature router" but otherwise didn't understand the technical mumbo jumbo Welsh was prattling on about. Frankly, Caspian didn't appear to understand much of it, either, but he was a glutton for information, even if he couldn't decipher it.

The sword came up next to me eventually, hovering at my shoulder, and watched the guys for a while, too. But even it got bored and went streaking out an open window.

"Are we worried about nanny cams?" I finally asked when Welsh started in on a dissertation about the spec difference in two computer brands. "Isn't that a thing in Airbnbs—paranoid and/or voyeuristic hosts spying on their guests?"

Welsh's head popped up from behind a monitor positioned at the opposite end of the table. "Vanessa is a *superhost*," he said indignantly, as if I'd just slapped his mother. When all I did was stare blankly at him, he added, "This listing is also on Forage. Vanessa is a bighorn sheep shifter. I told her we're from Luma and I paid an extra fee for her to shut down the cameras."

Honestly, out of all that, I was most hung up on the concept of a sheep shifter. "So you sweet-talked a sheep? Did you promise not to be a baaad boy?"

"Don't you have a siren to seduce?" Welsh asked sharply. "Bold choice to not only wear *that*, but to not shower."

I inspected myself, glad to see my beloved combat boots had returned from their interdimensional pocket after my glamour had worn off. The outfit *did* leave a lot to be desired, but I almost wanted to leave it on just to spite Welsh.

Stalking back toward my claimed room, I said, "I'm only humoring you because you're so fragile right now!"

"Don't forget to brush your teeth!" he called after me. "*We* don't mind if you look and smell like a bog witch, but the siren most certainly will!"

I snatched my go-bag off the bed, stomped into the bathroom, and slammed the door. It really *was* like having a brother I never wanted. A brother I both wanted to punch squarely in the face and protect at all costs.

Not only did I shower, but I also brushed my teeth. Twice. I washed my hair, styled it, put on a dress and flats, and even managed mascara, eye shadow, *and* lipstick.

I employed my best sashay as I exited my room. The boys were both seated at the table. Welsh was positioned behind a monitor, and Caspian sat kitty-corner, nose buried in a book. They both glanced up as I strolled in.

"The bog witch cleans up nice." Welsh lightly slapped Caspian's arm with the back of his hand. "You're welcome. Reverse psychology always works on the weak-minded."

"Sword!" It was in my face in an instant. I thrust a finger at Welsh. "Impale!"

The sword, in the inverted position, floated toward Welsh a few inches, stopped, hovered there momentarily, then zipped back out of the room. My shoulders sagged.

Caspian, laughing, got to his feet. He tucked the tab-laden book he'd been reading under his arm. "Ready?"

I sighed. "I guess so."

We said goodbye to Welsh—who was staying behind to "work on some stuff"—and then I, Caspian, and the sword headed back out of the fancy house. Caspian opted to drive this time. The sword decided to lounge on the back seat since it now had the whole thing to itself.

It wasn't until we were on the curving road that would lead us back down the hillside that Caspian said anything.

"You know him harassing you means he likes you, right?" Caspian asked.

"You'd think he'd have more maturity than a boy pulling a girl's pigtails on the playground," I muttered, though I knew I turned into just as much of a child around Welsh as he did with me. I wasn't even sure why. I gasped and turned abruptly in my seat. "Am I as emotionally stunted as Zander Welsh?"

Caspian cut me a sidelong look that suggested he wasn't sure how to answer that without running the risk of being decapitated by my very loyal sword. "Welsh is emotionally stunted because he's got severe mommy issues. You resort to humor because you've got severe trust issues."

I wrinkled my nose. He wasn't wrong, but I didn't want to talk about me. "Please describe these mommy issues in excruciating detail."

"Let's just say they were bad enough that he ran away from home when he was twelve and never looked back."

My mouth slightly dropped open.

"Don't ask me anything else about his childhood because I won't tell you."

I idly worried at the inside of my cheek, debating whether or not I wanted to accept the challenge of wearing down Caspian's resolve.

"He likes bantering with you because you're quick, keep him on his toes, and see through his grouchy attitude," Caspian said. "You see his walls and climb over them. Most people don't. I just don't want you to think him acting like a petulant brat means something it doesn't."

"It's all good. He puts up with me, too." I chewed on my bottom lip as I studied his profile. "How are *you* holding up?"

He shrugged one shoulder. "I'm … I'm trying to say thank you for still treating him the same, despite everything. You're keeping us both sane, frankly. I know I haven't been the most agreeable person over the last couple of days, and I'm sorry for that."

Caspian hadn't been remotely disagreeable as far as I was concerned. Moodier, sure, but if anything, that had been welcome—it was good to see the sides of him that existed beneath the academy–trained sorcerer veneer.

"I'm …" He sighed. "It's been a while since I've had someone other than Welsh—who, as you say, isn't the most stable emotionally—to help shoulder anything. I wasn't in the best shape after the fiasco at the academy, and somehow Welsh, of all people, helped me get through it. He's like a second brother. I just appreciate not doing this alone."

"Well, you're in luck, because you're never getting rid of me," I said.

I really wasn't sure what else to say. He'd sounded supremely uncomfortable saying any of that, but I also knew he'd meant every word. It had sounded a bit rehearsed, as if he'd practiced the speech several times before he'd haltingly gotten it all out of his mouth.

Part of the problem was that I truly didn't know what I'd done to help either one of them. If anything, I felt like a burden half the time. But maybe always being there, no matter what, was enough, regardless of the fact that I didn't have heightened senses, superior strength, or any magical skill.

"We're all emotionally stunted in a complementary way," I said. "Between the three of us, we almost make a well-adjusted person."

"'Almost' feels like a stretch most days," Caspian said. "But I'll take it."

We settled into companionable silence as Caspian drove us back across the dam and up the other side of the fork toward Lake Nacimiento. As we approached the kiosk barring our entrance, I eyed the rust-colored canoe to our right sitting atop a small pile of rocks, the canoe's body filled with a few flowering plants, a smattering of fake red-capped mushrooms, and a sign whose left side said, LAKE NACIMIENTO RESORT. The right side of the sign sported a rendered drawing of "the dragon" as seen from the sky.

We followed the signs leading us to the marina and general store, passing several turn-offs for camping areas dotted with both RVs and tents.

"So, uh, Welsh and I were talking while you were taking a rather extensive time getting ready," Caspian said cautiously.

"Uh oh."

"We've got four points of interest here. Oak Shores is the location marked on the map we found with the cutlass's twin. We've got Christmas Cove where the portals have been reported. There are the sirens who were eyewitnesses to the portals, though the only clue we have is that at least one resides in one of the bigger homes overlooking the lake."

"Hence the vacation rental," I said.

Caspian nodded. "Correct. And the fourth location is one Welsh suggested. There are reports of pysid in a spot known colloquially as The Narrows. The land around there is all private property, but we don't need access to the land anyway. We just need to get into the pysid's territory and then entice them to talk to us. They'll be easier to track down than the sirens and will hopefully be able to point us in the right direction."

"All this is sounding a lot like we need to get in a boat," I said. "I've never been on a boat!"

Not even I was sure if I was excited or terrified by the prospect.

Caspian pulled up outside the general store. The dragon image was stamped on the sign for the shop, too. He turned to me and squinted. "Can you swim?"

"Is it like riding a bike? Because I learned how to swim when I was a kid, but I haven't been in a pool, let alone a whole-ass lake, since I was twelve." My heart thundered. I placed a hand over it. "Oh no. I might have just unlocked a phobia."

Caspian tucked his lips between his teeth.

Now it was my turn to squint. "You're laughing at my deep-seated water phobia?"

"So deep-seated you didn't even know you had it until five seconds ago?"

"That's how deep it is! It was buried! It's even deeper than the depths of that lake." I clapped a hand over my throat. "What else is in that lake? *Fish?* Fish are slimy!"

Caspian crossed his arms and sat back in the driver's seat, letting me lose my shit for a few more minutes until I'd run out of steam. "You finished?"

"For now, I think," I said, feeling suddenly drained.

"I reserved a pontoon boat before we left. We'll have life vests. I've operated a boat before, *and* I know how to swim. I know where we're going. All I need you to do is hold on. You can even lie in the fetal position on one of the seats."

I finally asked the question I'd been avoiding. "Okay. So what is a pysid? Because if it's a demon fish, I'm staying in the car with the sword."

The sword hummed from the back seat.

"A pysid is somewhere between a selkie and a mermaid—they're creatures that shift from aquatic creatures, mostly fish, to human. But the type of creature they are varies wildly—bass, salmon, eel. They can start as a salmon, shift to human, and when they revert back to their aquatic form, can choose another form entirely. A seahorse, if they wanted. They usually stick with types of creatures that make the most sense for the body of water they're inhabiting, largely to help avoid detection. A bluehead wrasse in a freshwater lake, for example, would be ludicrous."

"Yeah," I said, deadpan. "Ludicrous."

He, as usual, was unfazed. "Luckily for your overwhelmed nerves, pysid are very friendly. They're easily distracted, though, and need to be constantly redirected back to the conversation via snacks. And the snacks are … live bait." He got a distant look in his eye. "They're not always the most mindful of their teeth."

"Do I want to know how you know this much about pysid?" I asked.

"When I was about ten, and Aiden was eight, my parents took us on a trip to Alaska for the summer. My parents were enamored with Alaska well before they took a Collective job there," he said. "That was the summer I learned how to drive a boat, by the way. Anyway, we had many run-ins with pysid on that trip. They're the golden retrievers of aquatic shifters. Very helpful if you can keep them on topic long enough. They liked me quite a bit." He paused, chewing on his bottom lip. "It was very disconcerting to fall asleep in my bunk alone one night, only to awake spooning an eel."

I blinked dumbly at him. "They … they don't need to be in water?"

"They do. This one was young and almost desiccated herself because she became so fond of me. She wanted my family to adopt her." He sighed. "Her mother realized after an hour where the girl was, and moments after waking with an eel in my arms, a very angry woman wearing nothing but a few strands of kelp was in our room, demanding I unhand her daughter."

"I bet that little eel girl is still pining for you," I mused. "That would be quite the star-crossed interspecies love story."

Caspian shook his head. "I truly doubt she'd remember me. I can't overstate how *abysmal* their memories are. As in, the girl was lying beside me as an eel because she'd simply forgotten it would have been prudent for her to shift into an oxygen-breathing human when out of the water for prolonged periods."

This was going to be a mess.

Releasing a fortifying breath, I said, "Okay, let's do this. I'm absolutely petrified, but let's do it anyway."

"We'll get seasickness medication for you, just in case," Caspian said. "And we can see if they have any bathing suits, if you want. Would be quite a shame to ruin the dress." He coughed awkwardly, then quickly climbed out of the minivan.

I instructed the sword to stay put, then hustled after Caspian. I suddenly remembered what Mom had told me earlier. "*It's not common to sell pig repellent, so if you see any, grab some. It means the locals know their pig population is aggressive, even if they don't under-stand why.*" I sent a prayer to the Goddess that the store didn't carry the repellant. Between the impending siren seduction and my inevitable demise via drowning, I really didn't need to add fae-born boar to my list of threats this place posed.

Twenty minutes later, we left the general store with bathing suits, Dramamine, a veritable truckload of "comfort snacks" I'd assured Caspian I desperately needed to help combat my phobia, two containers of fish bait—and, regrettably, a jumbo canister of Boar-Be-Gone.

CHAPTER TWENTY-FIVE

HARLOW

After changing into our bathing suits in the outdoor bathrooms attached to the general store, stowing the sword in Caspian's duffel bag, and a quick safety and boat operation orientation at the marina, I was on a lake in a boat for the first time in my life. Though we weren't moving at a crazy speed, and I felt comfortable having Caspian at the helm, I was also immediately thankful Caspian had insisted I take Dramamine. My stomach wasn't exactly churning, but it wasn't calm, either.

We cruised at twenty miles an hour or so, as per the recommendation of the chipper elderly guy who gave the orientation. Caspian waved amiably at nearby boaters as we passed. He looked strangely at home on the boat, clad in swim shorts, a plain white T-shirt, and a bright orange life jacket, his hair being gently tossed by the wind. I'd tied my hair into a pineapple bun atop my head to keep the curls from constantly whipping into my face.

If I closed my eyes and basked in the feel of the sun on my skin and the wind buffeting my face, it was almost easy to forget that we glided over dark water full of untold mysteries. It didn't help that I knew at least some of those mysteries were fae in origin. The sirens we sought could be in this water at this very moment in their aquatic form, circling the boat as one of them decided how best to lure me from the relative safety of the boat. I tightened my hold on the railing beside my seat with one hand and my life jacket's chest piece with the other.

Before we'd taken off, Caspian had unzipped his duffel and left it on the deck by his feet, instructing the sword to stay inside until given the all-clear. I watched now as one of Caspian's hands left the steering wheel to begin casting an array. I wasn't sure how he'd manage it, not only while multitasking but with the wind working against him, but he soon cast a small array down toward his bag.

Returning his hand to the wheel, he said, "Come on out, cutlass. The camouflaging glamour is up, and the lake isn't too busy right now."

I watched the odd movement of the bag—as if it were trying to sprout legs and wander off—more than I saw the sword itself. A shimmering anomaly in the air above the now-deflated duffel was the only clue I had that the sword was on the move.

"Keep it slow and controlled—and don't go swimming!" Caspian called, craning his neck in a way that implied the sword had already harpooned toward the front of the boat. "I really hope it stays out of sight when we get to the pysid. If they spot the cutlass, there's no way we're getting their focus back."

"You're really selling these things as reliable informants."

Caspian merely grunted in response.

Though the lake was beautiful, the coves, low vegetation-dotted hills, and crisp blue water all largely looked the same to me. I saw no discernible landmarks, yet Caspian eventually muttered, "Ah, here we are," and he cut the engine. Nothing alarming happened in the slightest. We floated gently in the water. A tiny wave lapped a little louder against the hull, and all of sudden my chest seized. My panicked brain yelled, *"Is this is it? Are we capsizing?!"*

My face must have telegraphed what my brain was thinking, because a breath later, Caspian was in my face. His hands were on my shoulders, and he shook me until my wide eyes were locked on his.

"You've literally faced eight-foot trolls," he said calmly. "And feral vampires. And Welsh when his blood sugar is low. You can handle this, too. And if somehow you inexplicably pitch overboard and sink like a stone, there's no way the cutlass or I will let you drown."

I smacked my lips to lubricate my dry-as-the-desert mouth. "First, I appreciate that. Second, what if there's something in this water *aside* from pysid? There could be something horrific down there you've never heard of! There could be—"

Splash!

I squawked in terror, flailed, and clocked Caspian right in the jaw with an elbow. He staggered back, tripped over his duffel, and went down hard on the deck—miraculously without whacking his head on anything and giving himself a concussion or cracking his skull open. I had just lurched to my feet, intending to hurry to his side, when another great splash made me whirl around.

The sword, fully visible, was jumping in and out of the water like a metallic dolphin. On either side of it were *actual* dolphins, though these ones were a pinkish color. I clapped a hand to my forehead, quickly scanning the immediate area, worried a mundane local was watching this. The last thing we needed was footage to end up online.

Even though I'd heard of pink river dolphins, I highly doubted they naturally existed in Lake Nacimiento. Caspian might think it would be ludicrous for a bluehead wrasse to be in freshwater, but this was so much worse.

The dolphins and my dumb sword had finally stopped jumping, but they were currently booking it away from the boat, their fins slicing through the otherwise still surface of the lake. The sword's "fin" was the curved edge of its blade.

No one was currently in the vicinity, but there was a boat on the other side of The Narrows that looked to be heading our way. Freaked out, I dove for one of the plastic bags of supplies we'd gotten from the general store. They'd been wedged under the seat I'd been glued to since we left the marina.

Caspian was flat on his back, hand cupping his cheek while he moaned piteously.

"So, I'm super sorry," I said, grunting as I pulled out the bag. The life jacket was bulky and hindered my mobility, which only stressed me out further. "But the pysid are in a ludicrous form and the sword is matching their freak."

"Are you speaking in slang again or am I having a stroke?" Caspian asked as he got up, stumbling again when a foot got caught in a strap of his duffel. "I don't *think* I smell burnt toast ..."

"Aha!" I said, pulling a pint-sized canister of fish bait aloft. I popped back to my feet. "Okay, how do I summon a pysid?"

"Normally they need something magical in nature to entice them away from the safety of the water's depths, but the cutlass has already done that for us. I'd been planning on a method with more finesse and subtlety, of course, but—"

"Cas!" I flapped a hand in the direction of the quickly departing dolphins. "How do I get them back?"

"Call for the cutlass then toss a few of the worms in the water," Caspian said, sidling up next to me. "Distraction works wonders."

Cupping a hand around my mouth, I shouted, "Get back here, you fool sword!" I pried the lid off the plastic tub, winced at the mass of wriggling earthworms, grabbed a small handful, tried not to yak, then chucked the small writhing ball. The worms landed with a series of muted plops.

I winced at Caspian's disheveled state. "Sorry about your face."

"Just the kind of thing every guy wants to hear," he said, rubbing his jaw. "Those elbows of yours should be classified as lethal weapons. Oh, looks like they're on their way back. How in all the realms are they moving that fast? *Oooh* shit … you might—"

In one breath, Caspian had wrapped his arms around me, pinning my arms to my sides, and in the next there was an almighty crash—and then we were *in* the lake. The water was a surprisingly comfortable temperature, but it was hard to appreciate that when said water was *over* my head. I was still in the life jacket, but somehow I was going down instead of up. Caspian's hold on me had broken as soon as we'd hit the water. I'd completely lost sight of him.

I kicked and flailed, mentally chastising myself not to panic so badly that I opened my mouth and took in a lungful of water. But kicking and paddling my arms, open eyes locked on the rapidly vanishing light from the surface, seemed to be having the opposite intended effect.

And unfortunately, when I thought "Eff it, Goddess take the wheel" and stopped paddling, I only sank faster.

I glanced down, convinced my legs or clothes must have somehow gotten snagged. A pair of ghostly pale hands were hooked on my life jacket, the fingers clutching at the band of the cinched belt. The hands were coated in tiny, iridescent, bluish scales. *That* was when I screamed. Water flooded into my mouth in a terrifying rush.

My chest seized, my throat burned, and my body convulsed violently. Blackness crept into my vision.

Another surge of sheer panic squeezed out what little oxygen was left in my lungs as a silver torpedo shot toward me out of the depths. This had to be one of the many unknown mysteries lurking in the water. I *told* Caspian there had to be more down here than pysid!

Bubbles and pulses of water assaulted me, clouding my already taxed vision. Something tugged even more ferociously at my life jacket. A last gasp of air exploded out of my mouth.

This was it.

I was dead.

My back slammed into something hard, and the sheer force of it startled a gasp out of me. Warm hands turned me onto my side just in time for me to vomit up enough water to fill a second lake. By the time I was no longer racked by deep coughs, my throat and chest felt like they were on fire.

Someone helped me sit up so I was resting against a side wall of what I assumed was the boat. I still hadn't opened my eyes. I was too tired. Everything hurt.

Warm hands cupped my face.

"Harlow?"

The voice sounded far away.

"Harlow, can you look at me?"

I whimpered, but managed to pry one eye open, and then the other. Caspian's concerned expression blurred into view. I squinted against the influx of light. A long breath rasped out of my fatigued throat.

Caspian's hair was plastered to his head, and his clothes were soaked through. I noted then that, while he was still in his life jacket, mine was gone.

Someone wailed dramatically on the other end of the boat. The person sounded both female and very young. "I didn't mean to hurt her, swordfish. I wanted to introduce her to my father. It is a great honor to meet a goddess!"

I swallowed hard, wincing. "What happened?" I asked Caspian.

"A series of very unfortunate events," he said unhelpfully. His voice didn't sound as shredded as mine, but he didn't sound like he was in top shape, either. He was still examining my face and neck. I was too drained to swat his probing fingers away. "The pysid managed to forget that the cutlass was a cutlass and not a fellow pysid at the same moment you summoned it back. The pysid believed you must be a goddess who had come to visit them. When the cutlass turned on the proverbial jets to get back to you, the pysid followed suit so as to not upset their visiting deity. The cutlass is capable of incredible maneuverability that the pysid lack. By the time the cutlass shot out of the water to safely make it onto the boat, the pysid had both forgotten what they were doing and had run out of time to divert themselves, which sent them crashing headlong into the side of the boat, thereby tossing us overboard."

I processed that for a moment. "If they thought I was a visiting deity, why were they trying so hard to drown me?"

"I suppose if they thought you were able to command the sea, they didn't consider drowning a possibility," Caspian said. "After I hit the water, nothing came after me—honestly it felt like something ripped you away. I was able to climb back up into the boat without issue."

A wet squelch made me jump, and my head whipped to the side just as a catfish as long as my thigh flopped onto the boat. My vision went swimmy for a second before everything solidified again.

The catfish thrashed there a moment, mouth opening and closing frantically, its whiskers quivering, before it abruptly shifted into a middle-aged man in the fetal position. He sported an impressive jet-black handlebar mustache. Though he wasn't wearing clothes, he was covered in a thin layer of pearly white scales, as if he were wearing a bodysuit that covered him from neck to slightly webbed toes.

"Ah!" he said cheerfully, moving from the fetal position to squatting on the balls of his feet in one fluid motion. He got so close to my face, I jerked back, thunking my skull on the lip of the bulwark. My already throbbing head throbbed harder.

"Are you truly Goddess Anobay?" he asked, his owlish eyes blinking rapidly. His head jerked from side to side as he regarded me, his handlebar mustache quivering.

Severe oxygen deprivation was the only explanation for what I did next. I reached up and squeezed the curly end of his mustache, suddenly finding it imperative to know if it was made of hair or not. Was it shellacked into place with heavy-duty gel? Glue?

Dozens of eyes blinked open on his mustache. What had been several wormlike creatures twisted around each other suddenly unwound and flailed about under the man's nose, issuing high-pitched shrieks. The pysid's owlish gaze shifted downward, widened at the sight of his terrified face anemones, then unleashed a blood-curdling wail. I shrieked. Caspian fell backward onto his ass again.

The pysid's and his mustache's caterwauling died abruptly a breath later, the sword at the man's throat. He was sprawled on his back. The eyes on his mustache had gone dark, but the anemones all hung loosely on either side of the man's mouth. Perhaps they'd simultaneously fainted. I slammed a hand over my chest, thankful for the confirmation that my heart still beat, though it was doing so too fast.

Caspian cursed ferociously as he got himself to his hands and knees. "He must have forgotten his facial hair is alive."

I was going to ask how one could possibly forget such a thing but decided against it. "No more screaming, all right?" I asked the pysid, who nodded vigorously. "Sword, let him go."

The sword backed off.

The pysid gasped, wide eyes flitting between me and the sword and back again. He scuttled toward me on his knees, grabbed my hand, and kissed the back of it noisily. I recoiled as he gently licked it, too. His face anemones still hung limply, grazing my wrist on either side. My stomach heaved.

"Goddess Krenu!" the pysid said. "The honor is all mine! I must show you our mirror pool. If you show us which realm is yours, we can send you gifts!"

In the matter of a breath, the pysid had scooped me into his arms like a groom intending to cart his new bride over the threshold. He would have thrown my ass back into the damn lake had the sword not whipped around in front of us, blade tip aimed at the pysid's forehead. The sword lunged forward, causing the pysid to stutter several steps back.

Caspian grabbed the pysid's forearm. "She's neither Goddess Anobay nor Goddess Krenu. Unhand her."

The pysid instantly dropped me and I probably would have shattered my tailbone had Caspian not swooped over to throw an arm around me before I hit the deck. I still managed to land funny on my ankle, though. I sagged in Caspian's hold.

"I can't help but think," I said, using Caspian as a crutch as I got myself more firmly onto my feet, "that Welsh came up with this pysid idea solely because he knew it would be a nightmare."

"I suspected this would be messy, but I didn't think you'd get—"

I straightened as something the pysid had said earlier caught up with me, and I turned toward the fishman. "When you say 'mirror pool,' do you—"

My question died on my lips when I didn't immediately see the pysid. I looked down; the pysid had inexplicably shifted back into a catfish. It lay flat on its side, its gills hardly fluttering. Had the sword inflicted a killing blow while I wasn't looking?

The sword hovered blade first, as if it were staring down at the fish as well, its blade a purplish color that I was starting to interpret as confusion.

"Pysid?" I asked.

The catfish morphed back into the mustachioed man with a wet pop. "Hello, my queen."

Good grief.

"You said you have a 'mirror pool' that lets you see into other realms?" I asked.

"Oh, yes! Would you like me to take you there?"

I raised both arms, palms out, to stop the pysid from trying to drag me to the bottom of the lake. Again. He dropped his scaly arms to his sides, dejected. Thankfully his face anemones had gone back into stasis, curled into their handlebar mustache config-uration.

"Just tell me about it," I said. "What does it look like?"

"She is not always there," the pysid said. "But when she appears, she is round, like this." He made a circle with his arms, roughly the size of a beach ball. "She glows as bright as the sun! Sometimes we can see through the mirror pool into other places. Some have water. Some have land. Some are sky. Some are—" The pysid's eyes glazed over for a moment. When lucidity returned, he grinned brightly at me. "Hello, my queen!"

"Oh my god," I muttered.

The pysid's owlish eyes widened, and he pressed his scaly palms to either side of his bald head. "He's behind me, isn't he? Please tell God Orue that I didn't mean what I said about his tail."

I glanced over at Caspian in bewilderment, but he was busily prying the lid off another canister of bait. A fragrant whiff of fish hit my nostrils, and my stomach pitched once more. Caspian grabbed an anchovy by the tail, holding it toward the pysid. The pysid's gaze snapped to the small fish. His pale bluish tongue snaked out to lick scaly lips. *My* lip curled at the possibility that I was enabling cannibalism.

"Are you able to change what realms you see in the mirror pool?" Caspian asked.

In an almost robotic voice, as if the anchovy had hypnotized the pysid, he said, "Oh no. We do not control the mirror pool. We only tell the siren when it opens. Especially when something comes through."

As Caspian looked sharply at me, the pysid lunged and clamped his mouth around Caspian's fingers, like a fish would bait dangling from a fishing hook. Caspian yelped and pulled his hand free, wiping his fingers on his life jacket. The pysid happily slurped down the anchovy. I swallowed down bile.

Turning to Caspian, I asked, "So did the siren in the report actually *see* portals where he claimed he had, or did he make something up so the agents wouldn't suspect portals opening somewhere else?"

Caspian's brow pinched. "I have no idea. Maybe being *in* the lake helps hide, if not wholly cloak, a portal from detection."

"That, or the underwater portal *does* give off a magical signature, but the water distorts it." I grabbed an anchovy out of the canister Caspian still held and waved it in front of the pysid. The fishman had been idly picking his nose slits but slipped back into that hypnotic state at the sight of the snack. "Do you know of any mirror pools *outside* of the water?"

The pysid angled a scaly finger toward some spot behind Caspian and me, vaguely in the direction of The Narrows's shore, though his eyes never left the fish. "Siren Red, when he thinks Siren Yellow is not listening, asks us to tell him about the land mirrors. Siren Yellow says no one can know about the mirror pool because they will send us to another realm if … if they find out the … uhh … the mirror pool exists."

I hastily tossed the anchovy to the pysid, who caught it out of the air. I grabbed another fish to reset the connection. "Is Siren Red nicer than Siren Yellow?"

"Oh yes," the pysid said. "We thought Siren Yellow was a god at first, because Yellow commands the water much like you do, my queen. But the fish flee from Siren Yellow. The water darkens when Siren Yellow is near. Siren Yellow can drown us on land or in the water without using anything but the power of the lake. If we obey, if we report what we see and hear from the mirrors, Siren Yellow does not harm us. We do not want to leave this realm, so we listen."

I tossed him another fish for his efforts.

Caspian picked up the next line of questioning. The pysid licked his lips in anticipation of another treat. "Can Siren Yellow open and close the mirror pool?"

"Yes, yes," the pysid said, head bobbing. "Sometimes Siren Yellow comes to look into the mirror, and a man from another place opens the mirror to speak to the siren. Siren Yellow sends us away, so I do not know what they speak about, but the water around the mirror turns black as squid ink for as far as the eye can see while they meet, so we wouldn't be able to see anything even if we tried to spy."

Caspian gave the pysid two fish for that.

Without prompting, the pysid said in a small, sad voice, "We don't always remember. Siren Red knows this and helps us stay focused. Siren Yellow laughs at us, and I've heard Siren Yellow tell the mirror man that we are the best spies because we're too stupid to remember we didn't get anything we were promised. We might not remember much, but it's hard to forget the hand that punishes you."

Caspian and I frowned at each other. A moment later, Caspian thrust the entire canister of anchovies at the pysid, who took it reverently, as if he'd just been given a sack of priceless gemstones.

The pysid shoved his entire hand in the tub and pulled free a handful of fish, which he promptly shoveled into his mouth. Several slimy fish slipped free, hitting the deck with soft splats. Without a word, he launched over the side of the boat with a belly flopping splash.

Since the canister was missing its lid, the fish hit the water in a cascading wave. A catfish mouth lurched from the depths to snatch up several of the now-sinking anchovies. The catfish was joined by two pink dolphins, a bass, and a sea turtle the size of a small car.

A sharp pain assaulted my ankle, and I lurched away from the side of the boat to find what I could only describe as a flying fish flopping around. A thin red line marred my shin, just above my ankle.

"Shit!" I said as the pain finally hit me. "What the hell, fish?"

The flying fish morphed into a young girl. She was covered head to toe in a thin layer of bluish scales that matched her previous fish form. She was completely devoid of hair but was rocking elaborate eyebrows similar to fish fins. The iridescent scales flared yellow or green depending on how the light hit them.

"I'm sorry, Your Majesty!" the girl said, sounding much like the young person I'd heard when I'd first regained consciousness after my near-death experience. The sword had had her pinned to the deck while she'd begged for forgiveness.

I crossed my arms and stared down at her bowed, bald head. "Were you the one who tried to bring me to your father?"

"Yes, miss," she said. "I throw myself before your mercy!"

She hit the deck on her hands and knees. Even if she'd intended initially to show me reverence, the anchovies lying on the deck soon proved too much. The young girl began crawling around, shoving wayward fish into her mouth.

Caspian plucked up the last anchovy just before the girl could. She, like the mustachioed pysid, became entranced and slowly got to her feet, wide eyes fixed on the fish. Caspian nodded at me, granting me the final round of pysid interrogation. We'd purchased two tubs of bait, but who knew what had happened to the first one. I'd been holding it just before we'd been tossed overboard.

"Do you know where Siren Red or Siren Yellow live?"

The girl gave a full-body shudder. "Siren Red lives in the blue house with the rooster on the shore with the oaks." She jabbed a finger back the way we'd come.

"Oak Shores?" I asked.

The girl bobbed her head.

We still had no idea what exactly the connection was between Oak Shores and the sword's dormant twin. Especially since that map, the sword, and the box they'd been buried in had been underground for at least twenty years. Who knew how much Oak Shores had changed since then.

"And Siren Yellow?" Caspian asked.

She shivered again. "I know not. Siren Yellow only comes out at night and turns the water black. Siren Yellow smells like metal. My mother says we must always listen and obey, but we cannot look at Siren Yellow because our insides will turn as black as the siren's eyes."

Caspian and I *both* lost our hold on the conversation that time. The young girl snatched the fish from his hand, shoved it into her mouth, and then dove into the water. She quickly disappeared from view.

The only sound was water lightly lapping against the undoubtedly dented hull of the boat. An engine roared to life somewhere near The Narrows's shore. The boat I'd seen earlier had disappeared into one of the lake's many secluded coves. Hopefully no one was on the hillside or hiding behind shrubbery with a camera running. Late morning on a weekday near the tail end of summer was far less busy than it would be on the weekend, at least.

I cleared my throat. "Why do I have a really bad feeling that this Siren Yellow is a shadow vamp?"

Caspian nodded absently. "And was he a siren before he was turned, or was he a water witch and the pysid are merely *calling* him a siren?"

Given how easily the pysid were confused, it was a fifty-fifty chance in either direction.

"The question now is," Caspian said, "do you want to head straight for Siren Red, or do you need to regroup after all ... *this*?"

My hair was a soggy mess. What little makeup I'd put on had washed off by now. My ballet flats were ruined, I stank vaguely of fish, my cut ankle throbbed in time with my pulse, and it still felt as if someone had taken a blowtorch to my esophagus and chest.

But my chances of seducing a siren had already been improbable, so what difference did any of this make now?

"Operation Siren Seduction is still a go," I said.

Caspian nodded and headed for the helm of the boat. The sword must have tuckered itself out because it had already wedged itself back into Caspian's duffel.

I flopped onto one of the seats as the boat's engine turned over, hoping today wouldn't get any worse.

CHAPTER TWENTY-SIX

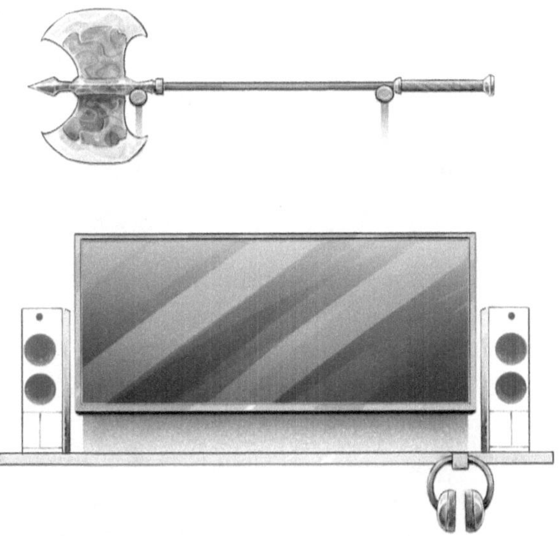

The trip from Luma to the back room of the Something of Note piano shop in San Diego went off without a hitch. An hour later, Kayda, Marisol, and Quaid were pulling into the warehouse that served as San Diego's VHoA headquarters. A small fleet of black SUVs were parked inside to the right, in the middle of the space was a collection of electronics-laden tables, and to the left were a few picnic tables where a couple of people were eating. The wall behind the picnic tables had a small kitchen area with a fridge, stove, coffee pot, and a couple of credenzas that provided counter space. Cots positioned behind freestanding curtained partitions took up the back of the room. That was it. Efficient use of space. No frills.

Marisol pulled the rented SUV beside one of VHoA's black Jeeps. "We gotta track down Akio."

With that, Marisol climbed out.

Kayda, who sat in the passenger seat, and Quaid in the back didn't move.

"I'm kinda nervous," Quaid said.

"Yeah, me too."

"If we never get out of this car, then we'll never know what happened to Kessler. But if something awful *did* happen to him, not moving means we get to hold on to the hope he's all right."

Kayda sighed. "There are other Kesslers out there, though. Kessler could be the cautionary tale to protect the ones who come after him."

"Dammit," Quaid muttered.

They both threw their doors open. No going back.

Kayda spotted Marisol near the makeshift kitchen area chatting with a middle-aged Asian guy. By the time Kayda and Quaid reached them, others had wandered over to openly eavesdrop. Within a minute, from what Kayda could tell with her dialed-up hearing, the entire small team of eight who had been in the warehouse had joined them. Kayda leaned against the fridge, arms crossed, as she waited for Marisol to finish telling the group who she, Kayda, and Quaid were, as well as their interest in Kessler.

A buff, bald, twenty-something guy sitting on top of a nearby picnic table was more riveted by Kayda than the conversation at hand. She couldn't tell if he was intrigued by her or outright frightened. She tried to ignore him, but her main source of distraction was the top of the fridge—which was filthy. Not enough people were mindful about the tops of their fridges, Kayda thought. The average person couldn't *see* the top of their fridge on a regular basis like she could, but that was hardly the point.

"Tony!"

The bald guy and Kayda both jumped, their gazes swinging toward the middle-aged man Kayda guessed was Akio.

"Stop ogling the guests." Akio's attention shifted to Kayda. "We don't get a lot of draken around here. Nearly half of us have never been in a hub. I apologize in advance if anyone acts like an uncultured asshole."

A few more cautious looks slid her way.

She sighed, weighing her options. Harlow had taught her that, for a lot of mundanes, information settled their anxieties. Imaginations were great at making up fantastical shit when they needed to fill in gaps in knowledge. Kayda wanted to do her due diligence to find Kessler and hopefully uncover something that could help Welsh. In order to do that, her new temporary coworkers needed to *not* be scared of her.

Kayda made a show of checking a watch she wasn't actually wearing. "All right. I'm giving y'all five minutes to ask me anything you want. Nothing is too stupid. Nothing is too offensive. But after those five minutes are up, you gotta knock this shit off. I don't want the group to be compromised because someone is freaked out that I'm going to go Hulk on them and turn into a fire-breathing lizard or something." She stabbed a finger toward a young blond lady whose hand had just shot into the air. "No, I can't turn into a dragon."

The young woman dropped her hand and pouted.

The questions were pretty basic. No, she didn't dye her hair white; that was its natural color. No, she didn't shave off her eyebrows; she'd never had any. No, she couldn't see through walls, but she *did* possess strong enough hearing to know there was currently a rat or mouse chewing through someone's bag in the back of the room.

A guy went booking it across the warehouse, muttering about his secret stash of Canadian KitKats.

Kayda assured them that she didn't possess any magic ability whatsoever, and she reiterated to the same young lady that no, no draken in the earthen realm could shift into a dragon.

"Do you know for sure, though?" the lady asked, her eyes wide and hopeful.

Kayda shrugged. "I mean, I guess it's possible? Any draken who discovered they could shift would become a celebrity overnight; it's unlikely they'd keep it to themselves."

The woman pouted again.

"Not everyone seeks notoriety, I suppose. So there could be a draken who can and is keeping the secret close to the vest," Kayda added, not sure why she wanted to cheer the lady up.

That tiny kernel of hope puffed the woman back up, and she smiled gratefully at Kayda. "I sure hope so," she said dreamily.

Kayda sensed the woman had read one too many fantasy novels.

There were a few questions about hubs, too. No, there were no flying cars, flying people, or a fleet of pegasi used to commute to work. No, it wasn't like a fantasy Wild West movie where people were murdered willy-nilly by magic projectiles simply because you looked at a sorcerer the wrong way. That very specific question had come from the dragon-obsessed lady. Kayda was half tempted to kidnap the woman and shove her into a telepad just to help disabuse her of her very wrong, and possibly romanticized, notions.

Kayda thought the group had finally run out of questions since the room had gone quiet, but then Akio cleared his throat. She guessed he was fifty or so. White peppered his jet-black hair —both at the temples and in his short-cropped beard. She pegged him as at least part Japanese. Since he didn't have an accent, she assumed that meant he'd been born in the States and/or one of his parents was Caucasian. His dark eyes flitted between Marisol and Kayda a few times before he spoke.

"Are you the contact of Mari's who witnessed Lachlan Shade come out of that portal?" Akio asked.

Kayda pursed her lips as she eyed Marisol, who was looking everywhere *except* at Kayda. As much as Kayda appreciated how freely VHoA shared intel, it was a little like living in a small town: Everyone seemed to know your business. Marisol was also exceedingly chatty in the forums—possibly *too* chatty, even by VHoA standards. That was probably a symptom of a bigger problem with her friend, but it was a problem for another day.

"That was me," Kayda admitted reluctantly and was met with another flood of questions.

Most were about the elfin kids—ages, magical skill levels, any known details about their home lives. None of the inquiries were about Kayda's inability to stop Lachlan from getting out. Several even commended her for being able to save two of the kids.

Kayda felt someone watching her, quickly spotting Quaid in the small group.

"Told you," he mouthed.

She supposed the guy wasn't *all* bad.

"Okay, okay. Let Kayda come up for air," Akio said. "Now, most of you know about Kessler since he was from our neck of the woods. We've been actively searching for information about him for a while, but I admit he's slipped from the priority list as of late. Mari and I have been pooling resources on Kessler in preparation for her visit. In all likelihood, the vamps found and reclaimed him, which would mean he's back on Bliss and doing their bidding.

"Hopefully most of you have watched that video I emailed of Kessler and the few glimpses of his magic. Ferals are bad enough, but if the vamps are able to turn fae now, we've gotta get ahead of this sooner rather than later. The organization as a whole—especially chapters that operate more in the mundane world than in the hubs, like us—will need to reevaluate weapons, tactics, gear, all of it. As much as we're helping the Luma chapter with their quest to find Kessler, it's worth the effort to find the guy for the sake of the bigger picture.

"Now, it's highly probable the vamps have already trafficked him somewhere else, but we can still ask around in known vampire haunts. We'll question bartenders, waitstaff, and janitors. I'll send recent photos of Kessler to everyone so you all have them."

Tony, the bald guy, asked, "And what about the nest on Briar Road?"

Several people murmured agreement.

Emboldened by his colleagues' support, Tony continued. "You keep saying we need more reason to raid the place. If we need to confirm Kessler isn't in San Diego anymore, leaving the Briar nest untouched would be stupid." He gestured at Kayda. "Plus, we have a personal tank now. What other reason do we need?"

Normally such a comment would rankle her, but for some reason it didn't when coming from Tony.

Akio shot Kayda a questioning glance.

"I'll go wherever you need me, but I'm not any better equipped. If the nest has fae-born shadow vamps in it, I'm as fucked as the rest of you," Kayda said. "But I'd be of more use there than trying to be inconspicuous at a club. If someone looking like me starts asking questions in a mundane place, it'll get noticed." Her head tottered back and forth. "Which could work in our favor, depending on the results we want."

"Fair point," Akio said. "I'd like to put most of our efforts into going after the nest, then. We'll keep a few people here, send two or three small teams out to the most frequented bars and clubs, and the rest of us will tackle Briar. Start calling people in. I want to be twenty strong for this one."

Akio's group of eight split off, most pulling out phones, but a few plopped into chairs before computers in the middle of the room. Tony and the dragon-obsessed lady jogged to an SUV. After someone got the roll-up door open for them, the SUV took off to Goddess knew where.

Quaid pushed his glasses up his nose and asked, "Need us to do anything while you rally the troops? Pack up vehicles?"

"We can do that in a minute." Akio contemplated Kayda, his expression telegraphing cautious trepidation more than unease. "Mari mentioned your friend Zander?"

No one really referred to Welsh as Zander, so that at least showed *some* restraint on Marisol's part.

"What about him?" Kayda asked.

"What I told the others is true—I think what's going on with Kessler and this shadow vampire thing is possibly a precursor to something that we frankly can't handle yet," Akio said. "As much as I'm thrilled to have someone like you on our side, the idea of a shadow vamp version of you running around is fucking terrifying. Shade's recruits are rumored to be elves, vampires, and folks who have been kicked out of the hub system." He paused. "He's also recruiting draken, trolls, and orcs. Having elephantine fae in the Shades is smart as far as sheer muscle power goes, but what if Lachlan's been recruiting those people for *this* reason—to turn them into shadow vamps and have an army that's even stronger?"

Kayda hadn't once considered any of this. It all made her sick to her stomach.

When it was clear Kayda wasn't going to comment, Akio pressed on. "I've been looking into this stuff for a few months now. All we've got are anecdotal stories, but I have a reliable source who believes that, in addition to the blood-poisoning side effect, there also might be something off about their shadows. As in, the shadowy fog that follows them around may be providing a method of communication."

Kayda cocked her head. *"Explain."*

Akio flinched minutely and Kayda chastised herself to take it down a notch. "There's a pretty famous case of a witch getting turned and the poison rotting the poor sod's brain. Granted, 'famous' in our circles means a few hundred people know about it. Anyway, the guy's brain was so cooked, he was convinced he'd found the burning rainbow bridge to Asgard and was going to walk there."

Whoa.

Harlow had told Kayda that very story just this morning. Kayda supposed that "few hundred people" included Camila, since she was the one who'd told Harlow.

"The witch was captured by a VHoA team in Texas near the hub in San Augustine County. They shot him fifteen times, and he didn't slow—even after two head shots. But elephant-strength tranqs knocked him out," Akio said. "They chained him to a table, locked him in a basement with a steel-reinforced door and no windows, then left him there while they brainstormed on what to do with him. VHoA tends to take out vamps first and ask questions later, but he was so hard to classify, they kept him alive.

"They were only able to contain him for about twenty-four hours. He broke both wrists and both ankles to get out of the shackles. After his bones mended themselves enough that he could walk, he used fire magic to melt the steel door into a puddle, then took off."

Kayda blew out a breath that puffed out her cheeks. If Kessler was at full nyad power, or any other fae in the Briar Road nest was a shadow vamp with functioning magic, she and the others were screwed.

Akio said, "Thing is, as they were strapping the guy down—since the tranqs only kept him down for about twenty minutes—they noticed two things. One, there was a dark mist all around the guy, like black fog was seeping out of his pores. And two? My buddy said the witch sounded like he was having a conversation where only the witch could hear the replies. He'd go, 'No, I can't do that. I'm too weak, and these bonds are too tight.' He'd pause and say, 'I'm not like you. My bones can't mend that fast without healing tonics.' Another pause, then he'd say, 'Why would I trust a talking cloud?'"

Kayda chewed on her bottom lip, her heart thumping hard. Harlow had mentioned a text Welsh had sent. *"I don't have a hankering for blood yet, but shadows whisper to me now, which I can't imagine is a good thing.*"

"I've heard at least two other stories about these sick, poisoned fae claiming the shadows around them can speak," Akio said. "Now that's hair-raising all on its own, but is that a side effect of the poison? Is it eating away at the victims' brains and they're hallucinating?"

"Or is someone talking to the victims *through* the shadows?" Kayda filled in.

Akio nodded. "Exactly."

Marisol chimed in. "Which would suggest a level of puppet and puppet master, especially in a case like Kessler, who is hooked on Bliss. There's always been something in vampire lore that suggests a mental bond between sire and progeny. There certainly seems to be one between hybrids and ferals, but I haven't seen evidence of it elsewhere. Which is why I think vampires created Bliss in the first place. They're artificially creating that bond through the victim's addiction to the drug."

Quaid said, "Yet another reason why pures hate the hybrids so much—hybrids are addicted to fae blood and then force their victims to stick around by forcing *them* into an addiction as well."

"My real concern in all this," Akio said, "is that if hybrids are successfully turning fae, who the hybrids can then control via shadows, it's not just a matter of us being instantly outmatched by a new opponent. It's that, in order for the hybrid to control their progeny—like in the case of that witch who tried to walk to Asgard—the hybrid has to sense what their progeny is seeing or hearing in order to know what to instruct them to do, right? If that witch's sire *truly* instructed him to break his own bones to get out of his shackles, that means the sire *knew* he was shackled. So either that hybrid was nearby with a pair of binoculars that could see through walls, or the sire was watching through their bond."

Kayda's mind spun.

Not only was that thought scary as shit, but there was a very important detail she'd just remembered about Welsh's case in particular. His sire, if one could call the vampire that, was dead. *Extremely* dead. So dead that creepy-ass Erik currently had the vampire's severed head in his refrigerator.

So that begged the question: If Welsh's sire *wasn't* the one giving voice to the whispers ... who was?

CHAPTER TWENTY-SEVEN

HARLOW

Despite the pontoon boat being rammed into by a pair of pink river dolphins that absolutely should not have been in the lake, it hadn't sustained any damage. Whether that was due to magical intervention or exceptional craftsmanship was a mystery. Either way, Caspian was delighted he wouldn't be forced to purchase the boat in a very inconvenient version of "you break it, you buy it."

"I must say I'm a little troubled by how surprised you are that the boat *isn't* damaged," the elderly man behind the counter told Caspian. He was the same chipper guy who had given us our safety and equipment orientation. He was more baffled now than chipper. "I got a call here from one of the residents who said they thought someone might have run into some trouble in the water in a boat of ours. She was watching through binoculars and didn't have a clear view, but she kept using the words 'really strange' to describe what she saw."

"And what *did* she see?" I asked, hoping the man didn't notice that my life jacket was inexplicably absent. My best guess was that the sword had cut the jacket off me when the confused pysid had latched onto me and tried to drag me to my watery grave. Caspian and I were both unsure who or what had gotten me from the lake onto the boat, especially when I'd hit the deck with such force. My bets were on the sword, even if Caspian doubted the possibility of the feat.

"That's just it—the woman didn't seem to know *what* she was seeing," the man said. "She said she'd heard what might have sounded like a crash, but when she found the boat in question, she saw people in outlandish shiny wetsuits on the deck. She, and I quote, said, 'I think it's those mermaid reenactment people. You know the ones—the ones who pretend to live life as fishpeople.' She also mentioned an oddly shaped drone that kept crashing into the lake. I honestly didn't know what to make of any of it." His mouth bunched up. "But if she was concerned someone's life was in danger, she would have called the rangers, not the marina, right? I'm not sure what she expected *me* to do."

The concerned woman had likely somehow sensed that what was happening around our boat hadn't been life-threatening so much as bizarre. She'd clearly missed my near drowning.

I'd been told countless times that mundanes unused to magic had an uncanny knack for convincing themselves they hadn't seen something they most assuredly had. It was a plot point that came up in shows like *Faet of the Heart* all the time. Sometimes to hilarious effect.

Since this woman had never seen a pysid in human form, she'd convinced herself that she was watching a band of mermaid LARPers—which was strange to many in its own right but also a real thing in the mundane world.

The man leaned forward and glowered at Caspian and me

each in turn. "Your eyes don't *look* off. The woman never said as much, but she heavily hinted that she thought there might have been drug use aboard. I'm not going to find any drug paraphernalia on my boat, am I? I have your information, Caleb Berkshire, *and* I have access to drug-sniffing canines. If they find even a *flake* of cocaine, you'll be in a world of hurt."

I wasn't a street drug connoisseur, but I didn't think there would be "flakes" of cocaine anyway. It was unlikely the man would appreciate the comment, though, so I kept it to myself.

Caspian put his hands up. "No drugs, sir. It wasn't my intention to alarm you about the condition of the boat. I suspect I got too close to the shore and grazed a sandbar. As for the shiny suits … we have a few friends in the area who LARP as sea creatures on the weekends. They know boats, so they checked out the hull for us and assured us everything was fine, but I just wanted to be sure. Can't be too careful with other people's property, can you?"

The man stood ramrod straight now, his gaze flicking between me and Caspian. "You have … friends who … *live* as sea creatures? Is this like those furry things I keep hearing about? Are they having *fish orgies* or something? There are families out there! That's not a thing kids should see. Flopping around in the sand touching each other's fins and such. Maybe I need to call the rangers after all."

I said, "Orgies wouldn't be accurate to their lifestyle, what with the way fish fertilize eggs and all."

Caspian shot me a mildly scandalized look. Yeah, I had no idea what I meant, either.

The man's mouth puckered, his eyes going a little glassy as his imagination ran rampant with the implications of my statement. "I almost wish it *had* been drugs."

"Well, have a lovely day, sir!" Caspian said, grabbing me by the elbow and yanking me out the door. I squeezed Caspian's duffel bag tight to my side.

Just as we stepped onto the pier, the sword buzzed angrily from the bag's depths, setting my teeth to chattering.

Though it must have made us appear even guiltier, we quickly jogged down the pier, across the sand, and up the grassy hill that led to the parking area shared by campers, boaters, picnickers, and shoppers of the Lake Nacimiento General Store. Caspian waited in the minivan while I took my meager belongings into the bathroom to change out of my wet bathing suit. The relief I felt at peeling the suit off was dampened somewhat by the anchovy head that tumbled out and hit the cement floor with a splat. It was a marvel that my horrified retching hadn't sent the sword slamming its way through the restroom walls to save me from my latest foe. My mom's advice to always have a pair of extra underwear in a separate sealed bag helped make the world feel more manageable, at least.

I did what I could with my hair, but even with the aid of a copious amount of water from the sink in an attempt to get it slicked back, I knew, as soon as it started to dry, it would frizz up without any product in it.

I scrutinized my reflection, watching a war of indecision play out across my features as I continued the mental argument I'd been having with myself ever since Caspian started our return trip across the lake. The so-called Siren Yellow sounded like he was one of Lachlan's—whether he was a Shade by choice or design I couldn't say. I also didn't care.

Mom, Soren, Kayda, and VHoA were all hunting for answers about what was happening to Welsh. All of them frankly knew more about ferals and side effects of vampire bites than I did. Caspian and I had brought Welsh along on this side quest in part to help him gain distance from the reality of his new ailment— and yet we'd managed to bring him closer. If Siren Yellow was indeed a successfully turned siren or water witch, I wasn't sure Caspian, Welsh, *or* the sword would be enough to stand against him. I sure as hell wasn't.

I could only think of one person whose resources we hadn't tapped yet. Making a phone call was one of the few skills I could offer the cause at this point. Blowing out a breath, I dug around in my bag for my cell. My screen, thankfully, wasn't full of notifications of missed calls and SOS text messages.

After selecting one of the few numbers I had programmed in, I hit call, grabbed my bag, and with the phone pressed to my ear, walked out of the restroom. I walked to a spot where Caspian could see me from the minivan while also staying a good distance from a boisterous family of at least twenty. Someone was grilling, a stereo blasted hip hop from the nineties, and a gaggle of kids played a very intense game of dodgeball.

"Hello, Daughter of Camila," came a voice through my phone, startling me. Some part of me hadn't thought he'd answer.

"Hi, Vaughn," I said, clearing my throat. "I thought we decided 'Daughter of Camila' had too many syllables."

"The moniker isn't for ease, but to maintain a level of societal distance. Obviously it isn't having its intended purpose if you're calling me for a … chat."

He said the last word as if it were something as detestable as kicking puppies.

"Don't make assumptions. I could be calling with an emergency," I said.

Vaughn's sigh, though slight, was frustrated. "The sound of merriment in the background would suggest otherwise. What is it you need, Daughter of Camila?"

"Did you know hybrid bites are starting to turn fae?" I asked.

Vaughn's silence was charged. "We've heard rumors."

I gave him a condensed version of Welsh's current predicament, as well as what the pysid had just told us about Siren Yellow. The faint rustle of wind was the only commentary I got from Vaughn's end of the call. Maybe he was taking a stroll while he listened to me ramble. "We're planning to track down Siren Red next. We're pretty sure Siren Red is your run-of-the-mill siren, so we just have the usual things to worry about with him."

"Being seduced so thoroughly that you allow yourself to be conned out of everything you own save your name?" Vaughn asked. "And some even lose that."

"Is it still considered a con if you let it happen?"

"Is it considered voluntary if the interaction begins with magical coercion?"

"Says the guy who can't even *eat* without magical coercion," I muttered.

In a dangerously low tone, he said, "If you know what you're doing, there's no coercion necessary. *My* food comes to *me*."

My heartbeat ratcheted up. Right. Ancient vampire who only lightly tolerated me because his boss—best friend? sire?—had the hots for my mom.

"I do find this shadow vampire business to be quite troublesome," Vaughn said absently after a long beat. Birds twittered in the background. "And you say your witch's shadows … speak to him?"

"He said he can't understand what they're saying, and if he keeps his glamours up, he can keep the shadows away. But the poison is weakening him, and his hold on his magic will fail eventually." My throat tightened. I swallowed the lump down.

"Would it help if I spoke with your witch?" Vaughn asked.

"*Really?*"

"Who better for him to speak to than a vampire?"

Oh, I don't know, I thought. *Literally anyone else, since Welsh hates pure vampires even more than hybrids and ferals.*

"I can ask him if he'd be up for that. He's desperate not to turn, but I don't know if he's desperate enough to *chat* with a vamp—especially a pure one."

"Drop me a pin of your current location."

I was momentarily baffled. Why would he need a location pin for a phone call?

This was odd.

It was weird enough that I was talking to a vampire on my cell phone as if we were good buddies. The fact that he was up to date enough on technology to know about dropping pins, though, was doing a number on my brain. "Uhh … one sec."

After I sent it, I pressed the phone to my ear again. "Not sure if that worked. Reception is spotty out here."

"Got it," Vaughn said. "I believe talking to your witch would be helpful for both of us. I can be very persuasive."

Persuasive about what? I was so confused.

Movement out of the corner of my eye made me look up. A strikingly handsome man had just emerged from the men's restroom and was strolling toward me. He was dressed in loose-fitting beige linen pants and a long-sleeved white shirt. His dark hair was in an intentional state of curly disarray. Though the outfit was the same, this time he was wearing shoes. I surveyed him from beige boat shoes to lean frame to dark eyes. He stopped in front of me, hands in his pockets.

I still had the phone pressed to my ear, so I pulled it away, staring down at the screen. Vaughn had ended the call before he'd, what, teleported over here? My gaze snapped back to his face.

I remembered how fast he'd moved the first time I'd met him —so fast that he'd slipped a note into Caspian's pocket, deposited two travel talismans at our feet, and returned to his previous spot in the span of a blink. Had he really traveled over a hundred miles in less than a minute? Mom had said that surviving magical malaria had made Vaughn "preternaturally fast," but this was next level.

Vaughn placed a finger under my chin and guided it up so I closed my mouth. "You'll catch flies."

I snorted. It was such a dad thing to say, it broke the spell. "You can't enthrall Welsh," I blurted. "He's going to be *fuming* that I brought a freaking vampire back with us, but if you, like, enthrall him and force him to tell you stuff against his will, he'll probably kill me in my sleep."

Vaughn, hands back in the pockets of his linen pants, stared at me impassively.

Slowly, as if he were a child, I said, "If I die a gruesome death because of you, my mom will be super mad. Then she'll tear Roch a new one, and then *you'll* have to deal with the fallout."

Vaughn wrinkled his perfect nose. "Fine. No enthrall. Off to visit this Siren Red first, then?"

I waved a finger in a circle in front of his face, squinting at him all the while. "This is all very suspicious, you showing up like this."

"Do you want my assistance or not? Because I would prefer to be *literally* anywhere else." He smiled tightly. "That is to say ..." Deep breath. "I'm *at your service*, Daughter of Camila."

Ah. So he was here because of either Roch or my mom. If not both. Which somehow made me feel better. It also potentially meant he'd been nearby already, and him getting here in record time, even for a vampire with superhero speed, wasn't nearly as impressive—disquieting—as I'd originally thought.

I headed for the minivan. Caspian was already outside, resting against the passenger-side door with his arms crossed.

My smile was more of a grimace when I reached him. "Cas, you remember our good buddy Vaughn, right?"

"Vampire," Caspian said in greeting, tone flat.

"Sorcerer," Vaughn replied.

"Human!" I chirped, suddenly not wanting to be left out.

Both men shot me questioning side-eyes. Maybe the two could bond over how odd I was.

"I will climb into this disgusting vehicle now, close the door, and pretend not to hear every word of your conversation with your sorcerer lover as you explain my presence, Daughter of Camila." Vaughn pulled open the side door of the minivan, muttered something about the unsettling number of desiccated french fries, offered the sword a relatively cordial greeting as he sat down, then shut the door.

Caspian, I realized then, had already changed out of his swim trunks and was back in a familiar pair of khakis. Instead of one of his usual white button-up shirts, though, he wore a black Lake

Nacimiento T-shirt. He must have grown bored waiting for me to get changed.

Misinterpreting the reason I was eyeing his shirt, he said, "I got you a hoodie. Both items were exorbitantly expensive."

Though I knew Vaughn was listening, since he'd readily admitted to it, I still dragged Caspian away from the car. I explained everything as quickly as I could, as we were rapidly losing daylight, and I really didn't want to have to bust out the Boar-Be-Gone. Caspian didn't interrupt me, but he did cast quite a few wary glances toward the minivan.

Silence descended between us.

"Welsh is going to be apoplectic," Caspian said.

"He hates pure vamps that much, huh?" I asked.

"You have no idea."

"In my defense," I said, "the *undead creep* just showed up. I only called him for advice."

The door to the minivan trundled open a fraction. "I'm not undead—that's a hurtful, inaccurate label!"

I might not have known Vaughn long, but I knew him well enough to know he didn't care one iota about labels. He'd said it solely to befuddle the elderly woman who had just left the restroom.

Vaughn flapped a hand in my direction as the woman spotted him sulking in the minivan. "Youth these days, amiright? Just because I'm of an older generation doesn't mean I'm so old I'm practically dead." He even feigned getting choked up.

The woman curled a lip at me in disgust, then walked away, shaking her head.

Vaughn's face went flat the moment the woman was gone. He rattled the car's door closed.

Caspian gusted a sigh. "And here I thought the most upsetting part of my day was having my fingers sucked by a pysid."

"*Wowww,*" I said, stalking away from him. "Me almost drowning didn't even get an honorable mention?"

Caspian cursed under his breath and hurried after me. I wasn't actually mad, but I needed to distract Caspian about the whole, "We're going to ambush Welsh with a pure vampire" thing.

Even after we'd settled into the car and Caspian had turned the engine over, Caspian hadn't spoken.

"*Ouch,*" Vaughn said from the back, sounding uncharacteristically pleased. "Someone is sleeping on the couch tonight."

The sword tapped once on the side panel of the back door. I stayed quiet, refusing to take bait offered by a petulant vampire.

Caspian backed out of the parking spot and headed toward the exit.

Sulkily, Vaughn said, "Needling you is decidedly less entertaining if you don't even react."

Even minutes later, Caspian's jaw was still set. It was his deep-thinking face. I guessed he was as rattled by Vaughn's sudden arrival as I was.

HARLOW

Did you ask Vaughn to babysit us?

MOM

Of course not. Why?

I whirled in my seat. "Say cheese!" Vaughn did not comply. Despite his deep scowl, it was still a good picture. Like a super-model advertising designer jeans or cologne—but moodily.

I turned back around and sent the picture to my mom.

HARLOW

We've got company.

MOM

Goddammit, Roch.

With Vaughn's speed and stealth abilities, he could have watched us without tipping us off. Hell, he'd been spying on the Washington chapter of VHoA for a while before he'd revealed his presence. He hadn't done so until he was convinced that the situation with the Shades had grown so serious that he was willing to facilitate a meeting between Roch—a freaking *elder* vampire—and my mom, despite how livid they'd both be.

"Dammit, *Vaughn*," Mom had said. *"You told me he was expecting me and was willing to talk."*

Vaughn had shrugged. *"I lied. This is too important."*

Which meant that Vaughn was here now, willing to work on our much slower timeline, because he thought *this* was important, too. He was just as worried as we were about the emergence of shadow vampires—not because he cared a whit about Welsh, but because the pures, a species who had been alive for over five hundred years, were currently as clueless as the rest of us.

A pit formed in my stomach.

What the hells did this mean for Welsh's chances?

CHAPTER TWENTY-EIGHT

HARLOW

On our way to Oak Shores, we had to pass the turnoff that led to the rented house where Welsh was presumably still holed up. Caspian had checked his phone a few times on our ride back to the marina, and since he hadn't mentioned anything about Welsh, I had to hope no news was good news. That, or Caspian had gotten news, but it hadn't been worth mentioning.

Remembering the coolers I'd seen in the back of the minivan, I hoped now that they'd been packed with groceries. Maybe Welsh had been cooking for hours and food would be waiting for us when we got back. My mouth watered.

Though the curving road that led to the community of Oak Shores had been peaceful and relatively traffic free, we hit our first snag in our plan when the helpful signs dotting our drive led us to a gatehouse with a keypad out front and a gate blocking our entrance. Caspian pulled up to the box and cranked down his window.

The gatehouse was lined with stones a third of the way up the walls, while the rest of the one-room building was layered in wooden siding painted a bright white. The accents were blue, and a smattering of plants lined the small swatch of cement outside the blue door. It was a cute, tidy building that quietly stated this place didn't welcome randos.

Caspian's idling beside the keypad for a full minute finally triggered curiosity from inside the gatehouse, and the blue door swung open. A trim, clean-cut middle-aged man in a dark uniform strode toward us.

From the back, Vaughn asked, "Does your moral compass allow me to enthrall the gate code out of this fellow lumbering from the shack?"

Neither "shack" nor "lumbering" were accurate descriptors.

"My moral compass is currently on the fritz as long as you don't hurt the guy," I whispered.

"Hi, folks," the man said when he reached the minivan, hinging at the waist so he could give Caspian and me a quick scan through the open window. I hoped the sword had stowed itself in a seat pocket by now. "What can I help you with this afternoon?"

Vaughn yanked the side door to the minivan open without warning, startling the security guard so much, his hand instinctively strayed toward something holstered on his belt. At this angle, I had no idea if it was a gun or a taser. Given the quiet, peaceful community we sat outside of, I supposed it could be a canister of pepper spray.

The vampire stepped out of the vehicle with the languid grace of a cat. As unnerved as the security guard had been by what he'd in all likelihood assumed was an ambush by a band of miscreants, he was instantly entranced by the otherworldly man standing before him. "We're here visiting family," Vaughn said in an even, almost robotic tone. "The code we've been given must be old. You rotate your codes, do you not?"

A vampire's enthrall power wasn't visible like a sorcerer's array or witnessing the spontaneous manifestation of a fireball in the palm of a fire witch. I'd been enthralled by disgusting-ass Yannick so thoroughly, it was as if my brain had been hijacked. But I hadn't seen anything, hadn't sensed the pheromone fog Mom had equated a vampire's power to. Like the last time I'd been in the presence of Vaughn's power, the air around me felt electrically charged. The hairs on my arms stood on end and goose bumps skittered across my skin.

"*Damn,*" Caspian muttered under his breath, his gaze leveled out the driver's-side window. He hadn't experienced Vaughn's power before since he'd been left off the Terclan guest list.

The sword started up the discordant hum that I hadn't heard since the day we'd met Roch.

The security guard had gone slack in the face, his arms hanging limply by his sides. He gaped at Vaughn with something akin to devotion, but it felt creepier than that. It looked like *mindless* devotion—as if the man had been lobotomized. "Welcome to Oak Shores, sir. I will fetch you a visitor's pass. The code is 1-5-8-3-4. One moment." The man jogged into the gatehouse, arms unmoving, and returned a minute later with a printed receipt. He handed it to Vaughn. "Keep this on your dashboard. Is there anything else I can do for you, sir?"

Vaughn took the receipt. "If you see any one of us, or this car, you will recognize us as welcome visitors who were kind and funny when you met them. You will reiterate this to anyone who asks about our identities. Once we are out of your view, you will promptly forget us until you see us again."

The security guard nodded dumbly. "Understood, sir."

I shouted, "We're looking for a blue house with a rooster. Does that mean anything to you?"

The question temporarily broke the trance the security guard was in, and a hint of his natural professional scrutiny swiveled to me.

"You don't know what house your family lives in?" the guard asked.

"Her memory is a bit faulty," Vaughn said, and the guard's face went slack again as he stared adoringly at the vampire. "Now, where is this blue house with the rooster?"

"That's Doherty's place," the guard said. "Sky blue house on Raven's Cove. Take Oak Shores to Lakeview, make a right onto Shoreline, and then a right onto Raven's Cove. His is the only house on that road. There's a giant metal rooster in the yard— nearly eight feet tall. Doherty made it himself. You can't miss it."

Vaughn jutted his chin at Caspian. "Key in the code."

The electric charge in the air didn't change, and I somehow knew Vaughn hadn't used his enthrall ability on Caspian. He was just pushy.

The keypad gave a long *beep* after the last punched-in number, then the gate began to trundle open.

"You've done well," Vaughn told the security guard. "Go back inside the gatehouse now and wave amiably at us as we drive past the window."

The guard abruptly turned on his heel and marched back inside, closing the door behind him. Once Vaughn had climbed back into the minivan, shutting the door with a rattling clang, Caspian eased the car forward.

The guard, standing before the window like a department store mannequin, broke into a friendly grin as the car passed the gatehouse, his hand up in greeting. It wasn't until we were through the gate and picking up speed once again that the crackle in the air puffed away like dandelion fluff on the wind. The sword's off-kilter humming stopped.

Vaughn said, "As I told you before, Harlow, I've never once enthralled you. Granted, I prefer a more subtle approach than what I used with the rent-a-cop, but we're in a time crunch. If I had wanted to influence you one way or another, you would have been, and you'd have never known."

I didn't think Vaughn was trying to creep me out—though it was working anyway. He wanted me to know I could trust him.

Which I did not.

Caspian, thankfully, remembered the instructions the security guard had rattled off, allowing me to simply admire the picturesque lakeside community. Though I missed Luma more the longer I was out in the "real" world, places like this made it tempting to find a safe, unassuming town like Oak Shores to live in. I wouldn't be able to afford to live here in this lifetime or the next, but it was a nice thought, nevertheless.

Caspian turned onto a road that took us up a hillside. I remembered then that the security guard had said that Doherty—hopefully otherwise known as Siren Red—had the street to himself. According to Caspian's albeit limited knowledge, sirens possessed the ability to influence individuals into believing whatever they wanted to hear. It was possible Doherty had influenced any number of people that granting Raven's Cove to Doherty and Doherty alone in perpetuity was in the best interests of Oak Shores.

As we crested the hill, I spotted the massive metal rooster well before my gaze settled on the McMansion nestled among the towering pines. Sunlight glinted off the thing so brightly, I had to avoid looking at it head-on. The fact that Doherty had crafted the monstrosity himself was impressive, but it was a bit of an eyesore. There was also something decidedly off about it being a rooster— shouldn't it have been a fish or mermaid or something? Maybe that was too on-the-nose. I was sure sirens contained multitudes just like anyone else, and stereotyping them was racist. Speciesist?

"*Harlow.*"

I flinched hard. "What?"

Vaughn asked, "Did you want me to join you from the start or merely eavesdrop nearby and save you from yourself when you inevitably wind up filling a bathtub with ice to aid in the theft of your own kidneys?"

The minivan was stopped at the curb in front of the baby-blue three-storied house. A low stone wall ran around a sloping lawn that stretched before a wraparound porch. From the metal gate in the wall hung a wreath made of the same silvery metal as the giant rooster, who, from this angle, appeared to be caught in mid-charge from around the side of the house—like an avian Godzilla hell-bent on squashing intruders beneath his massive foot. The wreath was decorated not with metal flowers and leaves, but with chickens. The detailed birds had been painted in whites, browns, and reds.

"What's with this guy's fixation on poultry?" I asked.

Vaughn sighed. "Your human may already be compromised, sorcerer."

"I'm observant, *vampire*." I turned in my seat. "Is it possible for you to be less ..." I waved a hand in his general direction. "You?"

Vaughn's expression somehow flattened further.

"Can you give me any advice on how to deal with a siren?" I asked. "Refrain from a snarky answer if you can help it. I get the impression you're playing babysitter and you deeply resent me for it. But remember: I didn't *ask* you to come here. I called asking for advice, and you showed up. If you're pissed at Roch, go take it up with him. Either you're here to help us or you're not. Which is it?"

Caspian's posture had straightened sharply in my peripheral vision. Probably because the car had started to fill with that fuzzy static electricity feeling again—the same feeling I'd gotten when Vaughn had been enthralling the security guard. The sword resumed its off-kilter humming.

I was vaguely concerned that my oxygen deprivation from earlier had compromised my decision-making skills. A vivid image of my brain bobbing on the surface of a lake before sinking into the unfathomable darkness filled my mind.

A muscle ticked in Vaughn's jaw as he regarded me. Then, all at once, the crackle in the air vanished as if it had escaped out an open window.

"Sirens technically can't lie," Vaughn said in a tone that was almost friendly. "They've found loopholes in the rules mostly through interpretation of language. Humans often speak in metaphor or butcher the meaning of words entirely. As modern language evolves, sirens root out more and more loopholes. They will exploit those loopholes via anything you say that isn't direct, precise, and literal. It's similar to the lore about faeries from mundane stories. Sirens don't speak in riddles, but words are what will get you into trouble the quickest."

"Caspian will have a better time with that than I will," I said.

"I am quite intrigued by this," Caspian admitted. "The use of precise language is going the way of the dodo."

Vaughn said, "My advice is to not beat around the bush. You shouldn't pretend to be a couple in the area chatting up residents of Oak Shores to assess if this is a place you'd want to settle down. Don't pretend that you're budding artists interested in his metal-work or a neighbor looking to commission a piece for your yard. As much as sirens aren't able to lie, they're able to sense lies from others. If you start the conversation on the wrong foot, you'll be hard-pressed to reel him back in."

I frowned at how many metaphors and idioms he'd purposely used. Not even pretending to be a mute would work if Siren Red could tell I was bullshitting him from the get-go.

"I grow less intrigued," Caspian muttered.

Vaughn hiked his brows, silently asking if he'd done enough to prove he was here to help, even if he wasn't happy about it. I nodded once. "I will wait here," he said.

"Excellent," Caspian said and threw open the driver's-side door.

The sword shot out the opening before I'd even gotten my door open.

Vaughn provided no more commentary as I exited the vehicle. I couldn't imagine the guy would stay seated alone in the minivan for long, but at least I knew the vamp could be as quiet as death when he wanted to. Only problem was, I didn't know if the siren had senses that rivaled the vampire's and would know we had a spy lurking around his property.

I met Caspian at the gate. The sword remained hovering in the inverted position beside him instead of venturing off on its own. It was always hard to know if the sword's rare cautious behavior was for its protection or mine.

Steeling myself, I pushed open the gate and trudged up the slight incline to the porch. The damned monster rooster grew more disturbing the closer I got. The top of one of its round eyes was level with the porch's ceiling. The eye was black and shiny, with a circle of red dots ringing the area where the pupil would be. A camera.

The wooden porch steps creaked under my feet, officially giving away our approach, assuming the siren wasn't actively watching his security feed. The wraparound porch was decorated with the standard fare—Adirondack chairs positioned to provide a prime view of the lake, low-lying tables dotted with potted plants, and a welcome mat sitting before the red door. I canted my head as I stared down at the mat. In the middle of the brown fiber mat was a black silhouette of a chicken. Above the chicken was the word "WELCOME," and below it read "MOTHER CLUCKERS."

I knocked on the door. We twiddled our thumbs for a minute before I tried the doorbell. The muted crow of a rooster sounded beyond the door. I turned to Caspian, who leaned against the porch's railing. "Didn't consider the possibility of him not being home."

The sword issued a buzz, took off down the porch, then disappeared around the corner.

"We can always go back to the gatehouse and have Vaughn enthrall Doherty's phone number out of the guard," Caspian said flippantly. "I don't suppose you brought your lockpicks? We can hole up in his kitchen until he arrives. Lie in wait like assassins in a bad thriller movie."

"You all right?" I asked.

Caspian's shoulders drooped, and he leaned more heavily on the railing. "I'm just tired. Forced insomnia would unquestionably be a more effective method of torture than waterboarding."

I was about to ask when he'd last gotten a decent night's sleep when a series of rapid knocks sounded in the direction the sword had gone. Standing there in post-apocalyptic gear, curls whipping about in an unseen wind was ... me. My likeness pointed the sword toward the back of the house like an incensed signpost.

"What is it, boy?" I asked, as if the sword were a precocious dog. "Is Timmy stuck in the well?"

The expression on my face twisted into one of mild distaste, and then the sword shot out of sight again, my visage breaking up in the air like ink in water.

"Let me go first," Caspian said, heading across the porch. As he walked, he started up a rune array, adding rune after rune to the glowing golden disc in front of him, like adding pieces to a puzzle.

By the time we reached the back porch, Caspian had one of his signature wind arrays primed and ready to be thrown. A long set of stairs led down a cleared slope of the hillside, ending in a flat swatch of land. The area was surrounded by a chain-link fence, so I presumed this was Doherty's back yard, though the base of it resembled a junkyard. The area was dotted with worktables, piles of rusted metal, an entire rusted car, and freestanding shelving units butted up against the fence and stuffed to the gills with metal poles, rods, sheets, and misshapen lumps. Dozens of metal-work projects in various stages of completion sat on the ground and tables. The hillside to the left of the staircase was a wild tangle of bushes interspersed with young pine trees.

A man stood hunched before one of the worktables, the handle of a contraption in one hand as the other held a piece of curved metal. Sparks flew in a cascade of white. The man wore a helmet with face mask in place, sparks bouncing harmlessly off the reinforced plastic.

"Welding machine," Caspian commented.

Even from the top of the long staircase, the welder was loud, which explained why Doherty hadn't heard us ring the bell. We stood there for a minute or two until the guy finally turned off the welder, placed the welding gun on the table, and flipped up his face mask. It must have been hot as hell under that thing.

"Mr. Doherty?" I called out.

The man whirled toward us. He placed his helmet on what little free space the table had, pulled off his thick gloves, and headed toward us, weaving around the maze that was his outdoor workspace. "Who are you?"

I involuntarily grinned like a fool. He had the most delightful Irish brogue. It somehow took the edge off the biting suspicion in his tone.

"We wanted to talk to you about portals in the area," I said.

"Oof," Caspian whispered next to me. "Really wasting no time, huh?"

"Are you from Portal Relations?" Doherty asked.

I started down the steps, keeping my eyes glued to my feet, as the wood was a bit rotted and there were no handrails. A few young trees and bushes whose leaves tickled my arm as I descended the steps grew to my right. The chain-link fence encircling the yard separated Doherty's property from the empty lot next door. Caspian followed me, cursing under his breath. He had to be especially careful not to lose his footing or he'd also lose his hold on the array.

I stopped on the last step; Doherty stood a few feet away, hands on his hips. He wasn't much taller than my five eight—possibly a smidge shorter—had a wild mop of red hair, a stubbly beard, a healthy smattering of freckles, and tortoiseshell glasses perched on his nose before bright-green eyes. A leather apron covered most of his front. He wore worn, dark-brown boots.

I didn't have any idea how old he was—he could have been anywhere between twenty-five and fifty.

"We don't work for Portal Relations," I said. "We're both average citizens from Luma."

Doherty eyed me for a long moment before his gaze cut to some spot behind me. "Average citizens can't craft arrays. You with the Collective, then?"

"No," Caspian said behind me. A soft puff of air told me he'd just dropped his array. I had no idea if he'd done so because Doherty wasn't threatening or if Doherty's siren powers had convinced Caspian he wasn't. "I trained with the Collective but forfeited my right to graduate when I refused to complete my final exam."

"Why?" Doherty asked, sounding genuinely curious.

"I'd prefer not to discuss it."

Doherty looked like he was considering pushing the matter further but then decided he didn't care. Addressing me, he asked, "How did an average mundane citizen of Luma end up in Oak Shores asking me, of all people, about portals?"

My usual instinct when nervous was to ramble incessantly until I eventually arrived at the point. Though Doherty was being friendly enough, all things considered, Vaughn's crash course in sirens left me leery about saying too much. I also didn't want to inadvertently lie to the siren, or give off the *impression* I was lying, and end up kidney-free in a bathtub of ice. Would a siren even *want* my kidneys?

"So you *do* know about the instances of portals seen around Lake Nacimiento, then?" I asked, figuring bypassing his question altogether would be safer.

Doherty narrowed his eyes. The longer the silence stretched on, the more nervous I became. And now that his welder wasn't creating a ruckus, the natural sounds of the area grew louder—the wind gently rustling leaves, the distant warble of songbirds, the buzz of a nearby insect.

"I'm surprised you don't have chickens," I blurted.

The siren's manner softened a fraction. "I travel for work so much that it seems unfair to keep them. This is a summer home.

Until I have a more stable schedule, I must abstain from pet ownership, though it pains me not to have a companion."

Speaking of companions, where the hell was mine?

"Do *you* have a companion?" the siren asked, as if reading my thoughts.

"I do! You'd like it, since you're so skilled with metal," I said.

He smiled, lighting up his whole face. He had lovely, straight white teeth. "Are you a metalworker as well?"

"Me?" I asked, giggling. "Have you seen these hands? These are not the hands of a crafter."

He was on the bottom step with me a breath later, my hand clutched in his calloused ones. I had been right—he was a smidge shorter than me. He had dirt under his short fingernails, and despite wearing gloves while welding, his strong fingers were dirty, too. "Oh, I don't know about that," he said, examining my hands as a jeweler would a rare gem. "I could help you put these things to proper use."

I giggled again.

"Hi. Hello, Mr. Doherty," a voice said behind me.

I glared up at Caspian for interrupting us. "Can you go … do something? Find the sword, maybe?"

His pinched expression suggested he considered slapping me.

"A sword?" the siren asked.

I regarded him. He was already a very attractive man, but my goodness, that accent! It was like bathing in a pool of warm caramel. My lip curled. That sounded … sticky. And probably impossible to move in. Would it harden around me if the temperature of the caramel dropped or if I remained too stationary?

The siren gently squeezed my hand. "Love? What's your name?"

"I'm Harlow Fletcher. What's yours?"

I want to tattoo it over my heart.

"Ronan," he said. "Ronan Doherty. It's lovely to meet you. It's been such a long time since someone has come to visit."

"That's unfathomable. You're … you're incredible. You know that, don't you?"

"You are too kind, Harlow," Ronan said. "Now what was this about a sword?"

"Oh! Yes. My sword. It's alive. It's powered by dragon magic, but it listens to me as a dog would." Something incredibly loud buzzed in my ear, like a mosquito the size of a foghorn. I stumbled back, the heel of my shoe hitting the step above me. I went down hard. My tailbone and an elbow hit the unforgiving edges of wooden steps. A cry ripped free, aggravating my already tired lungs. The burning sensation in my throat and chest reignited like an ember given oxygen.

A warm hand landed on my shoulder, and a delicious voice asked if I was okay. That accent stirred familiarity in me like a punch to the gut. I squeezed my eyes shut, hoping that keeping my eyes diverted would somehow keep the siren from getting his hooks into me again. Then I recalled that Vaughn said a siren's power came from the manipulation of words. Keeping my eyes closed wouldn't do any good.

I quickly sat up and clapped my hands over my ears.

Ronan's face was a few inches from mine. The concern there *seemed* genuine, but I also noted that, even though he was an attractive guy, he wasn't nearly as attractive as he had been a couple of minutes ago. I *hated* magic that influenced the mind. Ronan's ability to enchant me wasn't as powerful as Yannick's, but I didn't hate it any less. That hatred must have played out across my features because Ronan quickly backed away, standing at the base of the stairs again, palms up in placation.

Before I could even consider taking my hands off my ears, my sword was in my face. It was evidently buzzing hard because it felt as if the very air around me vibrated, even though I couldn't fully hear it. It formed an image of Caspian this time, who wagged the pointer of his free hand like a disappointed parent.

Caspian!

I scrambled to my feet as best I could while keeping my hands over my ears. "Cas!" I yelled, my voice tinny to my own ears. I scanned the immediate area—the porch, the stairs, the junkyard of metal. No sign of him. I whirled toward Ronan.

The siren did his best to look contrite and went through a series of hand signals as if we were playing charades. My best guess was that he was silently assuring me he would behave if I lowered my hands. That was exactly the kind of thing a sneaky siren would say, though. I considered the fact that he actually hadn't *said* he'd behave. Did their "I can't lie" rule only refer to *spoken* words?

"Sword," I said, "if the siren makes me act weirder than usual, you have permission to maim him."

The sword's blade glowed so blue, Ronan and I both squinted against the light.

I offered Ronan my best menacing glare. "The sword's ability to discern the intricacies of human behavior is dubious at best, so I suggest not giving it a reason to stab you."

Ronan pushed his tortoiseshell glasses up his nose, then shot me an enthusiastic thumbs-up.

I slowly lowered my hands.

"I do apologize, Harlow," Ronan said. "You likely will not believe me, but I've never had the best control of my powers. I'm naturally charming, and with American women, the accent alone does most of the work. If the woman and I have a connection, no matter how slight, my power takes on a mind of its own. I end up with a legion of devoted women wherever I go."

I rolled my eyes. "Oh, boo-hoo. 'I am adored without even trying. I am the Goddess's gift to women. The tragedy.' Said no man ever."

Ronan crossed his arms, his auburn brows smashed together. "A siren cannot lie."

"Why exactly do you sound this upset about needing to beat women off with a stick?"

"Because it's nearly impossible to tell which ones are actually interested and which ones are there solely because my power lured them in," he said. "Don't get me wrong. It was incredible in my twenties and thirties. And forties. My fifties had quite a few stellar interactions as well …"

"*All* right," I said, waving my hand in the universal sign for "let's speed this along."

"But I'm getting older. My priorities have changed. It would be nice to find a woman who *wants* to be with me, who wants children, who wants to build a life," he said. "As you can see, I've chosen to live in a gated, remote community on a street by myself. Sometimes it's easier to be alone, though it can be incredibly lonely."

My shoulders sagged. "Shit, dude. Now I feel bad for you."

The corner of his mouth lifted, and little butterflies took wing in my belly. "*How* bad?" he asked.

The accent really was a crime. I bit my bottom lip. "Pretty bad."

He took a couple of steps toward me. I took one step down the staircase, the rotting wood spongy beneath my feet.

"What could we do to make us *both* feel better?" he asked.

"I have a few ideas."

"Oh yeah?" he purred.

I shrieked anew as a conjured copy of Kayda towered over me. I'd seen Kayda enraged countless times, but the sword had taken my best friend's scowl to a petrifying level. I stumbled once more but managed to grab hold of a sapling's trunk before I crashed onto my ass again.

"Thanks, sword," I managed, heart thrashing. I was grateful that it had deduced my behavior was slightly strange and not maim-worthy strange. I didn't know what it said about my behavior scale that the sword had only been *partially* sure I'd been acting off.

"Goddess," Ronan muttered, rubbing the spot between his eyes. "I apologize again. Perhaps it would be best if we talked quickly and then you went on your way." He paused. "Unless, of course, you'd want to stay for dinner?"

I licked my lips. "You cook, too?"

"Ever tried boxty? I have a fresh loaf of barmbrack cooling in the kitchen as we speak."

"I have no idea what any of that is," I said. "But you could tell me we're having a feast from Taco Bell and I'd be into it."

He was on the step with me again, my back pressed against the sapling that had saved me only moments before. He wrapped his arms around me and nuzzled my neck. In my ear, his breath warm on my cheek, he whispered, "How do you feel about … *chalupas*?"

I moaned.

Ronan issued a small, startled yelp, then was sailing through the air like a chucked football. Vaughn glowered down at me, and I cowered against the sapling. Ronan crashed into bushes somewhere on the other side of his yard. I supposed that was better than smashing into a tree or landing in the junkyard. Did ailments like tetanus affect sirens?

The pounding of footsteps sounded, and I offered Caspian a toothy grimace as he jogged down the stairs toward us. His hair was damp, and he'd changed back out of his Lake Nacimiento tourist shirt. Good to know he was off partaking in self-care while I was left to my own devices with a damned siren.

"Vaughn's been watching you for a while but was instructed only to intervene if you couldn't be trusted by yourself with Doherty," Caspian said. "I've been watching from the porch."

My face heated. "You could have hit the horny siren with one of your arrays or something!"

"I did!" Caspian said. "Multiple times. He flung them aside with a wave of his hand. He shot a firehose of water at me and blasted me up the steps at one point. That's when I went to get Vaughn."

It was beyond upsetting that I had no memory of any of that.

Vaughn whirled around, shielding me with his back. I peeked around him, spotting Ronan a few moments later as he stalked around the trunk of a young pine. His face had gone nearly as red as his hair. He angrily plucked a pine needle out of his beard and tossed it aside.

"Who do you think—" Ronan started, only to gag as he clawed at his throat.

Vaughn's hands hung loosely by his sides, but it was clear he was the culprit. "We haven't formally met. I don't care to change that. All we want is information. Harlow and Caspian will ask you a series of questions, and you will answer them honestly. The instant you deviate from this, I will kill you. I will leave your body in this slag heap of a yard to be scavenged by wild animals. I will enthrall anyone who may come looking for you so they believe that you are, in fact, fine. No one will discover your body until you're a pile of bones bleached white by the sun. Is that understood?"

Ronan's only reply was a choked gurgle.

Vaughn released the siren, who collapsed to one knee, coughing. Water seeped up from the ground around Ronan's knee, bubbling like lava spewing from a volcano as if the water table was reacting to his distress and was rising to aid him.

"Think very carefully about your next move, siren," Vaughn said.

After another racking cough, the water receded, leaving a patch of dampened earth below the siren. He slowly got to his feet.

As much as Vaughn's arrival had been both off-putting and worrying, I realized how screwed we'd have been—possibly literally for me—if he hadn't shown up when he did. Did I owe Roch a thank you? How annoying.

Jaw tight, Ronan ground out, "What do you want to know?"

CHAPTER TWENTY-NINE

HARLOW

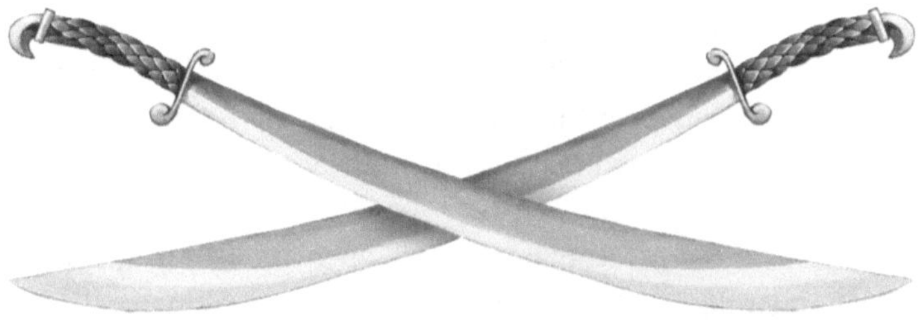

Caspian spoke first. "Have you witnessed unstable portals opening in Christmas Cove?"

Ronan's lip curled at the sound of Caspian's voice, his complete disdain evident in every line of his face. Dismissing Caspian just as quickly, he refocused on Vaughn. "Yes. I enjoy fishing in the cove. I've seen four unstable portals open there over the past three years."

I asked, "Have you seen anything *in* the portals? Has anything come out?"

Though he didn't break eye contact with Vaughn, a small smile graced his face at the sound of my voice. I resisted the urge to leave the safety of the vampire meat shield and run to my soulmate.

I gave my head a violent shake. This was getting ridiculous.

"Only lesser fae. A dragonfly from here flew into a portal once —poor bastard musta got the scare of its short life," Ronan said. "A brownie came tumbling out one day. Absolutely nasty buggers —this one came tumbling out cursing something awful—so I tossed her wrinkly little arse back in before she could get stuck here and ruin the lives of everyone she met."

Caspian muttered, "Sounds like you two would have gotten along swimmingly."

"What was that?" Ronan snapped. Water pooled and bubbled forth from the earth below him.

"Have you ever seen inside the portals?" I asked, hoping to defuse the temper that seemed to flare in Ronan every time Caspian spoke. Until a few minutes ago, I'd been sure that the siren who had been causing so many problems in town had been Siren Yellow, what with the shadow vamp revelation. But now I was starting to suspect that my redheaded, *hot*headed Siren Red was the one who was breaking up marriages when he needed a break from crafting metal giants.

The water below Ronan receded once more. He graced me with a soft smile. "Only once, love. A face was looking back at me. It was a creature I'd never seen before—some combination of human and reptile, heavy on the reptile. The portals are only ever as big as a basketball, and short-lived, so I've not seen much inside them. But the background behind the creature was as bleak as it gets—like a desert but somehow drier. The creature spoke briefly, but I honestly don't know if he was speaking to me or just muttering to himself."

"What did he say?" Vaughn asked.

Ronan's expression suggested what he *wanted* to say was something along the lines of "Get fucked, you bloodsucking gobshite," but he visibly calmed himself down. "His English was really broken, but he said something like, 'Would you look at that? He wasn't lying. Such beautiful colors. So much water.' I waved my hand in front of the portal trying to gain his notice. I can't be sure, but in the split second before the portal snapped shut, I swear he looked right at me—like he'd been ignoring me until that point. There was something really spooky about him. It felt like a lion was sizing me up, and the only reason he didn't tear my throat out was simply because he wasn't hungry."

Caspian and I exchanged a wary glance. Was the reptilian creature a Shade trying to make contact with the earthen realm? Was it the one who kept opening unstable portals, or were several beings from several realms trying to reach this one? In either case, why did the portals keep appearing in the same remote place? And were those portals at all connected to the one in the lake?

Caspian worked his jaw before addressing Ronan, visibly gearing himself up for being verbally berated. "Who is this Siren Yellow the pysid mentioned?"

The color leached from Ronan's face, making his red hair stand out in sharp relief. His gaze flicked left and right, as if the siren in question were lying in wait the way Vaughn had been earlier. "I … she … she can't know I've spoken to you."

"Not that you deserve it," Vaughn said, "but we have no intention of disrupting your sad little life—as long as you cooperate."

"She … she's … she *was* a good friend of mine," Ronan said. "We met about forty years ago when I moved to the States to pursue my art. I wanted to take lessons from a renowned armorer in Anderson—the hub in New York."

"Grantham?" Caspian blurted.

Ronan straightened. "You know of him?"

"Are you kidding?" Caspian asked. "He handcrafted the armor for all eight seasons of *Rengal's Army*. He's won *fourteen* Tillys!"

"*And* a Sheba."

"Did you actually train with him?" Caspian asked, awed.

Ronan puffed up. "For ten years."

"Incredible."

"I have an autographed copy of his *Ancient Techniques for the Modern Armorer*. Would you like to see it?"

"Would I!" Caspian said.

Ronan tipped his head from side to side. "It's even more diffi-cult to find like-minded individuals with a healthy appreciation of metalcraft. Now please be aware that I don't find you the least bit attractive."

"That is understandable. I am a wretch," Caspian said.

Ronan huffed, annoyed. "I can't say self-deprecation is an admirable quality in a friend."

"I am magnificent," Caspian corrected dutifully.

Vaughn issued a small, pained noise.

Ronan, thoughtful, tapped his chin. "My instinctive reaction to you is unadulterated hatred, as rival males are to be put down like the dogs they are, but you can't be *that* detestable if you're aware of Grantham ..."

"I would be most honored to be your best friend until the day I perish," Caspian said.

Ronan brightened. "Really? How do *you* feel about barmbrack?"

Vaughn sighed so loudly, I worried he'd pass out from lack of oxygen. Which I now knew something about.

Caspian coughed, hard, and gaped at me, eyes wide. "It happens so fast!"

"I *know*!"

"This is quite possibly the worst day of my life, and I've been alive for five centuries. I survived the Black Death, for fuck's sake," Vaughn said. "I need you all to keep your hormones and insecurities in line so I can get the *hells* out of here."

We bowed our heads like properly chastised children.

"Oh!" I said. "Oh, wait. Oh, oh! My brain is doing a thing."

"That's called a *thought*, love," Ronan said with complete sincerity.

The sword poked Ronan in the side with its hilt, then zipped out of range. Ronan looked torn between wanting to snap the sword over his knee and wanting to study it under a microscope.

The sword likely had been offering its version of "Hey, that's not nice!" but it was impossible to know.

"Armor ... Oak Shores ... metalwork ... welding ..." I muttered, frustrated that my brain had been glitchy ever since the near drowning. Which was, you know, admittedly bad. My ass should have been in a hospital and not in the back yard of a ginger siren. "Oh! Bernard!"

As supportive as Ronan wanted to be, he seemed to be at a loss now, seeking clarification from Vaughn and even, begrudgingly, from Caspian.

"Hold up," Caspian said. "Let her cook."

The correct use of modern-day slang was so startling, I turned on my spongy step to goggle at him open-mouthed. Was it all an act? Could Caspian *actually* be more in tune with the modern world than his outward stuffy professor persona would suggest?

The pieces all of a sudden snapped into place, and I peered around Vaughn to address Ronan. "Did you know a Margaret Fengast or Bernard Rex?"

Ronan reared back slightly in surprise. "Well, if *that's* not a blast from the past! I haven't heard those names in, blimey, twenty-five years? Back when ..." He trailed off as his gaze slowly swiveled back to the sword. "Is this ... no, really? Is this one of Bernard's?"

"It is," I said. "How did you know him?"

"I met him at Grantham's academy, actually. His mother had passed by then; he was in his late fifties. He'd only been at the academy for a few years before he left. Grantham told me Bernard died of a heart attack a year or so after his departure." He frowned, lost in thought for a moment. "Anyway, Bernard told me that the weapons he and his mother made, save for their ax, had been stolen from surrounding properties years before. He'd been working on a new cutlass when he was at the academy, trying to solve the conundrum of giving the weapon autonomy without risking the possibility that it could be incapacitated with the silver alloy powder like the others. He was trying to develop a rune and/or a steel composition that would work to negate the silver alloy's effect on the magic that came from the dragon scales on the hilt. He'd hoped Grantham could help him figure out the steel part of the equation."

"And did he?" I asked, opting to leave out the tidbit that the alloy wasn't the weapons' only kryptonite. Their "minds" could still be hacked by beings with mental manipulation abilities. I didn't know if a siren's powers worked similarly to a vampire's, and I didn't want to give the guy any ideas.

Had Bernard somehow known his days were numbered? It could be why he'd buried the box with the unfinished sword and the map of Lake Nacimiento under a thick layer of concrete. He hadn't wanted the wrong people to find it. He and Margaret must have gone to their graves worried about who had stolen their sentient weapons and what they'd planned to do with them. Had such worries led to Bernard's heart condition? Even if his mother had come up with the original plans for the weapons, Bernard had been the one who'd crafted them.

I said, "The map we found with the incomplete cutlass is the main reason we're here right now. I think Bernard wanted whoever found the box to then find *you*. Unless, of course, there's another fae tied to Bernard Rex in Oak Shores?"

Ronan shook his head. "Other than the so-called Siren Yellow and the pysid, there aren't any fae in the area. None with notable power, anyway."

"Did you share something with him while you were both at the academy that would explain why he'd point people here rather than at, say, Grantham?" I asked.

Ronan's green eyes glazed over behind his glasses as he went back in time in his mind. "Oh!" he said suddenly, eyes wide now. "We had a working theory about how the steel composition might change if we added arctic freezing temperatures into the mix— either from runes during the forging process or from a direct magical source."

"Like a siren?" I asked.

He smiled at me as if I'd hung the moon. "Like a siren," he confirmed.

Ronan then went into a very technical ramble about the high conductivity of silver as compared to steel and how runes that subtly altered electric currents could hold the key to the composition Bernard sought. After ten minutes, I stared up at the sky, mouth agape, as I counted the number of leaves on the tree's canopy above me. The sword spun in a lazy circle like a ceiling fan kept on low.

Vaughn finally interrupted when Ronan tried to invite Caspian to dinner again. Caspian, naturally, had found the conversation titillating, and Ronan's siren powers had tried to convince Caspian that their bromance would be the stuff of legend.

The siren needed a magic-canceling collar or something. Talking to the man for longer than a few minutes without an interruption to break the spell was damn near impossible. Now it seemed obvious why Ronan kept himself isolated: He was a menace to himself and everyone he met.

Caspian cleared his throat. "I *have* considered the possibility that what we need to reveal the runes on the second cutlass's blade is a high *cold* source rather than heat. Though the two blades appear identical, it makes sense that they'd bear striking differences once one delves below the surface."

Ronan opened and closed his mouth in rapid succession, something clearly dawning on him. "*That's* not the cutlass in question?" he asked, pointing in my sword's direction.

"*That* is one of the original five," I said, feeling a bit proud of my sword for some reason.

The sword tapped its hilt once on the ground. It sort of wiggled as it rose to shoulder height again, the blade blazing blue —a sword strut. It was proud of itself, too.

"Where is the second one, then?" Ronan asked.

A few strands of curls that had come loose from my messy bun inexplicably blew into my face.

Vaughn the meat shield lifted his arms a fraction. "In here."

I craned my neck to peer around him. Sure enough, he held out the metal box that, the last time I'd seen it, had been sitting in the trunk of the minivan. I tried not to think about how easily Vaughn could snap all three of our necks, enthrall the sword to dutifully follow after him like an obedient duckling, and be in the next county before our lifeless bodies hit the ground.

"May I?" Ronan asked, gesturing to the box.

"I wish you would," Vaughn snapped, which didn't make a lick of sense as a reply, but the lot of us had decided not to push the vamp's buttons if we could avoid it.

Ronan plucked the box from the vampire's grip and headed back toward his work area. He shoved aside a few odds and ends on a table in the middle of the junkyard and plunked the metal box atop it. We surrounded the table, me choosing a spot across from Ronan, as distance was ideal and the table was four or five feet wide. Vaughn stood to one side of me while my sword buzzed in agitation by my other shoulder. Caspian took up a spot at the head of the table, as Ronan's siren power couldn't seem to decide whether Caspian needed to become Ronan's bestest pal in the whole wide world or dead. Talk about mixed signals.

Ronan reverently opened the box, letting the lid fall all the way open. He wrapped his hand around the hilt, paused, and then dramatically hoisted the sword into the air as if he expected lightning to strike the blade and bestow on him powers from the heavens. My sword started pumping itself in the air while issuing a high-pitched screech. I wasn't sure if it was offering encouragement to its twin or to Ronan.

A whole bunch of nothing happened.

Ronan sniffed and lowered the sword, his cheeks reddening. "Had to try."

Holding the hilt in one hand, with the sword positioned horizontally, he placed two fingers from his free hand below the flat curve of the blade. At first, I thought he was merely admiring Bernard's handiwork, but the temperature around me suddenly dropped twenty degrees. My teeth chattered. From the point of contact with his fingertips, snowflake-shaped patterns skittered across the blade, riming the metal with crystalline frost.

Even from my spot across the table, I saw deep blue runes begin to materialize on the metal along the sword's fuller. As the metal grew colder, the runes became more pronounced, almost burning their way through the ice coating.

Safety be damned, Caspian's curiosity about the newly revealed runes sent him to Ronan's side. Thankfully, the siren was so preoccupied by his task at hand that he hardly noticed Caspian.

"My goodness!" Caspian said. "All of these appear to be norvinic pairings! A yin and yang of core sensory components of boranig chains, if you will."

"I will not," Vaughn grumbled.

"What now?" I asked, getting on tiptoe and leaning forward to get a better look at something I didn't understand from any distance. "You mentioned electric currents earlier. Do you need to zap it now or something? I wasn't really listening."

Ronan smiled up at me. "Either electricity or fire, we're unsure which. Electricity and water normally don't pair well, but with the steel composition of the blade, we might—"

I giggled softly at the way Ronan's fingertips trailed up my forearm. We were both leaning toward each other across the table. He had been talking about electricity and how sirens often had an innate control over it. I asked him to show me. A little spark of electricity surged between two of his fingers before he touched them to my wrist. I half laughed, half moaned, as the zap tickled my entire nervous system. My toes curled.

A loud slap on a hard surface startled me like a cattle prod to my chest, and I flailed out of Ronan's light hold. Caspian stood heaving at the head of the table. He was soaked again—his hair plastered to his head and his feet squelching loudly in his shoes as he shifted his weight. One palm lay splayed on the table; that must have been the sound that snapped me out of the spell. The burst of black lines that radiated across the wood from each of his fingers suggested that a fire array had aided in the assault on the table.

I felt a presence behind me and spun to find Vaughn sitting on a table, legs swinging, as he took a healthy bite out of a large chunk of a fruitcake-looking dessert he held in his fist like an apple. "This broombreak is actually pretty good, siren."

"Barmbrack," Ronan corrected mournfully.

I swiveled back toward Caspian, but my gaze skated past him and up toward the house. All the windows on the back of the house had shattered. Had Vaughn done that when he decided to pilfer the cake? "Uhh …" I muttered. "Did you get any closer to waking the sword?"

Caspian worked his jaw. I took an involuntary step back. I wasn't sure if he was furious with me or Ronan. "No. We got close and then …" He dramatically gestured between me and Ronan, and then to his own soaking-wet person.

"I, uh, think it'll be safer for all involved if I go … over there." I pointed toward the other end of the junkyard. "Give a holler if you get it to work."

"You don't have to—" Ronan started but cut off when he got beaned in the head by a very tightly packed ball of spiced bread.

The sword and I paced the far end of the junkyard like nervous fathers waiting for news about the birth of our child. As boredom set in, I started chucking the sword at a nearby tree. Though my overhead throw was consistently wildly off course, the sword always corrected its trajectory so I hit the tree dead center every time. I suspected the sword also slowed its approach so it didn't inflict too much damage on the tree.

During one such throw—and one that looked damn good without the sword's assistance—the sword halted a foot before the tree, turned on a dime, and shot back the other way. It zipped over the top of my head like a torpedo.

"I think it worked!" Caspian shouted.

I darted over to the guys, finding them all huddled around the sword lying on its side on a table. It wasn't moving, but the runes on its blade were glowing a brilliant gold. Slowly, the gold dimmed to a deep black. Just as I was wondering if the runes would remain visible, they faded altogether, leaving behind smooth, unblemished steel.

I chewed my lip as I waited for the sword to rise from the table like a helicopter taking off from a helipad. Nothing happened.

My sword tentatively approached its twin and gave its hilt a gentle nudge with its blade, just as it had done when we'd first found the second sword. Still nothing.

Caspian made the same suggestion he had that day. "It may be something to do with you, Harlow. See if your touch wakes this one as well."

Ronan muttered something under his breath about wanting to experience my touch, but my curiosity about the sword's twin kept my concentration from deviating.

I wiped my sweaty palms on my shirt, wrapped my hand around the hilt, and held the sword out in front of me. I considered trying my dramatic "Awaken!" command once again, but I didn't need to.

The hilt warmed in my hands. Magic—thick and heady— poured into me, the sensation somehow reminding me of drinking decadent hot chocolate on a blustery day. The magic felt right, like it was something I'd been missing all my life, filling in the empty places in my soul and psyche. Had Bernard somehow known decades ago that I would be here one day, holding this sword that was meant for me and me alone? Had he—

UNWORTHY!

The word slammed into my head like a ten-ton brick. I howled in surprise and let the sword go, stumbling backward. My lower back hit the lip of the worktable behind me and sent several tools rolling off the table and thudding onto the hard-packed dirt. Nausea roiled in my stomach, but I swallowed down the bile.

Caspian was there, cupping my face in his hands. He'd been doing that a lot today. "What happened? Are you all right?"

Over his shoulder, I surveyed the pair of hovering swords. The new one hovered in the inverted position, but there was something oddly still about it. My sword was floating a foot away from it, humming and buzzing. It kept turning the flat of its blade toward the other and then away, as if it were sneaking peeks at the newcomer but didn't want to be caught ogling. The new sword either didn't notice or didn't care.

Some part of me had been sure I'd feel deeply bereft about the magic fleeing my body and the sword itself wholly rejecting me, but I didn't. I only felt leery of the weapon. It had been so vehement in its opposition to my handling it.

I explained what had happened. I expected a snarky comment from Vaughn and an overly flattering one from Ronan, but both men seemed as troubled by this development as me.

"Maybe you can try, Cas?" I asked. "You're the one who did the hocus pocus with the boring chains thing."

He smiled ruefully at me. "*Boranig* chains."

"Yeah, that."

Caspian had let my face go, and I was easily standing on my own two feet again, but he still eyed me warily. "You're sure you're okay? We honestly should have gone straight to a hospital. Goddess above, Low, you almost drowned. *Drowned*. I truly didn't expect you to get beaten up this many times in one day."

I tried my best to act nonchalant, when in reality all I wanted to do was sleep for a week. "I'll have Welsh make me a healing tonic, and I'll be right as rain."

He huffed a sigh out of his nose, then headed for the swords. "It's a pleasure to make your acquaintance, cutlass the second. I would like to try my hand—literally, I suppose—at gaining your favor."

My sword pulsed red. The new sword merely floated toward Caspian and then hovered a few inches away, waiting.

I had no idea how long *I'd* been holding the hilt of the new sword, but what felt like moments later, Caspian had let the sword go and was backing away. "I appreciate the opportunity," he said, bowing once to the new weapon.

Caspian hadn't screamed in terror at a bellowing voice sounding in his head, and his voice had sounded steady just now, so maybe the sword had been as polite with him as Caspian had been with it.

Yet when Caspian turned toward me, his face had drained of color, and his lips had gone a little gray. He angled his hand, palm up, my way, revealing an angry red burn slashed across his skin.

"Oh, shit," I said, grabbing his hand to better examine it. Though the burn looked painful, it wasn't hot to the touch. The intensity of the burn faded before my eyes. Letting his hand go, I asked, "Did it yell at you, too?"

"Indeed," Caspian said tightly, swallowing.

"I'm always up for a challenge," Ronan said, then tried his luck.

The sword rejected him almost instantly, which sent Ronan into a near-apoplectic fit of rage. He unleashed an absolutely vile string of obscenities at the sword, which didn't show any indication whatsoever that it was bothered. In fact, as Ronan continued to rant and rave, the sword floated toward Vaughn and waited for the vampire to try.

When the sword rejected the vampire too, the only comment from Vaughn was, "You have unequivocally atrocious taste."

I nearly shit a brick when the sword floated toward me next. I didn't want to touch the damn thing ever again. It hovered there, its hilt aimed toward the sky, then suddenly slammed blade first into the ground. I flinched hard, waiting for it to do something horrible. But the only thing that changed was that the iridescent hilt lost all color, the dragon scales fading to mundane steel.

Apprehensively, I slowly bent to pluck the sword from the ground. There was still a hint of warmth in the hilt, as if the sword had merely gone into sleep mode as opposed to spontaneously dying because it didn't see fit to live in a world full of unworthy reprobates. A voice sounded in my head again, but it lacked the volume or vitriol.

Unworthy, but sufficient for now.

"That's not very nice," I muttered.

I'd hoped I'd get a response, but apparently I was so unworthy, I didn't even deserve that much. I didn't have anything on my person to carry the thing, so I decided to treat it like a walking stick. We'd see how it felt about *that*.

"Just when I thought you couldn't be more magnificent, you get chosen by yet another sentient weapon," Ronan said, as if he hadn't just gone completely off the rails a few minutes ago. I had a feeling that the rejection from the sword had greatly bruised his ego, and now he wanted me to stroke it.

A faint pulse of magic from the hilt of the new sword blissfully batted the siren's magical attempt away. Ronan audibly grumbled, like a ticked-off bear. My sword took up a spot by my shoulder as an additional line of defense.

"Well," Ronan said dismissively, "this has all been quite exciting, but it might be best if you all scamper off now."

Vaughn tsked. "There's one topic of conversation we haven't finished with yet."

Ronan scratched the side of his neck and pushed his glasses up his nose. Maybe he'd been hoping we'd forget about Siren Yellow. Now that I could fend off the siren's advances, he spoke with a general air of indifference. "Ugh. Fine. But you swear this won't get back to her?"

"We care little for your personal squabbles. You said Siren Yellow was an old acquaintance of yours?" Vaughn asked.

Ronan gusted a sigh. "The pysid call her Siren Yellow because she's blonde. They're not the best with names. Hers is Filomena Rossi."

Something that really should have registered sooner clicked for me now. "Wait, Siren Yellow is a woman? Cas, I thought you said the two sirens mentioned in the Portal Relations reports were male."

"I convinced the sorcerers we were both men for Filomena's sake," Ronan said.

I shook my head, confused. "Why?"

"Filomena was dating a man in town who was … not good for her," he said, eyeing Vaughn. "Whatever this man was … he was a different breed than yours, vampire. I've always tried to avoid your kind. His enthrall power was even more powerful than her siren abilities. He conned her into believing that the only way for them to be together was if he turned her. Sirens live a long time, but not as long as a vamp.

"She wouldn't listen to reason. And no matter what I did to track the bastard down, he'd always slip away—like mist. I've still never laid actual eyes on him. And now the piece of shite is long gone.

"One day she showed up here, so sick I was sure she wouldn't survive the night. Her skin was so pale, it was nearly translucent. The blood in her veins had turned black. A literal dark cloud, like a fog, wafted around her, like her very essence was rotting. She stayed here with me while she was sick, too ill to walk most days.

"She started talking to herself, but it was like listening to only half a phone call. I was unsure if she'd gone mad. One day I tried to sneak up and listen at her door. I heard her say, 'Ronan would never violate my privacy by eavesdropping. Of course he's not listening at the door.' That black fog crept under the door then. From inside the room, I heard her say, 'I don't think he even owns orange Crocs. And even if he did, I wouldn't tell him they're hideous.' I was indeed wearing orange Crocs; I'd just purchased them that morning. She hadn't seen them yet."

I grew more confused by the second.

"Portal Relations showed up during one of Filomena's especially bad days. I knew by then that the bite from her vampire lover had grown infected and that it would either turn her or kill her. Portal Relations had come here to ask a few follow-up questions about my latest report. I got caught in a line of questioning that forced me to admit another siren was in the house. I was able to talk my way out of allowing them inside, but I also led them to believe Filomena was a man, in part to help hide her identity. Filomena didn't want Portal Relations to find out about her condition. She'd been exiled from her home hub decades before and was convinced the Collective would come take her away if they knew. So I manipulated the truth to grant the dying wish of a cherished friend."

I chewed on the inside of my cheek.

"She survived her ailment," Ronan said, gazing distantly into space. "But she's been so changed by the transition, I hardly recognize her. Every day that goes by, she remembers less and less of her life before. She's become something of an antagonist now. What I know of her antics comes almost exclusively from the pysid, though the pysid aren't the most reliable source. The Filomena I knew *never* would have treated the pysid the way she does now. The pysid are our lesser fae—beings of the sea who should be cared for like the innocents they are. I stay in Oak Shores in large part because I want to be the one to take Filomena down should her transition into this unholy version of a vampire get too out of hand. If I had done more to help her before that swindler made her think he loved her, I may not have lost her."

This was the most sincere Ronan had been since our arrival. As he spoke of Filomena, he didn't speak in the literal way of sirens. There were no hints of his magic trying to influence anyone. There was no flirtation, no desperation to manipulate.

I had a feeling that the family—the *life*—Ronan had wanted had been with Filomena. She'd not only chosen someone else, she'd trusted a man who had killed her in many ways. And now Ronan was losing her bit by bit every day. Maybe it was true that he was out here by himself to maintain distance from anyone he may ensnare in his web under false pretenses, but it was likely also true that he stayed removed because he was heartbroken. Any connections he made would ring false, not only because of his manipulative magic, but because no one would ever be the Filomena he'd lost.

"It may already be too late," Caspian said.

Ronan glared at Caspian, ready to defend Filomena's honor, even though it was evident the old Filomena was long gone.

Caspian told Ronan about Lachlan Shade and shadow vampires. He spoke of our suspicion that Filomena was a Shade who was in contact with Lachlan through the portal at the bottom of the lake. "We don't know the extent of Lachlan's plans, but she's purposefully keeping the existence of the lake portal from Portal Relations because she's assisting Lachlan."

"She's also killed a few of the pysid. One of them told us that Filomena can drown them on land *or* in water," I said softly. "They obey her because they're terrified of her."

"Goddess be damned," Ronan muttered, hands clasped atop his head. "How have I been so blind?"

I said, "Because you love her. Do you think she would listen to you if you confronted her? Maybe you can convince her to leave with you. You could get her—"

Ronan shook his head. "No. If she's killed pysid, she's beyond saving. I cannot overstate how much of an affront it is to our kind to kill a pysid."

The fact that Ronan currently *wasn't* raging out of control was more discomfiting than his meltdown from earlier. He was preternaturally motionless. My sword started up a soft, off-kilter hum.

"If you do not wish to dispatch her yourself, I'd be happy to do so," Vaughn said, his tone genuine and sincere. Granted, he was offering to murder someone, so that wasn't great, but it was good to know he could be nice when he wanted to.

"No," Ronan said, shaking his head tightly once more. "This is something I must do. Clearly Goddess Anobay sent you here today." When he looked at me this time, that undeserved aura of pure adoration wasn't present. His soft smile told me he was truly grateful, though. "Anobay wants me to protect the innocent pysid. I have let this go on too long because of a foolish hope that Filomena could be absolved. I thank you for showing me the way."

Without warning, Ronan morphed into a terrifying amalgam of fish, human, and bird that stood six feet tall. While his face remained somewhat human, he bore the beak of an eagle, two clawed feet that would befit an ostrich on steroids, and the body of a red-scaled fish, and a pair of sleek, black wings sprang from his back. He unleashed a piercing screech and then shot straight into the air with a great burst of speed. A single black feather drifted to the ground, landing on the torn-up and damp earth where Ronan had just been standing. As Ronan reached the tops of the trees, his entire body shimmered out of existence. I didn't know if he'd teleported or employed a cloaking ability.

Vaughn trudged back toward the stairs as if we hadn't all witnessed one of the most jarring and disturbing things in my life. Even Caspian looked stunned. The sword hovered a few feet away, its blade a sickly yellow. The hilt of the second sword still felt warm in my palm, but it otherwise remained quiet.

A chill wind swept past me—this one a natural one and not one crafted by a siren. I shivered as I took in the junkyard. The shadows cast from the piles of metal were long and spindly. The undulations of the shadows made chills skitter down my back anew as I recalled Ronan's claim that the shadows that seeped from Filomena could communicate with her. Would that be the sign that Welsh had reached the point of no return—if the whispers that wafted from his shadows began to speak to him coherently?

Vaughn, halfway up the stairs, called out, "Did you want to get back to your rented abode now? Or did you want to stop for chalupas first?"

Caspian snickered.

But any witty retorts I might have come up with died on my lips.

Because the sound emanating from the darkening trees beyond the flimsy chain-link fence that ringed Ronan's yard had turned my blood to ice.

It sounded again.

The violent snorting of a pig. *Several* pigs.

With my new unfriendly sword in hand, I sprinted all the way back to the car.

CHAPTER THIRTY

KAYDA

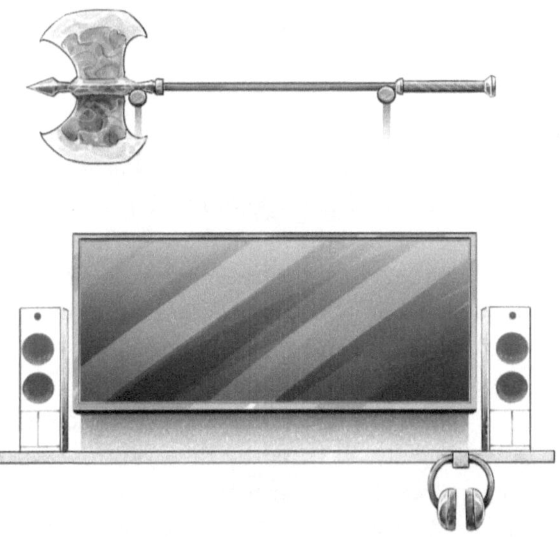

The San Diego VHoA chapter waited until ten p.m. before they loaded into their tinted SUVs and Jeeps. The small group staying back at headquarters was in charge of getting the roll-up doors opened for the fleet to leave and then sealing headquarters back up.

When all was said and done, six members were headed into downtown San Diego to question staff at two local vampire hangouts, and a twenty-person team was headed to the Briar Road nest.

Kayda was bundled into an SUV with Marisol, Quaid, Tony, and the blond dragon-obsessed lady who, she informed Kayda, went by the name Ocean. Kayda had a sneaking suspicion that the woman had given herself the name to help her manifest her deep desire to inhabit a fantasy world. Tony looked like the kind of guy who wouldn't suffer fools, so Kayda was banking on Ocean being an adept fighter even if her head was otherwise in the clouds.

Everyone had been outfitted in tactical gear, charmed weapons, and earpieces so the team could constantly stay in contact. Kayda had rightly assumed tactical gear in her size wouldn't be available, so she'd stuffed her set into her go-bag before she'd left Luma.

Kayda had put the earpiece in when Marisol first eased the SUV out of the warehouse after Akio's, but the chatter on the coms was near constant, giving Kayda a headache. Even with the earpiece lying in her lap, her sense of hearing was so strong, she might as well have still had the damn thing in. So she'd dialed her hearing down to near zero and turned her sight up, scanning the dark world outside the windows in case anything other than mundane wildlife was out and about tonight.

It took roughly forty-five minutes to reach the now-infamous Briar Road just outside of Bonsall in San Diego County. The sign for the road was mostly obscured by the overgrown canopy of a massive mulberry tree. They'd been on the deserted dirt road with no streetlights for nearly twenty minutes, the rutted road lined by the spindly remains of a long-abandoned apple orchard. The only things that stood out in the darkness during the drive had come from the SUV's headlight beams reflecting off the slashes of white paint decorating each tree trunk. Kayda didn't know if the paint meant anything—maybe they'd been marked for removal. Was the vamp nest hidden behind these rotting trees because the area was abandoned, or had they made it *look* abandoned to keep others away?

Marisol elbowed Kayda in the side and motioned to the earpiece still lying in Kayda's lap.

Reluctantly, Kayda adjusted the dials on her senses so she could comfortably wear the earpiece without being so distracted that she compromised the mission.

"Pulling over in roughly four hundred meters," came Akio's voice. "We'll hoof it for the next half mile. Keep your eyes peeled for ferals. If they're out here, they've heard us by now. Kayda, I'd appreciate any extra help those draken eyes of yours can give us."

"Haven't sensed anything yet, but I'll make adjustments once we're on foot," Kayda said.

"Keep the com channel clear once we're on the move," Akio said. "Baxter, get your fucking horrible jokes out of your system in the next minute, then I'm going to need you to shut up."

A smattering of amiable laughter came through the com so loudly, Kayda winced. She further finessed the dials on her senses.

"Did you hear about my job making plastic Draculas?" Baxter, presumably, asked.

"At least he's staying on brand with it being vampire themed," someone muttered.

"There's only two of us on the production line," Baxter said, already chuckling at himself. "So I have to make every second count!"

A chorus of enthusiastic boos came down the line. Kayda groaned, but she was laughing, too.

Akio's SUV pulled onto the soft shoulder. Marisol followed suit. Spindly branches scraped at the side of the vehicle, like the nails of some great beast trying to get in. Chills skittered across Kayda's skin.

"All right, everyone," Akio said. "Going radio silent. Keep the line open for vital intel only."

Kayda's phone buzzed in her pocket. She quickly pulled it out, smiling like a fool at the sight of Henri's name.

HENRI

Good luck! I need you to come back in one piece, okay?

KAYDA

I'll do my best. Sorry I couldn't see you before we left tonight.

HENRI

All good. The stress of you being three hundred miles away fighting monsters has resulted in me marathoning Mangrin's Gate. I just hit level 63.

KAYDA

Did you do the naga cave run already? You were supposed to wait for me!

HENRI

You brought this upon yourself, woman. Picture me atop the widow's walk, staring out at the sea as I wait for my lady love to return home from war. I've developed a debilitating drinking problem and an ulcer.

KAYDA

I'll make it up to you when I get back. And also replenish your stash of antacids.

HENRI

You're so good to me.

She stuck her phone back in her pocket and climbed out of the SUV.

She'd felt relatively Zen when she exited the car—talking to Henri, no matter how briefly, usually did that. But the sounds of the VHoA team's heartbeats were pumping hard on the fringes of her hearing, like a discordant drum solo. She wasn't able to hold on to the Zen feeling for long.

People were light on their feet, but she could hear every footfall, every squelch of rotting fruit underfoot, every puff of breath. She blocked it all out as she fell into step with the others jogging along the side of the road. Marisol was in front of her and Quaid was behind. Kayda's beloved battle-ax was strapped into the reinforced belt loop at her hip. The faint crackle and glow of other charmed weapons flickered ahead—reds and yellows and greens seeping out from beneath their shoddily made magic-dampening hoods. VHoA overall needed better hoods. There had to be a way to get Jo a business deal with the organization. If Jo then got Snowdrop on board, they could get a nice assembly line going.

After five minutes, Akio's hushed voice rang out in Kayda's ear. "Farmhouse is up ahead. Team A, head toward the back now. Team B, keep charging ahead."

Kayda was on Team B. Her ears pricked as ten pairs of feet peeled off from the line and ducked into the trees. The air seemed thick with the smell of rotting apples—and something else. Something metallic.

"Shit," Kayda muttered. "I smell blood."

The footfalls around her didn't stumble.

Akio asked, "A normal amount of blood for a nest? Or a worrying amount?"

Kayda wanted to say that *any* amount was worrying, but these people lived a much different life than hers.

Before she could answer, a soft chitter carried to her on the wind. She stopped dead in her tracks. Quaid deftly wove around her without breaking stride. Kayda closed her eyes for a moment and further tweaked the dials on her hearing. The chitter came again, sending her forward a few steps as her eyes popped back open, willing the nebulous shapes to solidify in the dark.

Team B kept up their steady, slow crouch-walk toward the house's front door.

The two-story farmhouse was made of limestone bricks. Wooden pillars held up black-roofed awnings over the patios in front of the house and along one side. A chimney stretched high into the dark air, its height dwarfed only by a pair of nearby oaks.

The house had once been pristine, Kayda guessed. The owners had been wealthy. A tire swing, the rubber weather-worn and cracked, swayed lazily from the branches of one of the oaks. Kayda hoped the family who had once lived here had left of their own volition and not been forced out by vampires seeking a secluded area to make their nest.

The chitter sounded again, and Kayda's gaze snapped to the chimney. A dark figure scuttled around near the column, then leaped.

"Incoming!" Kayda bellowed. "Feral above us at twelve o'clock."

The group of three nearest the front patio turned on a dime and backtracked, expertly getting out of the way before the feral hit the ground inches from where they'd been. The feral got out a chittering cry, but charmed weapons divested of their dampening hoods were already swinging for the beast. In a matter of seconds, it was dead.

"Three o'clock and nine o'clock!" Kayda shouted out as she heard three more monsters come charging in from each direction.

The light chatter on the coms suggested that Team A had run into a pack of ferals as well. Kayda had been about to charge to the left, in the direction Marisol and Quaid had gone, when a snarl sounded from behind her. She whirled just as a feral darted into a weak beam of moonlight filtering between the bare branches of an apple tree. She took off at a dead run, back in the direction of the entrance road, calling into the coms that at least three more were coming from the apple orchard.

As she ran, she yanked her battle-ax free, tore off its hood and swung the weapon, shearing off the top of the first feral's skull without breaking stride. She leaped over the tumbling body, the scent of rotting flesh overpowering the stench of rotting apples as the feral's black blood gushed from the fatal head wound.

By the time she'd reached the other three ferals, five VHoA

members—including Akio—had joined her. They dispatched the ferals with ease. Six against four had frankly been overkill. Kayda came to an abrupt halt, chest heaving, as she scanned the area. She couldn't hear or see any more ferals. The animated chatter in her earpiece had died down—not because the team had been taken out, but because they'd cleared their horde, too.

"Horde" felt like too big a word. Small contingent?

Akio strode up to her, shaking a chunk of gore off the blade of his machete as he did so. "Picking up any others?"

"Nope. It's … kind of spooky. This feels too easy …"

Akio's lips compressed into a deep frown. "I was thinking the same thing."

"But if this is a trap, everyone in that house is being *deathly* quiet," Kayda said. "I haven't faced off against any hybrids, so I don't know if being utterly silent is a thing they can do, but my gut says that house is empty."

Akio stared off into the middle distance for a beat, pensive. "Team A, move in through the back. Team B will breach the front door."

Kayda's team regrouped in front of the house. Everyone's charmed weapons were out; the crackling magic emanating from the team made it look as if they all held monstrous glowsticks. She kept to the back of the group, constantly adjusting the dials on her hearing as if she'd somehow be able to hear the quiet exhalation of someone huddled in an upstairs closet if she just concentrated enough.

Less than two months ago, Marisol had lost two-thirds of her team when a hybrid had blown his hideout up, sacrificing several of his own vampires solely to take down a team of vampire hunters at the same time. Kayda didn't detect the tick of a bomb—hells she couldn't even hear a wall clock. There was no buzz of electricity, no hum of a running refrigerator—not even the soft patter of a mouse scampering in the walls.

Even so, when Akio threw open the front door and a group of VHoA members streamed into the house, weapons raised, Kayda held her breath, half convinced the house would erupt in a ball of flame—all because they'd trusted her assessment.

The only thing that exploded from the house was a veritable wall of putrid air.

She loitered alone on the front porch, casting her senses out in all directions, but she still couldn't detect anything. Even the rodents were quiet, as if not even they wanted to be anywhere near this place. Claw marks and deep gouges marred the wood of the columns and patio floor, but the ferals could have made those marks in the last hour for all Kayda knew.

"Clear!"

"Clear!"

"Clear!"

Kayda inched into the house, stomach roiling at the pungent cloud of rot that was so strong she could taste it on her tongue. It coated her throat.

Blood, decay, death.

Team B streamed up the stairs, clearing rooms just as quickly as Team A had cleared the first floor. Within ten minutes, the entire team of twenty loitered in the modest living room. The décor was a bit dated and covered in a thick layer of dust, but if Kayda had been in this house for any other reason, she would have thought no one had been here for years.

Akio instructed Team A to head back outside to scour the orchard and surrounding wooded areas. Half the assembled group filed out, seemingly grateful to escape the stink of the place. "Split up. Check for an attic, a basement, hidden doorways, false walls—the smell's gotta be coming from somewhere."

With no electricity in the house, team members soon swapped their weapons for flashlights. Outside among the trees, flashlight beams sliced their way through the dark apple orchard. Kayda stowed her battle-ax back at her hip but opted to keep her hands free and used her natural night vision to see instead of a flashlight.

While Kayda had been letting her ears guide her so far, now

she needed to rely on her nose. She hadn't trained her olfactory skills as much as the others, but now was as good a time as any to start.

Her nose eventually led her to the enormous kitchen. Maybe the place had been a bed and breakfast at one point, or a popular location for weddings. Kayda opened the fridge, checked under the sink, and peeked into the pantry. Everything was empty save for a desiccated, rotting bulb of garlic sitting on a shelf in the middle of the refrigerator. Green shoots had begun to grow from the individual cloves, but those had dried and withered, too. Was someone fucking with them? Garlic in the fridge in a vampire nest?

The more she let her nose be her guide, the more she kept coming back to the massive ten-by-five-foot island in the middle of the kitchen. The cabinets and drawers were empty. Frustrated, she placed a hand flat on the scrubbed-clean marble top, baffled about the origin of the smell that was definitely strongest in this room. As she shifted her weight from one foot to the other, the toe of her boot snagged on something. She squatted, cocking her head at what looked like a faint groove dug into the wooden floor. Brow creased, she placed her hands on the side of the island and pushed.

The island was heavy, but not so heavy that she couldn't move it a good foot on her own. And below the island was the outline of a trapdoor, complete with handle. The putrid smell ratcheted up exponentially.

"Trapdoor in the kitchen!" Kayda said in a normal volume, knowing the coms would pick it up and carry it through the group at large.

A flood of footsteps pounded across hallways, down steps, and across the lawn outside. Four members ran into the kitchen in record time, one of whom was Tony. All four gagged violently at the smell but quickly got to work helping Kayda shove the marble-topped island out of the way.

A minute later, most of the team had filed into the kitchen.

"Ready?" Kayda asked.

"Do the honors," Akio said.

Kayda grabbed the handle and pulled it up. The damn thing was thick as hells and must have weighed at least fifty pounds. The underside, she noted, was made of reinforced steel. With some help, she got the door all the way open and rested it against the island. A dark set of stairs stretched into pitch black.

Someone noisily vomited into the sink as the absolutely horrific smell blasted out of the basement like a silent bomb. Two others clapped hands over their mouths and bolted from the room. Kayda found Quaid and Marisol in the crowd, and though they both looked decidedly green, they each nodded at her in turn.

Kayda pulled her battle-ax back out, got a good grip on the haft, then started the descent into the basement. Though her night vision had served her well so far, she appreciated the cascade of light that accompanied the single-file line of VHoA members coming down the steps behind her, assuring she wouldn't go tumbling down the steps. Though the further she got into the basement, the more she wanted to turn around and run back up.

This nest hadn't been a squalid disaster like the one she'd seen in the last video of Kessler when he'd wielded the power of a tsunami. The spacious basement was nearly as large as the house above, conjuring up a ludicrous image of vampires in construction gear, complete with hard hats.

The half of the room closest to the stairs had been set up like a decadent lounging area—thick tapestries depicting bloody battles lined two of the walls, while bookshelves lined the others; pillows as large as couch cushions and upholstered in red or black silk were piled on the floor surrounding low tables that had once been topped with trays of snacks and bowls of fruit. The carpet was the color of wine.

The farther half of the room was lined with beds—most twin-sized, but there were a few larger ones wedged into corners—piled high with fluffy comforters and pillows. A cooking area ran along the far wall to the right—a setup that reminded Kayda a lot of the ones in the VHoA warehouses.

Overall, it looked like the kind of place that would be a great shelter should some calamity befall a large group of people.

That was all dampened by the sea of headless bodies. Blood and gore were splashed across tapestries, walls, the floor, the beds. It pooled and soaked into the cement. The wine-colored carpet squelched under Kayda's boots as she skirted around upended fruit baskets, blood-soaked books, and bodies. She stashed her ax back in its loop; no one here had any life left in them to fight.

The team behind her was largely silent save for the squish of the bloody carpet. Kayda felt mildly relieved when she finally made it to the other half of the room where the floor was cement. Bloody footprints trailed after her as she scanned the beds and the floor, searching for any sign that Kessler had been felled in the massacre. Though she didn't know how they'd be able to identify him, considering that all the bodies were missing their heads.

The more she searched, the more she was sure that the bodies had belonged to hybrids or ferals. Feral blood was a deep black, while hybrid blood was a purplish-red. Kayda knew old human blood dried a darker color than the vibrant red that spilled from a fresh cut, but none of this *smelled* human.

"Anyone seeing blue blood?" Kayda asked softly, though she knew there was no chance of waking the dead.

Replies came back in the negative or some form of "It's hard to tell," especially with only flashlights to see by, but most agreed the blood was all too dark to belong to a fae.

Did that mean Kessler hadn't been here when the killing started? Had he ever been here at all?

Kayda kept her head on a swivel as she slowly made her way to the far end of the room. When she reached the last row of twin beds, she stopped dead in her tracks as her gaze settled on something that was impossible to see from the entrance—especially in the dark. "Found the heads …"

Piled along the far wall were a dozen severed vampire heads. They'd been arranged in a vaguely pyramidal shape, with a single head topping the macabre shrine. Kayda didn't know if the vampire would be recognizable to the San Diego team who were familiar with this particular nest.

All Kayda knew was that there were two very disturbing things about the topmost head. First, it didn't look like his head had been sliced off by way of a blade. Part of the head's jaw was missing, and the skin of his cheek was torn in a jagged line rather than in a straight one. The more she studied the heads, she realized the way some of the skulls appeared caved in at the temples implied the heads had been palmed like basketballs before being *ripped* off their necks.

If that wasn't bad enough, the head atop the pile also had his eyes gouged out. An object protruded from each socket. Reluctantly, she inched toward the pile, trying to avoid stepping in the gelatinous puddle forming below the heads, and gently pulled one of the objects free. Half of it was coated in a thick purple-red blood, but the part that had been sticking out of the hole was a clean white. Covered in blood or not, Kayda knew what the object was.

A domino.

Through the earpiece, someone said, "I think I found the bed that belonged to Kessler. Baxter and I have been checking under each of the mattresses. Nest captives usually keep personal items hidden there. There are a few *Bioframe* manga here. They all star Echo."

Bouncing flashlight beams grew closer, painting the walls around Kayda with white-blue light. As she stared blankly at the pile of heads, she absently turned the bloody domino over and over in her hand, so much that the blood was mostly transferred to her palm.

Marisol reached Kayda first, cursing softly under her breath at the disturbing scene. Others slowly joined them, each one as horrified as the last.

"What's in your hand, Kay?" Marisol asked in her motherly voice—the tone she used when she thought Kayda might snap if she was pushed too hard.

Maybe such a tone was necessary. Something *had* gone unsettlingly quiet in Kayda, but she wasn't sure if the hollow feeling was disappointment or horror. Perhaps both.

Kayda handed the domino to her. "That mean anything to you?"

Someone else plucked the second domino free. People speculated that the numbers on the tiles might mean something. Number combinations and totals were whispered about on the coms. Others theorized that the numbers on each tile could represent a letter—the building blocks needed to solve a cipher.

Kayda finally peeled herself away from the pile of severed heads, needing to think, needing to get the cloying stench of death out of her nose. Needing to shake off the feeling that she'd failed Kessler the same way she'd failed those sixteen elf teenagers.

"It's too messy," Kayda muttered to herself.

"What was that, Kayda?" Akio asked. "Hey, everyone shut up."

"What's too messy, Kay?" Marisol prompted when Kayda didn't immediately reply.

Kayda found herself leaning against another refrigerator. The kitchen somehow felt removed from the carnage, allowing her to think a little more clearly. "What do vamp hunters do after they clear a nest?"

There was a long stretch of silence from the group.

"Burn the bodies," Akio finally said.

Kayda asked, "What do bounty hunters do after they've cleared a nest?"

"Call in a cleanup crew of sorcerers and witches to use magic to scrub the place clean." That answer had come from Quaid.

"And werecats?" Kayda asked.

Marisol answered. "Cleanup crew for them, too."

"There was a slaughter here, and when the killers were done, they blocked off the basement *and* assigned ferals to prowl the outside." Kayda worked her jaw. "VHoA, bounty hunters, werecats—none of them would leave a scene like this. The only bodies in here are hybrids and ferals. No humans. No fae. That's weird. Killers this brutal wouldn't leave witnesses behind. And *fuck*. That head with dominos shoved in the eyes? That's a message."

"A message from who, Kay?" Marisol asked.

Kayda shrugged even though she knew no one could see it. They were all huddled around the pile of heads. "I don't know. But whoever left it? That's who has Kessler."

The mood was somehow even more somber after that.

VHoA took pictures, loaded a few of the heads into pillowcases for reasons unfathomable to Kayda, and collected the personal effects from below all the mattresses. Then they filed out.

The fresh, cool air outside the farmhouse felt delicious in Kayda's lungs. She feared that the smell, though, would haunt her forever. Kayda wanted nothing more than to burn the entire house to the ground, but Akio convinced her that the risk of setting the whole county on fire was too high. He assured her that he and another team would be back out tomorrow to take care of the basement. Kayda had no idea what that entailed, but she didn't care.

Everyone was quiet on the drive back, lost in their thoughts.

She couldn't shake the feeling that someone had *torn* the heads off those hybrids. Sorcerers with the right set of arrays could manage the feat, but casting specific spells like that would take time. *Too* much time.

The so-called elephantine fae, however, were more believable culprits.

Before leaving for the nest, Akio had said it would be smart for the Shades to have draken, trolls, and orcs in their employ, simply because they supplied sheer muscle power. But he'd also postulated a disturbing theory about Lachlan. *"What if Lachlan's been recruiting those people for* this *reason—to turn them into shadow vamps and have an army that's even stronger?"*

Could that be who murdered all those hybrids and ferals?

If so, why *this* nest? Why leave what almost looked like a calling card?

Kayda kept circling back to the same reason: Kessler.

The video of Kessler commanding a tsunami of shadows replayed in her mind. Any number of people could have watched Kessler's vlog. If Marisol had been able to find that clip of Kessler, if VHoA could track down clues that led to this very farmhouse, then someone else could have done all that internet sleuthing, too. Kayda desperately hoped it had been an orc or troll with serious tech skills who'd made the discovery and then tracked Kessler here and not someone in VHoA who had *sold* the information to some unscrupulous type. A mole in VHoA could be disastrous. The forum would be an absolute goldmine if someone was willing to exploit the organization's policy of freely shared information in exchange for cash.

If the Shades had been the ones behind Kessler's kidnapping, there was a very real possibility Kayda would never find him.

Kayda was realizing that the hollow feeling in her chest came not just from feeling like she'd failed Kessler, but that she'd failed Welsh, too. He was a grouchy asshole, but he'd also saved her from being arrested, given her a place to stay when she'd had nowhere to go, and gone out of his way countless times to protect Harlow. Hells, he'd even helped Aster perfect her baking recipes. He was a good guy deep down, even if he didn't want anyone to know it.

Kayda had wanted to return the favor—to find Kessler and somehow uncover the magic cure for Welsh.

But if powerful fae were being *purposely* selected as part of Lachlan's master plan, Welsh could end up in that monster's clutches, too.

And Kayda had no idea how to stop it from happening.

CHAPTER THIRTY-ONE

HARLOW

As I unlocked the door to the rental house, the scent of garlic and bacon wafted past me. My stomach gave a happy jump —Welsh *had* cooked. I'd hardly eaten anything today, and now I was starving.

"Honey, we're home!" I called out.

"About damn time!" Welsh called back over the sound of the TV, which he paused a moment later.

I walked into the living room just as Welsh was swinging his legs off the couch. A quick peek at the TV revealed he'd been watching *The Great British Bake Off*.

Welsh's gaze bounced from me to my floating sword and then to the one in my hand.

Caspian's shoulder clipped mine as he barreled past me and

speedwalked into the living room. "Hey, buddy. Hi, my good old pal. How about we scootch on over into the kitchen, and you can tell us what you made!"

I was so flabbergasted by whatever in the hell awkward-ass nonsense had just come out of Caspian's mouth, I couldn't even be annoyed that he'd practically shoved me out of his way.

Caspian had only succeeded in getting Welsh to move a single step across the black rug before Welsh's attention snagged on who was loitering in the foyer. Welsh slammed on the brakes.

My sword darted around behind me, humming. The second sword's hilt pulsed once in my grip but otherwise remained dormant. It was good to know the thing was aware of its surroundings but incredibly annoying that it was actively avoiding intervening, solely because it had decided none of us were worthy of its time.

Jaw set, Welsh yanked himself out of Caspian's loose hold and took several steps away. He tore his focus away from the vampire and settled on Caspian for a moment before glaring at me. "Did *you* do this?"

Welsh was grumpy on his best days. I'd seen playful, irritated, silly, annoyed, deeply amused, and disgusted. It wasn't until that second that I realized I'd never truly seen him angry—until now.

"Do not blame her, Zan—"

Welsh jabbed a finger toward Vaughn. "I don't recall asking for *your* fucking opinion."

All that stood between the two was a low, glass-topped coffee table and a stretch of shiny hardwood floor. I stood just in front of the open doorway of the kitchen, several feet away from ticked-off witch and impassive vampire. Shinnying out the window over the sink was my closest available exit. I briefly considered folding myself into one of the cabinets.

"I asked him for advice, and he just *showed up*," I said.

"That's when you *send him away*," Welsh said. "If you want a mangy stray to go away, you stop feeding it."

I wasn't sure what that meant, but the sudden crackle of

Vaughn's power flitting through the air said Welsh had hit a nerve.

Gesturing at Vaughn with a whole-body thrust of his arms, Welsh asked, "Of all the people in all the Goddess-damned world you could have contacted, Harlow, why did it have to be *him*?"

A sinking feeling in my gut made me begin to question everything up until this point. This wasn't an "I don't like vampires" reaction. This was a very specific "I violently despise *this* vampire" reaction. I'd seen a brief text conversation between Caspian and Welsh about pure vampires and how Welsh thought pures were the worst of the lot. I hadn't thought much about it, if only because Welsh had a healthy hatred of just about everyone.

But I remembered now how Roch's eyes had glinted at the mention of Welsh's ability. No names had been used, but I supposed names weren't strictly necessary when glamourers, according to Roch, were "as rare as they come." Roch had downplayed his interest by saying he'd only asked about my glamourer friend in a veiled attempt to appear interested in me, as a person, to further "butter up" my mother.

Slowly, I asked, "Vaughn, how do you know Welsh?"

"*Know* is such a relative concept," Vaughn hedged.

"I can't believe I'm saying this," Caspian said, "but skip the semantics and just answer the damn question."

"Swoon." I flushed; that had been ninety percent involuntary.

Vaughn and Welsh made twin sounds of disgust.

I gasped. "Oh, holy shit! He's not, like, your long-lost dad or something, is he, Zeef?"

The look Welsh shot me was one of unfiltered bewilderment. "Why are you like this?"

"Who can say?"

Welsh gusted a loud sigh. "No, for fuck's sake, he's not my father."

"But I *did* know his mother," Vaughn said. "Young Zander and I crossed paths often when he was a boy."

Welsh's jaw had gone tight again.

Caspian gawked at his friend, though Welsh was still pointedly ignoring him, despite their current proximity. "*This* is the vampire Thalia was working with?"

"Among others," Vaughn said. "But we were also the only ones who extended an offer to house you when you had nowhere to go, Zander. Instead, you disappeared into the hub system, ensuring we'd lose track of you. Incredible that you've been a mere twenty miles away this whole time. I suppose this is all fitting, though. That is what you do for others now, isn't it? Help them disappear? Your mother would be *very* disappointed."

Strangely, that last sentence had been uttered with an air of pride. Caspian *had* said that Welsh's plethora of defense mechanisms were borne out of his "mommy issues." I should have forced more details out of him then.

"Don't try to flatter me," Welsh muttered.

"If, uh, Vaughn, and presumably Roch, offered to help you," I said slowly, knowing just shutting up would be smarter, "why are you so mad at him?"

If looks could kill, the one Welsh fired my way would have done the job.

"An excellent question," Vaughn said.

"Oh, *fuuuuck* you, Vaughn." Welsh pressed the heels of his palms to either side of his head, as if he were trying to crush his own skull like a melon to get out of this conversation. He paced back and forth in a tight line.

Caspian backed up a few steps, looking fearful of his friend for the first time since I'd met them.

"I'm sorry, Welsh," I said quietly, and frankly a little desperately. "I didn't know there was history. I was just trying to help. I told you we'd figure this out. And to me, that means leaving no stone unturned."

"I'm sure he'll make a quip now about a cockroach like me skittering out from beneath one such overturned stone," Vaughn said.

Welsh dropped his hands. "Generally, most people would

agree that exploiting a child is a pretty cockroach-like thing to do. So, yeah, Vaughn, I wasn't about to hole up with the same people who saw what my mother was forcing me to do and not only didn't stop her, encouraged her."

I chewed on my bottom lip.

Caspian hazarded a single step toward his friend. "You don't have to get into this, Welsh."

Welsh whirled on him. "Oh, *now* you think ambushing me with this fucking guy was a bad idea?"

"You say that as if I had any idea you had a history with Vaughn!" Caspian snapped. "You're not exactly loquacious when it comes to divulging pertinent personal information."

"Stop with the fucking SAT words already, Caspian. Goddess above!"

Welsh had never had much of a foul mouth before, but he was dropping f-bombs like a B-52 tonight.

As the boys bickered, I studied Vaughn, who was watching the argument with his usual quiet detachment. This entire scenario still didn't sit well with me; the odds of Vaughn being connected to Welsh by mere happenstance were slim.

Vaughn, after I'd told him about Welsh's predicament, hadn't said something like "Let me consult with Roch and get back to you," or "I have no idea what's going on with shadow vamps, but let me know if your friend gets any worse," or "Why do you think I give a shit about your personal quibbles?"

What he'd asked was, "Would it help if I spoke with your witch?"

I should have known then that something was off. Vaughn didn't make house calls. He didn't involve himself unless it was vital to him and his kind.

"While we have no vested interest in the well-being of the humans in the hubs, we're certain that once Lachlan perfects ripping away veils from hub cities like one tears a shower curtain from the rod, enclaves like Tercla will be next," Vaughn had said the day we met. Despite the significant threat to humans inside the veils *and* out, Vaughn had

readily admitted that he didn't care about their fate. So why hadn't I been more suspicious when Vaughn had volunteered to talk to Welsh with no coercion from me? Hell, *he'd* done most of the coercing.

"Who better for him to speak to than a vampire?" Vaughn had asked me.

The suggestion had thrown me off, but while I'd surmised that a phone call with a vampire wouldn't be on the top of Welsh's Top Ways to Spend My Time list, it could have still proven useful.

"I can ask him if he'd be up for that. He's desperate not to turn, but I don't know if he's desperate enough to chat with a vamp," I'd said.

"Drop me a pin of your current location."

Why hadn't I fought his pushy behavior?

But then I remembered something else Vaughn had said. *"If I had wanted to influence you one way or another, you would have been, and you'd have never known."*

Had he enthralled me to get me to agree to yet another of his little meetings between people who normally wouldn't want anything to do with each other? Had he wanted to make sure I'd comply so he wouldn't have to deal with less-than-welcome, pesky human emotions? And, given Welsh's vehement and instant rage upon seeing Vaughn, it would make sense that Vaughn would want to assure compliance from at least one of us. He must have concluded that, if I was on board with this plan, Caspian would take my lead.

When I'd called Vaughn out on being butt-hurt over his babysitting assignment from Roch, he hadn't corrected me. I'd assumed Vaughn was here on Roch's orders and that those orders had been about *me*. Roch, I thought, had made the call in an effort to get back into Mom's good graces. She'd saved Roch's kid, so now he was going to protect hers.

Which was egotistical of me, honestly.

Because maybe Vaughn's sudden arrival here, and his willingness to assist us, had been about Welsh this whole time.

"Did you enthrall me?" I asked, my voice quiet. I knew

Vaughn could easily hear me over the ranting boys, but they stopped at the sound of my question anyway. "Did you make me agree to this without consulting Welsh first because you knew he'd say no?"

When Vaughn didn't reply, Welsh let out a hearty laugh.

"Unbelievable," Welsh said, chuckling darkly and shaking his head. When he glanced at me, the silver rimming his eyes scared me even more than his obscenity-laced bitching from mere minutes ago. "I'm sorry, Harlow. And … Cas. I …" He sighed and clasped his hands behind his own neck. After a few calming breaths, he dropped his hands to his sides.

His malice from earlier had gone out of him like an ebbing tide. While his tone was decisive, he was more straightforward now, rather than infuriated. "I'm going to need you to leave, Vaughn. I don't know why you're here. I assume you know about the infected hybrid bite. Maybe you're intrigued by the possibilities of what a shadowy version of my skills would be. I'm sure Roch would fucking *love* to use me as his political spy or something, but the answer is no, okay? No. No amount of money would be enough. I can't be bought. Maybe I could have been when I was twelve, but not anymore. I would rather die than deal with you fuckers on a regular basis again."

I was practically vibrating with how desperately I needed to ask Welsh nine billion questions about his horrible-sounding mother, being exploited as a child, and how he'd survived after taking off alone at the very young age of twelve because he'd felt safer by himself than with any of the adults in his life. No wonder he was a curmudgeon.

I *had* been curious whether there was a family member to blame for Welsh's grouchy ways, and now I had my answer. His mother needed a shiv to the kidney if she wasn't already dead.

Mission accepted.

"Wha?" I muttered out loud.

The hilt of the second sword warmed in my hand, and the scales instantly turned iridescent and shimmery instead of dull and lifeless. The sword quickly lifted to shoulder height, sword tip pointing in the vague direction of the front door. Suddenly I was being pulled forward. I tried to let the hilt go and couldn't. I clapped a second hand around the hilt for added leverage, only for that hand to get stuck as well. I leaned back, trying to counteract the sword's albeit slow momentum. It had accepted my "mission"—whatever the hell *that* meant—but its acceptance felt reluctant.

Probably because I was so unworthy.

All at once, I realized what was happening.

"No! Abort mission, abort mission!"

Mission assignments unclear.

"Oh, sweet lord, can you read thoughts? I didn't mean we had to murder his mother literally. It was a figure of speech! If I'm actually *giving* you a mission, I'll make it explicitly clear."

The sword's tip was a mere few inches from Vaughn's forearm when the hilt went dark. I stumbled forward as gravity yanked the sword's tip back toward the floor. My palm no longer felt superglued to the hilt, either.

Understood. Mission aborted.

All three men stared at me with varying levels of curiosity. My sword donned Kayda's visage once again, apparently solely to glare menacingly in my direction. Why was it mad at *me*?

I was in the process of figuring out how to explain that the second sword was both a snob and a psychopath when Welsh suddenly issued a grunt of pain. Caspian rushed to his side and caught his friend by the arm before Welsh hit the floor and brained himself on one of the sharp corners of the glass coffee table.

"Welsh? Welsh, what's wrong?" I asked, taking an involuntary step forward.

My question was answered by the sudden appearance of the blackened bite on Welsh's neck, the spiderwebbing tendrils of black that radiated from it, and the ghostly pale pallor of his skin. His glamour glitched for a moment, and a series of faces cycled over Welsh's face, like someone flipping through a stack of headshots.

Caspian helped Welsh sit on the couch. I deposited the psychopath sword on the table, then darted into the kitchen to fetch a glass of water.

When I returned, handing the glass to Welsh, my stomach twinged. His face had stopped flickering and had settled on the boy-band hottie version of him I knew best. Only the persona was toned down—less-perfect skin, a slightly crooked nose, brown eyes instead of a striking green, and a scar that ran through his upper lip. His lips were so pale, they were nearly blue. Sweat beaded on his forehead.

I sat on his other side and forced him to wrap his fingers around the glass. I helped him take a sip. He coughed and sputtered, spraying my lap with droplets. When his coughing fit subsided, I helped him take a few more sips.

"He's overexerted himself," Vaughn said blandly.

"And whose fucking fault is that?" I asked, deciding that if Welsh was too weak to curse at the manipulative vampire, then I'd do it.

Hey! One more thing for me to add to my growing list of useful skills: inexplicably bonding with murderous swords, making phone calls, and cussing out vampires.

Welsh chuckled next to me, which soon turned into a wet-sounding cough—like his lungs were full of fluid. My eyes welled up. I didn't know what to do. He looked and sounded terrible. Keeping his glamour in place had pushed away the shadows, but had it also hastened the effects of the poison since he was constantly wearing down his energy stores?

I recalled what Ronan had said about Filomena when she'd been in the throes of her transition. *"One day she showed up here, so sick I was sure she wouldn't survive the night. Her skin was so pale it was nearly translucent. The blood in her veins had turned black. A literal dark cloud, like a fog, wafted around her, as if her very essence was rotting."*

The one thing Welsh had going for him so far was—

Caspian and I scrambled to our feet and away from Welsh at the same time. We somehow ended up on the other side of the coffee table, hands clasped, as we gaped in horror at Welsh. An opaque cloud of swirling black, like living ink, swirled around Welsh's feet and legs. In the span of a breath, it had engulfed him to his waist, as if the undulating shadows were consuming him.

My breaths were coming too quickly. I couldn't get enough air in. "What … what do we do?"

Caspian squeezed my hand hard.

There was a hopelessness in the fact that Caspian hadn't once tried to craft a rune array. He must have known, deep down, that nothing in his extensive arsenal would suffice here. We didn't even understand what was happening.

Vaughn sidled up beside me on my other side. His lack of reaction was wholly disconcerting, too. None of us knew what to do. Did we just have to wait it out?

My gaze roamed over Welsh's sweaty face and the tendrils of black on his arms and neck that snaked under too-pale skin. His eyes were closed and his head lolled to the side. If it wasn't for the steady rise and fall of his chest, I would have thought he was dead.

Suddenly the shadows shot up and over Welsh's head, consuming him completely, like he'd just been stuffed into a giant black garbage bag. The giant, amorphous black mass writhed and thrashed on the couch—a foot here, a hand there, the sharp point of an elbow. Was Welsh fighting back? Was he trying to break out?

Just as suddenly, the blob seemed to implode, the force of its thrashing turning inward.

A person sat on the couch—a person who was *not* Welsh.

Caspian and I fell back a step.

Vaughn didn't move, but his voice wavered when he spoke. *"Teo?"*

The man on the couch laughed—a deep, jubilant sound that warred horribly with the dread in my belly. "We thought you might try to claim this one for yourself. We've been searching for him high and low but had resigned ourselves to the reality that he'd forever be holed up in a hub out of reach." The man—Teo—held his arms out in front of him and turned them this way and that, marveling. "It *is* spectacular what he can do, isn't it? Ciro, may peace find his soul, recognized him at once, despite the nearly two decades since he'd seen him last. Snatched him even though it hadn't been his mission that night. But Ciro was always a quick thinker. Sacrificed himself for the greater good. He will be missed, but this …" He twisted his arms from side to side again. "*This* was worth it. We used to have such fun with Zander, did we not?"

"Stand up, Teo," Vaughn said.

I shot an incredulous look at the back of his head. What, did he want to partake in fisticuffs and slap this Teo guy out of Welsh?

Because the more I watched the man, the more off he looked. Every color on him—olive skin, navy-blue button-up shirt, brown slacks—was muted. There was an image of another person—though it was so faint, I lost my grasp on it every few seconds—that was superimposed *over* Teo's shape … like a ghost.

I gave my head a shake. I refused to think of Welsh as a ghost. He was still *here*, dammit. We just had to get to him.

"Stand up," Vaughn repeated.

Teo sighed heavily. "If you wanted to know if I'm really here or if I'm merely using Zander's shadow-powered glamour to speak to you, you could have just asked."

"Let him go," I snapped.

Teo's muted brown eyes shifted to me for the first time. His lip curled, dismissing me. "Ah, a brave human. How quaint. I don't —" His attention snagged on something behind me. The off-kilter hum of my sword started up a breath later. Teo suddenly found me quite intriguing again. "Is that one of Likho's weapons? How interesting!"

"Any day now, sorcerer," Vaughn muttered.

A wind array was hurtling toward Teo a breath later. The

vampire's eyes widened as the golden disc hit him center mass, blasting the ghostly shadow of the man out of Welsh, through the back of the couch, and into the space beyond it. Teo floated there, stunned. He reminded me of a cartoon rendering of a genie—body tethered to its host by smoke.

Welsh woke with a start. In a raspy, pained voice, he said, "Knock me out! He can't get back in if I'm unconscious."

Vaughn was by Welsh's side in a millisecond. "Sleep," he said simply.

The crackle of Vaughn's power made goosebumps skitter across my skin. Welsh gave a little gasp, then slumped, his chin on his chest. The ghostly form of Teo vanished.

"Ohh my god," I said in a rush, letting Caspian's hand go so I could prop my hands on my knees. My stomach roiled.

"I'm not going to lie and say we have a cure for this," came Vaughn's voice.

I was too nauseous to stand. The faint sound of Welsh's gentle snores was the only thing keeping my sanity intact. He was still alive. He was still breathing.

"But we have more resources in Tercla than you have in Luma. There's also the added bonus that, even if Teo attempts to hijack Zander again to deduce where he is, hybrids can't get into Tercla."

I slowly stood to full height. Caspian wrapped an arm around my waist, and I circled mine around his shoulder. I wasn't sure who was holding up who at this point. "Ferals can, though—ferals whose bites are even more fatal to you than whatever in the hell is happening to Welsh."

"There aren't degrees of fatal, Harlow," Vaughn said. "Fatal is fatal."

"Again with the semantics?" Caspian snapped.

Vaughn said, "We can shield him. I can guarantee you that if Teo gains access to Zander enough times he *will* find you. He will kill Harlow outright. He will drain Caspian for his blood—hells, he might find you strong enough, sorcerer, that you end up in circumstances identical to Zander's. I have known Teo for a long time, even by vampire standards. He had an entitlement problem well before he was corrupted by fae blood. His addiction made him a more extreme version of the vampire I knew." He paused, composed himself. "I have no doubts that he's a Shade."

My stomach pitched again.

"Do you really want to risk Shades getting their hooks into Zander the way they did with Filomena?" Vaughn asked.

Caspian started to say something, stopped, tried again, sagged. He stared vacantly at Welsh. "He'll never forgive me."

"Would you rather him dead? Harlow dead? You turned?"

Every question felt like a slap. I knew now that it was impossible to know when I was being enthralled. I only felt the telltale crackle of it in the air when Vaughn used a flood of his power at once. When he went for the slow-drip method, I was clueless. But right now? Vaughn sounded a touch desperate. My gut told me to believe that a small part of him was doing this for Welsh and not himself, but I also knew my gut could be duped by someone like Vaughn.

"You both know that the hubs aren't safe for him," Vaughn said, his tone gentler. "He was bitten while in a hub. Hybrids can find you in Luma. Teo and the Shades can find you outside of the hubs. Let me take him back to Tercla with me—it's the only safe place left."

"And if we refuse?" I asked.

"Then I'll leave you to your own devices," Vaughn said.

Caspian and I turned to each other at the same time. He looked gutted—whether from what he'd witnessed Welsh go through or the decision he had to make, I wasn't sure. Likely both. We stood nearly toe to toe, hands clasped in front of us.

I spoke to Caspian as if Vaughn wasn't in the room with us. "I don't know the right answer. I don't trust him. I didn't before this, and I *really* don't now. But I trust my mom, and she saw something in Roch that made her feel safe. He *could* enthrall her, and he actively doesn't. She calls all the shots, even when it's in his power—*literally*—to make her comply. If he's got someone like

Vaughn in his inner circle, it *has* to be because Vaughn isn't a total monster. Morally gray, sure, but not a monster."

Caspian asked, "Are you trying to convince me or you?"

I shrugged hopelessly. "I don't know."

We stood there for a long time, holding hands, lost in our thoughts. Vaughn didn't interrupt us or hurry us along or grumble. He simply waited.

Voice shaking, Caspian kept his gaze on me when he said, "Take him."

"I will keep you updated as often as I'm able," Vaughn said.

A strand of loose hair tickled my cheek, blown by a sudden shift in the air. Vaughn was beside us, cradling Welsh's unconscious body. I could only look at Welsh for a moment before I had to avert my eyes.

There was a long stretch of silence before Vaughn spoke.

"I don't have many regrets in my long life, but what happened to Zander was one of them. I want to do right by him now."

A gust of wind blew across the foyer from the ajar front door.

Welsh was gone.

CHAPTER THIRTY-TWO

HARLOW

Caspian and I had tried to stay in the rental house after Vaughn had whisked Welsh away. When we sat down to eat the food he'd left for us, I'd only eaten one bite of the ramen dish before I burst into tears.

Caspian poked around the electronics display Welsh had set up. There was a series of notes on a legal pad detailing the tasks he needed to complete for a few of his clients. One such client was one Welsh had told Caspian about recently. It was a twelve-year-old faun boy named Arlan who had run away from an abusive mother—and had crossed multiple state lines to do it. Welsh had agreed to help the boy pro bono, which was unheard of for Welsh, Caspian said, but Welsh had insisted on waiving the boy's fees simply because so much of the boy's story had mirrored Welsh's own.

Now Welsh couldn't help the kid.

What would happen to him—to either of them?

After only a few minutes of sitting at Welsh's makeshift work-station, Caspian had hastily pushed away from the table, muttering that he needed to take a shower.

Once he was out of the room, I rounded the table to take a look at the legal pad. At the bottom of the to-do list was the note, "Check up on Noah. Make sure he's going to school every day."

I'd burst into tears again.

I plopped onto the couch, hoping to find an escape in an asinine TV show. Except Welsh's paused episode of *The Great British Bake Off* was still on the screen.

When Caspian emerged from the bathroom, I was a wreck. He sat with me, letting me sob openly on his shoulder. Caspian, in contrast, had turned into somewhat of a zombie, hardly speaking.

I let out a shuddering sigh after what felt like an eternity and pushed away from Caspian, feeling wrung out. "Can we go home? I don't think I can stay here."

So we packed up everything—me keeping the Boar-Be-Gone nearby—loaded the car, hit the lock button on the door's keypad, and left. Caspian drove. The swords lay silently on the empty back seats.

I knew I should warn Mom and Kayda that we were heading back, but I didn't have the energy. I didn't want to have to say or type the words that, not only was Welsh gone, but we'd *let* him be taken. It wasn't as if Tercla had visiting hours. The only way in was to be invited and they didn't exactly pass out invitations like coupons.

The silence on the drive back wasn't awkward so much as charged. Caspian must have wanted to take back what he'd said —that he was grateful I was around to keep him and Welsh, his second brother, sane. He'd thanked me for helping him shoulder the emotional load. Now I felt like the *cause* of his emotional burdens. If I'd never contacted Vaughn, Welsh might be riding back to Luma with us right now.

Granted, Welsh was so sick—hiding it from us to some degree with his glamours—that moving him might not have been safe. Not that sending him off like a lamb to slaughter with a bunch of vampires was safe, either.

When we were half an hour outside Luma, I received a text.

VAUGHN

The patient is sleeping peacefully. I promise I'll do everything we can for him.

I started crying again. Which was incredible, because I wasn't sure how I had any tears left. It also said a lot about Caspian's deteriorating mental state that he didn't even ask what had set me off.

The one other thing Welsh had left for us, in addition to the ramen that had no doubt been delicious, was another set of glamour tonics. Yet when I asked Caspian if he wanted to pull over to take the tonics to turn us back into the Duns, he'd simply said, "No. Can you hand me the remaining vehicle travel talisman from the glove box?"

I'd done so, noting that this one looked twice the size of the one we'd gotten from the guard outside Morning Meadows—the disguised mundane neighborhood that served as an extra layer of protection for Luma.

As he drove, he rolled down his window and clapped the metallic box on the outside of his door. Instead of heading for Morning Meadows, he drove through a more rural area where the roads were pitted and disused. He gunned the minivan through one of the back entrances of the city, punching through into the Warehouse District. The minivan had given a great shuddering jolt as we passed through the veil. The sword had issued a hum of disgruntlement. Its twin remained silent.

Caspian's silence started to knot my stomach. I'd asked him a handful of times what his plan was, seeing as the werecats still had to be loitering outside his residence. He, as far as I knew, hadn't been in contact with the Duns recently to ask if their garage was empty. It wasn't like Caspian to outright ignore me.

"Doesn't matter," he'd finally said as he turned into his neighborhood, his voice flat. "Our three days allotted by Sorceress Rhiannon are almost up anyway. We'd only have a twenty-four-hour stay of execution at best. Might as well let them see us show up and then try to ascertain where the hells we've been all this time."

"You know this is going to ruin your ability to sneak out as the Duns again, right?" I asked, sounding more pissed than I probably should have been.

"Doesn't matter."

"You want to tell that to the Duns?" I snapped. "You want them to get arrested for aiding and abetting criminals or whatever? Sounds like the Duns want to *avoid* trouble with authorities."

He'd cut me a look then that said, if I didn't stop talking, *he* was going to turn me in for the reward money, just to shut me up.

When we pulled up to his front gate, there weren't any cats sprawled in front of it. I didn't spot the eyeshine of any lounging in the bushes or up in the trees, either. Of course that didn't mean there weren't any. Caspian climbed out without a word to punch in his code.

I hastily pulled out my phone.

HARLOW

We're back. Cas is ... not doing well.

MOM

I think the pixies might have heard you coming because the pair of cats who got stuck with night shift duty are currently around back berating the pixies for "being a nuisance and impeding an ongoing investigation"

Caspian had just pulled into his driveway and killed the engine, the gate safely secured behind us, when I rounded on him.

"Will you just yell at me already and get it over with?" I asked. "The silent treatment is stressing me the hell out. The anticipation of you losing your shit over something minor because you can't just scream at me *now* is going to eat me alive."

He stared at me for a long time, expression blank. "I hate that he's so far away that we can't do anything for him. But you know what's worse?"

I braced myself.

"What's worse is that, as much as this whole thing is *unreservedly* fucked up, I know that if Vaughn hadn't been there today, there's a very real possibility I wouldn't have been able to get you away from Ronan's house *or* help Welsh. Going to Ronan's was *my* idea. Getting on that boat to visit the pysid was *my* idea."

"That last one was Welsh's …"

"You could have wound up *trapped* with Ronan, Harlow. Then Welsh would have been by himself when the infection took a sudden turn for the worse. He could have … he could have died *alone* in that house. I'm outmatched on all fronts here. Welsh is gone. *You* almost drowned." He pursed his lips, staring out the windshield for a short while before focusing on me again. Sharp shadows obscured most of his face in the dark cabin of the minivan. "Maybe I'm as great of a talent as my professors and my parents claim. I'm a quick study. I can lose myself in a task so thoroughly that I master a skill that might take someone else years. But none of that helps in the real world. I'm not the best at thinking on my feet. I might be book smart, but I'm not streetwise —as the youths say."

My throat tightened in relief at hearing a hint of his terrible humor.

"I don't know what I'm doing, Low. I could have easily lost you both today."

I picked up my phone lying in my lap and opened the text thread I had with Vaughn. I turned the phone to face him. "I don't know what I'm doing either, which is why our trust is currently in the hands of a pack of five-hundred-year-old vampires."

Caspian let out a shuddering sigh.

"All we can do is keep going," I said. "Together."

He nodded tightly.

We piled out of the car, intending to only grab the essentials out of the back. When I trundled the side of the minivan open, my sword shot out and beelined for the lawn, presumably hoping to visit with the pixies. I'd think most of them would be asleep by now, though—it was almost midnight.

The second sword didn't move.

"Uh, cutlass the second?" I asked, using the name Caspian had used for it earlier.

Still nothing.

Caspian was still around the back of the minivan, fussing with our luggage.

"Cas? We gotta come up with a better name for the second sword. What's a synonym for snob?" I asked, knowing how much he loved his word puzzles.

"Upstart, parvenu, braggart ..."

"Ohh, how about Gart?" I asked, trying my best to aim the question *at* the second sword, even if that didn't make a lot of sense.

UNACCEPTABLE! the sword bellowed in my head with such volume, I stumbled back several steps.

Seeing as Caspian didn't react in the slightest, he hadn't heard it. Good *and* bad to know that the psychopathic sword could speak in my head even when I wasn't touching it.

"Chill, dude," I hissed. "A simple 'no thank you' would suffice."

"What was that?" Caspian said as he closed the back of the car and came up beside me.

"He doesn't like any of those names," I said. "What about 'Eli'? It's short for 'elitist.' Or 'snicket,' which is short for 'persnickety.'"

Nothing from the sword.

"What if we try something more pretentious, like Rupert or Giles?" Caspian asked.

Silence.

"Gotta give me something, dude! Otherwise, I'm going to name you something real dull, like, I don't know, Tim."

ACCEPTABLE!

I sighed. "Cutlass the Second is now otherwise known as Tim."

"All right, Tim," Caspian said, unfazed. "If you're comfortable with it, you can float your way into the house on your own. The cutlass is allowed to roam the grounds as it pleases, as long as it lets Harlow know what it's doing."

Mission accepted.

The scales on the hilt went iridescent, the sword slowly lifted itself off the seat cushion, and then it eased its way out of the car and toward my sword who was … I sighed again.

"Sword, I don't know where you are, but keep a watchful blade on Tim, all right?"

A faint pulse of blue flashed at the far end of the lawn near a rose bush. Possibly *in* a rose bush. I didn't want to know what it was doing.

Mom opened the door for us just as we reached the welcome mat. Her gaze bounced from me to Caspian to a spot behind us that was conspicuously devoid of Welsh. "Oh, baby girl, what happened?"

I fell apart again.

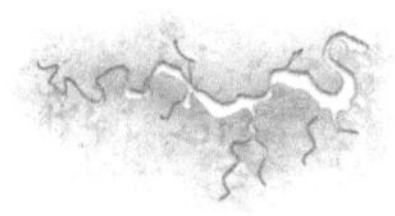

THE FOUR OF US—ME, MOM, CASPIAN, AND SOREN—SAT AROUND Caspian's dining room table for a few hours talking and raiding Caspian's liquor supply. Mom and Soren shared what they'd found in their research, which wasn't much, and we told them about the pysid, the siren, waking up the second sword, and, eventually, what had happened to Welsh.

"I'll talk to Roch," Mom said in her decisive way. "We'll find a way to stay in contact with Tercla so we have updates on what's going on with Welsh without also jeopardizing anyone's safety. My relationship with him was beyond complicated and messy as hell, but despite all that, I *do* trust him. Not fully, of course, but I do. I can't say that for a lot of people."

Soren's jaw tightened at that admission, but he kept his comments to himself.

We were all varying levels of intoxicated when I finally decided I needed to shower off the lake and anchovy residue and go to bed. Both swords had come back in hours before and were in their powered-down modes on the kitchen counter. A cursory glimpse of the microwave told me it was just after three in the morning. I hoped I was finally exhausted enough that I could sleep for five days straight.

I'd just reached the doorway to the kitchen when Mom's phone rang.

"Wait, Harlow," she said, words a little slurred. "It's Rhiannon. What the hell is she doing calling at three in the morning?"

Stomach pitching, I walked back toward the table. I was suddenly so tired, I worried I'd face-plant on the tile. I braced a hand on the counter to keep myself upright.

"Hi, Rhia … oh wait," Mom said, then pulled the phone away from her face, squinting at the screen. I think she was attempting to push the speaker button. Soren reached over to push it for her. She grinned at him—an uninhibited smile that made such an intense look of longing take over his face, I had to divert my eyes.

Sorceress Rhiannon's voice rang out from the phone's speakers. "Camila? I didn't mean to wake you. I was going to leave a voicemail."

"Hi, Rhi."

The sorceress sighed. "I should have presumed you'd be

drunk if you're answering at this hour. Does the tinny sound of my voice mean the others can hear me?"

Me, Caspian, and Soren all offered an enthusiastic greeting.

"Great, you're *all* drunk," Rhiannon said. "I've scheduled a private meeting at the Tower for us all tomorrow morning. There's a larger meeting scheduled for later in the day; there will be sorcerers present from hubs across the country to discuss the Lachlan Shade and feral problems." She lowered her voice, and we all leaned forward to hear her. "Sorcerers are choosing sides. I have a very select few I trust, and I want you to have the opportunity to have a frank, honest discussion with them first before we're all subjected to the bullshit political posturing that will happen in the official meeting."

"And you're still sure bringing the attractant to the Tower is wise?" Mom asked.

"Absolutely. I truly believe it can level the playing field for us, but I want the opinions of my trusted colleagues on the matter before we even consider bringing it up at the official gathering. Sober up. I expect you all here by 11 a.m."

I groaned. Not that I usually slept more than four hours at a time anyway, but still.

Rhiannon said, "And Harlow? Caspian? Two werecats reported that you were seen driving back to Caspian's residence this evening despite no one on patrol seeing you leave. Factions are cropping up among the cats, too, and one such faction is currently getting torn a new one for failing to surveil Caspian's house properly with such high-value targets inside. If you're not here at your appointed time, I'll personally give the cats permission to bring you in by force."

Caspian and I shared a look—mine hopefully telegraphing "Now I see where your reckless label came from" and his saying "I think I had too much tequila."

"Noted," I said.

Rhiannon disconnected the call without a goodbye.

CHAPTER THIRTY-THREE

HARLOW

After I settled into bed that night, finally clean after a wholly traumatic day, I texted Kayda. I typed out a novel-length message telling her about the second sword, Welsh, and my guilt. I'd still been wide awake when she sent back a long message of her own, telling me about Kessler the nyad and her, Marisol's, and Quaid's attempt to find him.

Neither one of us gave the other platitudes or promises that everything would be okay. We'd both needed unfiltered venting without the other trying to find a solution. We both needed to wallow first; solutions would come later.

Deep down, I knew we both felt like we'd had missions to complete—me to help find a cure for Welsh and her to rescue Kessler—and we'd both failed. Neither one of us knew how our respective charges were doing, or where Lachlan Shade was, or if Luma was safe. It all felt too big. The little pieces of the larger puzzle we'd been tasked with had slipped out of our grasp.

I felt unmoored. I had a sneaking suspicion Kayda did, too. I was glad she had Henri. A wave of missing my best friend hit me like a semi. And suddenly I missed everyone all at once—Kayda, Welsh, Felix. My dad.

My dad had been an absolute champ at making me laugh when I was feeling down, even when laughing was the last thing I wanted to do. The laughter would crack open something inside me, letting me talk freely about whatever it was that had been eating me up inside. He'd listen dutifully—regardless of whether the laughter had devolved into shouting, or ranting, or blubbering tears. No matter what it was, he always had the best advice.

It killed me that I couldn't hear his voice in my head the way I used to.

No one since had known me as well as Dad had. Felix had been a close second—until he wasn't.

Hanging out with Kayda would make this crushing feeling of loneliness ebb, but I was still too scared to risk her safety. The prowling werecats outside and the looming appointment—along with the accompanying threat of bodily harm should I *miss* the appointment—with the sorcerers in the Tower further assured I wasn't going to see Kayda for a while yet.

HARLOW

When all this calms down, you, me, and my mom are going to have a spa day

KAYDA

Only if you buy me ramen first

HARLOW

Deal

An hour later, I was still wide awake. I got up to use the restroom. Laid back down. Stared at the dark ceiling.

I sat bolt upright when a creak sounded in the hallway. The swords, the last I'd seen them, were powered down on the kitchen counter. Brow furrowed, I crept to my door and eased it open, expecting one or both of them to be doing something horrible.

What I spotted was Caspian a few feet down the hallway, back hunched and walking on his tiptoes like a cat burglar from a cartoon. "What are you doing?" I whispered.

He backtracked and stood before my door looking utterly miserable. The bags under his eyes were so dark, they looked like they hurt. He wore a black hoodie with the Lake Nacimiento dragon printed large across the chest.

I gasped in mock horror. "Is that *my* hoodie? You can't get someone a gift, Cas, and then take it for yourself."

He glanced down at himself, brows furrowed, as if he couldn't figure out how the hoodie had made it onto his person in the first place. He swung his bleary, bloodshot hazel gaze back to my face. "I just woke up from a nightmare. I was going to make a few dozen cups of coffee and forgo sleep entirely."

I frowned, more than a little concerned. He sounded a touch delirious. "A nightmare about Welsh?"

The faint sound of a voice told me Soren was awake. When words like "autopsy" and "necrosis" wafted upstairs, I had a sneaking suspicion he was on the phone with his Illinoisan contact who worked in a fae morgue.

I pulled Caspian into my room, closed the door, and forced him to sit on the side of the bed. After turning on the bedside lamp, I plopped down next to him, our shoulders touching. I'd been wanting to ask Caspian about his insomnia for a while, so I finally did now.

He sighed, his shoulders rounding. "I only sleep a couple of hours a night lately. Welsh has been cooking up sleeping tonics for me for a while, but the latest batch isn't working. And I can't exactly ask him for more."

"Is it usually nightmares that keep you from sleeping?"

"Sometimes. Sometimes it's just anxious, bouncing thoughts.

You know the kind that seemed perfectly reasonable and dire at 2 a.m., but are preposterous in the light of day?"

"In my pre-sword days, my anxieties were usually about my charmed weapons and being worried I hadn't used the right dampening hoods. The fear was always that I'd pick up something and short-circuit my heart. It wouldn't be *that* fear—the whole being dead thing—that would wake me up in the middle of the night, but the fear that Kayda would eventually come looking for me and find my electrocuted body on the floor. Sometimes there were maggots … in my eye sockets."

Caspian chuckled. "That's why your nightmares are so vivid—your imagination is a scary place."

I'd said something similar to Welsh. My throat tightened.

"My mom called today," he blurted.

My brows hiked. "Oh?"

"I missed the call since we were a bit preoccupied. She sent a text letting me know my brother and his wife are pregnant again."

"Uhh … so I'm guessing she doesn't know you and Aiden talk?"

"Apparently not. Aiden must have told her himself today, and she used that as an excuse to call me, assuming I didn't know."

I knew his relationship with his parents was on shaky footing, but it wasn't something he liked to talk about. What little I knew had come from Sorcerer Sweeney, of all people. Sweeney had tried to goad Caspian into going nuclear back in the motel in Washington by throwing the details of Caspian's fraught past in his face. It had almost worked, too.

Caspian hesitated for a few seconds more before he started talking. He told me that ever since his dramatic departure from the sorcery academy—namely leaving his parents in debt—their relationship had been strained. He'd paid them back tenfold, but the money hadn't been the main reason for the estrangement. That, he said, had been a long time coming.

"They said they hadn't been surprised I'd dropped out of school, just disappointed," he said.

"Ouch." I studied his profile, as he'd said most of this while staring in the direction of his bare feet. "I know we haven't known each other that long, relatively speaking, but were you an absolute menace as a kid or something?"

His smile was brief. "They were strict, and I didn't want to follow in their footsteps. I wanted to be a blacksmith."

As random as that confession was, it also somehow made total sense.

"So *that's* why you're so infatuated with Margaret Fengast. She was living your dream. At least for a while."

"I wouldn't say infatuated," he said, then flicked his gaze over to mine. "Okay, maybe a slight crush."

I grinned, strangely delighted that he'd admitted it.

"Blacksmithing isn't a cheap hobby, though. And it's not exactly a lucrative career path, either," he said. "So they agreed to pay for classes and the equipment for my own forge if I agreed to go to the academy. They swore I didn't have to take up a veil maintenance post like they had. They just *knew I'd thrive there* and didn't want me to miss out on *unlocking my full potential.*"

"They were hoping you'd fall for sorcery the way you did with blacksmithing?"

"Yeah ..."

I worried at my bottom lip for a moment. "Seems like it was a good call, no? You're really into sorcery. Like, *really* into it. So into it, I hope you at least bought it dinner first."

The look he angled my way was both amused and exasperated.

"I will only admit this to you, and if you try to bring it up later, I will vehemently deny it," he said, "but part of my resentment toward my parents for forcing me into the academy was *because* they were right. I *did* love my schooling. I loved the rigor of it. I loved that, once I had the basics mastered, the sky was the limit on what my magic could do. The only true limitation on where it can go is the caster's discipline and imagination."

"But ...?" I prompted when he fell quiet.

"But it was hard to reconcile my passion for sorcery with how stifling my upbringing *and* schooling were. The joke is that academy schooling completely strips you of your personality if you make it to graduation, and it's true, in a way. The level of dedication needed doesn't just border the line of obsession—it blows right past it. Friends dropped out. If someone failed one too many exams and was expelled, their dorm room would be cleaned out overnight, the student shipped back home to their disappointed family. You learned in later years not to get too attached to anyone because they could be whisked away. Teachers wouldn't make announcements about departed students; they didn't want to encourage quitting or seem sympathetic to failure. People burned out mentally. But if you succeeded? If you succeeded, if you were dedicated enough, the ability to change the very world around you was at your fingertips." His shoulder rubbed against mine as he shrugged. "But at what cost?"

Quietly, I said, "Marcus's life."

He heaved a shaky breath. "He died *right* in front of me. Did I tell you that?"

I shook my head.

"He died in front of the entire graduating class, actually. We sat in amphitheater seats while Marcus was alone on the ground floor, drawing his final array for his final project. We each had to complete one array that showcased an element. It was less about the element itself, or even the force behind it, but about showing control. A flock of fire barn swallows that flew around the theater in twenty different directions without any of them losing the quality of their feathers or the sharpness of their beaks. A detailed oak tree made of water and whose branches were loaded with plump apples made of ice ..."

I recalled the warring water and fire dragons that had clashed over the stage during Domino's auction.

"Marcus—being one of the few purely mundane students who made it to the final year—wanted to prove himself. He wanted to be flashy. Wanted everyone to know it wasn't my friendship or his parents' numerous donations to the school that had gotten him to that point," Caspian said. "He chose fire, which is the easiest element to call on, but also the most volatile. He crafted a common house cat at first. Students laughed, as it was a small cat, without much detail. He changed one section of the array drawn on the ground, and the cat doubled in size. Changing another section gave it stripes. He took slips of paper from his pocket and pulled pre-drawn arrays off the paper and into the air. He flung the arrays at the cat as if they were treats. The cat snatched them with its mouth, and the cat changed from ocelot to puma to tiger. It was a bit theatrical, but everyone was enraptured with the performance. After he settled on the tiger form, he returned to the array on the ground and altered it over and over and over. The tiger grew with every alteration. It didn't do much but sit on its haunches and occasionally lick its giant paw. But it grew to such monstrous size, its head nearly touched the ceiling twenty feet above Marcus's head. The room was sweltering.

"At one point, I could tell his energy was starting to flag. And worse still, I saw a power-enhancing ring on his thumb. I'd caught him with it before. It wasn't unheard of for students to use them in the later years of the academy, as everyone struggled to keep up. For someone magic-touched, a power-enhancing charm can work like several cups of coffee. For a mundane, it could be like taking one upper or twelve, depending on the magic level."

Kayda had mentioned that Snowdrop the elf had used a ring like that. It had taken the elf's wind spell and turned it into a gale-force blast.

"I left my spot, ran up the steps to the box seats where the professors were, and pounded on the door until one of them finally opened it. I told them about Marcus's ring and that I knew, if they didn't stop him, the expenditure of magic would kill him. Sweeney, that smug bastard, was the one who answered the door. He said Marcus knew the risks when he put the ring on, and if someone rushed in to *save his mundane ass* every time he made a mistake, he didn't deserve to be a Collective sorcerer anyway.

There was a lot of animated chatter behind him, but he closed the door in my face all the same.

"I ran back down the steps. Werecats blocked all the entrances to the ground floor from outside the amphitheater, so the best I could do was get to the first row and yell down at Marcus. He was almost in a trance by then. Swaying on his feet like he was drunk. He'd stopped adding alterations to the array and was using simple temperature-increase spells. Sweat poured off me while I leaned over the railing, yelling at him to snap out of it, to take the ring off. There was a magic barrier keeping me from physically or magically jumping over the railing to get to the ground floor. Helps prevent cheating." He punctuated that last sentiment with a sharp, bitter laugh. "A few others joined me when they realized what was happening. Eventually, the strain of it stopped Marcus's heart. His eyes rolled back in his head, and he collapsed. The fire tiger, nearly as tall as the amphitheater itself, exploded in a puff of scalding air and then was gone."

I slipped my hand into his, keeping our clasped hands resting on my thigh.

"Rhiannon found me later, still standing at the railing, even after Marcus's body was taken away and the floor was prepped for the next student. She told me she fought as hard as she could to intervene and pull Marcus out, but she'd been outvoted. I thanked her for trying, and then I walked out. I didn't even go back to my room to collect my things. I just … gave it all up."

"Jeez, Cas," I finally said. "That's … horrible."

"Yeah," he said on an exhale. "It really was."

"I don't blame you for being unsure if you want a relationship with your parents after they essentially sided with the school. You don't get to choose your biological family. Sometimes the family you get handed sucks," I said, thinking of Kayda's douche-canoe of a father. "It's okay if you can't forgive them. But it's also okay if you do. I don't think you'd be doing Marcus a disservice."

He nodded tightly. "My inability to do anything to save him is what haunts my nightmares. I don't have them as often anymore, but the call from my mom today brought it all back. And now everything that's happening with Welsh … I just … it's a lot."

"We probably both need therapy."

He laughed. "Probably."

I yawned so hard it physically hurt. My eyes itched. "I swear it feels like I can't remember the last time I actually slept well. What if this is my new normal? Sleep deprivation will either lead me to making dolls out of my own hair or going on homicidal rampages, right? There's no middle ground?"

"I remember the last time *I* slept well," he said, either ignoring my ramblings or not hearing them. "The road trip—the first one … the two nights I stayed up trying to crack the lock on the treasure chest notwithstanding. Maybe it was being away from all this, where no one knew who we were, and we had a relatively simple task at hand."

"Plus, you had direct access to your Ocean Sunrise Body Wash dealer."

"I'd feel bad for how uncomfortable I made Rachel feel, but she also broke into our room and sold our information to the trolls, so she kind of sucks."

I laughed.

He hesitated for a moment. "I think the sound of you sleeping in the next bed helped. I got used to the cadence of your breathing. You were like my personal white noise machine."

The silence that fell over us again felt different, but I couldn't say why. I wondered if he would have told me a fraction of this had he not been as worn out as I was and still a little drunk.

I cleared my throat. "What if you try sleeping in here tonight? I slept like a log during most of that trip, too. Especially that first night, in that fancy suite? Heaven."

"Ah, yes, the one I practically had to carry you into because you almost fell asleep on your feet just walking down the hallway."

"I'm surprised I didn't sleep constantly in the car with all that damn Bach or Beethoven or Brahms or whatever."

"Can you only name composers that start with B?"

I pulled my hand out of his so I could properly place both fists on my hips in righteous indignation. "Do you want to crash in here or not?"

"Yes."

He got up long enough to turn off the light and then skirted the bed to climb in on the other side. I worried I would feel wide awake once he was lying beside me, or that the situation would make a hard pivot into awkward, but I fell asleep almost immediately.

When I awoke to my alarm going off at ten, I quickly rolled over to silence it. Caspian hadn't stirred. The cadence of him sleeping had been something I'd grown accustomed to as well, I realized. He lay on his back now, with one arm thrown over his head, his mouth agape, and one leg kicked free from the comforter. He wasn't quite snoring, but he was out cold.

I let him sleep for a little while longer, feeling slightly less overwhelmed—less lonely—than I had even hours before.

I knew now how true my statement from earlier had been: We'd get through this—together.

EPILOGUE
LACHLAN

The term "phantom limb" had been in Lachlan's lexicon for decades, but he'd never experienced the truth of it until recently. From the elbow down, his left arm was nothing but a stump. It *felt* as if his arm and hand were still there—as if he could still reach out to grab a glass, wiggle his fingers, run his hand through his hair.

The more time that passed, and with it the inexorable reality that Blythe was gone for good, the more her loss felt like a missing limb, too. He'd been physically without her for decades during his exile, and though he'd talked to her via portal-sent missives, it wasn't the same as talking to her in the flesh. Wasn't the same as hearing her voice or her infectious laughter. Or feeling that tethering bond between siblings.

She'd been his rock for so long—even when she was furious with him and would go months, sometimes years, without speaking to him. But that tether always brought them back together. And now that cord was snapped permanently, like the bones, ligaments, and tendons that had once held the two halves of his arm together.

He thought of his severed limb lying on the desolate earth of the Goddess-forsaken realm he'd been trapped in for so long. Perhaps Dengrig would find the arm and mount it on the wall of his cave alongside his hunting trophies. He and Dengrig would be reunited eventually, if all went according to plan, but Lachlan's missing arm would be a dried-out husk of its former glory by then. Dengrig certainly couldn't have wasted the realm's most precious resource by putting the limb on ice.

Oh, how his friend would marvel at lakes, rivers, and oceans once he was here, though. He'd never believed Lachlan's stories about the earthen realm and how seventy percent of the planet was made up of water.

Lachlan pondered over how Dengrig's awe might compare to the showering adoration Lachlan had received when his Shades had found him a few miles outside Luma nearly two weeks ago. They'd practically carried him into the Californian base in a palanquin and thrown a ticker-tape parade in his honor. Over the next several days, though he'd been delirious with fever borne out of an almost fatal overexertion of his magic, Shades from across the country had come to pay their respects. They'd brought him gifts, professed their devotion to him and the cause, and some even branded themselves with the adopted symbol of the Shades: a fist grasping the middle of a horizontally oriented infinity symbol, with the entire image enclosed in a circle.

Lachlan had designed it one too-hot night in the barren realm. To him, it meant the Shades were taking the possibility of infinite worlds into their own hands. As Lachlan had thrashed under sheets in the throes of sickness, his attendants had whispered among themselves, unaware that Lachlan could hear them. They spoke of the Shades' symbol meaning Lachlan himself controlled a limitless power—a power that was once again testing him, now that he was back in the earthen realm.

Either interpretation suited him fine.

In those long nine or ten days, during the few hours when Lachlan was lucid, Teo had sat beside Lachlan's sick bed and praised Lachlan for his resolve under incredible pressure, for accomplishing what no one in the history of this realm post-Glitch had done. No matter what challenges were put before him, Teo had said, Lachlan rose to the occasion.

The Shades had *all* treated Lachlan's miraculous return with an air of reverence. He'd become something of a god to them. A man who promised the impossible and delivered.

But up until this morning, when the fever finally broke for good, Lachlan hadn't felt like a god.

The ghost of Blythe's absence haunted him during his waking hours, while a vengeful specter of his sister tormented his sleep. His parents took on demonic forms in his nightmares, cater-wauling like banshees about Lachlan failing the only job they'd ever given him: protecting his sister.

In his nightmares, he was a scared, naive, reckless little boy standing on that dais while his parents chose another world over him. Over Blythe. And then they eviscerated him for the choices *they'd* forced him to make.

With each passing day, his resentment grew, though he wasn't always sure who he resented most. When the fever lasted longer than it should, and lack of sufficient rest only worsened his condition, Teo began enthralling Lachlan into a sleep so deep, not even his own tortured thoughts could find him.

Teo had become his rock.

He shouldn't have *needed* to fill that role. But the role had been thrust upon him by that filthy draken and the army of lesser fae she'd commanded to tear Blythe to pieces.

Teo, he knew now, would keep Lachlan on track in Blythe's absence. He would help ensure The Restoration was a success. *Unflinching adherence to the plan was what Blythe would have wanted for you,* Teo had said, countless times over. *She wouldn't want you to lose sight of what's important.*

So, today, after days and days of being deathly ill, mourning the loss of his arm, of Ciro being lost to those monsters in Luma, and the brutal murder of his sister, Lachlan told his ghosts they were welcome to stay, but they could no longer distract him from his work.

Lachlan slowly left his quarters and made his way to the command center of the base. He followed the signs pointing him in the right direction, as this was the first time he'd walked its hallowed halls. The facility, based on Lachlan's many suggestions, had been modeled after a mundane military base. The Shades had been working to get this particular base—nestled in Sierra County in Northern California—up and running for years in preparation for Lachlan's return. His Shades wanted him to have a safe place to recover and regroup that wasn't too far from Luma. He'd hoped Blythe would be the one to give him a full tour of the place ...

When he finally stepped into the command center on his own two feet, the activity in the room died almost instantly. Though his Shades didn't wear a uniting uniform, as that might trigger recognition when they needed to remain hidden for now—Lachlan reveled in the sight of the Shades' logo painted in bright yellow on several of the otherwise plain, smooth concrete walls.

The silence only lasted for a breath, and then the assembled Shades erupted—with tears, adulation, and awe—as if he'd just risen from the dead.

And perhaps he had, in a way. The Lachlan Shade of old was gone. He was no longer a man with a beloved sister. He was no longer a whole elf.

But more importantly, now that he was firmly back in this realm, he was no longer a scared, naive, reckless child. He was the leader of the new Order—someone who'd finally gained the respect he deserved.

Teo eventually made his way to Lachlan through the crowd, deftly carving his path forward like a serpent through water. The Shades melted back, giving the pair room. "It is good to see you on your feet."

"It's good to *be* on my feet. You have my thanks."

Teo waved this away with one hand. The dark swirls in the whites of his eyes undulated and spun, like thunderclouds whipped by turbulent winds. Somehow the sight of it, even after all this time, perturbed Lachlan. His only companions had been reptilian beings for so long, speaking in English again had been more challenging than he'd anticipated, his words rusty and clumsy—so it only made sense that someone like Teo would seem foreign to him now.

"You have excellent timing," Teo said. "We have guests."

"What kind of guests?"

"They've made a bid," Teo said.

Lachlan's brows hiked, his curiosity piqued. "Lead the way."

Continued well-wishes buoyed his weary body as he followed Teo through the command center, past a few rune-reinforced training rooms, and toward an administrative center at the end of a long hall. One wall of the hallway was lined with thick glass, allowing easy viewing of the area inside. Lachlan stopped in his tracks and stood before the glass, scanning the makeshift hospital. It looked more like a sick bay than anything—the room filled with wheeled cots of varying sizes. Ten bodies lay under crisp white sheets. A few medical personnel made their rounds inside, tending to the patients. The sizes of most of the bodies implied they were humanoid, but there were two larger bodies. Green skin pegged them as either orcs or trolls.

"What happened here?" Lachlan asked, one arm tucked behind his back. The first time he'd attempted the position, his ruined arm had swung uselessly back to his side, as his right hand had only grasped air where his arm used to be.

If Teo had seen the blunder, he didn't acknowledge it.

"These are the products of the bid. Once you meet with the clan who submitted them, I thought it would be good for morale if you made your first official decree," Teo said.

Lachlan nodded once. "Excellent suggestion."

They resumed walking.

Teo informed him that Administration Room 4, where they were headed now, was the largest one on the base, constructed to help make their elephantine fae allies feel more comfortable. The doors alone looked large enough to accommodate a school bus. It was not a detail Lachlan would have thought of on his own, but as he stepped inside the room, he immediately understood its necessity. Seated in giant chairs around a gargantuan table were a dozen orcs, trolls, and a couple of downright unidentifiable, but no less massive beings. Most were taller than Lachlan's six two, even while sitting. The sheer size of them all sent Lachlan's heart racing—his instincts telling him to cow down to a superior predator.

Yet, all dozen of them quickly got to their feet and bowed their heads.

The orc closest to Lachlan—who still stood beside Teo at the head of the table—lifted his head and gazed down at him. The behemoth must have been at least eight feet tall. "It's an honor to meet you. I am Seven—the newest head of the Mrull clan."

The clan at large loosed a short, loud battle cry that was more of an impassioned grunt than words. Lachlan felt the vibration of it in the soles of his feet. It was all a bit barbaric, really, but he supposed he appreciated their enthusiasm.

"What happened to the original leader of the clan?" Lachlan asked, supposing he needed to know now if these Mrull neanderthals made it a habit of conducting military coups.

"Domino was slain, Master Traveler," the orc said. "Goddess rest his soul."

The neanderthals issued another bone-rattling battle cry in Domino's honor.

The orc leader said, "With all due respect to Domino, Master Traveler, he became too preoccupied with hosting auctions and throwing parties rather than issues important to the clan. Domino refused to consider making a bid to join the Shades. Many in the clan did not agree, but orcs are loyal to the bitter end. When I heard rumors that you were returning, I wanted to waste no time in putting in a bid from the Mrulls. It is the Goddess's doing that we arrived on the same day you bested your ailment."

Lachlan didn't love the fact that these overgrown beasts were as enamored of the Goddess as his parents had been—as the too-soft Order had been—but the orcs' strict adherence to a belief system, even if it was not one Lachlan bought into, showed they could be managed with the right messaging.

"So those people in the sick bay are your doing?" Lachlan asked. "What makes this bid any more noteworthy than the ones before it?"

Teo cleared his throat. "If I may ..." He produced a cell phone from the pocket of his slacks. "Mr. Mrull here had one of his human minions post a series of photos on a Forage website yesterday. It was these photos that triggered the interest of our recruitment liaisons in the first place."

Lachlan didn't have the faintest clue what half of those sentences meant. He stared at Teo's device as the vampire swiped through gory photograph after gory photograph. A warehouse of some kind had become the scene of a truly horrific slaughter. It was overkill, in Lachlan's opinion. Made even more so by the final few pictures of a pile of severed heads arranged in a pyramid. The eye sockets of the topmost head had what looked to be a white-tile domino shoved into each.

"Seeing as my right-hand man is a hybrid, Seven, it's a bit disconcerting that your bid involves murdering so many of his kind," Lachlan said as Teo calmly pocketed his phone. "Should I be concerned that you harbor a hatred of hybrids, and therefore your inclusion into the organization would jeopardize his life?"

Seven vigorously shook his head. "Never, Master Traveler. We attacked this nest because a reliable source told us that an anti-Shade faction of the hybrids had recently kidnapped a very coveted nyad who had been turned vamp. The nyad was *first* acquired by hybrids loyal to you, but vampire hunters captured him. The dumb kid had been posting videos for weeks about his reintegration into normal life. The videos led the anti-Shade group right to him. We figured if this many groups wanted the kid so much, you'd want him, too. You *are* collecting fae to turn, aren't you? That's not just a rumor?"

The orc hadn't been sarcastic; he sounded a touch concerned that he'd somehow miscalculated and his bid would be rejected because he'd been operating based on faulty intel. Truth be told, the fae-turned-vamp idea had been Teo's. He was a far better judge than Lachlan as to how the Shades could utilize vampirism to its full extent. When Teo had floated the idea for a new wave of live experiments, Lachlan had happily signed off on it. He was pleased to hear that decision had been a fruitful one.

"That's correct," Lachlan finally said, noting the beads of sweat forming on the orc's forehead. "The collection process can be time-consuming, so your assistance in the matter is appreciated."

The orc flashed a smile full of flat, yellowed teeth. "We gave all the hybrids a choice: change their allegiance to you or die. Most of them chose to die. Then we stole their human and fae food, as well as the nyad."

Teo said, "The nyad's power when the shadows take hold is … devastating."

Intriguing.

"And the dominos in the eyes?" Lachlan asked. "A subtle snub to your former leader?"

"A message," Seven said, though the darker green of his cheeks suggested he was blushing, a bit embarrassed by his own theatrics.

Seven could call the move "a message" all he wanted, but it was also passive-aggressive and a little petty. Lachlan couldn't say he minded either one, but it also meant he would need to keep a watchful eye on Seven. His emotions sometimes got the better of him, which could make him reckless.

Reckless, but effective.

Seven said, "It was a message to all fae outside the hubs that Domino is gone and the Mrulls have a new agenda. If they don't submit, we rip their heads off their shoulders."

Lachlan considered him for a long moment, quietly relishing the beast of a man's desperation to have his bid accepted.

"The side effect of Domino's favorite pastime," Teo said, "is that the Mrull clan amassed an immense stockpile of charmed weapons. The kind of stockpile that can be utilized for our own purposes *or* sold in black-market auctions in the very network Domino established. It would be a shame to leave that lucrative market untouched—both monetarily and as a means to spread the word far and wide about the benefit of joining the Shades."

"The whole cache would be yours, of course," Seven Mrull said, his thick lips pressed into a tight line, his bulging eyes pleading.

A few of the Mrulls quickly masked their shock at Seven's offer to cough up the weapons. Time would tell how strong a hold Seven actually had on this new clan of his.

Lachlan stuck out his one remaining hand, which was engulfed by Seven's a breath later. "Welcome to the Shades."

Leaving the clan of massive fae to celebrate their new alliance,

Lachlan and Teo stepped back into the hallway. The pair stopped before the window looking into the sick bay.

Lachlan scanned the space, his gaze snagging on an unmoving figure in the second row. "What's the nyad's name?"

"Kessler," Teo said.

"Take me to him. I'd like to see what all the fuss is about."

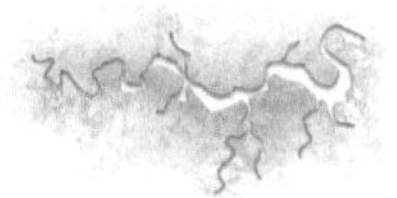

ALSO BY MELISSA ERIN JACKSON

Thank you for reading *Unholy Magic*! If you enjoyed this story, please consider leaving a review. Reviews mean the world to authors. Reviews often mean more sales, and more sales means more freedom to write more books.

If you'd like to read a **free** short story about how Camila Fletcher and Lachlan Shade first met, you can find *Veiled Threats* at: https://melissajacksonbooks.com/the-charm-collector/veiled-threats

Next up in Harlow and Kayda's adventure is *Monstrous Allies*. If you'd like to be notified when new books are released, you can join my newsletter at melissajacksonbooks.com.

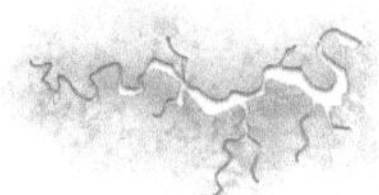

If you're interested in a lighter story, try *A Mythical Case of Arson*, the first book in a fantasy cozy mystery series set in the same universe as the Charm Collector series!

Just when she thinks her day can't get any weirder, she finds a baby dragon …

Deandra Hendricks works her fingers to the bone at two jobs to keep her Los Angeles apartment. With a rapidly dwindling savings account, the prospects for her future are bleak. So when her cousin invites her to visit Axia—the hidden, magical hub their grandparents retired to—she agrees. Deandra doesn't possess a stitch of magic herself, but a long weekend vacation in a strange new town might be just what she needs.

Her first day in Axia is so bizarre, though, she wonders if her bleak life in Los Angeles hasn't been so bad after all. And, just when she thinks her day can't get any stranger, she finds a baby dragon trapped in a dumpster. At a loss, she takes a trip to the vet, hoping they can help find the little guy's owner.

The dragon, it turns out, only appears in its true form to her, while everyone else sees a dire wolf puppy. She and the vet discover that as long as the dragon wears his bespelled collar, his true identity is hidden. Someone went to great lengths to keep this supposed-to-be-extinct animal a secret.

Then the "dog" is accused of arson and is seized by authorities.

Determined to help him, Deandra searches for the real arsonist. She catches wind of a thriving black market that's populated by those who would stop at nothing to claim an animal this rare. She must work quickly to clear her dragon's name, because if he falls into the wrong hands, she could lose him forever.

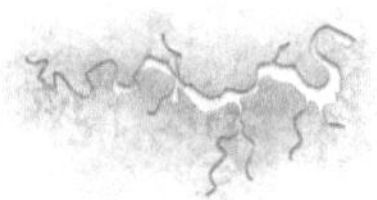

Also available as an audiobook!

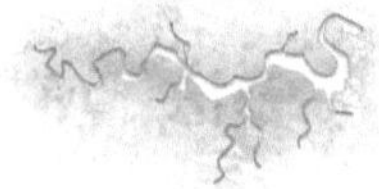

If you're looking for a ghost-filled paranormal tale, consider *The Forgotten Child*, a haunting mystery starring a reluctant medium.

ACKNOWLEDGMENTS

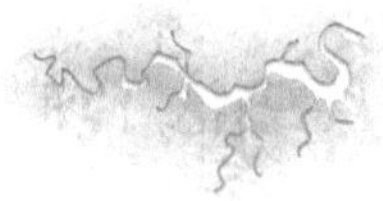

As much as I love writing this series, it's a constant struggle, y'all. I was determined to wrap this series up in three books. These characters did not agree. It wasn't until I was two years and 150k words into *Unholy Magic* that I finally accepted this series was bigger than I originally planned. More Luma for me! More Luma for you!

Thank you to the readers who have been patient with me since the beginning. These books are not coming out on any kind of a consistent deadline and I'm sorry. Hopefully they're worth the wait. Thank you to the beta readers who keep volunteering to read early drafts for me … even when there are years between books and you've forgotten half the character names. Whoops.

Thanks, Mom, Margarita, John, and Emilie who helped me in a pinch this time around. And thank you to Cyndi, my beta reader turned editor, who has been reading these books from the start.

Thanks as always to Danielle Fine for my covers, to Tom Madej for Luma's ever-evolving map, and to Etheric Tales for the chapter header and scene break art. So grateful to have so many talented artists in my corner—especially since ya girl can barely draw stick figures.

Thank you to Victoria Villarreal, Mac Fowler, Chris Johnson, and Connor Brannigan for sticking with me on this long full-cast audiobook journey.

This is a weird thank you … but thank you to the Tycho radio station on Pandora. The number of hours I've clocked on that station is … alarming. But for some reason, I can only write to atmospheric electronica now. Go figure.

And, as always, thank you to Sam for putting up with me. I lose my cookies at the end of every draft and you're always there to talk me off the proverbial ledge. Thank you for the brainstorming sessions, keeping the fire in the outdoor chimney roaring in winter when I can only seem to write in the back yard, and being unfazed when I need to pace in circles on the lawn. You're my favorite person.

Onward to *Monstrous Allies*!

ABOUT THE AUTHOR

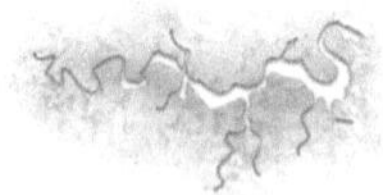

Melissa has had a love of stories for as long as she can remember, but only started penning her own during her freshman year of college. She majored in Wildlife, Fish, and Conservation Biology at UC Davis. Yet, while she was neck-deep in organic chemistry and physics, she kept finding herself writing stories in the back of the classroom about fairies and trolls and magic. She finished her degree, but it never captured her heart the way writing did.

Now she owns her own dog walking business (that's sort of wildlife related, right?) by day … and afternoon and night … and writes whenever she gets a spare moment. She alternates mostly between fantasy and mystery (often with a paranormal twist). All her books have some element of "other" to them … witches, ghosts, UFOs. There's no better way to escape the real world than getting lost in a fictional one.

She lives in Northern California with her very patient boyfriend and way too many pets.

You can find more of her books and join her newsletter at melissajacksonbooks.com